RETREAT HELL

Book One: The Empire's Corps
Book Two: No Worse Enemy
Book Three: When The Bough Breaks
Book Four: Semper Fi
Book Five: The Outcast
Book Six: To The Shores
Book Seven: Reality Check
Book Eight: Retreat Hell
Book Nine: The Thin Blue Line
Book Ten: Never Surrender
Book Eleven: First To Fight
Book Twelve: They Shall Not Pass
Book Thirteen: Culture Shock

RETREAT HELL

CHRISTOPHER G. NUTTALL

The characters and events portrayed in this book are fictitious. Any similarity to real persons, living or dead, is coincidental and not intended by the author.

Text copyright © 2017 Christopher G. Nuttall
All rights reserved.
No part of this book may be reproduced, or stored in a retrieval system, or transmitted in any form or by any means, electronic, mechanical, photocopying, recording, or otherwise, without express written permission of the publisher.

ISBN-13: 9781544261638
ISBN-10: 1544261632

http://www.chrishanger.net
http://chrishanger.wordpress.com/
http://www.facebook.com/ChristopherGNuttall

All Comments Welcome!

AUTHOR'S NOTE

Retreat Hell probably requires some explanation.

In my previous books in this series, even the mainstream ones, I tried hard to create books that could be read without having read the previous books. It is up for debate just how well I succeeded. However, *Retreat Hell* is probably completely incomprehensible without having read the previous four mainstream books; *The Empire's Corps*, *No Worse Enemy*, *Semper Fi* and *To The Shores*. The events surrounding the Fall of Earth, mentioned in this novel, were detailed in *When The Bough Breaks*, while the foundation of the Trade Federation was covered in *The Outcast*.

Retreat Hell also marks the start of the Commonwealth-Wolfbane War, an event I anticipate taking at least another two-three books to resolve. As such, it ends on a cliff-hanger of sorts. But don't worry. The Marines will be back.

As always, free samples of the previous books are available on my website (www.chrishanger.net) and full copies can be downloaded from Amazon Kindle. And if you like the book, please don't hesitate to leave a rating and a review on Amazon.

Thank you
Christopher G. Nuttall

DEDICATION

Over the past year, several of my readers have emailed me with spelling and grammar corrections for books in this series and others. As editing is a tricky task for a Kindle author, such assistance has been very helpful. This book is dedicated to everyone who has submitted a correction.

Thanks
Chris

PROLOGUE

Dateline – Two Months After the Fall of Corinthian

Admiral Rani Singh hated to lose.

She'd worked her way up the ranks through sheer stubbornness and native ability, forsaking all the shortcuts lecherous older officers offered her. She'd taken pride in not surrendering herself to the temptations, even when she'd been assigned to Trafalgar Naval Base by a particularly vindictive superior after she'd declined his advances. She'd even managed to turn a position that should have killed her career into a springboard to supreme power when the Empire started to withdraw from the sector, turning herself into a military dictator and ruler of a small empire of her own.

But then she'd lost everything, but her life and a handful of starships.

In hindsight, she saw – all too clearly – where she'd gone wrong. She hadn't taken the Commonwealth seriously, not at the time. It was a gathering of stars and human settlements towards the Rim, on the opposite side of her headquarters to Earth. The Commonwealth should not have been able to put together a challenge to her forces, not the sector fleet she'd snatched almost intact during the final chaotic days of the Empire's rule. But the Commonwealth had sent its people to Corinthian and undermined her rule. And when the ghost fleet had turned up, she'd panicked and lost everything.

Oh, she'd had plenty of time to think, she recalled, as the remains of her fleet had crept from hiding place to hiding place, fearful of an encounter that could have drained their finite supplies still further. Smaller and older ships had been cannibalised to keep the bigger ones operational, although she knew that even a victorious engagement could cost her everything;

her crews had grown more and more restless, their loyalty only assured by the looming presence of her security forces. One day, she'd known, they might rise up against her – and, if they took the ships, surrender them to the Commonwealth. She'd slept with a pistol under her pillow and armed guards at her hatch.

She'd known – she had never truly been able to lie to herself – that the situation was desperate. Battleships required constant maintenance and an endless supply of spare parts, which they no longer possessed. Sooner or later, she would have to abandon some of her crewmen or run out of life support. Maybe she could have found a world they could occupy – she did have far more firepower with her than the average Rim world could deploy in its own defence – but that would have been a form of surrender. And yet it had started to look like the only option. It had been then, when she'd been in the depths of despair, that they'd stumbled across the ship from Wolfbane.

Rani had known, vaguely, that another successor state was taking shape and form, coreward of Corinthian. She'd always known the value of good intelligence and her officials had interviewed the crews of every freighter that had made landfall within her territory. But she had always assumed that she would contact them from a position of strength, not weakness…not when weakness would invite attack. She knew that better than any of her former superiors, none of whom had realised the true scale of the looming disaster. And yet there was no choice.

She looked up from the screen as Wolfbane came into view, her ragtag fleet escorted by a handful of battleships. They weren't – quite – pointing their weapons at her ships, but she knew it would be a matter of seconds between the decision to open fire and the ships actually firing on her. She'd come to Wolfbane, after sending a message through the captured ship's crew, knowing that it could easily be a trap. But there was still no choice.

I do have cards to play, she thought, although she had no idea if they would be sufficient to win her a place on Wolfbane. *I have ships – and I have intelligence. And I have a few tools I dare not share…*

She gritted her teeth as the fleet finally entered high orbit. Wolfbane had been the most successful world in its sector, hence the Sector Government's decision to base itself there. It was surrounded by orbital weapons platforms, industrial nodes and starships – hundreds of starships. The general economic decline that had presaged the Fall of the Empire, it seemed, no longer cast a shadow over the Wolfbane Sector. She couldn't help feeling a flicker of envy – even her work on Corinthian hadn't produced so much activity – which she thrust aside ruthlessly. There was no time to waste on self-recrimination.

Her wristcom buzzed. "Admiral," Carolyn said, "the shuttle from Wolfbane is making its final approach."

Rani nodded. Her aide was loyal – but she had no choice. Rani's security officers had seen to that, conditioning Carolyn until she couldn't even conceive of betraying her mistress. But the price for such conditioning was a reduction in the woman's intelligence and ability to act without specific orders. Rani was all too aware of the weaknesses in the system, but she dared not take the risk of leaving her aide unconditioned. It would be far too dangerous.

"Understood," she said. "I'm on my way."

She straightened up and studied herself in the mirror. Long dark hair framed an oddly fragile face, her dark skin and darker eyes giving her a winsome appearance that belied her inner strength. Her dress uniform was perfectly tailored to her slender form, tight in all the right places. It should have been no surprise when her former superiors had tried to seduce her, she admitted bitterly. The recruiting officers had never mentioned *that* aspect of the military when they'd convinced her to join up. Nor had it been a problem, she had to admit, until she'd graduated from the Imperial Academy with the rank of Lieutenant.

Absently, she wondered what Governor Brown would make of her. There had been little in the files on him, including a note that he had strong ties to a dozen corporations that presumably no longer existed. *That* suggested flexibility, Rani knew. It was rare for an official to be beholden to more than one set of masters. But Brown had clearly managed it long enough to reach the post of Sector Governor. His word would have been law in the sector long before the Empire collapsed.

I'll seduce him if I have to, she told herself. It was a bitter thought, one she resented after everything she'd done to avoid trading sex for favours, but she was damned if she would not use all the tools in her arsenal to claw her way back to power. *And I will have my revenge.*

CHAPTER ONE

> If you start by reviewing a generalised (and highly sanitised) history of the three thousand years of the Empire's existence, you could be forgiven for thinking that between the Unification Wars and the End of Empire there was no war. Certainly, no major conflict threatened the existence of the Empire. But was there peace?
>
> - Professor Leo Caesius, *War in a time of 'Peace:'*
> *The Empire's Forgotten Military History*

Darkness wrapped the landscape in shadow, unbroken by the merest hint of mankind's technology. The moon had yet to rise, leaving the stars as the only source of light. And it was very, very quiet.

Pete Rzeminski sat on the edge of the clearing, looking up at the stars and waited, patiently, for his contacts to arrive. The darkness – and the sound of nocturnal wild animals coming to life now the sun was gone – didn't bother him. He'd been in far worse spots when he'd been on active duty. But that had been a long time ago.

Pete wondered, absently, what his Drill Instructors would make of him now. Would they understand, he asked himself, or would they condemn him for making his choice? Once, he'd sworn an oath to the Empire that had defined his life and his service. It had once meant everything to him, even after he'd quit in disgust and retreated to Thule, where his family lived. But now the Empire was gone. What was the point, he asked himself, of swearing to something that no longer existed?

And yet, it had taken him years to take sides. In the end, only the death of his wife and family had convinced him to take up arms.

He wrapped the thermal cloak around him tightly as the temperature continued to fall, pushing his recollections aside. The youngsters had complained when he'd insisted on meeting the outsiders alone – not all of them trusted him – but Pete had been insistent. He did have training they lacked, training in escaping pursuit and – if necessary – in resisting interrogation. There was still the very real possibility that the entire operation was a loyalist trap. If so, it would be foolish to risk more than one life to make contact.

They called him the old man, he knew. And he *was* old, by their standards, even if he was in excellent shape for a fifty year old man. His hair was slowly turning grey, but his body was still strong, the result of exercise and genetic treatments he'd undergone in the past. And his wife had never complained about his performance before she'd died…

Memories rose up unbidden as he forced himself to relax, mocking him. There had been the Slaughterhouse, where he'd first known true companionship, and then a series of endless bloody battles, each one only a symptom of the Empire's steady decline. And then there had been the final bloody cataclysm…and his departure from the Terran Marine Corps. In the end, he knew, he'd failed. He hadn't been able to stay in the Marines, knowing that they'd become the Empire's bully boys, the people responsible for fixing problems the Grand Senate caused for itself.

He pushed the self-pity aside as his ears picked up faint sounds, blown on the wind. High overhead, something was descending towards the clearing. Pete tensed, one hand reaching for the pistol at his belt, as his enhanced eyes finally picked up the shuttle. Despite himself, he was impressed. Thule was hardly a stage-one colony world, utterly incapable of detecting a starship in orbit or a shuttle passing through its atmosphere. Their contacts had managed to slip through a detection system that was rather more elaborate than anything Thule really needed. But then, the government had attempted to spend its way out of the financial crisis by investing in the local defence industry. It was just a shame that the crisis had proven well beyond the planet's ability to surmount.

The shuttle came to a hover over the clearing, then dropped down towards the ground. It was a boxy shape, coated in materials that absorbed or redirected sensor sweeps from both orbital and ground-based stations. The contacts had refused to discuss precisely how they intended to avoid the local defences, but Pete's private guess was that they'd hidden the shuttle on one of the freighters in orbit. He'd taken a look at the listings and seen several dozen that could easily have carried the shuttle, hidden away in a cargo hold or even bolted to the hull. It wouldn't be detected unless the inspection crew was *very* thorough.

Not that the government bothers to examine off-world ships unless they're independent, he thought, feeling a twinge of bitterness. He hadn't realised how closely he'd associated himself with Thule until after his extended family had been affected by the first political shockwaves sweeping across the planet. A system that had seemed logical – and a change from the Empire's maddeningly hypocritical ideology – had shown its weaknesses as soon as the winds of change had begun. *The Trade Federation would complain.*

The shuttle touched down, a faint hissing sound reaching his ears as the warm hull touched damp grass. Pete hesitated, then stepped forward as the hatch opened. No light spilled out – it was impossible to be *certain* that an orbital satellite wasn't looking for anything that stood out on the ground – but his eyes could pick out a figure standing in the hatch, carrying a rifle in both hands. The figure wore light body armour and goggles that enhanced his eyesight. A long moment passed, then the figure waved at Pete. Bracing himself, Pete walked up to the hatch.

"Alpha-Three-Preen," he said.

"Beta-Four-Prime," the contact replied. He stepped aside, inviting Pete into the shuttle. "And may I say what a relief it is to be dealing with professionals?"

Pete felt his lips quirk in silent amusement. The underground movements that had sprung up in the wake of the financial crisis – and mass unemployment, followed by disenfranchisement – had a cause, but no real experience. Most of their secret passwords and countersigns had come from books and entertainment programs, both of which sacrificed realism for drama. It had taken him years of effort to teach the youngsters about the virtues of the KISS principle. Maybe it lacked drama, but it was certainly one hell of a lot more effective.

Inside, the shuttle was dark, the interior illuminated only by the light from a single display monitoring the orbital situation. The hatch closed with a hiss, then the lights came on, revealing a handful of metal chairs and a single control stick. Pete felt a moment of nostalgia - it had been years since he'd ridden an infiltration shuttle down into hostile territory - which he pushed to one side. He couldn't afford the distraction, not now.

"We have weapons for you, as per request," the contact said. In the light, he was a bland young man, someone who could have passed unnoticed on any cosmopolitan world. Not too handsome and not too ugly. "And some intelligence as well."

He paused, significantly. "You are aware, of course, that both the Commonwealth and the Trade Federation plan to expand their activities in this sector?"

Pete nodded. He'd heard rumours, some of them more reliable than others. Joining the Commonwealth had seemed the ticket to economic recovery, but the Commonwealth either couldn't or wouldn't buy most of the planet's produce. He rather suspected the latter. The planetary development corporation - and then the elected government - had invested heavily in industrial production equipment, citing their belief that the sector would continue to grow and develop under the protection of the Empire. Now, Thule had more industrial production than she could use. Even throwing money into the planetary defences hadn't solved the growing economic disaster.

"We would like to come to terms with you, after you take over the government," the contact added. "Would that be acceptable to you?"

Pete kept his expression blank. No one did anything for nothing, not even the ivory tower intellectuals who'd provided the ideological base for the Empire's growth, development and slow collapse. Long experience in the Marine Corps had taught him that anyone who supplied weapons to underground movements wanted something in return. Sometimes, it was cold hard cash, paid in advance, but at other times it was political influence or post-war alliances. He would have preferred to pay in advance, rather than have the terms left undetermined. But he knew the underground could not hope to purchase advanced weapons systems with cash in hand. The planet's currency was almost definitely useless outside its star system.

"That would depend," he said carefully, "on just what those terms were."

The youngsters, he knew, would have been horrified at his attempt to sound out the contact. They would have protested, perhaps rightly, that the underground did not enjoy the luxury of being able to debate terms and conditions. Without advanced weapons systems, the underground could not hope to prevail. If worst came to worst, they'd argue, they could always launch another uprising against the contact's backers. Pete's caution would not bode well with them.

He smiled, a little sadly. Some of the underground might have made good Marines, once upon a time, while others were the kind of people the Marine Corps existed to defend. Now, they were forced to fight or accept permanent subordination...

The contact didn't sound offended. "We would like your political neutrality," he said. "If you do not wish to associate yourselves with us, you may avoid commitment, but you may not side with any other interstellar power."

Pete looked at him for a long thoughtful moment. He knew that the contact represented an interstellar power – no one else would be able to produce the weapons they'd offered – but he didn't know *who*. But the insistence on political neutrality suggested Wolfbane. There was no one else who had any interest in Thule remaining uninvolved. It was vaguely possible, he supposed, that the Trade Federation was covertly sabotaging the Commonwealth's operations, but it seemed unlikely. If nothing else, the Trade Federation benefited hugely from the current state of affairs. Why would they want to upset the applecart?

They wouldn't, he thought. Everything he knew about the Trade Federation backed up its assertion that it was not interested in political power, at least not to the extent of the Commonwealth or the vanished Empire. No, they were interested in interstellar trade and little else. They didn't benefit by upending the situation on Thule.

"Very well," he said, finally. "I cannot speak on behalf of every underground organisation, but my group will accept your terms."

"Good," the contact said. He turned to the collection of metal boxes at the rear of the cabin. "Once we have unloaded these, I will depart and you can begin your war."

Pete nodded. The youngsters couldn't think in the long term, but *he* could...and he couldn't help wondering if he'd just sold his soul along with the planet itself. But they had no alternative, no choice if they truly wanted to overthrow the government and create a new order. They needed outside support.

"Thank you," he said.

First Speaker Daniel Krautman, elected Head of State only weeks prior to the first financial shockwaves that had devastated the planet's economy, looked out of the Speaker's Mansion and down towards the empty streets. Once, they had been bustling with life at all hours, a reflection of the economic success the planet had enjoyed under his predecessors. Now, they were empty, save for passing military and police patrols. The city was under martial law and had been so for months. Even the camps of unemployed workers and students who had been evicted from their homes were quiet.

He shook his head in bitter disbelief, wondering – again – just what he had done to deserve such turmoil on his watch. He'd told himself that running for First Speaker would be a chance to ensure that his name went down in the planet's history, despite his comparative youth. He'd told himself that he would serve the fixed ten-year term, the economic boom would continue and he would retire to take up a place on a corporate board or simply write his memoirs. Instead, the bottom had dropped out of the economy only *weeks* after his election and nothing, no matter what he did, seemed to fix the problem.

Gritting his teeth, he swore under his breath as he caught sight of his reflection. He'd been middle-aged when he'd been elected, with black hair and a smile that charmed the lady voters – or so he'd been assured, by his focus groups. Now, he was almost an old man. His hair had turned white, his face was deathly pale and he walked like a cripple. The doctors swore blind that the constant pains in his chest were nothing more than the results of stress and there was nothing they could do, but he had his suspicions. There were political and corporate figures demanding a harsher response to the crisis and some of them might just have bribed the doctors to make his life miserable.

Or maybe he was just being paranoid, he told himself as he turned away from the window. He was lucky, compared to the men and women in the homeless camps, building what shelter they could from cardboard boxes and blankets supplied by charities. There, life was miserable and short; men struggled desperately to find a job while women sold themselves on street corners, trading sex for the food and warmth they needed to survive another few days. And the children...Daniel couldn't help shuddering at the thought of children in the camps, even though there was nothing he could do. Anything he might have tried would have been ruthlessly blocked by the conservative factions in the Senate.

But they might be right, he thought, numbly. *The founders set out to avoid creating a dependent society, like Earth.*

He shook his head, angrily. What good did it do to tell the unemployed to go get a job when there were no jobs to be had? What good did it do to insist that the government should create jobs when there was no money to pay the additional workers? What good did it to do to cling to the letter of the constitution when a crisis was upon them that had never been anticipated by the founders? But the hawks were adamantly opposed to any changes while the doves couldn't agree on how to proceed. And *he* was caught in the middle.

Daniel stepped over to his desk and looked down at the report his secretary had placed there before going to bed. It seemed that the only growth industry, even after contact with the Commonwealth and the Trade Federation, was government bureaucracy, as bureaucrats struggled to prove they were actually necessary. The report told him, in exhaustive detail, just how many men, women and children had been arrested at the most recent protest march, the one that had turned into yet another riot. Daniel glanced at the executive summary, then picked up the sheaf of papers and threw it across the room and into the fire. Maybe he should have offered it to the homeless, he told himself, a moment too late. They could have burnt the papers for heat.

There was a tap on the door. Daniel keyed a switch, opening it.

"First Speaker," General Erwin Adalbert said. "I apologise for disturbing you."

"Don't worry about it," Daniel said. He trusted the General, insofar as he trusted anyone these days. There were times when he suspected the only thing preventing a military coup was the simple fact that the military would have to solve the crisis itself. "What can I do for you?"

"We received an intelligence package from one of our agents in the underground," Adalbert said. "I'm afraid our worst nightmare has come to pass."

Daniel smiled, humourlessly. Protest marches, even riots, weren't a major problem. The various underground groups spent more time fighting each other and arguing over the plans to repair the economy – or nationalise it, or send everyone to the farms – than they did plotting to overthrow the government. His *real* nightmare was the underground groups burying their differences and uniting against him.

"They've definitely received some help from off-world," Adalbert continued. "There have been several weapons shipments already and more are apparently on the way."

"Oh," Daniel said. "Who from?"

"Intelligence believes that there is only one real suspect," Adalbert admitted. "Wolfbane."

Daniel couldn't disagree. The Commonwealth had nothing to gain and a great deal to lose by empowering underground movements intent on overthrowing the local government and reshaping the face of politics on Thule. Wolfbane, on the other hand, might well see advantage in trying to covertly knock Thule out of the Commonwealth. Given that the closest Wolfbane-controlled world was only nine light years away, they certainly had an interest...and probably the capability to do real damage.

"I see," he said.

"We can expect the various underground groups to start working together now," Adalbert added, softly. "Their suppliers will certainly insist on unity in exchange for weapons."

He paused. "First Speaker, we need to ask for assistance."

Daniel looked up, sharply. "Remind me," he said coldly, "just how much of our budget is spent on the military?"

Adalbert had the grace to look embarrassed. "We spent most of the money on upgrading and expanding our orbital defences," he said. "It provided more jobs than expanding troop numbers on the ground. We can expand our recruiting efforts, but we're already having problems training our current intake..."

"And we don't know how far we can trust the new recruits," Daniel finished.

"Yes, sir," Adalbert said. "And most of our new recruits are trained for policing duties, not all-out war. But that's what the underground is going to give us."

Daniel stared down at his desk. He'd wanted to go down in history, but not like this, not as the First Speaker who had invited outsiders to intervene in his planet's civil unrest. The Senate would crucify him, safe in the knowledge that *they* didn't have to deal with the situation. They'd voted him emergency powers, enough to call for assistance, but not enough to actually come to grips with the situation.

Damn them, he thought.

"Summon the Commonwealth representative," he said, finally. He honestly wasn't sure if the Commonwealth *could* legally help Thule. This was an internal problem, not an external threat. But there was no choice. "We will ask for help."

CHAPTER TWO

No, there wasn't. Peace is merely defined as the absence of fighting. In actual fact, there were very few years in the Empire's long history when the Empire's military forces were not deployed into combat. They might face rebels or insurgents, terrorists or freedom fighters, but they were never truly at peace.
- Professor Leo Caesius, *War in a time of 'Peace:'*
The Empire's Forgotten Military History

It was raining the day they laid Lieutenant Elman Travis to rest.

Colonel Edward Stalker stood by himself, away from the handful of spectators, and watched as the coffin was lowered into the ground. Traditionally, insofar as 'tradition' had a meaning on a world barely a hundred years old, those who had died on active service would be buried in a military graveyard on the outskirts of Camelot, but Lieutenant Travis's father had insisted on laying him to rest in a private churchyard. Ed had raised no objections, knowing that the grieving needed time to come to terms with the loss. Councillor Travis, he suspected, had yet to truly believe his son was dead.

The preacher started to speak, his words barely intelligible under the driving rain. Ed had never been particularly religious – a life in the Undercity, then in the Marine Corps had never predisposed him to believe in God – but he understood the value of believing that the dead were gone, but not *truly* gone. Councillor Travis clung to the belief he would see his son again, drawing strength from his conviction. Ed privately hoped he was right. But he couldn't escape the feeling that dead meant *gone*.

It had been his fault, Ed knew. Lieutenant Travis had died on Lakshmibai, victim of a treacherous attack that had claimed the lives of over a hundred Avalon Knights. Ed had looked at the files, such as they were, and decided that there was no reason to object to Wolfbane's choice of Lakshmibai as a neutral world. And really, what threat could Lakshmibai pose to two spacefaring interstellar powers? It had never really occurred to him that the locals hated the outsiders so much that they would rise up against them, even under the threat of colossal devastation when the starships returned. If the Commonwealth Expeditionary Force hadn't been deployed to Lakshmibai, Ed knew that he would be dead by now, along with the representatives from Wolfbane. Who knew what *that* would have done to relationships between the two interstellar powers?

Ed was used to death, or so he'd told himself. Being in the Marines meant the near-certainty of a violent death – and no one, not even the most highly-trained Marine, was immune. He'd lost far too many people over the years, from Marines he'd considered friends to Marines who'd served under his command...and then Avalon Knights and others who had joined the military and helped make the Commonwealth a success. But those deaths had taken place before he'd screwed up, badly. And he *had* screwed up. In hindsight, always clearer than foresight, it was alarmingly clear that Lakshmibai was a disaster waiting to happen.

"Hindsight is always clearer," the lecture had said, when he'd gone to OCS on the Slaughterhouse. "You will always be second-guessed by people who will have access to a much more accurate picture than you had at the time. The trick is not to let those people get under your skin, because they will find it very hard to filter out the information they gathered in hindsight from what you knew before the disaster occurred."

He shook his head, bitterly. There were just too many unanswered questions over the whole Lakshmibai debacle for him to relax, even if he had been inclined to let the dead go. Had someone *aided* the locals, promising assistance that would prevent either the Commonwealth or Wolfbane taking bloody revenge for the slaughter of their people? Had the locals believed that the starships would never return? Or had they just been maddened fanatics, too enraged to consider the long-term consequences of their actions?

The preacher finally stopped speaking and nodded to the friends and family, who stepped forward, picked up clods of earth and started to hurl them into the grave. Ed watched dispassionately as the coffin was slowly buried, part of him wishing that he could join them and help bury a young man who'd died too soon. But Councillor Travis had made his wishes quite clear. Ed could attend the funeral, but not take an active part in the ceremony. He blamed Ed for his son's death.

It was a bitter thought. Ed had cared little for Earth's cadre of professional politicians, from the mayors and managers of the giant cityblocks to the Grand Senators, who were – in fact, if not in name – an aristocracy that had succeeded, long ago, in barring outsiders from rising within the Empire's power structure. They'd known nothing, but politics; their actions were considered purely in terms of how they would help or hinder their endless quest for more and more political power. It didn't take hindsight – as Professor Caesius had demonstrated years ago – to understand that Earth's politicians were certainly part of the problems tearing the Empire apart. And now the Empire was gone.

But Councillor Travis was different. Ed and Professor Caesius had written most of the requirements for political service on Avalon – and the rest of the Commonwealth – and Councillor Travis qualified. Indeed, part of Ed rather admired the man for what he had accomplished, even before the Marines had arrived on Avalon and deposed the old Council. He was no professional politician...which made his new opposition to the military – and Ed personally – more than a little heartbreaking. But there was no point in trying to avoid the fact.

I never had children, Ed thought, sourly. It wasn't uncommon for Marines to have children while on active service, but the children tended to be raised by their mothers while the fathers were moved from trouble spot to trouble spot. But Ed had never found someone he seriously considered marrying until he'd been sent to Avalon – and they couldn't marry, not while they were holding important posts. *What is it like to lose a child?*

Losing a Marine was always a tragedy, all the more so when he had been in command, responsible for the lives of his men. But Marines were trained to the very peak of human capability before they were set loose on an unsuspecting universe and assigned to individual Marine companies.

Ed had never been responsible for training his men. A child, on the other hand, was raised from birth by its parents. There was a connection there that even the most loyal and determined NCO failed to grasp with his men. How could he blame Councillor Travis for his grief?

He caught sight of the older man, leaning over the grave and shuddered. Councillor Travis was older than Ed, his body carrying the scars of struggle with the old Council's stranglehold on Avalon's economy. His hair had faded to white long ago, but there was a grim determination in his eyes that had carried him far. Now, that determination was turned against the military itself – and the Commonwealth.

Ed sighed, bitterly. The hell of it was that he believed that Councillor Travis was right.

It felt strange, Brigadier Jasmine Yamane considered, to be wearing civilian clothes. She hadn't been a civilian since she'd turned seventeen and walked right into the Marine Corps recruitment station on her homeworld. At Boot Camp, she'd worn the khaki outfits the new recruits were issued by the Drill Instructors, while the Slaughterhouse had expected them to wear combat battledress at all hours of the day. Even when she'd gone on leave, which had only happened once between her qualifying as a Marine and being exiled to Avalon with the rest of the company, she'd worn undress uniform.

But the instructions for the funeral had been quite clear. No military uniforms. None of the guests were to wear anything that could even remotely be construed as a military uniform. And, for someone who had never really considered how to dress herself for years, even picking something to wear had taken hours. It annoyed the hell out of her that she could react quickly and decisively on the battlefield, but found herself utterly indecisive when trying to decide what to wear. There was no way she could talk about that with the other Marines.

She caught sight of her own reflection in the growing puddle of water on the grass and sighed, inwardly. Eventually, she'd settled for a black shirt and a long black skirt that swirled oddly around her legs. It was loose, but it still felt constraining. The first time she'd pulled it on, she'd had a flashback to one of the nastier exercises she'd undergone at the Slaughterhouse, when she'd been chained up and dropped into a swimming pool. It hadn't surprised her, afterwards, to learn that several recruits had quit when they'd realised what they had to do to proceed.

The preacher started to speak again, his words hanging on the air. Jasmine had once been religious, religious enough to understand why Councillor Travis and his family sought comfort from their belief in God. It had been a long time since she'd prayed formally, she reminded herself, although heartfelt prayers on the verge of battle were probably more sincere than anything she'd offered back on her homeworld. But listening to his words was a bitter reminder that over a hundred young men and women were dead – and most of them had died under her command.

I'm sorry, she thought, directing her thought towards the coffin, now buried under a thin layer of earth. *I'm so sorry.*

In the days of the Empire, she knew without false modesty, she would be lucky to have risen to Lieutenant by now. Promotion was slow, even within the Marine Corps – and a brevet promotion could be cancelled without affecting her career. It was worse, far worse, in the Imperial Army, where officers were often promoted based on their connections, rather than their actual competence. But Avalon needed experienced officers more than it needed to adhere to a strict promotion timetable and Jasmine had been promoted – faster, perhaps, than was wise.

She looked over at Colonel Stalker, standing on his own in the rain, and wondered how he managed to seem so impassive. Didn't the deaths bother him? He'd been in the Marines since before Jasmine had even entered Boot Camp, let alone the Slaughterhouse; hell, she rather suspected he'd been in the Marines long before Jasmine had even heard about them for the first time. Was he simply too experienced to truly *feel* each and every death? Or was he merely hiding his feelings and concentrating on the living?

Jasmine had known people died from a very early age, ever since her aunt had been killed in an accident on her homeworld. She'd served beside Marines who'd been killed in the line of fire, leaving their former comrades to mourn their deaths and move on as best as they could. But she hadn't had anyone die under her command until she'd been promoted for the first time. And yet, losing the young men and women of Avalon hurt worse than losing fellow Marines.

She puzzled over it as the preacher assured his audience, once again, that the dead had gone to a better place. Jasmine didn't doubt it. Lieutenant Travis had been a good officer, one of many young men to enter the army after the old Council had been sidelined...and his promotion had been well-deserved. Jasmine vaguely recalled meeting him once, during a review of the CEF's infantry companies. In hindsight, she rather wished she'd paid more attention to the young man. She'd had to look at his file to remember his face, before she'd even come to the funeral. The picture someone had placed on the coffin, before the pallbearers had lowered it into the ground, had been of the Lieutenant as a young child, smiling happily as he ran through the field. There had been endless promise in his smile, something that had made her start to tear up before she pulled herself firmly under control. Somehow, the picture hadn't been *him*.

He wasn't just young, she thought. *He was uncommitted.*

Maybe it wasn't fair, but *Marines* were committed in a way that few soldiers and civilians could grasp. She'd left her homeworld, spent seven months in Boot Camp and another two years at the Slaughterhouse, then signed up for a ten-year hitch as a Marine Rifleman. She had left her previous life behind, knowing that when she returned to her homeworld she would have nothing in common with her brothers and sisters. Hell, the Marines were her brothers and sisters now. But Lieutenant Travis could have gone home any time he liked – and no one would have looked at him as a potential monster in human clothing.

She shook her head, running her fingers through her short dark hair, cropped close to her skull. The Empire had had barely a percentage point of a percentage point of its vast population in uniform, even counting the vast number of uniformed bureaucrats and REMFs who added nothing to the military's ability to fight, but detracted from it at every conceivable opportunity. It was unusual for anyone on Earth to *know* someone who served or had served in the military personally, a pattern that was duplicated on most of the Core Worlds. Few of them had any real idea what the military was like, allowing themselves to be influenced by entertainment movies rather than reality. It had given them a skewed idea of what it was like to defend the Empire.

But on Avalon, almost everyone had served in the military, various local defence forces or knew someone who had served. There was little dispute over the value of the military...or the need to keep a formidable force at the ready. And yet...she couldn't help thinking that Councillor Travis was likely to cause real problems. What would it mean for the Commonwealth as a whole if the CEF concept was to be grounded without further exploration?

It was selfish of her, she knew, but she almost wished that she'd died instead.

When the service came to an end, she walked out of the churchyard and headed back to the apartment on the outskirts of Churchill Garrison. As the CEF's commander, she was expected to be near the base at all times, rather than sleeping on Castle Rock. And besides, it had other compensations. Some of them made sleeping away from her fellow Marines almost worthwhile.

Councillor Gordon Travis waited until the preacher shooed the remaining witnesses out of the churchyard, then walked over to the gravestone and knelt beside the hard stone. The muddy ground soaked his trousers, but he found it hard to care. His son was buried below the soil, his one and only son. What did a little discomfort matter compared to *that*?

Gordon knew he'd been lucky. His father's ticket to Avalon had been purchased by *his* father, who had gifted his wayward son with enough Imperial Credits to avoid the debt peonage that had blighted so many unwary colonists on Avalon. Gordon had grown up earning money without having to worry about it draining into an endless black hole of debt, money he'd swiftly invested in a shop when he'd finally realised he didn't want to spend his life staring at the back end of a mule. His father's farm might have been permanently hovering on the verge of bankruptcy, but Gordon's store had been a runaway success. It helped that he didn't have to save money to pay back loans he'd never taken out.

But when his father had been killed by bandits – and the old Council had done nothing – Gordon had sworn revenge. He'd joined the Crackers, funnelling money and resources to them, helping to keep the insurgency alive. It had seemed a dream come true when the Marines had arrived; they'd defeated the bandits, overthrown the old Council and come to terms with the Crackers. Gordon hadn't even raised any objections when his son had decided to join the Knights of Avalon. Every young man wanted to join.

I should have said no, he thought. God knew he'd had endless fights with his father over his reluctance to stay on the farm, fights that had resulted in them not speaking to each other for years. He'd known better than to bar his son from joining the military. How could he say no when the new elite were those who wore a uniform? But now...he knew he should have forbidden his son to join. Elman might have been mad at him, he might have stormed off and done something stupid, but at least he would have been alive.

Bitter hatred curled around his heart as he started to weep. Elman had been his only son and, as such, had been special in his eyes, even though his daughters had taken over the family business. Losing him *hurt*; somehow, Gordon knew he'd always assumed that he would die long before his son. But instead...he clutched the gravestone, feeling the cold stone against his bare skin. The Commonwealth had seemed a great idea at the time, one that would ensure that Avalon would never again be at the mercy of faceless bureaucrats thousands of light years away. But now... it wasn't worth his son's life.

And he didn't even die in defence of Avalon, he thought, bitterly. *He died on a world we should have known better even than to visit.*

Angrily, he stood up. It would not happen again, he vowed, as he marched away from his son's grave. *He* would make sure it never happened again, whatever it took. No more sons would die on foreign worlds.

CHAPTER THREE

This should not be surprising. The Empire did not provide solutions to most of the flashpoints within the Empire's vast territories. Unsurprisingly, the best the Empire could do was keep a lid on the trouble...which tended to flare up again when the Imperial military was withdrawn.
- Professor Leo Caesius, *War in a time of 'Peace:'*
The Empire's Forgotten Military History

In her slumber, Jasmine looked beautiful – and deadly.

Emmanuel Alves carefully – very carefully – lifted himself out of bed and moved away from her. Jasmine slept very lightly, he'd discovered, and making too much noise near her could have alarming and painful results. She'd been trained, she'd admitted after the first incident, to snap awake at the slightest hint anyone might be near her. Emmanuel hadn't been able to avoid asking how she'd managed to sleep in a small compartment with her fellow Marines, only to be told that was different. He wasn't sure how.

He looked back at her and smiled. She looked shorter, somehow, without her uniform, but there was no disguising the sheer strength of her body. Muscles rippled along her arms and legs, while her small breasts stood out against her flat chest. Longer hair might have set off her face nicely, he considered, but he knew she would never grow it out. All Marines, without exception, had their hair shaved close to their scalps or removed their hair permanently. It just made it easier to wear a combat helmet during fighting.

His smile grew wider as he stepped into the shower and turned on the tap. The apartment was small, but neither of them really cared. Jasmine was used to a Spartan existence, while Emmanuel himself had hidden from the old Council's goons in the badlands more than once, back before the old Council had been removed. Maybe it wasn't as heroic as service in the Marine Corps or the Knights of Avalon, but he *had* served a useful purpose. He'd kept people informed of what was going on before the end of the war.

He jumped as he felt a hand touch his shoulder, then heard a very feminine giggle. Jasmine moved silently, even on a hard wooden floor, so silently that he'd never heard her coming even when he was listening for her. She pushed him to the back of the shower, then directed the water to splash over both of them. Unlike him, she didn't seem to have any problems waking up in the morning. He felt himself harden as she washed the water over his member, then grunted as she pushed him against the wall and impaled herself on him. Somehow, her silence made it all the more exciting...

Afterwards, they dressed together, Jasmine donning her undress uniform rather than the civilian clothes she'd worn the previous day. Emmanuel had to admit that she looked better in her uniform, as shapeless as it was, rather than in civilian clothes, which looked rather ill-fitting on her. Unlike his previous girlfriends, Jasmine didn't seem to want to cuddle or talk after having sex, as if she was unwilling to open herself mentally as well as physically. It puzzled Emmanuel more than he cared to admit, but it wasn't something he wanted to share with anyone else. As far as he knew, he was the only person on Avalon dating a female Marine.

"Councillor Travis has requested my presence in two hours," he said, as he finished pulling on his jumper. There was no standard appearance for a reporter on Avalon, not like there had been on Earth – or so he had been told. But then, Earth had been a heavily stratified society for so long that most of its population was unaware there was *any* stratification. "Rumour has it that he's going to make a run for President."

Jasmine looked up, her face almost unreadable. Emmanuel had spent long enough with her to be able to read the signs of worry, almost concern. No one could escape hearing about Councillor Travis's campaign to build political influence in the month since they'd returned from Lakshmibai – or the speculation about what it might mean for the Commonwealth. The President of Avalon wasn't all-powerful, but Avalon was one of the most important worlds in the union. If Avalon started to pull away from the Commonwealth it had created, it was hard to see how the Commonwealth would survive.

"Pity you can't talk him out of it," she said, finally. Someone who didn't know her very well would have missed the self-recrimination in her tone. She blamed herself for the political disaster threatening to overwhelm the Commonwealth, even though no one else believed it was her fault. "Do you think he can win?"

Emmanuel hesitated. He'd followed Avalon's politics since the old Council had been defeated and exiled, but he had to admit that hardly anything was set in stone. It had been barely five years, after all. The Empire had taken nearly a century to settle all the issues that arose when the human race was united under one banner – and then started to ossify. But all that meant, he knew, was that someone with sufficient determination and political backing could rewrite the rules to suit himself.

"I don't know," he confessed, finally. "But he does have quite a following."

He mulled it over as he kissed Jasmine goodbye and strode out of the apartment, walking down towards the gate that led out to the city itself. Their relationship was an open secret, at least among the Marines, some of whom had teased Jasmine for sleeping with the enemy. Emmanuel had found that more than a little insulting at first – he'd supported the Marines ever since they'd deposed the old Council – but Jasmine had explained that reporters from Earth normally couldn't be trusted. And, even if they were experienced enough to produce reports that actually bore some resemblance to the truth, their editors would often rewrite them to suit their political leanings before the reports were published. Few in the military cared for reporters.

Outside the gate, Camelot seemed to have grown even larger and more populous overnight. He shook his head; between the Commonwealth bringing skilled workers to Avalon and farm children trying to move to the city to get in on the economic boom, the city was just growing larger and larger. His contacts had already told him that the Council was considering emergency legislation to limit the number of people who could move to the city, although Emmanuel suspected that would fall flat on its face. There were just too many people who wanted to share in the economic prosperity the Commonwealth had brought to Avalon.

Enough, he asked himself, *to prevent Councillor Travis from trying to separate us from the Commonwealth?*

The thought nagged at him as he made his way into the core of the city, the mansions that had once belonged to the old Council. Given Avalon's relative poverty before the collapse of the Empire, the mansions were nothing more than gross displays of conspicuous consumption on a colossal scale. Of the ones that had survived the Cracker War, one had been preserved as a museum, the remainder had been turned into government offices or emergency housing for some of the new immigrants.

He walked past the largest mansion and down towards a smaller block that served as the city homes for councillors. Unlike the Empire, which demanded the physical presence of Senators on Earth, Avalon insisted that the Councillors spend most of their time in their constituencies. Indeed, only the President and the four Councillors representing Camelot itself remained in the city more or less permanently. It was just their bad luck that Councillor Travis represented the business interests in the city.

There was only one guard at the gatehouse when he approached, something that always amused him after the old Council's paranoia about their safety. No one wanted to actually *kill* the new councillors, not when they could be recalled by their constituents. Politics on Avalon might be down and dirty, but they were safe. The victors certainly didn't take bloody revenge on the losers.

But they might soon, he thought, as the guard searched him thoroughly. *How many vested interests are tied up with the Commonwealth?*

"You're clean," the guard grunted. Judging by the way he moved, he'd been injured during the fighting and hadn't been able to reach a regeneration machine in time to recover full use of his leg. Probably a former Cracker, Emmanuel decided. "How surprising."

"I did shower this morning," Emmanuel said.

The guard snorted, then waved him into the apartment block. Councillor Travis owned one of the larger apartments, which doubled as his office as well as his living space. Emmanuel stepped through the door and nodded to the secretary, who waved him right into the Councillor's office. It was pleasant – and yet somehow worrying – to note that the secretary was a middle-aged woman with an air of formidable competence, rather than a young girl with more on her chest than on her mind. Councillor Travis didn't seem inclined to abuse his office.

And when, Emmanuel asked himself, *did I start taking a side?*

"It's always a pleasure," Councillor Travis said, as Emmanuel closed the door behind him. "I believe strongly in freedom of the press."

He meant it, Emmanuel knew. Unlike some of the other new businessmen, Councillor Travis had never tried to silence the newspapers or sue them into bankruptcy. But then, the privacy, libel and slander laws on Avalon ensured that the newspapers only printed the truth.

"Me too," Emmanuel said. It had been his cause ever since he had first read about the great crusading reporters in the Empire's past. He'd clung to it even after discovering that most of the great crusaders had been anything but independent seekers after truth. "And it is always a pleasure to speak to a councilman."

"We never get tired of saying that," Councillor Travis joked. He smiled, then nodded to a small chair. "Please, be seated."

Emmanuel sat and looked around the office. It was surprisingly bare, save for a series of photographs of the Councillor's children – and a large black-framed portrait of his dead son, wearing his military uniform. Emmanuel couldn't help wondering if the councilman had become more than a little unhinged by his son's death, although he had never lost anyone himself. Even his grandparents were still alive, down on the farm.

I wonder if Jasmine will want children, he thought, irrelevantly. *And would she want them with me?*

"Tea, coffee? I have some sweet biscuits, if you'd like."

Emmanuel looked up, broken out of his thoughts. "No, thank you," he said, quickly. It felt odd to have a politician prepare food and drinks personally. "I rarely eat anything before lunch."

"My son was like that too," Councillor Travis said. There was an odd note in his voice, one Emmanuel couldn't place. "But I didn't call you here to talk about my son. I called to invite you to the first hearing on the Lakshmibai Disaster."

Emmanuel blinked in surprise. "The first hearing?"

"I have convinced a majority of councillors to agree that we need to explore the circumstances leading up to the disaster," Councillor Travis said, with heavy satisfaction. "We will study everything we knew about the cursed world, reconsider every decision made by the authorities and then pass judgement."

"I see," Emmanuel said, fighting to keep his voice level. It wasn't quite the announcement he'd expected, but in hindsight it was more subtle. Instead of challenging the President directly, Councillor Travis would undermine her...and, if the hearing failed to produce the results he wanted, he could back off without losing anything. "And what sort of judgement do you expect?"

"It would be premature to rush to judgement," Councillor Travis said. "But there *will* be judgement. We *will* learn from this experience. The dead will not be allowed to die in vain."

"Good," Emmanuel said.

"I understand that you were there," Councillor Travis said, changing the subject slightly. "I read your dispatches with considerable interest. Do *you* have a view on the situation?"

Emmanuel hesitated, caught between loyalty to Jasmine and his sworn neutrality as a reporter.

"You may be called to testify," Councillor Travis warned him. "Don't leave the planet."

Emmanuel had to laugh. "I'll try not to," he said. "Who else are you going to call to testify?"

"Everyone who can reasonably be called," Councillor Travis said. "Do you have any questions?"

"Just one," Emmanuel said. "With all due respect, sir, your son died on that damned world. You are far from impartial. Should you be involved in the inquest?"

"I have already stated that I will not vote, unless there is a tie," Councillor Travis said. "It would be my duty, in that case, to cast a vote."

Emmanuel felt a flicker of reluctant admiration. If the vote was overwhelmingly in favour of one view or the other, Councillor Travis would either get what he wanted without voting or avoid being tainted by the unsuccessful attempt to condemn the Commonwealth. And, if he had to cast the decisive vote, he would look like he had been reluctant to make any decision.

"It would be," Emmanuel agreed, finally.

"The inquest will begin in three days," Councillor Travis said. "You would be welcome as my guest...?"

"Thank you, but I should at least *try* to be neutral," Emmanuel said. It would be easy, terrifyingly easy, to slant his reports in favour of one side or the other. And his relationship with Jasmine would leave him open to suggestions that he was doing just that. "But I will attend."

"Please do," the Councillor said. "And thank you for coming."

Emmanuel nodded, shook hands again and strode out of the office. Once he was back on the street, he reached for his wristcom and started to tap in Jasmine's code, before hesitating in doubt. *Should* he call her and explain what had happened? She'd pass it on to her superior, of that he had no doubt. But how could he keep it from her? She needed to know...

...And, it struck him suddenly, Councillor Travis might have *assumed* that he would tell her. But why? It wasn't as if anything he'd said to Emmanuel was a secret. There was no way the hearing could be held in private. By law, the media would be there along with public witnesses. Hell, if the hearing was already organised, it had probably been announced on the datanet by now.

Grimly, he finished tapping in her code and lifted the wristcom to his lips. He'd tell her...

...And, whatever happened, he'd deal with it.

"I was blindsided," President Gabriella Cracker said, sourly. "He got thirteen of the councillors to back a demand for a hearing before I even heard a whisper about it."

Ed nodded. "I think he must have assumed that you would automatically take my side," he said. They'd been lovers for over three years. By now, he rather doubted there was anyone on Avalon who hadn't heard that the President and the Marine Colonel were lovers. "And they didn't have to inform you, did they?"

"No," Gaby said. "Bloody politics!"

"You *are* a politician," Ed reminded her. "And you've been one since birth."

Gaby made a face. Her grandfather had been the legendary Peter Cracker, the leader of the first insurgency against the Avalon Development Corporation. Her father had carried on *his* father's legacy and, when he'd died, Gaby had been the only person all of the various factions could agree on to replace him. And, when the old Council had been defeated and the Crackers had come to terms with the new government, Gaby had run for President and won.

"How long will it be," she asked, "until we get a cadre of professional politicians?"

Ed hesitated, taking the question seriously. One of the charges Gaby's enemies threw at her, regularly, was that *she* was a hereditary politician. Never mind the fact, he considered, that she'd signed laws into the books that prevented partners, children and grandchildren of previous politicians from holding political office. Or that she'd already announced that she wouldn't attempt to run for President a second time.

"I don't think we will," he said, finally. "Travis certainly isn't a professional politician."

"I know," Gaby said. "The bastard is almost *admirable*. Hell, he *was* admirable."

She stood up and started to pace her office, her tread shaking the wooden floorboards. "The hearing will start in three days, Ed," she said. "I can't stop it. They will interrogate you thoroughly on everything that went wrong on Lakshmibai – you and your senior officers. And I have no idea what will happen if they vote to punish you."

"I will have to step down," Ed said. It was odd to admit that a local government had the power to force a Marine to resign from his position.

Yet another sign, in his opinion, that existence as he'd known it was over. "And they might take you down too."

"They might," Gaby agreed. "And with the tension between us and Wolfbane..."

Ed gritted his teeth. Nothing had been decided on Lakshmibai – and, in hindsight, he had to wonder if Wolfbane hadn't *wanted* to decide anything on Lakshmibai. Had they agreed to allow the CEF to travel to the border world to see how the Commonwealth's armed forces handled a challenge? They'd set the terms and conditions for the negotiations, after all. And all they had gained from the brief furious battle on Lakshmibai was a note of where the border ran between the two interstellar powers.

"I know," Ed said. The Empire hadn't had to worry about a peer power – but the Commonwealth's intelligence department suspected that Wolfbane had enough ships and men to give the Commonwealth a very hard time. "We may have a distraction at the worst possible time."

Gaby looked up at him. "Do you think he's right?"

Ed didn't need to ask about *what*. "The mere presence of the cloud-scoop makes us targets," he said, simply. "We either try to impose our own order on the surrounding sectors or they impose their order on us. Isolation isn't an option."

"I know," Gaby said. "So why does Travis feel differently?"

CHAPTER FOUR

> For example, the conflict on Janus began when a large-scale drought afflicted half of the main continent, causing famine on a colossal scale. The planetary government failed to provide assistance; in fact, it made the problems considerably worse. It should not have been surprising that the starving masses rose up against the rest of the planet, causing bad feelings that continued to plague the planet long after the drought came to an end.
> - Professor Leo Caesius, *War in a time of 'Peace:'*
> *The Empire's Forgotten Military History*

They hadn't managed to remove the smell.

Or maybe it was just her imagination, Commodore Mandy Caesius told herself, as she settled into *Sword's* command chair. None of the other crewmen, even the ones who had been liberated from various pirate strongholds, reported the stench of human urine and faeces pervading the ship. But for Mandy, who had spent several months on *Sword* as a pirate slave, there was no escaping the memories of the time her life hadn't been her own. Even now, as a confident and experienced spacer, the memories still haunted her.

Sword, largely thanks to Mandy's efforts, had been badly damaged when she'd been captured by the Marines. It had taken two years of hard work to replace most of the systems she'd destroyed, two years and plenty of resources that might have been better spent building starships from scratch. But the Commonwealth needed as many hulls as it could produce and an ex-Imperial Navy heavy cruiser was too valuable a prize to scrap.

When *Sword* had finally re-entered service, she'd been thoroughly cleaned and all of the evidence of pirate occupancy had been removed. Mandy still had nightmares.

"Captain," the tactical officer said, breaking into her recollections. "The freighter is in position."

Mandy nodded, then glowered over at the tactical display. A single light freighter, over five hundred years old, hung several thousand kilometres in front of *Sword*, waiting for the heavy cruiser. The freighter had been in a disgusting condition when she'd been captured, during a raid on a pirate-held asteroid; there hadn't seemed any point to refitting her, not when she was nothing more than a hull with engines. But now, thanks to the Commonwealth Navy and the Trade Federation's advanced weapons research program, she would serve a useful purpose once again.

"Confirm with the scientists," she said. "Make sure they're off the ship."

"Aye, Captain," the tactical officer said.

There was a long pause as he worked his console. Mandy smiled, remembering just how woolly-headed her father could become when he was working on a new thesis. He tended to forget everything from his wife and daughters to even something as simple as eating when he got hungry. Professor Caesius would have been happy in his ivory tower on Earth, if he'd been allowed to remain there. But, if the rumours were true, the family had been very lucky when they'd been expelled from Earth. Humanity's homeworld had collapsed into war and anarchy only months after their departure.

"The scientists have all left the ship," the tactical officer confirmed, finally. "They're currently on the observation barge."

Mandy allowed her smile to widen. She might be hellishly inexperienced compared to the Imperial Navy's ideal, but she was about to do something that few of the Empire's former commanders had ever been allowed to try. If there was one advantage to the fall of the Empire, it was that universities and research labs on the Rim had been able to escape the strictures and start genuinely original research. There were, she'd been told, all kinds of promise in gravimetric research, but the Empire's established interests had always blocked research into such technology. Who knew what would be the results of a sudden improvement in the Empire's technology?

But now the Empire was gone and those strictures no longer existed. Who knew where *that* would lead?

"Confirm that the shield generator is in place," she ordered. "And then send the activation signal."

On the display, the image of the freighter seemed to distort, slightly. Mandy watched, feeling an odd chill running down her spine. It was simple enough for a powerful starship – heavy cruisers or battleships – to create a gravimetric shield they could swing around to block incoming fire. Hullmetal was tough, but it couldn't take everything. But all the enemy ships had to do was fire from multiple vectors and stagger their fire to render the shield useless. It had been one of the great limiting factors of space combat.

But now...

"Shield in place," the tactical officer reported. "Target locked."

Mandy sucked in a breath. "Fire one," she ordered. "I say again, fire one."

Sword didn't even shudder as she launched a single missile towards her target. Mandy watched, her heart in her mouth, as the missile entered attack range and detonated, sending a single spear of energy towards the targeted freighter. The beam of energy hit the freighter's shield...and splashed. For a moment, the visual feed showed the freighter wrapped in a glowing bubble of light, which swiftly faded away to nothingness. The freighter, which should have been melted to molten debris, was intact.

"My god," the tactical officer breathed.

Mandy understood. She'd never even *considered* working in space, let alone joining the navy, until after she'd been exiled to Avalon. The tactical officer, on the other hand, had been an Imperial Navy officer who'd been kidnapped and pressed into service by the pirates. He had enough experience to feel, truly feel, just how radically space combat had just changed. But Mandy took it in her stride.

Not that we were ever in a major battle, she thought. *Only pirates...and raiders.*

The thought made her scowl. Over the past two months, more and more reports of *incidents* along the border with Wolfbane had arrived on Avalon. Starships disappearing, unknown starships detected inside various Phase Limits...even reports of outside interference on a dozen worlds. It took a month to make the round trip from Avalon to Thule, which was *on* the border; God alone knew how badly the situation had changed by now. Mandy knew her father had hoped otherwise, but she had a nasty feeling that the Commonwealth Navy was about to face its first major test. Wolfbane, positioned between Avalon and the former Core Worlds, might well have conquest in mind.

"Report," she ordered. "Just how successful was the test?"

"The shield generators held," the tactical officer reported. "Projections indicate that the freighter would have survived at least five more hits before the shield generators overloaded and failed. Overall, the system is less effective than gravimetric shields, but more protective."

"Impressive," Mandy said. In short battles, the shields would give her ships a decisive advantage. "And the power strain?"

"As projected," the tactical officer said. "Larger ships will presumably require more power to operate the generators, but will also be able to carry multiple generators to provide additional layers of protection."

"We'll see," Mandy said. She stood. "Contact Avalon; inform them that the test was a success. Then take us back to the shipyard, best possible speed."

"Aye, Captain," the helmsman said.

Mandy allowed herself another smile as she felt the heavy cruiser coming to life around her. It wouldn't take more than a few months, she had been assured, for the entire navy to be fitted with shields, as well as modified missiles. By then, their combat power would be greater than an Imperial Navy fleet of comparable size. And they had other advantages too, she knew. Her crews actually knew what they were doing, while the average Imperial Navy repair technician barely knew anything more than how to take out one self-contained component and replace it with another. But the Empire was gone.

She shivered as she headed off the bridge, walking into her office. The real question was more urgent – and it had no answer. Had Wolfbane advanced too? And, if so, what had *they* discovered?

The hatch hissed closed behind her and she caught her breath, forcing herself to breathe through her mouth. Maybe, just maybe, she understood the strictures now. There was something terrifying about the thought of going into battle against an enemy of unknown capabilities, an enemy who might be armed with something so devastating that your entire fleet would be blown to atoms before you ever realised you were under attack. Maybe the Imperial Navy hadn't wanted to run the risk of someone stumbling over something that would render its thousands of hulls instantly obsolete. After all, most tactical innovations – she'd been told – tended to be modifications of weapons and technology that were already well understood.

Sitting down at her desk, she composed a report to her senior officer, then opened her mailbox and discovered a brief note from Jasmine. It was a shame she hadn't been able to join the older Marine on a clothes-shopping expedition, but Jasmine seemed to think she'd done alright. Mandy carefully refrained from laughing at the picture the older woman had sent, then wrote back quickly. *Sword* was due back in Avalon orbit later in the week and they'd have time to meet up then. Perhaps they could go shopping again.

"I just received a hand-delivered message for you," Command Sergeant Gwendolyn Patterson said, knocking on the half-open door. "It looks alarmingly official."

"Pass it over," Ed grunted. He'd been busy trying to determine just how many Marines he could pull away from detached duties to make up another platoon and it was proving a frustrating task. His Marines had been meant to fill in holes until civilians were trained up, but half of them didn't even have replacements on the way. "Is there anything from the local police?"

"Apparently, the two missing soldiers were last seen entering a brothel," Gwendolyn said, her voice heavy with amused disapproval. "I think the mystery of their disappearance is about to be solved."

Ed didn't bother to disagree. Last night, two soldiers hadn't reported back to their barracks after a night on the town. Camelot's civilian police had been alerted – it hadn't been *that* long since a Marine had been kidnapped by the Crackers – but if they were last seen in a brothel, the chances were that they'd simply overslept or forgotten that they were meant to report back to the barracks. They'd face a week of punishment duties when they were found – unless, of course, something more serious had happened. But it didn't seem too likely.

He took the envelope and opened it, slowly. Earth rarely used paper for anything other than official communiqués, but Avalon still used paper for almost everything, despite the growth of the planetary datanet. The old Council had controlled the system they'd installed, using it to maintain their grip on power. Even now, few people who remembered life under their rule trusted the datanet. It was something, Ed knew, that would only fade in time.

Gwendolyn leaned forward. "Bad news?"

"Bad enough," Ed said. The councillors had finally sent him a note stating that he would be required to testify before the hearing on the following day. He had to admire their speed, he reluctantly admitted. On Earth, it could take years to organise the hearing; hell, the question of what shape the table would be could occupy them for months. Unless, of course, someone with enough political clout was pushing the issue forward. "They want me to talk."

He shook his head. Back on Earth, most military officers who had to face a hearing were forced to undergo a pre-hearing hearing called a Murder Board, where PR officials would force them to rehearse answering questions that ranged from the stupid to the perceptive. He *hadn't* faced a Murder Board before facing the Grand Senate himself, which might be why his Marines had been exiled from Earth. Given what they'd heard since then, they might well be luckier than any of the Marines or civilians who had remained on Earth. God alone knew what had happened to them.

"Good luck," Gwendolyn said, sympathetically. "These guys will probably be more focused than the Grand Senate."

Ed made a face. In OCS, they'd been forced to watch recordings of hearings held by the Grand Senate on Earth. Half of the Grand Senators had spent their allocated time making speeches rather than asking questions, let alone listening to the answers. Somehow, whatever else could be said about the Council, he doubted it would have that problem. All twenty-one councillors had a long experience of practical work, rather than professional politics.

Strange, he thought cynically, *how something that works well can work against us*.

"True," he said. He put the envelope down, then looked up at her. "Is there anything new from Training Command?"

"I believe the Drill Instructors would prefer you didn't keep harassing them for details," Gwendolyn said, dryly. "They *are* responsible for the recruit training program."

Ed nodded, abashed. The temptation to micromanage was overpowering, all the more so as the training program expanded and became more complex. Soon, they'd have to give serious thought to building their own version of the Slaughterhouse. The traditions of the Marine Corps would live on, in one form or another. But would it be the same when the soldiers served on their own homeworlds, when they could go back home at any time? Or would something be lost along with the Empire the Marine Corps had once served?

"They probably would," Ed said, reluctantly. Training was vitally important – and badly-trained soldiers were hard to retrain to acceptable standards. And yet, there had been surprisingly few problems...which might be about to change. Ed rather suspected that Councillor Travis intended to shine a light into every last section of the military on Avalon. "Is there anything else I can use to distract myself?"

"There's a couple of updates from Corinthian," Gwendolyn said. "The provisional government is looking forward to sending new recruits to Avalon – and has expressed interest in the Stormtrooper program. And support for the Commonwealth as a whole remains at an all-time high."

Ed smiled. If there was one definite advantage to being on Avalon – apart from not having the Grand Senate meddling in his operations – it was that they genuinely *did* manage to do some good for the sector. Admiral Singh's regime had been deposed and a new regime, a provisional government, had taken over, long enough for Corinthian to join the Commonwealth, along with the other worlds Admiral Singh had conquered. Corinthian alone represented a major boost to the Commonwealth's industrial base, while the starships they'd captured had strengthened the Commonwealth Navy.

Good thing we acted as fast as we did, he thought, ruefully. *If she'd invaded our space, we would have been crushed very quickly.*

He shook his head, wondering – again – just what had happened to the thousands of starships that had made up the Imperial Navy. Worries over just who had taken control of them were what kept him up at night – and drove him to invest vast resources in the advanced weapons development project. Avalon had started with nothing more than a handful of shuttles and an orbital station. It was a miracle that they'd managed to expand as far as they had – and yet, if a full Imperial Navy fleet survived, they would be badly outgunned. They *had* to enhance their technology.

"That's something I can mention at the hearing," Ed said, finally. "Anything else?"

Gwendolyn smirked. "Several requests for technical support, a couple of planets requesting the deployment of Marines or Stormtroopers to back them up against bandits...and the usual reports from the border," she said. Her face fell, slightly. "We're going to have trouble, boss."

"I know," Ed said. He'd hoped that sharing the perils of a siege would have formed a bond between himself and the Wolfbane representatives, but even if one existed, their superiors had different ideas. "I think we have to prepare for the worst."

His console chimed. Ed glanced at it, automatically, then blinked in surprise. The message had been sent from a courier boat that had just entered orbit – a courier boat, rather than a freighter or military starship. There were only a handful of such craft within the Commonwealth. The Empire had used them to keep the more populated star systems in touch, but they'd long since been largely withdrawn from the Avalon Sector and the surrounding regions.

Gwendolyn frowned. "Trouble?"

"I think so," Ed said. The message was from Thule, a world right on the border between the Commonwealth and Wolfbane. He downloaded the message, then skimmed it automatically. "They want help. A *lot* of help."

"I see," Gwendolyn said. "And can we help them?"

"That would be a question for the Council," Ed said. He gritted his teeth. The timing was terrible – assuming, of course, that it was also a coincidence. Long experience had taught him the more unpleasant a coincidence happened to be, the less likely it *was* a coincidence. "I'll have to raise it with them ASAP."

"Tomorrow," Gwendolyn said. Her face twisted into a grimace. "They won't make any decision tonight."

Ed nodded, reluctantly. Even if he had insisted on calling a full meeting, it would have been difficult to get them to read the message. Hell, the timing was just *lovely*. A debate over the use of the CEF away from Avalon, mixed with a request to deploy the CEF to another world...and away from Avalon. It was not going to go down well with the politicians.

At least it isn't an immediate problem demanding an immediate response, he thought, grimly. *But what will happen if we do have an immediate problem we have to solve?*

"I'll speak to Gaby tonight, anyway," he said. They'd already agreed that he would sleep in the barracks, although he suspected it was a waste of effort. "And then we will see how best to proceed."

"Good luck," Gwendolyn said, again.

CHAPTER FIVE

Or the mining colony on Stan's World, where the miners were permanently indentured to the operating corporation. They rebelled...and the military supported the corporation, without making any attempt to address the legitimate grievances of the miners. Unsurprisingly, the rebellion continued until Stan's World's entire ecosystem fell into ruins.

- Professor Leo Caesius, *War in a time of 'Peace:' The Empire's Forgotten Military History*

Ed slowed to a halt as he reached the heavy wooden doors barring the entrance into the formal council chamber. The two guards on either side of the door looked at him, then snapped to attention. Ed honestly wasn't sure if they were *meant* to show him any signs of respect, but he couldn't blame them, under the circumstances. The Commonwealth wasn't old or wealthy enough to develop separate military organisations with separate chains of command.

The door opened, revealing the Commonwealth Council Chamber. Unlike the Grand Senate on Earth – assuming it still existed – it was strictly formal, with no decoration beyond a large oil painting of the first Constitutional Convention. Ed saw himself in the painting, standing to one side as Gaby and the other Councillors signed their names to the document, and wondered – once again – just who the artist had used for a model. Even at the peak of his career in the Marines, he hadn't had muscles on his muscles.

He stopped in front of the council bench and saluted, feeling his dress uniform crinkling oddly against his skin. He'd been advised to wear all of his medals as well as his Rifleman's Tab, but he'd declined the suggestion. The Commonwealth Council would not be overawed by his awards, particularly not the ones they'd issued to him themselves. And, unlike the Grand Senate, they wouldn't play petty politics with military awards. A good third of them had military experience of their own. If nothing else, Ed considered, they would understand the limitations of the military as well as its capabilities.

"Please, be seated," Councillor Stevens said. She was chairing the hearing, as Gaby was Ed's partner. "There are two issues facing us today."

Ed had to admit that he rather liked her. She was a middle-aged woman who'd been neutral in the Cracker War, insofar as someone could be uninvolved in the conflict. She'd been a doctor who'd treated both sides equally – and, for some reason, the old Council had left her alone. After the end of the war, she'd revamped the public health service on Avalon and run for office. Her landslide victory had surprised no one.

A Grand Senator would have wasted time with a long speech, either praising himself or attacking his opponents. Councillor Stevens came right to the point.

"We have received a request from Thule for military assistance against an insurgency," she said. "Under the circumstances, the timing is particularly unfortunate, as we are here to debate the earlier deployment of the CEF and how it turned into a disaster of major proportions."

Ed couldn't disagree. Once, the Council would have accepted his decision. Now...they had their doubts about his competence. And, really, could he blame them? The buck stopped with whoever had been in command at the time and Ed, the Colonel of Marines and CO of the Commonwealth Military, had been in command. And *he* had made the decision to deploy the CEF.

Councillor Stevens pressed on. "Colonel Stalker," she said, "do you believe we should respond to Thule's request for help?"

Ed stood, clasping his hands behind his back. "The Commonwealth was founded on many agreements between its original member planets," he said. "One of those agreements was that the Commonwealth would respond to a request for help, should one be made. Thule *has* requested help and we have a legal obligation to provide help, if requested. We cannot back out of the agreement simply because we find it politically embarrassing now."

He paused. When it became apparent that no one was going to interrupt, he pressed on.

"We gave our word, Councillor, that we would respond to a cry for help," he continued. "If we break our word now, we will not be trusted in the future. The Commonwealth will eventually come apart if the treaties, the glue binding it together, are not honoured. We cannot run the risk of destroying the Commonwealth."

Councillor Travis held up his hand to be recognised. "I have reviewed the data on Thule carefully," he said, flatly. "The planet considers itself democratic, but in practice the franchise is restricted heavily. Do we really wish to prop up their government?"

Why, Ed asked himself, *did he have to be so...capable?*

"Thule once possessed the largest industrial base in its sector," Ed said. "Even now, it is still formidable – and, in the future, will grow to dominate the region. We cannot afford to let Thule slip out of the Commonwealth, let alone turn hostile. The Commonwealth needs them too much."

He paused. "The treaties were signed by the legitimately-elected – by their rules – government," he added. "Do we wish to break our own agreement *not* to intervene in local politics by *refusing* the government's request for help?"

Councillor Travis snorted. "But we would be supporting a government that isn't all-inclusive."

Ed took a breath. "The Commonwealth agreed not to intervene in the internal affairs of its member states," he reminded the Council. "We did not want to become like the Empire, which meddled whenever someone bribed the Grand Senate to intervene in their favour. We may not approve of how a member state comports itself, but we have no legal grounds to intervene. And, I might add, as no state can bar emigration, they will eventually have to modify their own system or find themselves running an empty planet."

He kept his face expressionless, despite his amusement. The Commonwealth had too many member states with restricted franchises, but several of them were already reforming. Their populations knew there were opportunities elsewhere in the Commonwealth, on Avalon and a dozen other worlds with no political restrictions, and were leaving in droves. And trying to prevent people, particularly skilled technicians, from leaving *would* be grounds for intervention or suspension from the Commonwealth. *That* would be political and economic suicide almost anywhere.

"Furthermore," Ed continued, "the local government's franchise is based upon employment or tax payments. As the economy of the Commonwealth grows larger, there will be more call for services from Thule, which will expand its own economy and thus its employment pool. Their crisis, caused by a vast collapse in the employment rate, will eventually be reversed by their involvement in the Commonwealth. It is our duty to support them long enough for them to get back on their feet."

"But you could be wrong," Councillor Travis pointed out.

"I agree that it is a possibility," Ed said, hiding his irritation at the jab. "But the Commonwealth's economy has doubled in size over the last year. Integrating Corinthian and the surrounding stars laid the groundwork for continued expansion. I believe that our economy will triple in size over the next two years."

There was a long pause. "I would like to raise an issue," Councillor Jackson said. He'd been a Cracker, one of the ones loyal to Gaby. Ed wasn't sure if that meant he would support Ed openly or if he would make a show of asking probing and incisive questions, just to establish his political independence. "There is a wolf at the door."

A low stir ran through the audience as they looked up at the starchart. On one side, the stars belonging to the Commonwealth shone green; on the other, the stars belonging to Wolfbane shone red. It was clear, from the display, that Thule was within a bare handful of light years from Wolfbane-held territory. The Commonwealth's expansion was bringing it up against another interstellar power of unknown size.

Ed scowled, inwardly. There were just too many unanswered questions about Wolfbane, questions he needed answered as quickly as possible. Just how many stars did they control, he wondered, and just how many starships had they salvaged from the ruins of the Empire? And, for that matter, just what did they want? Governor Brown's file hadn't suggested a rabid empire-builder, but someone who had built up relationships with no less than five massive interstellar corporations was clearly more formidable and ambitious than the file showed.

And if he truly wanted to reunite the Empire, he would have dealt with us openly, Ed thought, grimly. *Instead, we had the farce...*

Councillor Jackson's voice broke into his thoughts. "Do you feel, Colonel, that Wolfbane presents a threat?"

Ed met his gaze. "The unknown is always dangerous," he said. "We have no embassy on Wolfbane, no trading relationships; we don't even have a secure means of communicating with them. Our ships have been expelled from their space, as have starships belonging to the Trade Federation. *Their* freighters, however, have been permitted to enter our space at will, allowing them to spy on our deployments. I do not believe that they have dealt honestly with us."

He paused, then pressed on. "Assuming that their industrial base matches what our records show, before the Empire left us, they would be a formidable opponent," he added. "We have to face up to the possibility that they may mean us harm."

The Grand Senate, he knew, would have questioned that assertion. They'd been so secure in their power and supremacy that the thought of someone threatening them was inconceivable. None of the Councillors had any problems coming to terms with the fact that *some* people meant them a great deal of harm. It made them far more capable governors, Ed had no trouble admitting, than the Grand Senators.

"There is also the simple fact that Thule represents a major prize," he said. "And there are definite reports of off-world involvement with the rebels. Wolfbane may well be supporting them, hoping that they will win and then withdraw from the Commonwealth, removing their industrial base from our sphere of control. Even if they didn't join Wolfbane afterwards, it would still weaken us relative to them."

"We don't want another war," Councillor Stevens said, softly.

"With all due respect, Councillor," Ed said, "it only takes one party to start a war."

The discussion raged back and forth for several minutes. Even on Avalon, the councillors had to *look* as though they were doing their jobs, even if it meant asking the same questions over and over again. Compared to the Grand Senate, however, Ed had to admit they knew what they were doing. But no clear decision could be taken until all the facts were exposed and dragged out into the light.

"Deploying the CEF to Thule could be an open-ended commitment," Councillor Travis said, when the last set of questions had faded away. "Could you promise that the commitment would definitely be limited?"

Ed shook his head. "With all due respect, Councillor," he said, "war is a democracy. The enemy gets a vote. If things went according to plan" – the hasty deployment plan he'd sketched out yesterday, after the request for help arrived – "the CEF would provide a stiffening force to assist the locals in holding their ground while new soldiers were trained to take the offensive. Ideally, the deployment would take no more than a year.

"*However*, nothing ever goes quite according to plan. We can expect the rebels to understand what we are doing" – for more reasons than one, he admitted in the privacy of his own head – "and to work to counter it. Even with our...political advantages, we would still find it an uphill slog if the rebels oppose us at every turn. The deployment could last much longer than a year."

"The young men would be away from home for *years*," Councillor Stevens said.

Ed felt his temper flare, but he kept it in check. "Councillor," he said instead, "every soldier in the CEF *knows* that service away from Avalon is a possibility. The units attached to the CEF were built specifically for speedy deployment. Their personnel were told, when they were offered their choice of assignments, that they might be spending years away from home. They *volunteered* for the assignments, regardless."

Councillor Travis spoke, quickly. "You do not feel that we should establish a hard limit on deployment time? Or on our commitment? I must note that your war against the bandits and the Crackers resulted in victory in less than a year."

"In the bedchamber," someone muttered from the audience.

Ed felt the back of his neck heat, but refused to look round. "There are some similarities, I will admit, between Thule and Avalon, under the old Council," he said. "However, the problems on Avalon admitted of a simple solution, once the old Council was removed from power. Eliminating debt-peonage alone, Councillor, ensured that hundreds of thousands of settlers could claim their democratic rights. The Crackers no longer needed to fight to accomplish their aims. And, unlike many insurgent groups, the Crackers were actually *rational*.

"In short, we could forge a political consensus that provided a long-term solution to Avalon's problems. And we did.

"On Thule, however, there are many other problems. The population is considerably larger, there is a large supporting base for the government – and, to be fair, the government is not driven by a desire for personal power. There is a political solution already, Councillor; the local government merely needs to hold on long enough to implement the solution. And we have a commitment to support them."

He took a breath, then continued. "Insurgencies can be very difficult to destroy," he admitted. "If we tell the insurgents that our deployment will last no longer than five years, they will pull in their horns and outwait us. We may be successful in building up the local government to the point it can handle the insurgency on its own – or we may not. If we fail, the insurgency will resume operations as soon as we pull out."

The thought reminded him of far too many operations carried out at the Grand Senate's behest. Some problems could have been nipped in the bud, if the Grand Senate had been willing to make a commitment in time. Others needed political solutions as well as the application of military force, the carrot as well as the stick. At least the Commonwealth wasn't backing a particular faction, not like the Imperial Army had often had to do in the days of the Empire. There wouldn't be a need to do whatever it took to ensure that their faction won, just because the faction had won the bidding war.

"So you would have us make an open commitment," Councillor Travis said. "I confess this makes me very uneasy."

"That isn't the issue," Councillor Jackson snapped. "We made commitments to the Commonwealth. Are we going to abandon them merely because they prove inconvenient?"

Ed concealed his amusement with an effort. Both of them had been raised in an environment where their word was expected to be their bond. Even now, in politics, neither of them had devolved to the point where they believed in the tactical lie. But actually *keeping* their word – or Avalon's word – would cause them some problems. Would Travis vote to uphold the commitments, thus damaging his campaign against off-world involvement, or try to break the commitments and damage his reputation for keeping his word?

"Colonel," Councillor Travis said. "How do we know that the information we have in our databanks is accurate?"

"The crucial difference between Thule and Lakshmibai," Ed said, "is that we have a large presence on Thule. We have followed local politics ever since we made contact with Thule and they applied to join the Commonwealth. The situation on the ground is well-understood, Councillor, and we will not be going in blind. We know what we will face if we get involved. But we also know the price for *not* getting involved."

There was a long pause. "We will hold a vote after we take a break," Councillor Stevens said. "But then we must return to the subject at hand."

Ed sighed, inwardly. The Grand Senate could delay the conclusions of an inquiry until everyone involved was safely dead, if it felt like it. But the Commonwealth Council had no delaying tactics it could use. The Constitution specifically forbade any form of filibuster, let alone endless hearings and debates. Delay could not be tolerated.

He caught sight of Councillor Travis leaving the room, his face an expressionless mask that suggested he was trying to hide some strong emotion. Ed couldn't help feeling a moment of pity – he couldn't imagine what it was like to lose a son – which he ruthlessly suppressed. No matter the emotions driving the older man, he couldn't be allowed to tear the Commonwealth apart. But he was so *likeable*...

The old Council had been composed of power-hungry men and women, some of which had indulged themselves to the point of becoming pederasts and perverts. None of them had really *cared* about Avalon – or about anything other than themselves. The Grand Senate hadn't been much better. But Councillor Travis genuinely cared.

No one ever told you that you would only face evil men, he thought, bitterly. There had been a few deployments when he'd sympathised more with the insurgents than with the forces he was supposed to support.

They'd been murderers, rapists and thugs – but he'd been ordered to support them, because someone felt they deserved support. *Sometimes, even good men can disagree.*

Shaking his head, he strode from the chamber. There was a waiting room just down the hall, where he could get a cup of coffee and catch up on his mail. And wait, he knew, for the vote that would determine the fate of the Commonwealth.

And what will happen, he asked himself, *if they vote against the deployment?*

He couldn't help wondering if it would be the beginning of the end.

CHAPTER SIX

Or, perhaps worst of all, the ethnic/religious conflict on Morningstar, where one ethnic group became determined to convert or eradicate the other ethnic groups. The Empire attempted to keep the peace and so persistently refused to pass judgement (such measures were forbidden by the social scientists on Earth) that the net result was that all ethnic groups came to loathe the Empire more than their fellows.

- Professor Leo Caesius, *War in a time of 'Peace:'*
The Empire's Forgotten Military History

"There doesn't seem to be any choice," Suzanne said. "We do have a legal obligation to send assistance, if requested."

Councillor Gordon Travis glared down at the coffee cup in his hand, silently cursing the timing. He'd gone so far as to check and recheck the message, half-hoping to find proof that the whole affair had been faked by someone with a vested interest in undermining his position. But there was nothing...and besides, he had to admit, Colonel Stalker wasn't the type of person to fake a message just to interfere with the political system he'd designed. No, the request for help was real. But the timing was suspicious as hell.

He had to admit, when his anger cooled to manageable levels, that both Suzanne and the Colonel were right. An obligation could not be discarded when it became inconvenient, not if the person who had made the obligation wanted to be trusted in future. Part of him was tempted to insist on discarding the obligation anyway, but it wouldn't have helped his reputation on Avalon or off-world. The rest of him remembered the lessons of building a successful business and knew that the obligation had to be honoured. His political opponents wouldn't hesitate to use it against him during the lead up to the next election.

"Damn it," he muttered.

How many other young men, he asked himself, were going to die on Thule? He'd read the files carefully and noted, like Colonel Stalker, that the situation was likely to get very bloody very quickly. Hell, it would take roughly two weeks to get the CEF there, assuming that the formation was ready for instant deployment. And then...he gritted his teeth, remembering the moment he'd had to tell his daughters that their brother was dead. The scene would be repeated in countless more homes on Avalon. What good did it do to send their young men to Thule to die?

Suzanne kept wittering on, but he ignored her, tuning out her voice with the ease of long practice. It was a shame that he even *needed* a political advisor, but he was expected to manage his business as well as serve as a Councillor and someone had to keep tabs on what the other Councillors were doing. And yet she was far too careful for his tastes, far too focused on getting him into high office and keeping him there...but he needed her. He knew, without false modesty, that his first campaign might well have failed without her assistance.

"The vote will be taken in twenty minutes," Gordon said, glancing at his watch. It had been passed down from his father, who had claimed it dated all the way back to the pre-space era on Earth. Personally, Gordon suspected his father had lied through his teeth, but there was no doubting that the watch came from humanity's homeworld. Humanity's *wrecked* homeworld, if the rumours were true. "And I have to vote, one way or the other."

He briefly considered abstaining from the vote. It could be done, he knew, but he would pay a high price for it. And if the vote was drawn, he would have to get off the fence and cast the deciding vote, one way or the other. Either way, he would have to pay the price for abstaining without *actually* abstaining.

"Yes, sir," Suzanne said. If she was irked at being so blatantly ignored, then interrupted, she didn't show it. "I believe you should vote in favour of the deployment."

Gordon nodded. Avalon had given its word – and the Commonwealth had taken it. There was no choice, not if they wanted to maintain interstellar trust. Maybe the terms could be renegotiated again, later, but not now. But he *hated* it. How many young men were going to die because of his decision?

"I will," he said. "And then we can return to the issue at hand."

He put the coffee cup down before his grip cracked the ceramic. The hearing would be sharp, very sharp. And Gordon knew, without lying to himself, that he was going to enjoy it. His son might be dead, but he would ensure that the full story behind the fateful deployment was brought out into the open for judgement. And, if it seemed that someone had been careless, he would make damn sure they were crushed like bugs.

The whistle blew, calling them back to the Council Chamber. Sighing, Gordon nodded goodbye to his aide and strode over towards the door. The other councillors met him outside, exchanging brief greetings as they made their way up the corridor. It was tradition, almost, that the councillors couldn't talk to one another in the building, outside the Council Chamber. Gordon rather approved, even though it could be irritating. They couldn't do anything outside the light of publicity.

That was the problem with the Empire, he thought. *No accountability. And now I have to hold someone to account for the death of my son.*

President Gabriella Cracker disliked politics intensely. She'd never asked to be the granddaughter of Peter Cracker, let alone to be forced to take her father's position as rebel leader. And yet she'd had no choice. Despite her youth, she'd seen and heard enough to know the rebels would fragment into a multitude of smaller groups if she didn't step up and take command. For all their claims to fight for democracy, they'd only proved capable of uniting behind a Cracker.

It had placed no shortage of restrictions on her life. She had to move from place to place constantly, one step ahead of the old Council's hunters, talking to senior resistance leaders and pushing them to work together as a group. There had been no hope of a boyfriend; the boys she knew were all awed by her reputation or terrified at the prospect of dating someone who could order them killed if they put a foot wrong. Nor had there been any hope of a normal life. By the time she'd been captured, after the Battle of Camelot, it had almost been a relief. And then to hear that there would be a political solution...

Avalon had expanded, faster and further than she would have believed possible. Who would have thought that a comparatively minor colony world along the Rim of explored and settled space would wind up as the core of a new empire? *She* certainly hadn't assumed anything of the sort, not when she'd been in command of the Crackers. The best she'd known they could hope for was an agreement with the Empire that would allow them internal independence. And even *that* was a gamble. The last time the Empire had intervened openly in Avalon's affairs, the Crackers had been smashed from orbit.

But we're paying a price for our size now, she thought. *How can we continue to be representative if we swallow up several sectors?*

The Empire had based political representation on population size, she knew, something that had given the Core Worlds immense political clout. Even the entire population of the Commonwealth, put together, couldn't match the population of a single Core World. The Commonwealth had set out to change that, to ensure that each world got one vote regardless of its population size, but even that presented its own problems. Would Corinthian – or Avalon, for that matter – accept equality with farming worlds that had only a handful of settlers?

She thought she understood, now, why the Empire had become so undemocratic. The more space it controlled, the harder it was to have any form of accountability. They'd had to send out orders, then wait for months before they heard back from their subordinates. And the Commonwealth was growing larger every year. How long would it be, she asked herself, before they started issuing very strict orders to their subordinates? Even without the temptation to meddle – no, she admitted; the legal right to meddle – in local affairs, the problems would still prove difficult to surmount.

Bracing herself, she pasted a smile on her face as she stepped back into the Council Chamber and took her seat in the middle of the bench. As President, she had a vote – but she knew she couldn't use it. If she voted in favour of the deployment, she would be accused of supporting her lover; if she voted against the deployment, she would be accused of trying to avoid the *appearance* of supporting her lover. All she could do was abstain. She caught sight of Colonel Stalker as he returned to the room and sighed, inwardly. He was a good man, dedicated to his position – and she loved him. But part of her would have liked to go to an uninhabited island with him and stay there, far away from politics.

But he has a sense of duty, she thought, as the doors were closed. *He can't abandon his men, any more than I could abandon the Crackers after my father died.*

The thought nagged at her mind. What would happen when she left office? There would be no child of her body to take the presidency, even if her child had been legally allowed to inherit. What would happen when someone else became President? Would the system they had created, the system they had built to avoid the problems that had torn the Empire apart, remain stable? Or would public service be replaced by single-minded power grabs?

She nodded to Councillor Stevens, who stood. "The issue before us," she said, as if there was anyone who was in any doubt, "is the deployment of the CEF to Thule. We have debated the facts of the case in our prior session. I call upon you all to put politics aside and vote as you feel you should vote."

Gaby sighed. There was an idealism about Councillor Stevens that had never faded, something Gaby envied and distrusted in equal measure. After all, what could one make of someone who had never chosen a side? Stevens could have covertly supported the Crackers in more ways than just providing medical treatment to all comers. She hadn't done anything of the sort. But she had too many friends to be edged out of her council seat.

And here I am, she reproved herself, *considering removing someone because I don't like their politics. What does that make me?*

"All those in favour, raise your hands," Councillor Stevens said. "I repeat, all those in favour raise your hands."

Gaby watched as seventeen hands were raised, one by one. Seventeen. It was better than she'd feared, although she knew it wouldn't go down well with the Commonwealth. Four councillors on Avalon had voted against upholding the Commonwealth Treaty. God alone knew what the repercussions would be, in the long run. The only real surprise was that Councillor Travis had voted in favour.

"All those against, raise your hands," Councillor Stevens said. "I repeat, all those against, raise your hands."

She paused, significantly. "I must remind you," she added, "that refusing to cast a vote will be taken as an abstention."

There was a long pause. No hands moved. Gaby wasn't too surprised. With such an overwhelming vote in favour of the deployment, there was nothing to gain by trying to take a stand against it. It would be far better for the remaining councillors to abstain, whatever they'd intended to do. She shook her head, bitterly. Lord, but she hated politics with a white-hot passion.

"The motion is passed," Councillor Stevens said. "Seventeen in favour, none against, four abstentions."

A dull ripple ran through the chamber. "As it is late," Councillor Stevens continued, "I propose pushing the rest of the hearing back until tomorrow. Are there any objections?"

"I have one," Councillor Travis said. "Several of the officers I intend to call before the hearing will be dispatched with the CEF."

Councillor Stevens looked over at Colonel Stalker, who nodded. "That is a valid point," he said, evenly. Only someone who knew him very well would have noticed the irritation in his voice. The implication, that he was sending people who could testify against him away from Avalon, hadn't sat well with him. "However, the CEF will require at least a week before departure. Those officers can be called to face the hearing prior to departure."

"Acceptable," Councillor Travis said, surrendering the point. "I have no further objections."

Politics, Gaby thought. Councillor Travis probably wanted to get out to face the reporters. He would have to justify his vote to his constituents, after all. *God damn the lot of it.*

"Then this session is dismissed," Councillor Stevens said. "See you all tomorrow."

Ed allowed himself a moment of relief as he stood up and prepared to make his way to Churchill Garrison. The vote had been taken, the CEF would be deployed...and the Commonwealth would live to see another day. Tomorrow would be harder, he suspected, particularly when Councillor Travis got the bit between his teeth. He'd be summoning officers who'd been deployed with the CEF right, left and centre, looking for something he could use as a weapon. The hell of it was that Ed still found it hard to blame him.

He met Gaby's eyes, exchanging a silent message. They'd talk, tonight, planning a strategy for the following day. Perhaps the damage could be limited...he shook his head, grimly. Like it or not, he'd dropped the ball quite badly. The Council had every right to demand explanations, then changes in procedure to make sure it didn't happen again. But could such changes be realistically implemented?

We may be about to find out, he thought. He hadn't hidden anything from the Council; it was quite possible that Thule would prove a very different challenge, even with support on the ground. And with the other factor...somehow, he knew it was going to be nasty. But they had no choice. Thule could not be allowed to leave the Commonwealth.

"I suppose you're wondering," Councillor Travis said, "why I voted in favour of the deployment."

Emmanuel Alves could hardly disagree. He and his fellow reporters, who were now surrounding Councillor Travis outside the Council Chamber, had expected him to vote *against* the deployment. The whole matter had been intensely debated on the datanet and the general consensus had been that the Councillor would oppose the deployment tooth and nail.

"A man's word is his bond," Councillor Travis continued. "We – the Commonwealth – gave our word to our member states that we would provide military support upon request. I do not believe that we can discard our word, merely because we don't want to actually uphold it. The treaties *will* be rewritten, I suspect, but not now. Now, we have to uphold our word."

There was a long pause. Finally, one of the female reporters stepped forward. "Councillor," she said, "you have based your opposition to the Commonwealth on your son's death. What would you say to the parents of a son or daughter killed on Thule because of your decision to support their deployment?"

Emmanuel winced. *That* was a nasty shot, even by the standards of the Empire's media. It shouldn't have been considered permissible...although he did have to admit that it was a reasonable point to raise. Certainly, grieving families would raise it after their children were delivered home in sealed caskets.

"I would say," Councillor Travis said tightly, "that I honoured treaties that were created to support a new order."

"But that won't be any consolation," the reporter pointed out. Her voice seemed to grow stronger as she pushed onwards. "They'll have lost a child!"

Councillor Travis balled his fists, then visibly forced himself to relax. "It is never easy – and I speak from personal experience – to lose a child. However, I am forced to put such feelings aside and consider the matter as coldly and clearly as I can. In this case, refusing to honour the treaties would have ensured that other states *also* refused to honour the treaties, something that could easily rebound on us. The commitment to send military support upon request was, I feel, a mistake. However, it is one we are obliged to honour until we rewrite the treaties.

"I have the deepest sympathy for anyone who loses a child, particularly on a foreign world," he added. "It is my intention to have those treaties rewritten as soon as possible. Until then, people *will* lose children and

I *will* grieve for them, because of commitments that were made without careful forethought."

He turned, then strode away from the reporters. Emmanuel watched him go, wondering if any of his fellows would be so gauche as to give chase. But none of them did; instead, they talked briefly amongst themselves or headed off to the nearest datanet terminal, where they could start filing their stories. He wondered, absently, just what the newspapers would say in the evening. What sort of spin would they put on the vote?

The papers that support the Councillor will probably say he did what he had to do, he thought, answering his own question. It hadn't taken long for the newspapers on Avalon to take sides, even the ones that called themselves neutral. *Those that are against him will call him a hypocrite. Perhaps they'd both be right.*

Shaking his head, he strode off to find a terminal for himself. He had a story to file.

CHAPTER SEVEN

> These disasters – and many, many more – took place because the Empire rarely attempted to come to grips with the underlying causes of the conflicts. Instead, the Empire attempted to bring peace at gunpoint, order backed by the threat of force. But the force was clearly insufficient to prevent the conflicts from breaking out again when the force was withdrawn.
>
> - Professor Leo Caesius, War in a time of 'Peace:'
The Empire's Forgotten Military History

Jasmine had never been quite able to escape the feel of being called into the headmaster's – and then the Senior Drill Instructor's – office when her superior officers had called her into their offices. It was absurd; she was a grown woman, a fully-trained Marine and had been serving as a Brigadier for the last seven months. But the feeling persisted, no matter what she did. She'd never dared to ask her superiors if they felt the same way when confronted with *their* superiors.

"Please, be seated," Colonel Stalker said. "I assume you've read the briefing packet?"

"Yes, sir," Jasmine said. She'd gone through it in cynical detail, noting all the questions that were left unanswered. "It looks like Avalon when we first arrived, only worse."

"Almost certainly," Colonel Stalker agreed. "But there is a further complicating factor I left out of the briefing packet. Did you deduce it?"

"No, sir," Jasmine said. "I did find quite a few unanswered questions..."

"The leader of the insurgency – or at least one of the most powerful insurgent groups – is a man called Pete Rzeminski," Stalker said. He pressed his fingertips together as he leaned back in his chair. "Does the name mean anything to you?"

"No, sir," Jasmine said, puzzled. "Should it?"

Stalker laughed, humourlessly. "You weren't even born when he was a serving Marine," he said. "He retired from the corps thirty years ago, according to his file, and chose to live on Thule. I rather doubt the name is a coincidence."

Jasmine stared at him. "This insurgency is being led by a retired Marine?"

"Yes," Stalker said. "What do you make of *that*?"

Jasmine hesitated, still trying to come to terms with the concept. The media might create retired or rogue Marines as stock characters, but the former rarely involved themselves in politics and the latter were very rare. Not rare enough, in her opinion, yet she'd only ever heard of a handful of cases during her time in the corps. For a retired Marine to be serving with an insurgency, let alone leading it...

She shook her head. "Does he have good cause?"

"I don't know," the Colonel confessed. "What I do know is that this insurgency will have *professional* leadership."

Jasmine swallowed. Most insurgencies underwent a steep learning curve, discovering how to do everything the hard way. It was uncommon for military veterans to be involved, unless the entire planet was rising in rebellion. But a Marine, armed with the collective knowledge and experience of the Terran Marine Corps, could ensure that the insurgency skipped most of the learning curve. She'd done much the same thing on Corinthian.

"I see, sir," she said. Part of her found the whole concept offensive. How *dare* a Marine betray his oaths and side with the insurgents? The rest of her wondered just what had happened to convince him to join them. "This could get nasty."

"I'm afraid so," the Colonel agreed. He looked up, blue eyes meeting her gaze. "How long would it take for the CEF to board ship and depart?"

"I sent out the warning order yesterday," Jasmine said. "Assuming we start at once, we might be able to depart in five days if we work like demons. And if we can call on support from the crews in the spaceport."

"You'll have it," Stalker assured her. "You will probably be called to testify before the hearing, though. Make sure your XO is ready to take over at a moment's notice."

"Yes, sir," Jasmine said. She hesitated, then reminded herself that Colonel Stalker had never bitten anyone's head off for asking questions. "How did it go today, sir?"

"We have agreement that the CEF is to be deployed," Stalker said. "But the real hearing will start tomorrow."

"It wasn't your fault, sir," Jasmine said. She liked and respected the Colonel. He didn't deserve to be raked over the coals by a council he'd helped create. "They shouldn't be blaming you for it."

"But I was the one in charge," the Colonel said. He tapped points off on his fingers. "If I didn't know what my subordinates were doing, I damn well should have done; if I made the decision based on poor data, I damn well should have taken precautions in any case."

Jasmine nodded, recognising the quote. It had been made by the last Imperial Navy Admiral to retire early, without staying in grade long enough to collect a massive pension. But Admiral Vancouver had always had a sense of integrity his peers had lacked. His career, she'd been taught at the Slaughterhouse, should be held up as an example to be emulated. One poor judgement call shouldn't be allowed to override all of his successful decisions...

But people always remember the failures longer than the successes, she recalled. They'd been taught that too. *A failure can never be removed from the record.*

"In this case, I made a decision that plunged us into a full-scale war," the Colonel continued, seemingly unaware of her inner thoughts. "If I'd objected to the security demands they made, if I'd insisted on keeping even a single starship in the system, it wouldn't have happened. Even if I am blameless, we still have to go over the whole affair, just to ensure that it never happens again."

Jasmine frowned. "But wouldn't that mean that people would hesitate before making a decision?"

The Colonel shrugged. "There are some decisions that have to be made quickly," he said, "decisions when being half-right is better than being completely wrong. But the decision I made could have been made more carefully, after much contemplation. Better to hesitate then, I fancy, than get into trouble I might have been able to avoid."

He shrugged again. "In any case, your orders are as follows..."

There was a sharp knock on the door, interrupting him. "Come in," the Colonel called. "Now."

The door opened, revealing Mandy. Jasmine felt a warm smile spread across her face as she saw the girl she regarded almost as a little sister, now looking very grown up in a basic Commonwealth Navy shipsuit and uniform. The uniform looked a little larger than Jasmine recalled, hiding the shape of Mandy's body, but it wasn't too surprising. After what Mandy had endured as a pirate slave, she had never been able to have a proper relationship. At least she had managed to tough herself out of some of the other reactions to enslavement.

"It's good to see you again," Jasmine said, allowing her professional demeanour to slip, just slightly. "I heard about the successful test."

The Colonel cleared his throat, meaningfully. "Commodore Caesius will command a support squadron attached to your command," he said, "but she will also have another mission."

He tapped a switch, activating the holographic display. "We have good reason to believe that Wolfbane is supplying the insurgents on Thule," he said. "That, combined with the other reports, leads us to believe that Governor Brown is not feeling friendly. Depending on the assumptions we use, he may have decided to take us out before facing any threats from the Core."

"Assuming that anyone is left alive there," Mandy said.

Jasmine couldn't disagree. No one knew what had happened to the Core Worlds – or the Slaughterhouse – apart from rumours, each one wilder than the last. It was possible that they'd all been destroyed, wiped clean of human life...or that someone with enough firepower at his command had taken over the remains of the Empire. But with Wolfbane blocking their advance towards the Core Worlds, there was no way to obtain accurate data.

"I don't think the entire sector will have been wiped out," the Colonel said.

Jasmine had her doubts. Earth and the rest of the Core Worlds, all hideously overpopulated, had been dependent on their infrastructure for survival. If there had been a major war, it was quite likely that billions of humans had starved to death, if they hadn't been slaughtered by nuclear strikes or orbital bombardments. The Empire had kept one hell of a lot of tensions under control, but now the Empire was gone. Who knew what had happened, thousands of light years away?

The Colonel smiled, tightly. "Once the CEF has been delivered to Thule, Commodore Caesius and her command will be responsible for scouting the stars known to belong to Wolfbane," he said. "You will *covertly* enter their star systems, make passive sweeps near their planets, then withdraw without being detected. In the event you *are* detected, you are to break contact as fast as possible, preferably without being identified. Do you understand me?"

"Yes, sir," Mandy said. She sounded excited, rather than nervous. "It should be doable, unless they've made a breakthrough in sensor technology."

Jasmine remembered the little brat she'd been and smiled inwardly. Mandy had come a long way, even if her mother was still horrified at what her daughter had become. But it was her own fault, Jasmine considered, for refusing to recognise what a wonderful daughter she had brought into the universe. Or maybe not...Mandy had been a typical spoilt brat for much longer than she'd been a responsible starship commander. Her mother might not be in the best condition to realise that her daughters had finally grown up.

"Should you discover anything threatening," Colonel Stalker continued, "you will dispatch a courier boat to Avalon at once, then return to Thule and take what actions seem necessary, should the planet come under outside attack."

They were vague orders, Jasmine knew, and the Imperial Navy wouldn't have tolerated them for a moment. Their senior officers would have insisted on writing out a plan for every contingency – or at least every contingency they could imagine – which tended to result in disaster when something happened that wasn't covered in the contingency plans. But the Commonwealth Navy knew better. As the officers on the spot, Jasmine and Mandy would be expected to use their own initiative, within the broad outlines laid down by their superiors.

She leaned forward, thoughtfully. "Sir," she said, "do you think it will be war?"

"I would like to believe otherwise," the Colonel said. "But we shall prepare for the worst and hope for the best."

"Yes, sir," Jasmine said.

"You are to start embarking the CEF as soon as possible," the Colonel said. "If you can locate anyone with local knowledge, feel free to ask them to join you."

He hesitated, then looked at Mandy. "Our best estimates suggest that Wolfbane will have started with twice the tonnage of the Commonwealth Navy," he said. "We have no idea how...active that tonnage is, however."

Jasmine nodded. In theory, the Imperial Navy had deployed hundreds of thousands of warships; in practice, half of them had been classed as part of the reserve and placed in storage orbits around isolated military bases or cannibalised to keep the rest of the fleet operational. There was no way to know how many of the ships within Wolfbane's sphere of influence remained operational – or what they might have built, since leaving the Empire. If Avalon could make real progress on indigenous designs, there was no reason why Wolfbane couldn't do the same.

"That leads to the very real possibility that they will attack in sufficient force to take Thule," the Colonel continued. "If that happens, if there is no prospect of saving the planet, you are to fall back and avoid engagement – if possible. I do not wish to see you throw the lives of your crew away on futile gestures."

"I understand," Mandy said.

Jasmine wondered, absently, if she really understood what that meant. Mandy had been in danger herself – as a pirate slave, she ran the risk of being raped or murdered at any moment, even though she'd been one of the lucky ones – but she'd never had to cope with a situation where people under her command were at risk. How would Mandy cope when the time came to face an impossible situation?

"Good," the Colonel said. He looked over at Jasmine. "I will add sealed orders for you to open, should the shit hit the fan. Until then, good luck."

He passed a pair of datachips towards them. The Empire had insisted on writing out operational orders on old-fashioned paper, but it was one tradition the Commonwealth had no intention of retaining. Electronic orders were much simpler to use.

"Thank you, sir," Jasmine said.

"One other detail," the Colonel said, looking right at her. "I need you to give it back."

Jasmine knew, without having to ask, what he meant. She sensed, rather than saw, Mandy's puzzled look as she hesitated, then reached into her pocket. The Rifleman's Tab felt uncomfortably cold against her bare skin, the gold sheen discoloured by the explosion that had killed its owner. It should have been returned to the Slaughterhouse, Jasmine knew, but God alone knew when – if – they would see the Slaughterhouse again.

I'm sorry, Blake, she thought.

It didn't seem fair, somehow. Blake had been larger-than-life, a joker who would never see promotion...but was happy serving as a Marine. She remembered how he'd welcomed her to the platoon, just before the shit hit the fan on Han, and how they'd all played pranks on an Imperial Army unit that happened to share the same base. And how he'd saved her life, more than once, during the maelstroms that had swept over Han, Earth, Avalon and Corinthian. It didn't seem *right* that he should die on a world like Lakshmibai, during a pointless uprising that could only have resulted in disaster. Even if the locals *had* wiped the CEF out, the starships would have taken a brutal revenge.

Blake would have laughed at her, she knew. He'd never been sentimental, moving from girlfriend to girlfriend without bothering to mourn the loss of the previous girl. All he needed was fighting, booze and sex and he was happy. But Jasmine found it hard to let go of his memory. He hadn't been the first to die under her command, but he was the one she'd known the best before he'd fallen.

"Not every death seems meaningful," Colonel Stalker said, as he took the Tab. It had been pulled out of the wreckage of the Royal Palace, weeks after Blake's death. "But Blake died saving lives. None of us could ask for more."

Jasmine nodded, not trusting herself to speak. Blake would have teased her endlessly about sleeping with a reporter, then gently poked fun at her command style. And he would have commanded 1st Platoon on Thule...

She paused. "Colonel," she said. "Who will take command of 1st Platoon?"

"I'm going to give it to Joe Buckley," Colonel Stalker said. "There aren't many other qualified candidates right now, not when I had to swap out half the experienced Marines to create room for the ones who used to be on detached duty. Joe may screw up from time to time, but he's very good at recovering from his mistakes."

Jasmine nodded. Like it or not, she would probably never be able to command another Marine platoon. Besides, fitting in the newcomers would be a nightmare...thankfully, Joe Buckley could be diplomatic as well as bloody-minded. He was going to need it.

"I'll speak to you again, probably just before you depart," the Colonel concluded. He placed Blake's Tab in his drawer, then closed it. Jasmine couldn't help feeling that she'd just said goodbye to all that remained of her friend. "Let me know if you encounter any problems."

"Yes, sir," Jasmine said, tonelessly.

Outside, Mandy caught her arm. "Are you all right?"

"I think so," Jasmine lied. Blake's death *hurt* – and the unspoken reprimand was almost worse. "And yourself?"

Mandy gave her an odd look. "Jasmine..."

"I'll be fine," Jasmine said, sharply. The last thing she wanted was to have this discussion where someone – anyone – could hear it. "I have to see to the loading."

"Good luck," Mandy said. She gave Jasmine's arm a squeeze, then let go. "And tonight, would you like to join me for dinner? Or we could go shopping."

Jasmine had to smile at the eagerness in the younger girl's voice, even though she recognised that Mandy was only trying to get her to talk. God knew she'd needled Jasmine enough about her relationship ever since discovering that Jasmine was sharing an apartment with a man.

"We shall see," she said. There were no formal office hours in the military, no matter what some of the more ignorant politicians on Earth thought. She would probably wind up sleeping on a cot in her office, instead of back home with her lover. "Don't you have deployment work to handle too?"

Mandy smirked. "That's what XOs are for," she said, evilly. "I merely pass on the orders, then let them handle it."

"And you still get blamed if something goes wrong," Jasmine reminded her. She shook her head, running her hand through her short hair. As always, it felt vaguely itchy to the touch, but she'd never been able to work up the nerve to remove it completely. The treatment couldn't be reversed and her parents would have been horrified. Her mother, in particular, had been very proud of her long dark hair. "Watch your back."

"I will," Mandy promised.

Jasmine smiled, then headed back towards her office. There was no time to waste, not if they wanted to leave as soon as possible. And there was deployment planning to be done.

And a new aide to break in, she thought, ruefully. *Bad timing. Very bad timing.*

CHAPTER EIGHT

This seems obvious, you must admit, which leads neatly to the next question. Why did the Empire fail to recognise that this was the problem and that it had to be tackled?

- Professor Leo Caesius, *War in a time of 'Peace:'*
The Empire's Forgotten Military History

Violet Campbell prided herself on being the youngest spacecraft comptroller in orbit. At twelve years old, barely entering puberty, she was a solid three years younger than the next oldest comptroller. Indeed, she was young enough that half of the starship crews she met thought she was accompanying her mother rather than doing the job in her own right. But she didn't let that get her down. The excitement of meeting starship crewmen from hundreds of different worlds more than made up for them treating her as a little kid.

She stopped outside the airlock and waited, showing a patience few children from the planet below could master, while the giant starship linked hatches with Orbit Station. Violet had grown up on the station, even during the dark years when almost no starships had visited Avalon and her father - the station manager - had seriously considered either joining the RockRats or shipping his children to Avalon, where a single failure wouldn't risk ultimate catastrophe. Not that Violet wanted to go, of course. Half of what she'd heard about settled worlds made them sound hellish, while the remainder made them seem uncontrolled. Who would want to live in a wilderness when they could live in the infinite reaches of outer space? If her parents had seriously planned to send her groundside, she would have run away and joined the RockRats. They would have welcomed her.

Bracing herself, she checked her reflection in the hatch's porthole. She was slim, the protective shipsuit she wore revealing her lack of curves to the world. Her short dark hair surrounded a thin, almost elfin face. She honestly wasn't sure if she was pretty or not; her life on the station hadn't left her with many other women to compare herself to. But she did have the glamour of working in space, her father had told her, although he'd also told her that she was too young to date. And that anyone who tried to ask her out before she was sixteen would be hurled out the airlock without a spacesuit. Violet suspected he was joking, but she didn't want to test it. Her father could act rashly at times.

The hatch finally clicked, then hissed open, revealing a pressurised tube that linked the starship to the station. Violet checked the telltales out of habit – her father had drummed caution into her, time and time again – but everything seemed fine. None of the systems were reporting any atmospheric leaks or any other form of contamination. The starship might be a Trade Federation liner rather than something from the Commonwealth, but there was nothing wrong with it. Violet rather approved of the Trade Federation. *They* never seemed surprised at encountering a young girl manning the immigration desk.

"Welcome to Avalon," she called, as the first row of people emerged from the starship and made their way down the tube. They were rich, she knew, rich enough to travel in cabins rather than stasis tubes. "Can I have your papers please?"

One by one, they presented her with their credentials, which she checked against her datapad and then invited them to press their fingers against her scanner. Avalon was an open world, her father had told her when she'd insisted on taking up the job, but there were some people who were permanently barred from entry. If any of them appeared, he'd warned, she was to let them through into the station and sent a silent alert to the security team. She was not, under any circumstances, to attempt to tackle the unwanted visitor by herself. Violet found that rather insulting – she'd regularly taken top marks in armed and unarmed combat – but her father had been insistent. Recognising the signs of a father about to withdraw permission for her to actually work, she'd shut up and stopped arguing.

She chatted briefly to some of the visitors as they made their way past her. Most of them were coming on trade missions, opening up new lines of communication within the Commonwealth, while others were new to the planet. A handful of younger men cheerfully told her that they'd come to join the Commonwealth Navy; Violet pointed them towards the recruitment station, then wished them well. Who knew? Maybe she'd see them again as naval crewmen.

The next line of passengers appeared shortly after the first set had vanished. They looked rather more dishevelled, Violet noted; the bags they were carrying were all their worldly goods. She had no difficulty in recognising men and women coming to Avalon to look for work and political freedom, both unavailable on their homeworld. Most of them had no ID, so she took fingerprints and forwarded them on to the immigration office. None of them seemed to be on the banned list.

"Report into the office when you reach the ground," she told them, again and again. "They'll grant you residency permission and point you in the direction of some recruitment agencies."

She watched them go, hoping they'd find the life they wanted. New immigrants had plenty of opportunities to earn money, but some of them found themselves trapped in contracts that made them effective peons. Her father had been known to grumble that the shadow of the old Council – Violet was too young to remember the days it ruled Avalon – clearly lived on in some people. The big exploiters might have been removed, but there were plenty of others willing to exploit helpless immigrants just to save a few coins.

A final man emerged from the hatch, looking tired, thoroughly exhausted. Violet looked at him – and stared. He was tall, with short blonde hair and muscles that stood out even through the shapeless civilian clothes he was wearing. There was a faint scar on his face that drew her attention to the shape of his mouth. Violet flushed as she realised she was staring, then looked down at the datachip he held out to her. He was yet another immigrant from a farming world. Violet had heard about them from her father. The highest level of technology was something called a mule plough, which forced its user to walk behind a mule for their entire life. When she'd asked why, her father had gone on to rant about idiots who hated technology and were prepared to sentence themselves and their children to a hellish lifestyle, rather than admit they were wrong.

"Welcome to Avalon," she said, as she plugged the datachip into the terminal. There was a bleep as it recognised the man; apparently, one of the recruitment agencies had already cleared him through immigration and was waiting for him down below. "You were invited here?"

"I saved the recruiter's life," the man explained. His voice was almost completely devoid of an accent. Violet was impressed. Everyone was *supposed* to speak Imperial Standard, but there were so many different accents in the Commonwealth alone that some of the immigrants were almost incomprehensible. "He offered me a fast ticket to Avalon, but I had to wait until I had taken care of my family."

"Good for him," Violet said. She keyed her terminal, clearing the newcomer through to the first available shuttle to the surface, then smiled as she returned his datachip. "Welcome to Avalon."

"Thank you," the newcomer said.

"I feel naked," Joe Buckley commented.

Jasmine eyed him. He was wearing standard combat blacks, the uniform worn by Marines when location-specific uniforms weren't issued, which fell loosely around his wiry body. His belt was crammed with everything from spare clips of ammunition and medical supplies to a terminal and portable environmental sensors. Apart from his head, every part of his body was decently covered.

"You're not," she said, shortly "Or are you referring to actually being in command?"

Buckley scowled. Everyone knew he had one kind of luck – bad. Jasmine had watched in astonishment as Buckley stumbled from disaster to disaster, half of which should probably have killed him. Only a remarkable talent for adapting had kept him alive – and only a strong friendship with the rest of the original 1st Platoon had kept him in the company. Marines were rarely superstitious, preferring to leave such beliefs to spacers, but it was hard to deny that Buckley seemed to attract bad luck.

"It should be yours," he pointed out. "Or…"

Jasmine nodded. "I felt the same way when I was given command," she admitted. Marines weren't supposed to admit to doubts in front of outsiders, but they could confess to one another, if necessary. "I wondered if I could handle it, particularly with you and Blake under my command. But I have no doubt that you can do it too."

She smiled, as reassuringly as she could. Jasmine had been the youngest member of the platoon and, by rights, Blake should have taken command. But he'd blotted his record rather spectacularly during the Cracker War and would probably have been demoted, if there had been any demotion possible without dishonourably discharging him from the corps. As it was, he had been stripped of seniority and warned he might never be promoted again. But he had redeemed himself and taken command…long enough to die, only a few months ago.

"Thank you," Buckley said. He didn't sound convinced. "And the specific orders for 1st Platoon?"

Jasmine took a breath. "I have no specific orders as yet, apart from getting your asses onto the starships as soon as possible," she said. "I suggest you run endless drills to bond the platoon back together, after all the transfers. There will almost certainly be work for you to do on Thule."

"It sounds like Avalon, only worse," Buckley agreed. He gave her a grim smile. "But what if my talent strikes again…?"

"It hasn't, not since you married," Jasmine reminded him. "Speaking of which, how is Lila?"

Buckley grinned, openly. "Pregnant," he said. "She has a little Marine ready to make a forced exit from her womb."

Jasmine had to smile. "Congratulations," she said. She felt an odd flicker of envy, which she pushed aside savagely. Lila didn't have to worry about commanding troops in combat. "When's the baby due?"

"Seven months," Buckley said. He looked oddly worried. "We only found out a few days ago."

"I'm sorry," Jasmine said. She meant it. Buckley had stayed on Avalon as part of Training Command, but after he'd returned to active duty he could have been shipped off at any moment. And now...it was unlikely that he would return to Avalon before the child was born, even if the rebels on Thule tried to launch a stand-up battle and lost. "We could speak to the Colonel and..."

Buckley shook his head. "I don't want to leave the rest of you alone," he said. "God knows I felt badly enough for skipping the mission to Corinthian."

Jasmine winced, remembering the brief few hours she'd spent as a captive of Admiral Singh and her thugs. The torture hadn't been very imaginative, but it had left her a shaken wreck long enough to make her fear that she would never return to active service. And now she was unlikely ever to return to active service as a Marine anyway, now she was the CEF's commander. She was simply too important to be risked.

I didn't sign up to be a damn REMF, she thought.

But you know what has to be done, which is more than can be said for most REMFs, her own thoughts answered her. *And besides, who else has the experience to take command of the CEF?*

"It wasn't your fault," Jasmine said.

She shook her head. How could she blame Joe Buckley for marrying a girl on Avalon when it had become increasingly clear that they would never return to the Core Worlds? Marines did marry, they did have children...and yet, those children rarely saw their fathers until they left active duty. But the Slaughterhouse had provided a home for those families...she wondered, with a bitter pang of grief and rage, just what had happened to the Slaughterhouse and the families there. The corps had enemies who would happily take advantage of the chaos to strike at their very core.

"I still felt bad about it," Buckley confessed.

"Never mind," Jasmine said, bluntly. She picked up a datachip and passed it to him. "You will probably be deployed as raiders, capturing High-Value Targets and the like. One target in particular is at the top of the list."

"Our former comrade," Buckley said. "A Marine gone bad."

He paused. "*Has* he gone bad?"

Jasmine quirked an eyebrow, inviting him to continue.

"If I'd moved to Avalon ten years ago," Buckley said, "I might well have joined the Crackers. Would that have made me a bad person?"

"I wish I knew," Jasmine said. "But I do know that we need to keep Thule in our sphere of influence."

She sighed. Fighting the pirates and fanatics had been easy – and there had been no doubt over who was in the right. But most of the conflicts the Marine Corps had been involved in included a great deal of moral ambiguity. If *she'd* moved to Avalon, would she have supported the Empire-backed government – which just happened to be ruthlessly exploitative – or the insurgents resisting its control?

"Understood," Buckley said. He rose to his feet. "If you'll excuse me, then, I'll take the platoon through at least one run on the exercise field before we make our way to the starships. Let them hate, as long as they learn."

Jasmine nodded, wordlessly. That had been the motto of the Drill Instructors at the Slaughterhouse, men and women who had pushed the recruits to their limits. Only one tenth of them had passed through Boot Camp with the qualifications necessary to progress to the Slaughterhouse – and only one tenth of *them* had graduated as Marines. The remainder had quit, transferred into the Imperial Army, joined the Auxiliaries...or died. Their training was so realistic that it was quite possible for a careless recruit to kill himself – or get others killed.

She watched him leave the room, then looked down at the paperwork in front of her. Somehow, despite her best efforts, it was mutating, forcing her to devote more and more of her time to just filling in forms, reading reports and signing her name to pieces of paper she'd barely read. No wonder the bureaucratic-minded officers had so much trouble, she told herself; they were so busy doing their paperwork that they had no time to learn how to command their men in combat.

There was a knock on the door. Lieutenant Michael Volpe entered at her command.

Jasmine studied him, thoughtfully. He was a tall young man, barely out of his teens; he'd joined the Knights almost as soon as they'd been established and seen service against the Crackers. And then he'd joined the CEF, looking for more action. Jasmine recognised his type and knew, if they'd still had contact with the Empire, that she would have urged him to apply to the Slaughterhouse or a Special Forces Regiment. There were some men who were never happy unless they were in the thick of the action – which made what she was about to do the wrong course of action. But it would depend on his plans for his future.

"Be seated," she said, when Volpe saluted. "Where do you see yourself in five years?"

Volpe looked surprised at the question. "I would like command of my own regiment," he said, carefully. "I honestly haven't thought much about the question."

"Neither did I, when I was your age," Jasmine said. She couldn't help feeling old, even though she knew she was little more than six years older than him. "I have an offer for you."

She leaned forward. "I need an aide, someone who can work with me and pass on orders to subordinate formations," she said. "It won't be for more than a year, in any case, but it would give you valuable experience of high command. If you do well, you would have your chance at commanding a regiment after a little more seasoning."

Volpe frowned. "A year?"

Jasmine thought about how the bureaucrats on Earth would have responded to such a suggestion and smiled, inwardly. But then, one of the innovations the Colonel had introduced that she loved was the insistence that all officers were rotated in and out of the combat or deployment zones. No one would be allowed to spend too long at the rear, losing their awareness of what they actually needed to do – or what officers at the front required from them. Volpe would never have a chance to lose his love of a fight...even if, to such a young man, a year seemed endless.

"Yes," she said. "But it will be very useful to your future career."

She paused, then pressed on. "The CEF is deploying, as you know," she said. "I need an answer within the hour. If you say no, you will be returned to your unit and nothing more will be said about it. This isn't something that will be held against you, whatever answer you give."

There was another knock at the door. An officer stood outside, holding a plain white envelope. Jasmine took it without opening it, then looked back at Volpe. "You have an hour..."

"I'll do it," Volpe said. He hesitated, torn in two. "But will there be a chance at action?"

"You never know," Jasmine said. Perhaps she should recommend NCO training instead, if Volpe wanted to remain in the lower ranks. A Sergeant would command considerably more respect than a junior officer who'd spent too long in grade without being either promoted or discharged. "I'll speak to your CO. Gather your stuff, then report back to my office in an hour. You're going to be very busy."

CHAPTER NINE

There were, alas, many causes. One, perhaps the most important one, was that the Empire was truly unimaginably vast. The planners on Earth could not begin to handle the complexities of one particular conflict, let alone hundreds of them. They responded by general orders that were often ineffective, backed by threats made against military and civil service officers if they failed to carry them out.

- Professor Leo Caesius, *War in a time of 'Peace:'*
The Empire's Forgotten Military History

"The question before us," Councillor Stevens said, "is simple. Was the decision to dispatch the CEF to Lakshmibai a justifiable decision, *based on what we knew at the time*?"

She paused. "Hindsight is remarkably clear," she added, after a moment. "It tells us precisely what mistakes were made – and when. But foresight is nowhere near as clear. We must put hindsight out of our minds and approach the question armed only with what was known at the time.

"With that in mind, we must ask a second question. Was the decision to hold negotiations on Lakshmibai a mistake in its own right?"

Ed silently gave her points for recognising the difference between foresight and hindsight. It wasn't something he normally saw politicians doing, particularly when there was an opportunity to make political hay out of the disaster. But there were several points that had to be brought up, as quickly as possible, otherwise they would be forgotten.

He stepped forward when the Councillor recognised him. "With all due respect, Councillor, there are several issues with your statement," he said. "In particular, it was not us who decided that the talks should be held on Lakshmibai. It was chosen by Wolfbane's representatives and we accepted their suggestion. Had we not done so, it is quite possible that the talks would not have been held at all."

"But that leads to another issue," Councillor Stevens pointed out. "Was it wise to accept their suggestion?"

Ed kept his face expressionless. Inwardly, he wanted to scowl. "We had been attempting to open lines of communication with Wolfbane ever since we realised their existence," he said, calmly. "Matters were not helped by the degree of...paranoia Wolfbane showed when we tried to speak to them. In the end, they proposed Lakshmibai as a compromise – a world where we could talk without revealing more than we chose of ourselves and vice versa. We were not offered any alternative."

Councillor Roberson tapped the table for attention. "Could we not have arranged a meeting in interstellar space, light years from any reasonable threat?"

Ed shook his head. "Wolfbane gave us no choice," he reminded them. "The choice was to hold talks on Lakshmibai or have no talks at all. We discussed the matter extensively and decided that it would be better to have the talks, even on their terms, rather than risk failing to open diplomatic relations."

There was a long pause. "It has been alleged that outside powers – presumably Wolfbane – assisted the fanatics of Lakshmibai to rise up against us," Councillor Stevens said. "Do you believe, in hindsight, that we walked into a trap?"

Ed hesitated. "It's possible," he conceded, finally. "We do believe that the locals had some reason to assume that the starships would be unable to return, either to save us or take revenge for what they'd done. However, there were a number of oddities about their tactics that suggest otherwise. For example, man-portable drones are relatively easy to shoot down, even with primitive sniper rifles. Yet the locals made no attempt to engage them, even though removing them from the battlefield would have blinded us at a crucial moment. Nor, for that matter, did they move heavy guns into position to shell the Imperial Residency, which would have smashed us flat.

"However, almost all of the planet's royal family was either killed or knew nothing about off-world contacts," he added. "Other prisoners who were interrogated were either too ignorant to know what a starship was, let alone what it could do, or believed their superiors when they were told that the starships were rendered powerless. The mystery of just who, if anyone, backed the locals may remain unsolved."

He paused. "It is possible that they didn't anticipate the deployment of the CEF," he continued, after a long moment. "Without it, they would have overwhelmed the Imperial Residency and captured or killed all of the representatives."

"Which leads to another point," Councillor Stevens said. "*Why* was the CEF deployed in the first place."

Ed gritted his teeth, then pushed on. "The CEF was designed as a rapid reaction force that could be moved from Avalon to a threatened world and deployed at high speed," he said. "I decided that deploying to Lakshmibai would prove a more suitable test of its capabilities than deploying to a Commonwealth world, where there would be fewer surprises for its officers to handle. We asked Wolfbane if they had any objections and they offered none. Indeed, they have good reason to be grateful that we *did* deploy the CEF. It saved their representatives along with our own."

Councillor Travis leaned forward, threateningly. "Would the presence of the CEF not have worried Wolfbane, if they are such paranoid people?"

Ed sighed, inwardly. "The CEF is a formidable force on the ground," he said. "But if someone else controlled the high orbitals, it would be rapidly and completely destroyed by kinetic bombardment. Wolfbane, I believe, decided that it posed no threat to them. And they were probably right."

Councillor Stevens tapped the gravel against the table. "In foresight, Colonel, was there any reason to suspect that Lakshmibai would explode into chaos?"

"There were hints in the files," Ed conceded, "that the locals were not very fond of off-worlders. However, there was no reason to believe that the locals would be foolish enough to start a war against two interstellar powers, particularly when the planet's orbitals were completely undefended. The war could only end in the destruction of the local government and the victory of the rebel factions, at the very least. At worst, they would face the complete destruction of their homeworld. We assumed that the locals would ruefully accept our presence long enough to hold the talks."

"Which were held in their capital city," Councillor Travis said. "Could they not have been held at the former Imperial Garrison or an uninhabited island, somewhere away from the locals?"

"Wolfbane insisted on the Imperial Residency and made arrangements with the locals," Ed admitted. "We were not consulted on the decision."

Councillor Travis smiled at him, humourlessly. "All of this, Colonel, suggests that Wolfbane set a trap," he said. "A trap we walked into with our eyes firmly closed."

"But the CEF was deployed too," Councillor Jackson pointed out. "Why would they have agreed to allow us to deploy the CEF if they intended to capture our representatives?"

"Good question," Councillor Travis said. He looked at Ed, his eyes cold. "Colonel, is there a scenario where Wolfbane would benefit from our deployment of the CEF?"

Ed couldn't stop himself scowling, this time. "Yes, Councillor," he said. "We find them a mystery, but they may well have their own uncertainties about our capabilities. If they were to watch our deployment – and our response to the local attack – it would give them valuable insights into everything from preferred tactics to training drills. Should it come down to open war, they would find such insights very useful."

Councillor Yvette Hanson tapped the table. "Councillor," she said. "Wouldn't that mean they were prepared to risk their own representatives as well as our own? We know what happened to most of the prisoners on Lakshmibai."

She had a point, Ed knew. If Wolfbane had genuinely planned the whole Battle of Lakshmibai to gain insight into the Commonwealth's military, they definitely had put their own people at risk. He would have bet half his salary that the representatives he'd met – and the men he'd fought beside – had had no awareness of any ulterior motive. But Governor

Brown could easily have sent them to Lakshmibai, calculating that he would benefit whatever the outcome. And, if they didn't know anything about the overall plan, they could hardly betray it to the Commonwealth representatives.

"I see no reason for assuming that a former corporate stooge wouldn't have the cold-bloodedness necessary to send his own people to their deaths," Councillor Travis growled, crossly. "I believe that such people are quite willing to do whatever it takes to advance."

Ed nodded in agreement.

"I believe we have gone as far as we can this morning," Councillor Stevens said. "We will resume the hearing after lunch."

Jasmine couldn't help feeling nervous as she walked, in full dress uniform, into the Council Chamber and stopped in front of the witness stand. Councillor Travis hadn't wasted any time, she had to admit; he'd called the Colonel in the morning and Jasmine, the second-in-command on Lakshmibai, in the afternoon. There hadn't been any real time to plan for the hearing, but she'd been told by the Command Sergeant that a full body cavity search would be preferable to being raked over the coals by ambitious politicians. Jasmine could only hope she was wrong.

"Please, be seated," Councillor Stevens said. "Thank you for coming."

Jasmine nodded, then sat down, keeping her hands resting on her lap. She was tempted to look around for her boyfriend, but somehow she forced herself to keep her gaze on the councillors. Councillor Travis looked unrelentingly hostile, unsurprisingly; the others ranged from supportive to bored. She waited, patiently, as Councillor Stevens introduced her – purely for the benefit of the record, she suspected – and then asked the first question.

"Brigadier," she said, "did you have any reason to believe, prior to your arrival on Lakshmibai, that it might be a trap?"

"No," Jasmine said.

Somehow, she kept her face under control. She'd been warned to keep her answers as short as possible, which would ensure she didn't give them any rope to use to hang her. But she wanted, desperately, to explain that it wasn't the Colonel's fault. *No one* had seen the disaster coming until it was far too late.

"I see," Councillor Stevens said. "When did you first suspect that there would be trouble?"

"When we landed on Lakshmibai and heard from the Imperial Garrison," Jasmine said, remembering the odd group of people who'd maintained the base for years after the Empire had abandoned the planet. Most of them had been delighted to leave. "They told us that the locals were far from fond of off-worlders. If the locals had been able to cross the causeway to the island, the garrison would have been lynched."

It would have been worse than that, she knew. They'd seen what happened to local rebels who'd been taken prisoner by the government's troops. Rape, torture and death was the best they could expect. And there were still a handful of Commonwealth personnel unaccounted for on Lakshmibai. Jasmine had her suspicions about what had happened to them, but no sign of them had been discovered before the Commonwealth abandoned the planet completely.

Councillor Travis glowered at her. "Was there no option for intervening quickly when trouble started in the capital city?"

Jasmine took a breath. "No, Councillor," she said. "Without the starships, we lacked the ability to either land large amounts of troops in the city or provide fire support. Had I deployed what few helicopters and shuttles I had, I would have risked significant losses which would have crippled my ability to fight. I believed – and still believe – that fighting my way from the garrison to the capital city was the only realistic option."

There was a long pause. "Based on what you saw during your march up," Councillor Travis said finally, "do you believe that the uprising was pre-planned?"

"I'm not sure," Jasmine confessed. "On one hand, there was a sizable number of enemy military units blocking our path to the capital city. But on the other hand, that region had been unstable for years before our arrival and the enemy needed to deploy vast numbers of troops to keep the locals under control."

"Locals who might have been able to save our people without risking the CEF," Councillor Travis said. "Could you not have merely supported them?"

Jasmine felt her face heat with anger. "No, Councillor," she said. "I do not believe that would have produced acceptable results."

She pressed on before he could say a word. "The local rebels, sir, were very much a mixed bag. Few of them had any proper military training. Few of them really cared about what happened as long as the yoke of outside control was lifted from their territory. And few of them fought in what we would consider a civilised manner. Despite our best efforts, the rebels carried out hundreds of atrocities against captured enemy soldiers and high-caste civilians. The levels of hatred within their society had sunk so deep that bloody slaughter was the only likely outcome.

"In short, Councillor, we could not supply the rebels with arms and rely on them to capture the capital before the Imperial Residency's defenders ran out of ammunition. The only option at our disposal was to take the offensive and secure the capital city for ourselves."

She felt a twinge of guilt that, she knew, would never fade away. Even the worst Civil Guard units she'd encountered in her career hadn't matched the Lakshmibai rebels for cruelty or sadism. There was no escaping the fact that she'd enabled the rebels, armed them and prepared them for war...or that she bore some responsibility for the atrocities they'd committed against their hated oppressors. By the time the CEF had left Lakshmibai, the planet had been dissolving into a bloody mess. It might be years of blood-letting before a new order brought some semblance of civilisation to the godforsaken world.

"And so you did," Councillor Travis said. "Your superiors believed you conducted yourself very well. However, you made the decision to attack Pradesh directly, rather than trying to outflank the city. Was that necessary?"

Jasmine winced, inwardly. Pradesh, the bottleneck city...and where Councillor Travis's son had fallen in combat.

"I believe there was no choice, sir," she said, carefully.

The councillors exchanged glances. "Elaborate," Councillor Travis ordered.

"Pradesh sits in a pass between two mountain ranges," Jasmine explained. "While there were, apparently, a handful of smaller passes that allow men on foot to avoid the city, the only way to move a large military force through the mountains was to go through Pradesh, which meant storming the city and taking it by force. Outflanking it, as you suggest, would have forced us to add hundreds of kilometres to our journey, while opening our own flanks to enemy attack. No, the only option was to push our way through the city."

"Which proved," Councillor Stevens commented, "to be the most costly battle in the war."

Jasmine nodded. Her losses had been relatively light, all things considered. The enemy losses had never been counted, but estimates suggested that over twenty thousand local soldiers and militia had died or gone into POW camps. Guarding them had been yet another strain on her manpower, yet she'd had no choice. Letting the rebels guard them would have merely allowed the bastards to slaughter the prisoners.

"In an urban environment," she said, "our advantages – better training, better weapons, better surveillance – would be degraded. The enemy, I believe, knew better than to meet us in the field by then. Instead, they set a trap, knowing that we would have no alternative but to walk into it. We had no choice."

There were several more questions, but none of them seemed too focused on her and her conduct. The Colonel had been right, Jasmine realised; Councillor Travis was more interested in nailing him than anyone else. It was true, Jasmine had to admit, that they should have learned lessons from the Lakshmibai War, but not like this. Personalities would end up pushing the issues aside...

"Thank you for your time," Councillor Stevens said, finally. "Your testimony is greatly appreciated."

Jasmine saluted, then strode out of the chamber.

———

"She didn't do too badly," Gaby observed. "But if Councillor Travis hadn't been so bent on getting at you..."

Ed nodded. Jasmine hadn't had *any* training for facing politicians, even the relatively easy-going politicians on Avalon. Councillor Travis might think he was being a hard-ass, but compared to some of the politicians Ed had met in the past he was actually quite tame – and focused. The Grand Senators would probably have brought the issue of Jasmine's romantic life up as soon as possible, even though it had nothing to do with the issue under discussion.

"She did fine," he said, instead. It had been an hour since Jasmine's testimony, long enough for the councillors to make some private contacts outside the building. "Where do you think we stand?"

Gaby scowled, biting her lip. "It's hard to say," she confessed. "Right now, no one has been formally charged with anything. The hearing is just bringing out the facts, one by one. Once they think they know everything, they will decide what – if anything – should be done."

Ed sighed. Not knowing what was going to happen was a major problem – and it wasn't just the hearing that worried him. Wolfbane could attack at any moment...and they wouldn't even know about it until two weeks after the attack took place. Hell, with a little care, Wolfbane could overwhelm a number of worlds without word getting out at all.

"We just need to get it over with," Ed said. "We don't know what Wolfbane is planning to do."

"If anything," Gaby pointed out. "Governor Brown was a corporate officer. Wars are bad for business."

Ed shook his head. He'd met too many corporate drones who had believed that wars were very good for business. The hell of it had been that they'd been right. As long as they weren't at risk, profits were immense.

CHAPTER TEN

> Perversely, failure was not punished if the officers in question could prove that they had followed orders. Doctors used to say that the operation was a success, but the patient died. The Empire's military officers could say that their deployments were a success, yet the war was still lost.
>
> - Professor Leo Caesius, *War in a time of 'Peace:'*
> *The Empire's Forgotten Military History*

The house was smaller than Mandy remembered, although it was bigger than the one-room apartment they'd shared during their final days on Earth. That apartment had been nothing more than a box with some bedding; there had been no computer, no entertainer, nothing to do apart from bicker and fight. And it would have been worse, much worse, if the Marines hadn't offered them transport away from Earth. No matter how much she'd screamed and thrown tantrums at the time, she knew now they'd been lucky. If they'd remained on Earth, they would be dead.

Bracing herself, she walked up to the door and knocked, once. Her relationship with her parents had never really been good, although after Jasmine had knocked some sense into her their relationship had definitely improved. But the Professor and his social-climbing wife had little in common with their daughter – with both of their daughters, if she were to be honest. Mandy had been kidnapped by pirates, then joined the Commonwealth Navy, while Mindy had joined the Knights. The last Mandy had heard, her baby sister was going in for Stormtrooper training. It was the closest she could get to being a Marine.

Her mother opened the door and nodded at her, smiling wanly. Fiona Caesius was an older version of her two daughters, but her red hair was shading to gray and her body was alarmingly thin. She'd been determined to climb to the top of academic society on Earth – as the wife of a tenured professor, she had automatic entry into the system – and losing it through her husband's curiosity had almost destroyed her. Mandy knew, now, that her mother had fallen into deep depression, but back then she'd merely been a nagging mother to a pair of little brats.

"It's good to see you again," she said, as Fiona stepped to one side, inviting her in. "And it's good to see you recovered."

Her mother gave her the ghost of a smile. "I have been better," she said. "But I have been worse too."

Mandy followed her into the living room, which was littered with evidence of her mother's latest hobby. She'd taken up cooking and, according to her father's letters, had actually started work preparing food for short-term residents in a large communal flat. Mandy wasn't sure what she thought about that – the flats were tiny versions of Earth's cityblocks – but at least it gave her mother something to do with her life. An academic's wife, used to the environment of Imperial University on Earth, would be utterly unprepared for life on a colony world.

As was I, Mandy thought. She too had been unprepared for the dangers of living on Avalon – or anywhere away from Imperial University. And she'd come close to death before ever meeting the pirates.

She looked up as the door into her father's study opened, revealing Professor Caesius. He was an older man, so completely unlike his children that it was hard to believe they were actually related to him. His short brown hair was starting to grey too, but he'd taken his exile far better than any of the women. Unlike them, he'd found a useful position right at the start as a political advisor. Now, he spent half of his time advising the government in ways to avoid the Empire's mistakes and the other half writing books on political theory and practice that were eagerly devoured by people all across the Commonwealth.

"Mandy," he said. He pulled her into a hug that brought back memories of being a little girl, before she'd fallen victim to the Empire's public schooling. In hindsight, it was alarmingly clear just how thoroughly she'd been indoctrinated by her teachers. But she'd lacked the experience to know, at the time, just how badly they were leading her astray. "Welcome home."

There was a loud clunk as her mother put a pot on the table. "Sit down, please," Fiona said, softly. "It won't stay hot forever."

Mandy sat and watched as her mother ladled out something that resembled beef and dumplings stew. On Avalon, real meat was common, something she'd taken in her stride after she'd asked and discovered the truth. Mindy had spent a week refusing to eat it before finally surrendering to the inevitable and devouring the food. Fiona hadn't, as far as Mandy could recall, said anything about the fresh meat. But, as it would be massively expensive on Earth, she might just have decided that eating it was a sign of status.

"Thank you," she said, when Fiona had finished. "I'm sure it will be good."

It tasted better than she'd expected, thankfully. Her mother's first experiments with cooking had been unpleasant, to say the least. Mandy rather suspected that Fiona had tried to start with something complicated, rather than something simple, but she wasn't inclined to worry too much about it. After eating the slop the pirates had called rations, she'd permanently lost any impulse to quibble over the food.

"I understand that you're going on deployment," her father said, when they had eaten enough to satisfy the pangs of hunger. "Thule, isn't it?"

"Yes," Mandy said. It was no secret where they were going, unfortunately. "It's going to be a long trip."

"I have been watching the hearing," her father said. "I believe that the general consensus is that Lakshmibai was a trap. If so, Wolfbane is hostile."

"It seems that way," Mandy said. *Something* had to be driving their research programs onwards, apart from a desire to escape the strictures set by the Empire. "Do you know anything I haven't been told?"

"Not as far as I know," her father said. "I worry about you, though."

Mandy nodded, feeling another flicker of shame. She hadn't been a very good daughter – and she hadn't realised just how lucky she'd been to have such a gentle man for a father. Some of the children she'd known on Earth had had worse fathers – and there were children on Avalon who'd grown up *without* fathers after they'd been killed in the fighting. But, when she'd been a teenage girl, she'd sneered fearlessly at her father, ignoring his gentle rebukes and her mother's rages. She'd been an awful brat.

"Thank you, dad," she said, quietly.

"This could be bigger than Admiral Singh," her father said, quietly. "We know next to nothing about Wolfbane, apart from the fact they exist and that they're clearly powerful. Our best guesses are nothing more than estimates. Will a corporate stooge prove an effective leader, someone who can rebuild the sector after the economic crash, or will he be a failure, someone with no more imagination than Admiral Singh?"

"I wish I knew," Mandy said.

"So do I," her father confessed. "So do I."

He stood up and started to pace the room. "The best models we have tracking how the decline and fall of the Empire might have taken place are based on too much guesswork," he added. "We simply don't know the answers to the questions we need answered. All we know is that Governor Brown took control of Wolfbane and built himself an empire. We need information, Mandy, as much of it as we can get."

Mandy hesitated. He knew about her deployment to Thule, that was obvious, but did he know about the second part of her orders? Father or not, she couldn't tell him – or even ask for his advice. Colonel Stalker would be furious if she broke secrecy; she'd be lucky if she was allowed to spend the rest of her days on an asteroid mining platform.

"We may not get any unless someone defects to our side," she said, recalling the runaways that had first alerted the Commonwealth to Admiral Singh. "And Governor Brown seems to keep his people firmly under control. There have been no escapees..."

"That we know about," her father said. "But escaping isn't that easy."

"I know," Mandy said. She'd plotted hard to escape *Sword*, but she'd had to bide her time until the starship returned to a friendly star system. And a few moments either way would have cost her everything. "I will be careful, father."

"See that you are," her mother said. "I would hate to lose you too."

After the dinner had finally come to an end, Mandy sat down and wrote a note to her sister. It was unlikely Mindy would be able to read it until she went on leave – Stormtrooper training took place in complete isolation – but at least there would be *something*. And if Mandy didn't come home...

She shook her head, irked at herself. Her will was already written. Mindy would receive her savings, her parents would receive most of her possessions...apart from her commissioning coin, which she'd willed to Jasmine. If she didn't come back, she'd be remembered as more than the brat she'd been when she'd been exiled to Avalon. And her parents would mourn her death.

As soon as she'd said her goodbyes, she left the house and started to walk back towards the spaceport. Tomorrow...they'd be on their way.

"I wish I could come with you," Emmanuel Alves said. He lay below her, looking up. His face was flushed after a long bout of lovemaking. "But my editor wants me to remain here, covering the hearing."

Jasmine nodded. Part of her wished he was coming with them too – she'd been doing her best to make up for years of celibacy – but the rest of her knew that it would be awkward. Too many people knew they were lovers; too many people would be watching them, wondering if her command independence would be compromised by his presence. Or, for that matter, watching *him*. Would he stop being an impartial reporter simply because he was dating her?

"You'll probably be called upon to testify at one point," Jasmine said. She'd seen the list of people who had been called after her, all officers and soldiers from the CEF. Half the time, the questions went over the same information, time and time again. The only interesting moment had come when a supply officer confessed to accidentally mislabelling a couple of pallets of supplies. "You were there, too."

She gritted her teeth. Every entrant to the Slaughterhouse faced a full medical exam which included a great deal of poking and prodding in body cavities. The Marines joked that it was a test of nerve, that if you could handle having your cavities poked you could handle the rest of the Slaughterhouse, but she would have definitely have preferred repeating the exam than facing another hearing. She might even have preferred to face Admiral Singh's torturers again.

But I had to put those revenge fantasies aside, she reminded herself, firmly. If she'd allowed such emotions to influence her recovery, she knew, it was unlikely she would have been cleared to return to duty. Personal feelings had to be put aside when one was on active duty, no matter how tempting they were. *They were dealt with after the provisional government took power.*

"You didn't deserve such treatment," her boyfriend insisted. "I'm going to run an article on just how the hearing is treating experienced veterans."

Jasmine shook her head. "You'll compromise yourself," she warned. "You will have taken a side."

Emmanuel reached out and touched her right breast. "I think I took a side the moment I started courting you," he said. "I'm on *your* side."

He paused. "*Does* the hearing bother you?"

Jasmine eyed him. "Off the record?"

"Of course," Emmanuel insisted. "I don't tell everyone about this" – he waved a hand to indicate their nakedness – "either."

"Yes and no," Jasmine said. She hesitated, choosing her words carefully. "Learning from mistakes is a vitally important part of serving in the military. Everyone makes mistakes, I was taught, but we have to recognise them, admit they were mistakes and then make sure they don't happen again. Ideally, we should be learning from mistakes made by our enemies too – it's cheaper than learning from our own."

She paused. In hindsight, some of the reluctance shown by the Imperial Army's officers to recognise that they *had* made mistakes might have stemmed from an awareness that admitting the mistake might have cost them their careers. At least the Marine Corps normally got to handle such matters without political intervention.

"So, in this case, we allowed ourselves to become involved in a battle – which may or may not have been a trap – that could have ended very badly," she added. "We need to learn from that experience. Examining every last moment of the decision-making process will highlight the moment the process failed – or what we need to modify to ensure that future surprises don't catch us out so badly. Everyone involved with making the decision needs to be questioned so that we have as full an understanding of what actually happened as possible.

"But it's human nature to search for someone to blame."

"Like the Colonel," Emmanuel said, quietly. "Councillor Travis blamed him for the death of his son."

"I know," Jasmine said. "It's turning into a witch-hunt. Already."

"It should be over soon," Emmanuel said, reassuringly. "They can't prolong the process indefinitely."

"Not here," Jasmine agreed. She shook her head. "Be careful what you print, all right? You might well be accused of losing your neutrality."

She smiled, inwardly. No one could ever have called the Empire's hordes of reporters *neutral*, interested more in reporting the facts than slanting them in a particular way. But some of Avalon's reporters genuinely *were*...oddly, she suspected the Marines would find that more useful than either sycophants or politically-motivated enemies. There would be mistakes and setbacks, but the public would realise that nothing was being covered up.

"I'll take that chance," Emmanuel assured her. He shifted under her weight. "Ah...stand up?"

Jasmine concealed her amusement as she lifted her leg, then lay down beside him. She'd known, intellectually, that between the training and medical treatments she was considerably stronger than the average untreated man. But she had never really believed it, despite all the fighting she'd been involved in, until she'd started dating Emmanuel. It would be alarmingly easy to hurt him by accident.

It was odd, she realised, as she watched him stand up and make his way towards the shower. Logically, she should have been interested in a fellow Marine – although, she knew, such relationships were strictly forbidden. Emmanuel and her just weren't anything alike. But maybe that was the attraction; she didn't have to keep her game face on when she was with him. But what did he see in her?

"Perhaps he likes the thought of dating a woman who can kick his ass with both hands tied behind her back," Mandy had said, during one of their talks. Mandy had been delighted at Jasmine finding someone, going so far as to send Jasmine suggestions for underwear and date nights. "Or maybe you make him feel safe."

Shrugging, Jasmine swung her legs over the side of the bed and sat upright, reaching for her chronometer. She'd supervised her subordinates as they prepared the ships for departure, then given everyone the traditional Last Night on Avalon. In a few hours, they would be expected to board shuttles and return to orbit – or face disciplinary charges when they reported into the garrison and confessed they'd missed departure. Jasmine wouldn't be merciful to someone who overslept and nor, she knew, would any of the other officers.

Grinning to herself, she stood and padded naked into the bathroom. This time, Emmanuel was looking at the door when it opened. Jasmine smiled inwardly – no chance to surprise him this time – and walked over to where he was standing under the water. His penis stiffened when she touched it, growing harder within seconds. She recognised the signs and smiled, openly. Like many young men, Emmanuel was taking pills to enhance his performance in the bedroom.

"Sit down," she said, throatily. If she was going to be without him for months, she could at least enjoy herself before she left. The memories would help keep her warm at night. "Now."

Lucy McGhee had operated her boarding house for years, even during the days of the old Council. A combination of bribes and blackmail had ensured that the Civil Guard left her and her tenants alone, while her reputation for discretion had allowed her fame to spread far and wide. She asked no questions, as long as her tenants paid in cash and upfront, and shared no confidences with anyone outside the building.

But she had to admit that the tenant in Room 23 was behaving oddly. He'd paid for three weeks, in gold, then moved into the room...and hadn't been seen since. Lucy's cooking was just as famous as her discretion and her guests could have it in the dining room or have it sent to their rooms...

and yet her tenant had asked for nothing. Indeed, as far as she could tell, he hadn't left the room once, not even for food and drink.

She puzzled over the mystery, then put it out of her mind. Growing up under the old Council had left her with scant respect for law and order, let alone people who liked poking their noses into her business. Whatever the young man was running from, he'd paid for discretion and he would *have* discretion. She would leave him alone until his money ran out or his corpse started to smell. It was, after all, what she'd been paid to do.

CHAPTER ELEVEN

> Logically, the people in command of the deployment should have been given autonomy to act as they saw fit, without reference to Earth. It would certainly have reduced the message lag between Earth and the Rim. But there were reasons why commanding officers were rarely given that much authority.
> - Professor Leo Caesius, *War in a time of 'Peace:'*
> *The Empire's Forgotten Military History*

"You've done very well, Michael."

Michael Volpe glowed. He'd been aware that the Brigadier had been watching him as he struggled with the paperwork, but in the end he'd sorted it all out. At first, he'd thought that the smaller units that made up the CEF were supposed to submit their own paperwork, leaving him with nothing more than the task of ensuring that they all had the correct schedule for boarding the starships, but it turned out that he was supposed to sign off on hundreds of smaller pieces of paperwork, everything from time in the simulators to ammunition stockpiles and requisitions. He had no idea how the Brigadier's previous aide had handled all the requirements without driving himself mad.

"Thank you, Brigadier," he said, finally. He wished, now, that he'd turned down the job offer. It would have been easy to return to serving as a junior Lt. "Why...why do we need all of this paperwork anyway?"

"To keep everything in order," the Brigadier said. "And to make sure we all know what we're doing at the right time."

Michael shook his head in bitter disbelief. Even the schedule for embarking the troops – let alone loading their vehicles – had proven surprisingly complex. The armoured units had insisted on boarding last, even though their vehicles were not scheduled for early deployment once the squadron arrived at Thule. Michael had discovered, to his shock, that the Loading Officers were staging a small revolt, insisting on loading the armoured vehicles first rather than last. It had required reserves of tact and diplomacy he hadn't known he'd possessed to sort out the chaos and ensure that both sides retreated, fairly content with their results.

"You need a small army of staffers," Michael said, trying hard not to sound resentful. There was much more to the job than he'd realised when he'd been offered the chance to take it. "I can't handle everything."

The Brigadier snorted. "Do you know what went wrong on Earth?"

Michael shook his head. He'd been born on Avalon; his father had also been born on Avalon, while his mother had been an indentured colonist who'd found herself working for her husband rather than slaving in a brothel. From what he'd heard of Earth, it sounded hellish…but he didn't have the emotional connection to humanity's homeworld that the final generation of colonists had. Even the ones who had been kicked off the planet – or had foreseen the final disaster and made their escape before it was too late – practically worshipped the world. But Michael felt nothing for Earth.

"They did as you suggested and built up a corps intended to handle military supplies," the Brigadier said. "To be fair, they did have an immensely more complex job than the one you've been handling. God knows every single regiment attached to the Imperial Army had its own standards. But the supply officers found themselves more insistent on actually taking care of themselves rather than doing their job."

She gave him a wintery smile. "They didn't have any proper experience of what it was like to be serving on deployment," she added. "So when a request would come in for twenty pallets of ammunition, they'd insist on sending only ten – because that's what they believed would be necessary. Never mind that soldiers on active service burn through ammunition at a terrifying rate…they had to make do with what the supply corps insisted they could have, rather than what they needed."

Michael nodded in agreement. During his first trial of fire, against the Crackers, he and his mates *had* burned through ammunition alarmingly fast. If the old sweats hadn't insisted that they all carry extra magazines, despite the weight, they might well have been overwhelmed and slaughtered by the insurgents. What would someone who had never seen combat, never been within a hundred miles of a fight, think the military needed to do its job?

"The Colonel is very insistent that we will not repeat that mistake," the Brigadier explained. "Officers like you, officers who have seen the elephant, will spend a year or two of their careers in the supply corps, then return to their units before they go native. Would *you* refuse a request for extra ammunition?"

"No," Michael said. "I know they might need it."

The thought made him smile. He'd already had to handle several such requests, mostly from units that had already burned off their training stockpiles on the exercise ground. From what he'd heard, the Empire had demanded that each and every unit go through hours of paperwork before they could requisition training ammunition. Avalon didn't have that problem. If a company of soldiers wanted to spend a few hours improving their skills, they'd be able to draw the ammunition and use the training area without delay.

"When you have time," the Brigadier said, "read through the story of Dork's Defence. It's a cautionary tale the Empire forgot."

"But the Marines learned their lesson," a new voice said.

Michael looked up – and saw Colonel Stalker. Hastily, he jumped to his feet and saluted. "Sir!"

"At ease," the Colonel said. Despite his lowly rank, he was the senior military officer in the Commonwealth. Michael had heard he'd refused promotion when it had been offered to him. "I need to borrow your CO for a while."

The Brigadier smiled. "Return to work," she said. "No rest for the wicked, I'm afraid."

Jasmine had to smile as her young aide hastened out of the compartment. She'd had her doubts at first, particularly when it came to such a young officer, but he was showing definite promise. Absently, she wondered if he realised that half the snarls he'd dealt with had been caused deliberately, just to test him. It would be easier to return him to his unit – or another unit on Avalon – before the CEF departed the planet.

"He isn't doing *too* badly, sir," she said, once the hatch was closed. "Joe did better, of course, but Joe has years of extra experience."

"And a shot in OCS too," the Colonel said. Marine OCS was famed for being tough; it wasn't uncommon for almost all of the prospective candidates to be flushed out and returned to their units. Jasmine wondered, sometimes, just how well she would have done, if she'd been given a chance to go. "But he probably needs to study Dork's Defence."

Jasmine nodded, wordlessly. Dork – his name hadn't been Dork, but it had stuck – had been an Imperial Army officer assigned to command a company of soldiers on Han. The bureaucrats had insisted that he could only have a handful of pallets of ammunition and Dork had either failed to question them or hadn't had the connections to force the bureaucrats to disgorge more. When the uprising had finally begun, Dork and his men had fought with reasonable skill and bloody-minded determination until his men had run out of ammunition, whereupon the outpost had been completely overrun. The relief forces which had finally fought their way through to the outpost had discovered that the men had been beheaded and their heads mounted on pikes. No one had ever found the rest of their bodies.

The Imperial Army, as far as she knew, hadn't learned a thing from the disaster. Oh, the fighting men had probably understood the lesson, but the bureaucrats hadn't realised their role in the disaster. And even if they had…they'd probably have gotten in trouble for shipping all the ammunition the soldiers needed, no matter how desperate the situation had become. That, she knew, was what happened when priorities were set by someone light years away from the battlefield. They literally had no idea of just what was going on.

We have to do better, she thought. *The Commonwealth is growing larger…*

"I'll make sure he reviews the records," she said. As her aide, the young lieutenant would be expected to remain with her, rather than rejoin his former comrades. It was unfortunate that they would all be travelling on the same ships, but it couldn't be helped. "And a few others that need to be examined, such as our most recent experience of actual combat."

The Colonel nodded, then reached into his uniform belt and produced a datachip. "Your sealed orders," he said. "Keep them with you; in the event of Wolfbane starting a war, you are to access the orders and then carry them out to the best of your ability. If the situation refuses to allow you to follow them...I'll understand."

"Yes, sir," Jasmine said, feeling the weight of responsibility falling around her shoulders. It was impossible for any reasonable person to believe she could send for orders and then wait a month for them to arrive, assuming they were sent at once. Instead, the Colonel had given her permission to act as she saw fit. There would be no need to refer to higher authority, but she would be responsible. If she fucked up, the fault would be all hers. "I won't let you down."

She smiled, rather tightly. At least there wouldn't be multiple chains of command in the CEF, not after Colonel Stalker and his officers had carefully designed it to ensure that there was one recognised CO. She couldn't help thinking that the CEF would have several times the power of an Imperial Army deployment, simply because it had a unified command structure rather than dozens of competing officers. But they would never have a chance to find out.

The Colonel nodded, then stepped back and looked at the bulkheads. "Do you like the ships?"

"Yes, sir," Jasmine said. "There's room for improvement, of course, but overall they're workable."

They shared a look of silent understanding. The Empire's one great advantage – at least in its early centuries – had been logistics; the military had built up thousands of starships to rush troops from one trouble spot to another. But, as the Empire started its decline, fewer and fewer starships had entered service. The military transports had become massive starships, each one larger than a battleship, capable of carrying tens of thousands of soldiers...and equally capable of losing them, should they be intercepted in flight. Now, the Commonwealth had produced a series of smaller ships, hoping to recreate the flexibility the Empire had once enjoyed. But only experience would show how well the concept would work in practice.

"Good," the Colonel said. "Look after them, Jasmine. We may not get many more."

Jasmine grimaced, but understood. The Commonwealth's shipbuilding capabilities were still slender, compared to the Empire's vast network of industrial nodes and shipyards. Even with the integration of Corinthian and the rest of Admiral Singh's empire there was more demand than the Commonwealth could meet. If something were to happen to the Avalon shipyards, the Commonwealth would be almost certain to lose the war.

"Sir," she said slowly, "are the shipyards secure?"

"I believe so," the Colonel said. "But if something were to happen to them..."

"Too many point failure sources," Jasmine said. The Colonel nodded in agreement. "But do we have a choice?"

"No," the Colonel said, bluntly. "At least the modified cloudscoops are coming online."

Jasmine smiled. HE3 was the backbone of interstellar society, powering everything from fusion reactors to starship drives. Avalon had been almost unique in the Avalon Sector for having a cloudscoop, built by the ADC when their projections had indicated that the sector would become the centre of a new industrial expansion program. Ironically, Jasmine had to admit, they'd largely been right. But they hadn't predicted the fall of the Empire.

Cloudscoops – at least the ones the Empire used – were expensive cumbersome objects, difficult to establish and easy to destroy. Several pre-Empire interstellar wars had been decided, according to Mandy's father, by the destruction of one side's cloudscoops, ruining their economy. As interstellar shipping had dried up in the years before the Fall of Earth, the shortage of fuel had crippled hundreds of planets along the Rim. A new interstellar dark age had seemed on the cards.

But the Trade Federation had produced a far cheaper cloudscoop design – and, instead of keeping the design to itself, had shared it with every star system they'd contacted. The new cloudscoops were even more fragile than the originals, but they could be replaced easily and expanded rapidly. Given a few more years, Mandy had said once, the Commonwealth would be drowning in fuel.

The Colonel cleared his throat. "I have to get back groundside," he said, the regret obvious in his voice. This time, he would have to stay behind on Avalon while Jasmine and the CEF went off to do battle with the Commonwealth's foes. "Good luck, Brigadier."

"Thank you, sir," Jasmine said. She hesitated, then picked up a datachip of her own. "Can I ask you to pass this on, if I don't come back?"

The Colonel nodded. "It will be done," he said.

Jasmine watched him go, feeling oddly conflicted. Once, her last wishes had been recorded at the Slaughterhouse, where her body would be shipped if she fell in battle. Her family might have been shocked at her career choice, but she liked to think they were proud of her. They would have received her ashes...

...But now there was no contact between Avalon and the rest of what had once been the Empire. It was possible, she knew, that her family had survived...and equally possible that they were dead. There was no point in asking that her body be preserved for return to a home and family that might no longer exist. Instead, she'd asked for her ashes to be scattered on Castle Rock...and for her possessions to be turned over to the remainder of the Marines.

Not that there's very much, she thought, ruefully. Marines weren't encouraged to be packrats; even officers had strict limits on the number of personal possessions they could take with them from deployment to deployment. All she really had was her bank account and a handful of civilian clothes, all of which she'd purchased a few months ago. She wondered, suddenly, what her former comrades would have made of them. It had been Blake who'd led the panty raid on a barracks occupied by a regiment of female Imperial Army soldiers...

And didn't we all suffer for it, she recalled. Officially, no one had known who to blame, but Command Sergeant Patterson had known...and she hadn't seen the funny side. They'd been on punishment duty for weeks before Han exploded into war...

The thought gave her a sudden pang of bitter regret. Angrily, she pushed it aside and checked her wristcom. There was an hour until departure, just enough time to inspect the various units and make sure they were all squared away. And if someone was late boarding her ships, they'd regret it. Jasmine had no intention of tolerating someone who couldn't remember when they were supposed to board her ships, whatever excuses they offered.

She called for her aide, then headed for the hatch. If nothing else, she told herself, she could lose herself in work.

Sword hummed quietly as Mandy sat down in her command chair, then inspected the display as her crew brought the ship to full readiness. The Commonwealth Navy had been good to her, she knew; apart from the heavy cruiser, she had four light cruisers that had been captured from Admiral Singh, nine modern cruisers designed on Avalon and twelve destroyers. It was a mixed formation, but almost all of her ships had been intensively modified and upgraded. And, behind them, there were ten heavy transports, carrying the CEF and its supplies.

She smiled, rather wanly. Unlike the Empire's designs, the new transports were armed. They were still no match for a warship, but they'd be able to give a pirate ship a nasty surprise or two...if there were any pirates left. Between the Commonwealth, the Trade Federation – and, to be fair, Admiral Singh – the pirates had largely been exterminated.

"Inform the squadron," she ordered, once the checks were complete. "They are to follow us out."

"Aye, Captain," the communications officer said.

Mandy felt her smile grow wider. "Then signal System Command," she said. "We're departing on schedule."

She tapped her console, switching her display to a near-orbit view. Avalon had once had only a single orbital station and a handful of satellites orbiting her. Now, she had several dozen orbital installations, while others were clustered near the asteroid field or the gas giants. Given time, the industrial base they were building might rival Earth's legendary productive capability. It was already considerably more efficient.

"Take us out," she ordered, quietly.

The stealthed platform hung thousands of kilometres from Avalon, well away from the standard orbital tracks used by the traffic running in and out of the system. It emitted nothing, nothing that could be tracked back to its source. There was no way, its designers believed, that it could be detected save by the worst possible kind of bad luck. A starship could pass within bare kilometres of the platform and miss it completely. All it did was watch.

Its passive sensors noted the squadron leaving orbit, recording the size and composition of the squadron as it picked up speed. Once it had a complete record, the platform activated its laser communicator and sent a signal flickering across the void. It repeated the message ten minutes later, then waited. The acknowledgement arrived two hours later.

Following its orders, the platform resumed its silent watch on the planet.

And waited.

CHAPTER TWELVE

> In particular, there might be outside elements that had a vested interest in the conflicts coming to a particular end. On Stan's World, the corporation that owned and operated the planet had the ear of lobbyists who worked to sway the Grand Senate – and worked to ensure that the declared military objective was the restoration of the corporation's control over the planet, not a compromise truce that might have pleased both sides.
>
> - Professor Leo Caesius, *War in a time of 'Peace:'*
> *The Empire's Forgotten Military History*

"That's the latest intelligence report, Admiral," Lieutenant Foxglove said. "There won't be any update for at least another week."

"Thank you, Emma," Admiral Rani Singh said. "That will be all."

The younger officer nodded and retreated, leaving Rani alone with her thoughts. Emma Foxglove was young, a newcomer who had been conscripted into Wolfbane's expanding military shortly after the planet had lost contact with the Empire. Somehow, despite the chaos, her superiors had recognised that there was a capable intelligence officer hiding under her shy exterior and streamlined her into the military's intelligence section. Rani had taken the girl under her wing shortly after her arrival on Wolfbane, understanding the value of developing personal ties with intelligent and capable subordinates. Of such relationships, she knew, excellent command teams were forged.

And they will be loyal, when the chips are down, she thought, as she turned to stare out of the viewport. *When the shit hits the fan, it is always a good idea to have people who are loyal to you personally.*

She smiled as she studied the planet below. Wolfbane might be the most populated and developed world in its sector, but from orbit it was impossible to see any sign of human life, at least with the naked eye. Instead, Wolfbane was as blue and green as every other major human settlement. But, in orbit, it was surrounded by industrial nodes, starship yards and everything else required to sustain a major interstellar presence. Had the Empire survived, Rani suspected, Governor Thaddeus Brown would have gone far...if the Grand Senate, recognising a prospective rival, hadn't killed him first. Rani considered herself a military officer – she had nothing, but contempt for the shadowy world of corporate wheeling and dealing – but she had to admit that Governor Brown had done very well for himself. Before the Empire's fall, he'd played seven colossal interstellar corporations off against one another to ensure that he reached the coveted governorship.

And after the Empire's retreat he took control of the sector, she thought. *How many others could have done that without civil war?*

There'd been dozens of different competing factions in the sector, all suddenly freed from all restraints. Somehow, Governor Brown had manipulated all of them, so seamlessly that Rani couldn't help wondering if he'd anticipated the Empire's fall just as she'd done and made preparations before the collapse became obvious. By the time the dust had settled, Governor Brown was firmly in control, with a large military and a growing space fleet to back up his word. Rani was privately relieved that she hadn't encountered his empire prior to losing control of Corinthian. He would almost certainly have seen her as a threat.

But Governor Brown had his weaknesses as well as his strengths. Some of his military officers were restless, blaming him and his ilk for the fall of the Empire; some of his corporate allies thought they, not him, should wield supreme power. Rani, on the other hand, had come to him as a supplicant. Her pride groaned every time she admitted it, even in the privacy of her own mind, but she couldn't allow herself to cling to a delusion. He'd had a use for her purely because she had no power base of her own on Wolfbane. She needed him more than he needed her.

He'd been decent with her, Rani knew, even as he'd made it clear that she wouldn't be completely trusted until she'd proved herself. He hadn't humiliated her publicly, not like some of the Imperial Navy officers she'd known would have done, but neither of them were in any doubt where the power resided. Or *had* resided, Rani knew. The time she'd spent on Wolfbane hadn't been wasted. Building up the groundwork for a power base of her own had just been a matter of time.

She pushed the thought aside as she turned away from the viewport and examined the intelligence report. The Commonwealth – she felt a flicker of old anger which she ruthlessly suppressed – was sending a large military force to Thule, precisely as she'd anticipated. As always, principles had proved no match for political reality on a galactic scale. Whatever the Commonwealth might have said about not interfering in local politics, it couldn't risk allowing Thule to slip out of its grasp, let alone join Wolfbane. All they'd needed was the hint of outside involvement and they'd drawn the correct conclusions.

Rani had been a serving naval officer long enough to know that it was impossible to direct an operation from light years away. The Grand Senate might not have learned that lesson, but *she* had. Instead of trying to control events, she'd put her pieces in place and given them orders to take advantage of the developing situation as they saw fit. It would introduce an element of unpredictability into the equation, but it was a price worth paying. Besides, she knew – all too well – that the unpredicted popped up with monotonous regularity. All that really mattered was that the Commonwealth was taking the bait.

She looked through the report and found the second note, buried in the appendix. No one, apart from a handful of her staff, knew about the second part of the operation. It wasn't something she intended to let anyone know about, not when it was crucial to her private plans as well as the march to war. After all, war was inevitable. Wolfbane and the Commonwealth could not hope to co-exist, let alone Wolfbane and the Trade Federation. Rani fully expected to play a major role in the war...and use it as her stepping stone to galactic power.

And if that meant the deaths of untold thousands of people?

One can't make an omelette, she reminded herself, *without breaking a few eggs.*

She keyed her wristcom. "Contact the Governor," she said. For some reason, Governor Brown hadn't bothered to declare himself Emperor. She wasn't sure if it was an appeal to the Empire loyalists, such as they were, or a reluctance to state his power and control too openly. "Inform him that I have news."

There were Kings and Princes on a hundred worlds, Governor Thaddeus Brown knew, who had palaces less elaborate than the Governor's Mansion on Wolfbane. But then, he didn't inhabit *all* of the giant building, not when it was the centre of sector government as well as the governor's private residence. He kept one floor to himself, as his private territory, and left the remainder to his subordinates. There was no need to give himself airs.

He'd never really cared for the trappings of power. Some of his fellows had lost themselves in the pleasures brought with their ranks; the wine, the women, the drugs banned to the common folk...but Thaddeus had never really been tempted. They ate and drank the finest foods and most expensive wines until even the most careful tailoring could not disguise their bulging bellies. And yet Thaddeus was almost inhumanly thin. There were those who saw him, with his bald head and sharp blue eyes, who thought him a monk. But Thaddeus knew what was important.

Power. It was power that was important, power to break the universe to his will...and, compared to that, what was wine, woman and song? A man with power could take another man's woman any time he chose. Or anything else he happened to want.

But when you have the power, you don't want to threaten it, he thought, ruefully. *And that includes not stealing another man's wife.*

The thought made him roll his eyes. Sex had never been a particular interest of his; he'd married, because it was demanded of a man in his position, then insisted on remaining apart from his wife as much as possible. She hadn't objected; Thaddeus knew, without much concern, that she'd taken a long stream of lovers. That was expected of a woman in her position, particularly one who had entered an arranged marriage. As long as it didn't get out of hand, he didn't care.

He strode over to the window and peered out over Wolfbane City, the capital of Wolfbane itself. It was thriving – and he knew, without false modesty, that it was because of him. His measures to stave off the worst of the economic crisis had borne fruit, at the cost of political freedom and liberty. The Empire had never been particularly tolerant of free speech at the best of times, but Thaddeus had been worse. There was no way he could allow naysayers to undermine his work to save Wolfbane and create an empire of his own.

The intercom chimed. "Governor," his aide said, "Admiral Singh wishes to speak with you."

Thaddeus nodded and turned to walk over to his desk. Admiral Singh was one of his prospective problem children; loyal to herself, rather than the legacy of the Empire. In some ways, it was refreshing; Thaddeus knew, all-too-well, that half of his more competent senior officers wished for the return of the Empire they'd once served. But she was also dangerously ambitious. If she hadn't submitted herself at once, he would probably have had her killed. But now...

He sat down and tapped a switch. The dark-skinned officer's face appeared in front of him.

"Governor," she said. "The report from Avalon shows that they are about to dispatch their forces to Thule. They may already be on the way."

"Understood," Thaddeus said. He thought, rapidly. War was inevitable...and yet, war would bring a predominance to the military. Would Singh be able to use it to take power and execute Thaddeus himself? "You are ready to deploy?"

"I believe so," Singh said. "The new recruits are learning fast, Governor."

Thaddeus allowed himself a smile. Wolfbane's educational system had been better than Earth's for years, thanks to his careful monitoring and corporate influence. Earth's schools, which produced millions of highly-educated idiots every year, could not be allowed to contaminate Wolfbane. What use were such students in the corporate world? And now, with conscription to ensure that the military had no shortage of recruits, *his* students would show the universe what they could do.

"Good," he said. He took a breath. "You may deploy tomorrow, as per Plan Theta."

"Yes, Governor," Singh said. "Singh out."

She sounded respectful. Thaddeus knew. And yet there was her devilish level of ambition, glittering in her dark eyes every time he saw her. If she decided to move...

He looked down at the table and sighed. His security officers had ensured that her crew had been thoroughly infiltrated, with dozens of operatives on her flagship alone. If she showed the slightest hint of treachery, it would be easy to take over her ship and kill her. Or so he hoped. Whatever else he could say about her, Singh was a superb naval officer. She might have taken covert precautions against mutiny already.

Maybe I should have her killed, he thought. *But then I would lose her skills.*

Shaking his head, he brought up the latest set of industrial production reports. He couldn't hope to manage everything on Wolfbane – let alone the entire Consortium – by himself, but he wanted to keep an eye on his people. If something started to slip, if someone started to grow more ambitious than he was prepared to tolerate, he would have to move. The price of security was eternal vigilance.

And the price of survival, he added silently, *is to ensure that no one can threaten you.*

The Commonwealth was a threat, he knew. Even if they didn't plan to invade his territory, the mere fact of their existence was a deadly threat – and the Trade Federation even more so, because it didn't assert any political power over local governments at all. He'd told his people, the countless billions facing starvation or worse after the Empire's fall, that strong control was the only way to save their lives. His control had stabilised Wolfbane and made it the centre of a whole new empire. But if they started to see that there might be another way...

We have to wage war, he thought. *And we have to hope that the Commonwealth kills Singh before she moves against me.*

"I want every ship in the fleet ready to go within twenty-four hours," Rani ordered, as soon as the channel to the CIC had opened. "We will move to our forward base then."

"Yes, Admiral," Caroline – her aide – said. "A third of the crews are still on shore leave."

"Recall them," Rani ordered. It wouldn't be popular – but it couldn't be helped. Besides, Wolfbane had a rather more progressive view of what constituted an excellent shore leave than the more restrained parts of the Empire. Her crews would probably be ready to return to duty by now. "And then inform the other commanders that I will be holding a conference call at" – she glanced at the chronometer – "2100."

"Yes, Admiral," Caroline said. "I will inform them at once. Captain Gower, however, may not be available to take the call. He didn't return from his mandated shore leave period."

"I wouldn't worry about it," Rani said. If nothing else, she could relieve Gower of duty if he failed to join the conference. Shore leave was important, but so was attending tactical planning sessions. Besides, she knew Gower was reporting to at least two different people on her activities. "Just send the message and let him decide if he is to attend."

Rani allowed herself a tight smile as the connection broke, then stood. She could be on the command deck of her battleship within thirty minutes, then work her way through the rosters until every last man and woman of her crew was safely onboard. Then they could depart at once, if necessary; there was no real need to wait until tomorrow. Despite his undoubted skills, it was alarmingly clear that Governor Brown lacked the mindset of the successful military officer. But then, he'd never worn the uniform in his life.

Every military officer – at least every officer with real experience – knew the value of gambling. Even the most carefully planned offensive could fail – at least one of the Empire's offences, Rani knew, had failed because the planners had told everyone the plan in advance, including the enemy – and the Demon Murphy would make his appearance at the worst possible time. But civilians couldn't even *begin* to grasp the implications. Sooner or later, no matter how many variables you ruled out, you had to jump and trust to luck...and the competence of your subordinates.

She looked back at the display, noting the handful of strategically-important Commonwealth stars. For all of their undoubted industry – few states could introduce a brand-new class of starships so quickly, let alone at least four different new classes – the Commonwealth didn't have the sheer productive weight the Empire had enjoyed. If they lost their shipyards, they would be doomed to rapid and complete defeat. But Governor Brown had vetoed her plan to open the war by attacking Avalon itself. If the attack failed, he'd pointed out, the attackers would be trapped deep in enemy territory. Instead, apart from Thule, all the first targets of the war were unimportant worlds.

Rani had seriously considered proposing kinetic strikes on Avalon itself, but she'd dismissed the thought without ever suggesting it to the Governor. Rendering the entire planet lifeless would be relatively easy – an asteroid could be pushed up to near-light speed and aimed at the planet from the outer edge of the star system – but the Commonwealth would certainly retaliate in kind. Wolfbane was just as vulnerable, as were the other worlds in Governor Brown's little empire. Mass slaughter would leave both powers in ruins.

Smiling to herself, she picked up her terminal – loaded with secure data, she never went anywhere without it – and strode out of her office. Outside, she nodded to her bodyguards and allowed them to escort her to the shuttlebay, where her shuttle was waiting. She was marginally surprised she'd been allowed to keep the bodyguards, even when she wasn't visiting the Governor or his other senior officers. Perhaps the Governor hadn't realised that they were loyal to her personally...

...Or perhaps he thinks he can deal with them, if necessary, she thought. The twelve men who would take a bullet for her – she'd had them conditioned to ensure they wouldn't hesitate, if an assassin got close enough to shoot – could be outnumbered, if the Governor decided to have her killed. Or one of the orbital weapons platforms could have a 'malfunction' and her entire shuttle could be vaporised before she even realised she was under attack. There was no shortage of options for a quiet assassination if the Governor decided he wanted to be rid of her.

She didn't relax completely until they were back onboard her flagship, the battleship *Orion*. No matter how threatening she was, she doubted that

Governor Brown would sacrifice an entire battleship to kill her, not when there were other options. There were five thousand crewmen onboard, after all. Some of them were almost certainly his operatives...and others, probably, belonged to the Governor's other senior military officers. None of them liked or trusted Rani any more than she liked or trusted them.

But it doesn't matter, she thought, as she strode to the CIC. *I'll be in position to win the war...and then take Governor Brown's place for my own.*

CHAPTER THIRTEEN

Or, on Morningstar, several ethnic groups had their own off-planet backers (despite a moratorium on outside shipments of arms, imposed but not enforced.) Their belief was that, if their particular faction came out on top, Morningstar could be added to their factions scrabbling for influence in the Empire as a whole. They had no real concern for the planet as a whole, let alone its inhabitants.

- Professor Leo Caesius, *War in a time of 'Peace:' The Empire's Forgotten Military History*

Rifleman Thomas Stewart ducked his head as he stepped into the Brigadier's office, then stood upright and snapped out a salute. He didn't resent it, certainly nowhere near as much as an Imperial Army soldier would have resented it, even if he did have more years in the Marine Corps than the Brigadier. She'd proved herself in command of a platoon, then the entire CEF, while he'd been on detached duty working with new recruits. And besides, even if he had, it would have been unprofessional to show it.

"At ease," Brigadier Jasmine Yamane said. "We're both Marines here."

Thomas relaxed, slightly. It was true enough that the Marine Corps was surprisingly informal, at least by the standards of the Imperial Army, but every serving Marine had gone through the Slaughterhouse, giving them a degree of trust in one another's capabilities. On the other hand, while his career had been effectively frozen, Jasmine's had rocketed ahead. *And* he hadn't known her very well before he'd been detached from the serving Marines...

"Thank you," he said. "And thank you for the assignment."

"You're welcome," Jasmine said. Her lips twitched. "But I should inform you that it was the Colonel's decision."

"Understood," Thomas said. "Training was fun, but..."

"I know," Jasmine said. "It isn't quite the same, is it?"

Thomas nodded. He was a Slaughterhouse Brat, a child of a serving Marine who had grown up on the Slaughterhouse. He'd lived and breathed the Marine Corps since he'd been old enough to understand what a Marine actually *was*. Signing up at fifteen, the youngest age a man could join as a new recruit, had been an easy decision. After Boot Camp, he'd taken the Training MOS at the suggestion of his Drill Instructor. Ironically, it had made him too valuable to risk for the first five years of their exile to Avalon.

He enjoyed training, even though he swore the new recruits came up with new ways to kill themselves every year. Some seemed to breeze through Hell Week, others quit or tried to commit suicide...and still others, despite their problems, kept going, drawing on reserves of strength and determination they hadn't known they'd had. It was those recruits, he knew, who were the most valuable. They learned their lessons early enough to adapt, react and overcome. But still...it was a relief to be away from the training field for a few months.

"I may be about to stick a knife in your back," Jasmine admitted. "You may be needed to inspect the local training facilities on Thule."

Thomas made a face. "Must I?"

Jasmine snorted. "It will probably be embedded combat duty rather than training duty," she said. "But a lot depends on the situation on the ground."

"Oh," Thomas said. Embedded combat duty was either rewarding or hellish, not least because the local troopers the Marine was supposed to lead might just stick a literal knife in his back instead. He'd served long enough to know that one bad apple could tear apart an otherwise decent unit. It hadn't been too bad on Avalon, but the Crackers hadn't really had time to infiltrate the Knights before the war ended. "I will be at your disposal."

He recalled the briefing notes – Lieutenant Buckley had made them read their way through the notes in exhaustive detail – and felt his enthusiasm sink. Civil wars were always nasty, even when both sides were inclined to give the other some compromises in the interests of peace. *This* civil war looked like it was heading towards bloody slaughter. Maybe it wasn't racial or religious, both of which had been present on Han, but it was going to be quite bad enough. Who would have imagined a civil war based on *employment* prospects?

Thule, evidently, he noted. *Damn them.*

"It may come to nothing," Jasmine said, "but I want you prepared for the eventuality. The Colonel would prefer we had the situation well in hand before Wolfbane gets more openly involved."

"That may be difficult," Thomas warned. "We got lucky on Avalon, Jas. Here...we may not be so lucky."

He sighed. There were only two ways to win an insurgency; exterminate one side, root and branch, or make political compromises that would take the fire out of the insurgency's support, isolating the insurgents from the people. On Avalon, eliminating debt peonage and ending political disenfranchisement had weakened the Crackers to the point they'd surrendered and joined the government. But on Thule...the population was simply too large for such a solution to be enforced quickly. It was more likely that trying would merely add a third side to the civil war.

"I know," Jasmine said. "But we have to try."

"Understood," Thomas said. He grinned, suddenly. "Can I play hooky from training simulations?"

"Not unless you want Joe to come after you with a baseball bat," Jasmine said. "I don't think he'll be very pleased."

She passed him a datachip, then stood. "Do your reading, come up with plans...but don't get too attached to any of them," she added. "The situation on the ground might be completely different from what we expect."

―――――

"Thief," Buckley said.

Jasmine ducked the kick he aimed at her, then danced around him, watching for the moment he would lower his guard for a spilt-second. At that moment, she would have to knock him out of the circle or risk being hammered herself. Despite her training and enhancements, she knew she was no match for him in terms of sheer strength.

"That's a pretty serious accusation," she said, lightly. It was too, even though it was obvious that Buckley meant it in jest. A thief in the barracks could tear a unit apart. "Why, whatever do you mean?"

"You're going to steal Thomas from me," Buckley growled. He eyed her with cold calculation, despite the irritation in his words. "How am I meant to run training simulations with him when I may not *have* him."

"Needs must when higher command pisses on your hand and calls it golden rivers," jasmine said, remembering one of the cruder explanations for their hasty rush to defensible locations on Han when the shit had started to hit the fan. "There aren't many others I could call upon with the right experience."

"Still a major pain in the ass," Buckley said. He lunged forward with striking speed; Jasmine jumped to the side, almost falling out of the circle. "I can put him on reserves, but that's still a problem for training."

Jasmine sighed. The hell of it was that she knew Buckley was right. When she'd commanded the platoon, she'd had a fairly stable roster of Marines; Blake had had a couple of newcomers who had rotated off detached duty, but they'd had plenty of time to exercise with the rest of the platoon. Joe Buckley, on the other hand, couldn't make plans involving a tenth rifleman when that rifleman wasn't going to be there. Or even if he didn't *think* that rifleman wasn't going to be in the platoon.

Marines were taught to work together as a unit, right from the start. No single recruit could get through Boot Camp on his own. But they needed to train to ensure they knew their fellow Marines inside out, if only so they could compensate for their weaknesses. Jasmine had, accidentally, made it harder for Buckley to train his Marines.

"I'm sorry," she said, lowering her eyes. "Can you put him on reserve, for the moment…"

Buckley saw his chance and lunged forward, his fist slamming into her jaw. Jasmine felt herself thrown into the air, over the circle and down onto the hard deck. She grunted in pain as her legs came down hard, then rolled over instinctively. Buckley was still within the circle, waving his hand in a victory gesture.

"Bastard," Jasmine said, as she picked herself off the deck. Despite her training and enhancements, her jaw ached badly. She'd need to see the medic. "That was low."

"Dating a reporter has obviously taken some of the edge off you," Buckley countered, as he strode out of the circle. "You need to spend more time training."

He pointed a finger at her flat belly. "You'll be getting fat next."

"Asshole," Jasmine said, without heat.

She sighed. He was right about that too, she knew. The exercise she should be doing, every day, was often pushed aside to handle the endless stream of paperwork, no matter how much she passed down to her subordinates. No wonder REMFs got so fat, she thought, with an unaccustomed feeling of sympathy for the bastards who normally made deployments far harder than necessary. They had no time for exercise. Hell, they had even less time than she had because they had far more paperwork.

"Tell the reporter to withhold sex until you do at least two hours of hard callisthenics every day," Buckley added. "*That* should get you working again."

Jasmine stuck out her tongue, then started to remove her training outfit. "Do you think that would work on me?"

"It would work on *me*," Buckley said, as he followed her into the shower. "I'd hate it if my wife withheld sex for a day, let alone a week."

"*Men*," Jasmine said. "I'll tell her you said that, Joe. I'm sure she'll be very interested."

She snickered. "Don't do the dishes – no sex. Don't mow the lawn – no sex. Don't..."

"Point taken," Buckley said, hastily. "Please! Don't say a word to her."

Jasmine felt her snickers becoming laughter as she finished undressing. She tossed her sweaty outfit into the receptacle – the unlucky soldiers on punishment duty would have to wash them – and then turned on the water. As always, the temperature seemed to move between boiling hot and freezing cold. The technicians swore that it was a problem with the pipes, but Jasmine had her suspicions. Boot Camp's showers had been precisely the same. Maybe it was one of the secrets officer candidates learnt at OCS.

"I won't," she said, as she picked up a towel and dried her body. "But you should try to keep her happy."

Buckley sobered. "Blake used to tell me that it was the same in battlesuits as it was in fucking. Having a big one isn't as important as knowing what to do with it."

Jasmine nodded, remembering the bloody battle against the Nihilists on Earth. Somehow, they'd obtained enough military equipment to hold out for weeks, if they'd known how to use it. Hell, they'd probably outgunned Stalker's Stalkers when they'd plunged into the CityBlock, desperate to exterminate the terrorists before they could slaughter thousands of innocent civilians. If the terrorists had known what they were doing, Earth's government would probably have had to call KEW strikes from orbit and to hell with the collateral damage.

She reached for her uniform and pulled it on, rapidly. "That's an old joke," she reminded him. "A *very* old joke."

Buckley nodded. "I meant to ask," he said. "Is Commodore Caesius seeing anyone at the moment?"

Jasmine blinked. "Mandy?"

"Yeah," Buckley said. "There has been interest..."

"I'd suggest you tell whoever it is – and I don't want to know who – that Mandy went through hell," Jasmine said, tartly. She rolled her eyes, making sure he saw the gesture. Male Marines might not be allowed to hit on female Marines, but they were quite free to ask for dating advice. "She lost control of her life completely, Joe. It could have been a great deal worse...and she knows it. I could not recommend such a girl to anyone."

Buckley lifted an eyebrow. "That bad?"

Jasmine nodded. "Joe...we go through hell at the Slaughterhouse," she reminded him. "We are taught to shrug off trauma that would leave an ordinary civilian utterly broken. We're even tortured just so we know how to act under interrogation. And yet we keep going. I could have remained defiant if Admiral Singh's thugs had raped me while I was their captive, instead of just beating the shit out of me.

"Mandy grew up in one of Earth's better locations. She doesn't have our level of training, nor does she have the enhancements we take for granted. "She seems normal, she seems capable, but the wrong stimulus could easily cause a flashback – or worse. To the best of my knowledge, she hasn't dated anyone since her return from pirate hands, even though that was years ago. I would strongly suggest that you tell your subordinate to forget about it."

Buckley nodded, thoughtfully. "I will," he said. "But...if she's that vulnerable, why is she in command of a valuable starship? And the squadron?"

"Right of conquest," Jasmine said. By any definition of the term, it had been *Mandy* who had been the real victor of the Battle of Avalon. If she hadn't crippled *Sword*, it could easily have been the pirates who won the day. "And besides, we do have a shortage of experienced officers. At least Mandy had much less to unlearn."

"You should talk to her," Buckley said. "I mean...more openly than merely speaking to your subordinate. Ask her how she's coping. Woman to woman, as it were."

Jasmine nodded. "I intend to talk to her," she said. She checked her appearance, then headed towards the hatch. "I suggest that you place Thomas in the reserve, for the moment. And I'm sorry about the hassle."

The hatch hissed closed before Buckley could reply.

Mandy had been surprised when Jasmine had asked, during one of their brief returns to normal space long enough to run location checks, if she could shuttle over to *Sword* for a conference. She'd agreed, of course, and had then been surprised when Jasmine had come alone, without any staffers. Not, to be fair, that she had *many* staffers. One aide, Mandy had been told, was the maximum for any senior officer. There would be no small armies of aides in the Commonwealth military.

She received a second surprise, a moment after Jasmine entered her cabin, when the Marine produced a small bottle of wine and placed it on the table.

"I think we should talk," Jasmine said. She picked up a pair of plastic mugs and poured Mandy a generous portion. "How are you coping with the Commonwealth Navy?"

Mandy had to smile. Jasmine was never subtle, not off the battlefield. In some ways, Mandy had wondered if Jasmine was actually a lesbian, or a man trapped in a woman's body. She just didn't react like a typical woman. And then there had been the way Jasmine had taken her in hand, after the Sparkle Dust incident. It hadn't been until Jasmine had actually started an affair with a man that Mandy had realised that the Marine was merely trained and conditioned to a standard that admitted no trace of femininity.

"It's a great career," she said, slowly. "Is this about me?"

Jasmine nodded, then plunged on. "Are you recovering from your experiences?"

"It's a little late to ask," Mandy pointed out dryly. After a brief session, Jasmine seemed to have decided to ignore the whole incident. "It's been four years, more or less."

"Please," Jasmine said.

Mandy sighed. "I don't get many nightmares now," she said. She sniffed, loudly. "But I still think I smell the filth on this ship."

She shrugged. "I think I'm surviving, somehow," she added. "Was that what you wanted to hear?"

Jasmine leaned forward, meeting her eyes. "Have you had a relationship since you returned home?"

Mandy knew she couldn't lie, not when Jasmine was watching her so closely. "Not really," she admitted. "I...I couldn't take it any further."

The memory made her shiver. On Earth, she'd enjoyed near-complete sexual freedom. It had been fun to experiment, to see how many of the positions she saw regularly on the datanet were actually possible. She'd had friends who had been just as interested, boys and girls alike. She still recalled with a flush what had happened the day she'd found herself kissing her best female friend.

But things were more serious on Avalon. And then...

She'd been raped, to all intents and purposes, mentally if not physically. She'd given it up knowing that it could be taken from her at any moment, knowing that it was all she had to bargain with for the life of her friend. And it could easily have been worse...

Since then, she'd never been able to get past kissing a man. She'd panicked. She'd fled the room. Eventually, she'd just given up.

"I don't have much faith in psychologists," Jasmine said. "But if you can find one, you should probably go speak to her."

"I hated them on Earth," Mandy confessed. "They always asked such silly questions."

Jasmine nodded, ruefully.

"You are in command of a squadron of warships," she said. "That would not have happened if there had been more experienced officers at our disposal."

Her eyes narrowed. "If you have problems when the shit hits the fan – and it will – I want you to surrender command at once. Do you understand me?"

Mandy nodded. She knew her XO probably had secret orders to keep an eye on her, but she'd never dared ask.

"I understand," she said, when Jasmine seemed to be waiting for a verbal answer. "And I won't let you down."

"One week to Thule," Jasmine said. She stood, looking devastatingly intimidating in her skin-tight shipsuit. "If you have problems, you can call me at any time."

"I will," Mandy promised. "And thank you."

Chapter Fourteen

> A further problem was the sheer lack of military manpower. On the face of it, this seems absurd. At its height, the Empire could field over five billion soldiers (Imperial Army, Terran Marine Corps, Civil Guard (deployable). However, this number became vanishingly small when weighted against the sheer size of the Empire and the number of trouble spots that required attention.
> - Professor Leo Caesius, *War in a time of 'Peace:'*
> *The Empire's Forgotten Military History*

"They're ready for you, boss."

Pete Rzeminski nodded and stood, blanking the terminal and placing it carefully in his pocket. Carrying the device was a risk, even with the Marine Corps-grade security programs he'd uploaded, but there was no alternative. The only way for their backers to send messages was to insert them into the planetary datanet, where they could be recovered and forwarded to the terminal. And the message that had just arrived was important enough to justify the risk.

He picked up his mask and pulled it over his face, then checked to make sure that he wasn't wearing something – anything – that might lead the security forces to him. It was amusing to hear the young men who made up most of his fighting force brag about how they intended to resist interrogation, but Pete knew better than to assume they would be allowed to keep their mouths shut. Everyone broke, either through drugs, mental conditioning or even simple torture. The only way to keep a secret was to ensure it was shared with as few people as possible.

The living room was crammed with people, too many people. If Pete hadn't been aware that the entire district was packed with people, half of whom had moved in with their families when the economic crisis had really started to bite, he would have been more worried about concentrating so many of his subordinates together. He had no illusions about how effective some of the security forces could be, even if they were suffering problems from trying to expand too far too fast. Given enough time, they would start working out who was part of the insurgency and then use that person to lead them to others. And if they isolated a house...

He shook his head. One young man stood in the centre of the room, his hands cuffed behind his back. Two others stood behind him, weapons in hand; the remainder gave all three of them some room. Pete sighed, inwardly. Why was it always the young *men*? He couldn't help thinking that *he* hadn't been so stupid when he'd joined the Marines, although there was little room for youthful stupidity in Boot Camp. The Drill Instructors would have forced it out of him or given up and sent him to the Imperial Army instead of the Marines. But there was something about untrained young men that made them want to prove themselves, even if it meant breaking with the plan. Or, in this case, committing a major security breach.

It was *easy* to discipline Marines...or even soldiers. There was a chain of command backing up any commanding officer, no matter how weak-willed and feeble. If someone had decided to commit a military offence, if even the entire *unit* decided to commit an offence, the commanding officer would have support if he called for it. But insurgencies – at least the smarter ones - didn't have such chains of command. They could easily be penetrated and then used to take the entire group apart. But it did mean that disciplining its members was harder than it might have seemed.

Pete sighed, then looked at the young man. He *was* young, barely seventeen years old...and clearly torn between righteous indignation and fear. At least he wasn't a complete monster, thankfully; the quickest way for an insurgency to destroy itself was to prey on the local population to the point where the locals, desperate to escape their iron grip, called for help from the security forces. He'd seen insurgencies that had tormented their host populations to the point where the hosts had risen up against the insurgents, no matter what grievances they had with the outsiders. But this young man had just been an idiot.

"Tell me," he said. "Why are you here?"

The young man looked at him. "They said I broke security."

Pete allowed his voice to harden. "And *did* you?"

"I only told one person," the young man protested. "I..."

Pete interrupted him. "Let me see if I understand what happened," he said. "You were trying to get into a certain girl's panties, right? In order to impress her, you bragged that you were a member of the Voter Liberation Army" – one of the subgroups that had merged into Pete's unified force – "and that you were involved in a major operation against the government. But the girl, instead of opening her legs for you, went straight to her father, who happened to be one of our coordinators."

The young man gasped. Pete rolled his eyes. Honestly! What was the point of having a brain if one didn't use it? Girls might not, as a general rule, be as strong as men, but that didn't stop them from carrying out vital tasks for the insurgency. The girl in question had served as a courier more than once, simply because she was less likely to be stopped and searched than a teenage boy. And, unlike her paramour, she'd had the sense to keep her mouth shut about her involvement. Pete made a mental note to ensure she was kept somewhere safe for a few days – the young man might seek revenge on her, rather than recognising that he was the one at fault – and then leaned forward. The young man shrank back.

"You were told, time and time again, that certain details were not to be discussed," he said, coldly. "Or have you forgotten the oaths you swore, when you joined? Not a word to anyone, from your parents to your closest friends, unless you received permission to talk about your role in the war. Did you forget your oath?"

He took a step forward, and another, until their faces were almost touching. "Or was the sight of a pretty face enough to make you forget? Should we fear the government catching on and sending nude prostitutes dancing through the Zone? Should we expect you and your entire cell to go dancing after them with your tongues hanging on the ground, walking after the bitches until you walk right into a prison cell?"

"I'm sorry, all right!" The young man protested. "I didn't mean to say a word!"

"No, you meant to brag," Pete corrected him, rudely. "Was getting laid so important to you that you had to open your mouth?"

He sighed. The answer was almost certainly *yes*. Men, particularly young men, found themselves growing horny at the prospect of danger, excitement breaking down whatever barriers common sense and strict orders might provide. Pete still remembered the odd flow of excitement and anticipation that had gripped him, the day he'd gone into action for the first time...and he'd had drugs to help calm his mind. But was the lapse forgivable?

"You really should have gone to a prostitute," he said, tiredly. There was no shortage of prostitutes, in or out of the Zone. Some of them had been well established when the crisis had hit, others had been forced into selling themselves when they ran out of money and goods to pawn. "Do you understand what you did wrong?"

"Yes, sir," the young man said.

Getting caught, Pete thought, dryly.

He smiled. "Are you prepared to submit to our judgement?"

The young man shuddered, but nodded. Pete understood; they'd been warned, time and time again, that if they did something wrong, punishment would be severe. A traitor – and the movement had had its fair share of traitors – could expect to be brutally murdered. Several of the smaller groups had even targeted the traitor's family too, something that Pete had tried to discourage. The more they seemed like monsters, the more people would see the government as the lesser of two evils. But he had to admit that it was an effective warning to other potential traitors.

He sighed. Punishment was always a problem in an insurgency. Punish too lightly and others wouldn't be discouraged, punish too harshly and he would have an enemy for life. And if he killed the young man, his family would be outraged...particularly as he hadn't actually betrayed the movement to the government. Whatever oaths the young man had sworn, Pete doubted his family were completely unaware of his involvement in the movement. Families tended to be more observant than their younger members realised.

"There is a group of trainees leaving the Zone tomorrow," he said. "You will go with them to the camp and stay there for a month. While you are there, you will carry out whatever duties are assigned to you by the CO – and, let me assure you, there are no shortage of shit duties in the countryside. You will carry out those duties without complaint, even when you are called upon to shovel shit and clean up the campsites. If you serve well, you will be permitted to rejoin the movement."

"Thank you, sir," the young man said.

Pete concealed his amusement. The idiot thought he was getting off lightly – and he was, in the sense he wasn't going to be flogged to within an inch of his life, let alone killed. But shovelling shit for a week would be enough to determine if there was a useful person in there or if he was nothing more than a liability. If the latter...well, people vanished in the countryside all the time. There would be a quiet execution and the body would be buried somewhere far from civilisation.

"In addition," he added, "you are not to speak to anyone in the Zone, or attempt to communicate with any of them, without prior permission. You will be allowed to write letters to your parents, which will be carefully read before they're posted. If you attempt to break this restriction, there will be no further chances. Do you understand me?"

The young man nodded. Pete wondered, inwardly, if he realised he wasn't allowed to write to his girlfriend – his ex-girlfriend – or if that realisation would come later. Not that it mattered, he suspected. With her cover damaged, if not blown, the girl had already been hidden elsewhere within the Zone. She would never see the boy she'd betrayed again, which was probably for the best. A day or two of shovelling shit would probably have him blaming her for his punishment.

"Take him away," he ordered. The two young men behind the prisoner grabbed his arms, then turned and marched him through the door towards the cellar. He would be kept down there until the following morning, whereupon he would be attached to the group leaving the Zone. "Cell Leaders; stay. Everyone else, go down to the lower room and wait."

He waited for the group to sort itself out, sighing inwardly. The Zone – hundreds of thousands of cheap homes, warehouses and closed shops – wasn't a pleasant place to live, even at the best of times. In some ways, it reminded him of Earth, even though the comparison seemed absurd. But there were too many people crammed into too small a space, most of them unable to leave no matter what they did. If the Zone hadn't been so restive, he had a suspicion that most of the inhabitants would be homeless by now. They didn't own their homes, after all.

And it felt cramped. He would have preferred the farm. But that was no longer an option.

"We received a message from our sources," he said. He suspected that most of his allies knew that they had off-world support, but nothing had been said openly. "The Commonwealth has finally dispatched its forces to aid the government."

There was no surprise or expression of outrage from the group, merely a handful of muttered swearwords. Most of the excitable members had been killed by the government's forces or sidelined into places where they could do no harm. Pete still smiled at the member of the Thule Socialist League, who'd managed to alienate half of their allies through promising to nationalise all property and distribute it to the population. The government had barely needed to lift a finger to keep them from spreading outside the universities and college campuses, where the real world rarely intruded. *They'd* allowed the beauty of their cause to get the better of them.

"We would be looking at five thousand highly-trained soldiers, including a number of Terran Marines," he continued. "I've reviewed what information there is on their prior deployment, the Battle of Lakshmibai. Despite being caught on the hop" – he still wondered what sort of idiot hadn't realised that Lakshmibai was not going to be a peaceful deployment – "they fought their way over three hundred miles of countryside and urban areas and saved their fellows from a thoroughly unpleasant death."

"That doesn't sound like good news," one of the cell leaders said.

"Five thousand isn't *that* many," another objected. "It certainly isn't enough to occupy everywhere."

Pete nodded. He was right; Asgard alone would require thousands of troops to secure, while the miles upon miles of sprawling development surrounding the other cities would be a nightmare for even a million-man army to handle. But then, the government *did* have some forces of its own. The CEF would probably serve as a quick reinforcement, then a rapid reaction force, buying time for the government to train up its own troops.

"I believe that their commander is a Marine," he said. There had been a considerable amount of information available, but it hadn't been very specific. "She will go on the offensive as soon as possible, once her forces are deployed. I believe she will certainly attempt to take us on here."

He smiled. None of them seemed to like the idea – which was, he had to admit, sensible enough. Urban combat might limit the advantages of trained troops, but it would still mean a brutal fight which would count thousands of unarmed civilians as collateral damage. He liked to think that a Marine would hesitate before ordering such an operation, yet he knew better than to think the local government would have any such qualms. Even if the First Speaker objected, there were members of his faction who *hated* the Zone. It had, after all, defied them.

"So we will go on the offensive first," he said. He'd planned a knockout blow aimed at the local government, but there were too many variables. "Our objective will be knock the CEF out before it can be deployed."

"As far as I know," one of the older leaders grated, "we have no starships under our command."

"True," Pete agreed. "But they will be vulnerable while they are trying to deploy."

He felt his smile widen. The Terran Marines were – had been, he suspected – the ultimate in rapid reaction forces. They were trained extensively to deploy across light years as fast as possible, with all of their equipment standardised and lightened to make deployment and resupply an easy task. The Imperial Army had been far more cumbersome, often taking months to deploy to a single world. Reading the news reports, he suspected the CEF fell somewhere in between. But even the Marines had run into snags while they were deploying their forces.

"The current ETA is one week from now," he said. He'd worked it out from the data he'd been sent, cursing the absence of an FTL communicator as he did so. It had once been the Holy Grail of the Empire's science, although he'd suspected that progress had been deliberately stalled more than once. "We will have that long to prepare a warm reception."

He walked over to the table and picked up a sheet of paper. It would have to be destroyed, of course, once the meeting was over. He'd hammered into their heads, time and time again, that nothing was to be written down permanently. Marines, if no one else, knew the value of information pulled from a terrorist hideout. And whoever they were facing would not fail to learn that lesson, not when she needed to leverage only a small number of troops to their best advantage.

"I want all five of you to prepare cells for deployment," he said. "The spaceport will be our primary target, but we have to prevent the local forces from becoming involved. Ideally, we want to suggest that the local forces actually knew the attack was coming and did nothing."

"Might be tricky," one of the leaders observed. "They wouldn't want to ruin their relationships with the Commonwealth."

"Which leads to another point," another leader asked. "How many soldiers do we have to kill before the Commonwealth pulls out?"

Pete shrugged. The Empire had been indifferent to causalities, as long as the media hadn't caught wind of them. But when it had, the Imperial Army had been forced to protect its own ass first and fight the enemy second. Sometimes, a spectacular disaster that killed a few hundred soldiers had served as an excuse for withdrawal, while a steady loss rate had passed under the media's radar. There was no way to know what sort of loss rate the Commonwealth considered acceptable.

"We will probably have to find out the hard way," Pete said. He ran through the provisional plan, then listened to their input. Some aspects were dismissed as being too ambitious, others were modified slightly. "But if we can force the Commonwealth to withdraw, to abandon its commitment, we will be halfway to victory."

He smiled at them. "And once we win the war," he added, "we can create a new world."

CHAPTER FIFTEEN

> Finally, however, there was the baleful influence of the Empire's ivory tower social scientists. They had never carried out field work, never researched their subjects properly…and yet they branded themselves experts in social science. Their ignorance and incompetence would have been laughable, had it not been for the simple fact that they were believed.
>
> — Professor Leo Caesius, *War in a time of 'Peace:' The Empire's Forgotten Military History*

It was relatively easy for anyone, even someone who wasn't a trained navigator, to trace out the least-time course between two separate star systems. A civilian, however, might not realise that even the slightest error in calculation would be enough to make the starship miss its predicted arrival point by millions of kilometres. It was this reason, Mandy knew, that ensured that the standard pirate ambush tactic was to lurk just inside the Phase Limit and wait patiently for a prospective victim to arrive. After all, if the ambush was triggered while the starship was still outside the Phase Limit even the quickest pirates wouldn't be able to prevent their victim from escaping.

Not that I expect to run into pirates here, she thought, as *Sword* started to move towards the Phase Limit, followed by her squadron and the military transports. *Pirates rarely dare take on a warship.*

"Send System Command our ID and our planned ETA," she ordered. "And then take us in, best possible speed."

She settled back in her command chair to watch as the squadron crawled inwards, its passive sensors picking up signs of industrial activity from all over the system. Despite the economic crunch, Thule still possessed a formidable industrial base; given a few more years, it was quite likely that the planet would be supplying the entire sector. Jasmine, in one of her more pensive moods, had suggested that their real task was to support the local government long enough for the economy to recover completely, undermining the rebel position and destroying their support base. Mandy had her doubts – the crisis wouldn't be forgotten so easily – but she would do whatever she could to support her friend.

"Picking up a signal from System Command," the communications officer said. They were still far too far from the planet for regular communication. "They're welcoming us to the system and directing us to assume high orbit in seven hours."

"They're in a hurry," Mandy muttered. So was she, of course. Jasmine had been urging her to plan the deployment of her forces as soon as possible, pointing out that they were hopelessly vulnerable while inside transports. "Send back an acknowledgement and our revised ETA."

She had to smile as the system revealed more and more of its secrets. There was an old-style cloudscoop orbiting one of the gas giants and two new-style cloudscoops orbiting the other gas giant. Dozens of asteroids were radiating hints of settlements, including a number of RockRat colonies; even the outer planets and moons seemed to have moderate settlements established on their surfaces. And it was all politically united, apart from the RockRats, or so the file had claimed. Normally, a system as developed as Thule wouldn't have a completely united government. Someone always wanted independence from the capital world.

Their corporation knew what the hell it was doing, she thought. *It helped that they didn't have any debts to the Empire too.*

The Empire, according to the files, had once counted Thule as a success story. And they would have been right, if the economy hadn't collapsed. A combination of local independence and political ideology had turned Thule into a powerhouse, boosting its industrial capability forward far faster than anyone had believed possible. They'd even managed to keep the Empire's interstellar corporations from gaining controlling interests, a remarkable feat in the waning years of Empire. If the Empire hadn't fallen apart, Thule might well have risen to dominate the entire sector.

It still might, she reminded herself. It's industrial base might not have any of the improvements the Commonwealth or the Trade Federation had devised, but they had a head start on anyone else within the Commonwealth, even Corinthian. Given a few more years, they were likely to recover completely from the economic crash...which meant, if Jasmine was right, the end of the war. *And who knows what will happen then?*

She'd been raised, by the Empire's educational system, to believe in the innate goodness of the universe and its rulers. It had been badly-prepared propaganda, but she hadn't recognised it as such until she'd been exiled to Avalon. There, she'd started to question the underlying assumptions she'd been taught to accept...and her servitude with the pirates had destroyed whatever remained of those misconceptions. Power was all that mattered, in the end; the power to save a world was also the power to destroy it. What would happen, she asked herself, when Thule took the place it had earned in the new order? Was it possible that some elements within the Commonwealth would be interested in quietly sabotaging the planet's recovery?

No, she told herself, firmly. *Jasmine wouldn't go along with a scheme like that – and besides, we need their industrial base.*

But the thought refused to fade from her mind.

Jasmine had seen Earth, which had – had had – the most densely populated high orbitals in the Empire. There had been hundreds of settled asteroids orbiting the planet, joined by thousands of industrial nodes, dozens of orbital defence stations and countless shuttlecraft moving from space stations to starships. The four orbital towers had sent a steady stream of emigrants – some willing, some otherwise – from humanity's homeworld to the outer colonies. Thule was nowhere near as developed...

...But she had to admit they were getting there. There were seven asteroids in orbit, three of them hollowed out and converted into settlements, while the remainder were still being mined for raw material. Dozens of industrial platforms orbited beside the rocks, sucking in the raw material and turning it into useful goods, while freighters moved in and out of the system, carrying its produce to less fortunate star systems. Beyond them, there were nearly a hundred orbital defence platforms. In many ways, Thule was more heavily defended than Avalon itself.

They started earlier, she reminded herself. Avalon hadn't been prepared for an industrial boom, certainly not after the cloudscoop had bankrupted the development corporation. *And they're not as advanced as us.*

She smiled as she looked down at the green planet below. Starship transport was all-too-familiar to her, but she wouldn't be happy until she was down on the ground. It was unlikely that they would have time to explore the countryside, not when the rebels would probably take advantage of the opportunity to kidnap any of her people who wandered off alone, yet at least it would be groundside. She had always felt a little helpless on starships and shuttles, knowing that a single missile would be enough to vaporise her and the rest of her unit.

"Brigadier," Volpe said, "we're settling into high orbit now."

Jasmine turned back from the porthole, then carefully schooled her features into composure before she turned to face him. "Good," she said. "And have we had an update from the local government?"

"We're being assigned the military spaceport," Volpe said. "They're asking us to get down on the ground as fast as possible."

Jasmine wasn't surprised. The local government had sent her an update as soon as they'd started their long crawl towards the planet, which she'd skimmed rapidly. It was growing alarmingly clear that the rebel leadership was growing in power, uniting the smaller insurgent groups under its banner...and it had done almost nothing. That bothered Jasmine more than hundreds of tiny pinprick attacks. An insurgency that did nothing was almost certainly plotting something. But it's silence did give the locals a chance to take the offensive.

"Order the lead elements to start prepping for deployment," she said. She saw his expression flicker and sighed, inwardly. His unit – his *former* unit – was in the lead. "Then check with the local flight control, make sure we're cleared into their system."

Michael nodded and reached for his terminal. While he fumbled with it, Jasmine picked up hers and ordered the transport's optical sensors to examine the spaceport. It was larger than she'd expected, almost as large as the facility on Mars or the Slaughterhouse. Twelve massive landing runways, for shuttles that couldn't land vertically; nine massive barracks for deploying troops...and a security fence that should keep out anyone, but authorised personnel. The only worrying detail, she couldn't help noticing, was that the urban sprawl had advanced to the spaceport and overwhelmed it.

They must be very confident in their safety, she thought. Avalon's main spaceport was several miles from the outer edge of the city, even after five years of expansion. A single shuttle accident could be disastrous, if the shuttle crashed in the middle of a town. *Or maybe they don't care about the folk who live near the spaceport.*

Michael looked up from his terminal. "The lead elements are ready to deploy," he said. "The locals have confirmed that we are cleared to land; they've keyed us into the military flight control system."

Jasmine nodded. "Inform them that they are to launch in five minutes," she said. "We will go to the CIC."

Cold logic – and sound tactics – told Pete that he shouldn't take command of the operation personally, let alone be far too close to the spaceport. The area wasn't *entirely* friendly, after all. Smuggling was common and the criminal gangs that operated the smuggling trade didn't like the insurgents very much. After all, if the insurgents won, the high taxes that made smuggling profitable would be abolished. But he wasn't about to send people into danger without sharing it himself, at least to some extent.

"I just had the word passed to me," his aide said. She was staring down at a portable computer, which they'd spliced into one of the underground cables that handled data traffic for the planetary datanet. According to the hackers, who were practically an underground movement in their own right, the tap was completely undetectable. "The Commonwealth has arrived."

"Good," Pete said, as enthusiastically as he could. He knew better than to be so enthusiastic in truth. Wars were inherently unpredictable, no matter how carefully one planned. It was quite possible that the movement would lose. "Pass the word. The operation is to begin on my mark."

Cary Thornton had worked at the spaceport before the economic crash had forced him and his comrades out of work. Unable to find another job, despite more than a passing knowledge of electronics, he'd been forced to move in with his parents and try to avoid leeching off them more than strictly necessary. Humiliated by his unemployed and unemployable status, he had been an easy mark for the movement's recruiters, who had seen a promise in the young man his former employers had not. He'd been taken out of the Zone, given a crash course in how to use a portable HVM launcher, then sent to find somewhere to live near the spaceport and wait. Finally, the waiting had come to an end.

The five members of his team looked alike in their masks, he noted with some amusement, as they took up position under an awning on a warehouse roof. They'd been warned, time and time again, that the government was peering down on Thule, twenty-four hours a day. They didn't dare bring the launchers out into the open until it was too late for the local forces to intervene...although Cary had his doubts about their willingness to intervene even if they'd had advance knowledge of the plot. The criminal gangs that dominated the area were quite happy to turn on the cops if they tried to enter without permission.

"That was the mark," Kay said. Cary didn't know her story, but she was the most determined of them all just to hit back at someone – anyone. "And here they come."

Cary stepped away from his fellows, then lifted the HVM to his shoulder and activated the sensor head. It started bleeping at once, picking up the emissions of four shuttles dropping through the planetary atmosphere and heading towards the spaceport. A brief datanet formed between the three launchers, designating targets and ensuring that two missiles wouldn't go after the same shuttle, then faded away as Kay removed the awning. Bracing himself, Cary pulled the trigger. The missile launched into the sky and roared towards its targets.

He stared after it, despite the smoke it had left in its wake. The shuttles were barely visible to the naked eye, but the trail pointed directly towards their position. Kay grabbed his arm, swore at him and pointed towards the hatch. Catching himself, Cary dropped the remainder of the launcher on the ground – it was a one-shot; there was no point in trying to salvage it – and then jumped down the hatch. They'd been told, in no uncertain terms, to make their escape without worrying about anything else...

Jennifer Fallow had been cautious ever since she'd guided the shuttle into the planet's atmosphere. Every planet was different, every planet had unpleasant surprises for unwary pilots, from Earth's super-polluted atmosphere to the high winds that ravaged Yellowstone and drove its inhabitants into underground cities. But she hadn't expected the threat receiver to start screaming at her as she dropped down towards the spaceport.

Instinctively, she pulled at the stick, yanking the shuttle to one side as she started to launch flares. But it was too late; the shuttle rocked violently, then tilted to one side and started to fall. Jennifer felt a moment of absolute terror, then tried to retake control. The damage, she realised within seconds, was too extensive to allow her to guide the shuttle down to a crash-landing. Quickly, she reached for the ejector switch, hoping desperately that there was time to launch her passengers into the air. It would be a rough landing, but there was no alternative...

And, once again, it was too late. She saw, just for a second, the urban sprawl coming up at her...and then the universe fell into darkness.

"Two direct hits," his aide cheered. "Two shuttles down!"

Pete nodded, glumly. In the distance, he saw two plumes of smoke rising up from the other side of the spaceport. It was easy to imagine that the falling shuttles had crashed on top of inhabited houses, crushing or incinerating innocent men, women and children. The fires would spread rapidly too, he knew, unless the fire department responded in time. It wasn't likely, not when the gangs opposed *all* evidence of government authority. They'd prefer to let the whole district burn down then concede control for a few hours.

"Send the second signal," he ordered. He'd taken a week to set up the attack, with hundreds of pawns prepped for the moment they received the order to move. It would shake the local government to the bone, although Pete doubted it would be enough to destroy it. "And then order the mortar crews to engage."

―――――

It had taken some careful arguing – and an agreement of future services – but Rifleman Thomas Stewart had managed to convince Lieutenant Buckley that he should be allowed to join the 1st Avalon Mechanized Infantry Battalion as its lead elements landed on Thule. He might be attached to local units, after all, and their landing would be his first chance to actually *see* the locals. Buckley had been pissed, but he'd conceded the point. Thomas *would* be allowed to go.

He swore as alerts flashed up in his combat helmet, warning of incoming missiles. One shuttle was hit before the news even sank through his mind and started to plummet towards the ground, a second exploded in midair, showering wreckage over the area. His shuttle dropped sharply, launching flares and other decoys as a missile closed in on them. God was looking after them, he realised; the missile, thankfully, fell prey to one of the decoys and exploded harmlessly, some distance from the shuttle.

The craft rocked again as it dropped violently towards the ground, then slammed down and hit the ground roughly enough to be mistaken for a crash-landing. Thomas thrust himself to his feet, clutching his MAG-47 in one hand, and started to bawl orders. The unit's CO had been in the second shuttle, while the senior surviving officer was completely untried. Making a mental note to apologise later, Thomas chased the soldiers out of the shuttle and bellowed for them to secure the surrounding area. Training, thankfully, reasserted itself as they recovered from the landing.

He snapped out a report as he surveyed the surrounding area, noting the plume of smoke from where the shuttle had crashed. It would have to be secured as quickly as possible, he knew, but the spaceport was his first priority. The local soldiers looked just as surprised as his own people, which didn't bode well. Clearly, there hadn't been any warning at all…

"Secure the gates," he snapped. The first moments of an attack were always chaotic…and the enemy, if they *were* facing a former Marine, would know to take advantage of the confusion. "Call your people; get me some air support!"

If they have any, he thought. *HVMs and helicopters don't go together.*

The second shuttle landed, a little less violently than his own. Hatches sprung open and soldiers ran out, heading away from the shuttle at speed. Thomas blinked in surprise, then heard the telltale sound of incoming mortar fire. The enemy, damn them, hadn't just prepared a HVM ambush, they'd prepared mortars as well. It was a textbook ambush, he conceded, and it had already claimed the lives of seventy soldiers.

"Get under cover," he snapped, as the shells started to crash down on the spaceport's landing pads. "Hurry!"

Chapter Sixteen

> The Grand Senate was quite happy to allow the social scientists to propose remedies for conflict across the Empire. After all, conflict was bad for business – and therefore tax collection. However, their remedies were, in most cases, largely useless at best and downright harmful at worst.
> - Professor Leo Caesius, *War in a time of 'Peace:'*
> *The Empire's Forgotten Military History*

Mara Schuler had slaved – she wouldn't say worked – as a cleaning lady for nearly two years, despite the pressures of her job. No one really questioned why she stayed; employment was scarce, after all, and she *was* a voter. She was just part of the background, the cleaning lady who swept the police barracks clean, washed the toilets and put up with their smutty jokes and innuendo without ever answering back. They didn't even know she was twenty-seven, not when she looked old enough to be her own mother. Two years of hard work and exposure to cleaning chemicals had turned her red hair stringy, her face pale and her hands flaky, her skin drying and falling off like dandruff. Somehow, she'd endured two years of hell.

But the order had finally come!

It hadn't occurred to the police that she might have family who *had* suffered the indignities of being unemployed and thus disenfranchised. After all, Schuler was hardly an uncommon name. None of them had thought that she might be politically minded, not when she was just the cleaning lady. And none of them had really understood the potentials in the chemicals she used to carry out her duties. Mara did. The one time she'd been allowed to take a short holiday, she'd spent it in the countryside, learning how to turn ordinary chemicals into bombs.

The architect who'd designed the police station had done a good job, she'd been told; he'd designed the building to ensure that it would survive even a large bomb blast outside its walls. But he'd never anticipated a bomb going off *inside* the building, or that the materials he'd used to shield the policemen from outside threats would contain a blast inside their base, ensuring that it would do more damage.

No one noticed as she pushed her trolley of cleaning supplies into the basement. It was part of her job, after all, to clean the holding cells, once the prisoners were moved on to detention facilities a long way from the Zone. Sometimes, the prisoners were mistreated and she had to clean up blood and piss, sometimes they were treated fairly decently. She'd watched, unseen and unnoticed in the background, as some prisoners were tortured. It had helped to convince her, when the order finally came, that she had no choice.

She mixed the explosive together quickly and efficiently, then set the timer and placed it at the bottom of the liquid. One spark would be enough to detonate the bomb; they hadn't even bothered to search her when she'd come back from holiday. It wouldn't have revealed anything – she wasn't stupid enough to try to carry the timer into the station on her first day back on the job – but it still annoyed her. They *really* didn't take her seriously.

Gritting her teeth, she turned and walked out of the cell. It was all she could do to walk slowly and steadily towards the entrance, feeling sweat pricking at the back of her neck. Some of the policemen were thugs, true, but others were experienced officers with years on the streets. Surely they would sense that something was wrong...

...But no one moved to stop her as she left the building and headed down the street, passing the homeless bums as she walked. She wondered, absently, if any of them were actually observers, or if they were just what they seemed to be. The police sometimes ignored them, sometimes treated them as criminals and sometimes tried to help. Mara reached the corner, glanced at her watch, then looked back at the police station. She was just in time to see the blast.

The entire building shook, violently. Windows, made from reinforced glass, exploded outwards, shattered by the sheer force of the blast. The walls, unsurprisingly, remained intact, almost undamaged. Flames roared through what remained of the building, glowing an odd series of colours as chemicals – both hers and the chemicals used for forensic work – caught fire. If there were any survivors, Mara didn't see them in the wake of the explosion.

She felt an odd pang of regret as she turned and made her way towards the Zone. Some of the cops hadn't been too bad to her; they'd almost been friendly, even to the point of making cups of tea and coffee for the cleaning lady. Others...others had only been deterred from cornering her by the disapproval of their fellows. But, in the end, both the decent cops and the bastards had been working to uphold a system that needed to be destroyed. It might have started out with good intentions, but it had mutated into a monster.

And Sandi will cheer, she thought. Her cousin had been arrested – a case of mistaken identity, as it turned out. She'd still been badly abused by the time she was released. *The guilty have been punished.*

Turning her back, she walked on. Behind her, the city started to fall into chaos.

Constable Gunter Schmitz liked to think that he was doing his duty by his city. His father had been a policeman, his grandfather had been a policeman...and his great-grandfather had been an immigrant from Earth, who'd once been in the Civil Guard. Being a policeman meant more than just policing, he'd been told; it meant being a friend as well as a supervisor to the public. If they trusted you, his father had said, when he'd graduated from the academy, they were likely to bring matters to you, rather than try to take them into their own hands.

But it was different now, Gunter admitted, in the privacy of his own mind. The world had changed, hundreds of thousands of people had found themselves out of work...and they had grown to hate authority. Once, there had been nowhere a policeman couldn't go; now, entire districts were judged too dangerous for the police unless they were in force. The weapon on his belt was just another sign that times were different. His grandfather had never carried a weapon on the streets, while his father had eventually joined the SWAT team. *They'd* backed up coppers who'd needed armed support.

He sighed as he peered into an alleyway. Technically, the homeless shouldn't have been there, not when it was against the law to block public access ways. But they had nowhere else to go and he was damned if he was ordering them to move. They weren't just bums, after all; some of them had once been decent families, reduced to poverty. Even their children were trying to sleep in the alley. God alone knew how long it would be before the children fell into even worse conditions. Rumour had it that some desperate families were even selling their children to *pimps*. It was disgusting, but they were desperate to survive.

It was worse elsewhere, he knew. He'd been part of the police force that had dispersed the rioters outside the First Speaker's Mansion, watching grimly as young men and women were cuffed and led away to detention camps. Most of them couldn't be held for long, but by the time they were released they'd probably hate the police even more than they had before the riot started. There were rumours, whispered among the cops who liked to think they were still upholding the rules, that some of the prisoners had been abused by the guards. But anyone who asked too many questions tended to be put on shit duty...

He froze as he heard the first explosion, then swore as he heard several others in quick succession. Everything had been quiet, too quiet. Now... he reached for his radio and clicked the switch, only to heard nothing but static. Had something happened to the radio network or...he caught sight of the plume of smoke and realised, to his horror, that it was alarmingly close to the police station. Gritting his teeth, he started to run towards the scene of the crime.

The building was in flames by the time he reached it – and totally deserted. There should have been a pair of policemen guarding the outer door, but they were gone. The waves of heat drove him back, convincing him – at a very basic level – that everyone inside the building was dead. Policemen had died along with their prisoners.

There was a low growl behind him. He turned, slowly, to see a mob of people slowly filing out of the nearby buildings, their gazes fixed on him – and his uniform. Once, it would have allowed him to calm them. Now, it was a symbol of their oppressors...marking him as a target. Gunter hesitated – it was beneath his dignity to run, wasn't it? – and then made up his mind as cold ice filtered down his spine. He turned and started to run...and then saw another mob forming in front of him. Panic gripped him as he reached for his weapon, but it was already too late. The mob closed in, pushing and shoving at his exposed face and hands. He fell to the ground, trying to shield himself...

...And then someone kicked him in the face. There was a moment of intense pain, a sudden chilling awareness of his skull cracking, and then nothing at all.

The entire building shook. Alarms started a moment later, underscoring the shouts that seemed to be coming from all around the giant mansion. First Speaker Daniel Krautman blinked in surprise as several armed men appeared from a side door, then relaxed slightly as he realised they were his security officers. The insurgents couldn't have managed to get men on his personal security detachment, could they?

"This way, sir," the leader said, opening a hidden doorway hidden behind a portrait of the planet's spiritual founder. She was an odd-looking woman, Daniel had often thought, but no one had removed her picture from his office. Now, he understood why. "We have to hurry."

Inside, there was nothing more than a flight of metal stairs leading down into the basement. Daniel hesitated, then followed the leader as he led the way downwards, weapon firmly in hand. At the bottom, there was a sealed metal door, a security sensor blinking ominously beside it. The leader caught Daniel's hand, pressed it against the sensor, then let go as the door hissed open. Daniel caught his breath in surprise. He'd been First Speaker for years and he'd never known there was a secret complex under the mansion.

"First Speaker," a familiar voice said. Daniel turned to see General Erwin Adalbert, carrying a terminal in one hand. He couldn't help noticing that his security advisor was wearing a holster at his belt, with the flap unbuttoned. "Welcome to the Underground Bunker."

Daniel looked around, shaking his head in disbelief. There were a dozen computer consoles, manned by a team of operators, a large electronic map of the entire planet, a holographic display of near-orbit space and several displays that blinked for attention. He knew that there were parts of the mansion that were devoted to the military, but he'd never seen *this* one before. How had it been kept a secret?

"It was installed when the mansion was originally built," Adalbert explained. "The First Speaker at the time insisted that the secret should be held by the senior military officials – and even then, kept on a strict need-to-know basis. Those who work here" – he nodded to the operators – "are conditioned to keep its secrets. You would only have been brought here if there was a military or civil disaster you couldn't handle in the mansion overhead."

Daniel glanced up at the bare ceiling, then followed Adalbert into a smaller briefing room. It was barren, compared to the briefing rooms in the mansion itself, but somehow he found it surprisingly reassuring. A pretty female officer poured him a mug of coffee, then helped him into a seat. Adalbert stood on the other side of the table, looking down at his terminal.

After a moment, Daniel cleared his throat. "What's happening?"

"A series of major attacks," Adalbert said. "We're still pulling together the reports, but there was a major explosion outside the mansion and an ongoing situation at the military spaceport, as well as hundreds of minor attacks all across the continent. Right now, we're looking at upwards of seventy police or military installations that have come under attack, followed by rioting and uprisings that have crippled our response. Shootings in the city, several more bomb attacks in vulnerable places...we've even had a report of soldiers firing on policemen."

Daniel swore. "Panic? Or rebel spies?"

"We're unsure as yet," Adalbert said. He turned to look at the map. "Right now, our communications network is suffering the effects of a chaos virus, so we're actually having to depend on makeshift communications systems just to pass messages. My belief, however, is that the overall objective of the attack is to engage and destroy the Commonwealth forces as they land. Everywhere else, the rebels have used hit-and-run tactics. The spaceport seems to be the only place under constant attack."

"I see," Daniel said. He stared down at his hands, bitterly. The military aspects of the sudden series of attacks were beyond him, but he could see the political aspects all too clearly. His political enemies would insist on harsher measures, while the Commonwealth might think twice about honouring their commitments if they couldn't even land their forces, which would be disastrous. "Can we win?"

"We're pulling our forces back together," Adalbert assured him. "I don't think we're in danger of losing any more ground; we just need to gather our forces, then restore security to the city. After that, we can go on the offensive."

Daniel knew it wouldn't be that simple. In politics, perception was often reality – particularly when someone *wanted* perception to be reality. The rebels wouldn't hesitate to use the attack to showcase their ability to attack anywhere, wherever they wanted to attack, while his political enemies would use it to undermine his position. There were even some of them who wanted to turn orbital weapons on the Zone, vaporising rebels and innocent civilians alike. They didn't seem to care about the prospect of mass slaughter...

But it's so much easier, he thought, *to propose solutions if you're not the ones responsible for carrying them out.*

"Do what you have to do to restore security around the spaceport," he said. They'd hoped – even if they hadn't quite admitted it – that the criminal gangs would keep the rebels away from the spaceport. Clearly, that hope had been worse than futile. "And then let me speak to the Commonwealth commander directly."

"Understood, sir," Adalbert said. "I believe that she will speak to you."

Gudrun Gerhardt watched, feeling excitement and terror mingling in her breast, as the convoy of military vehicles headed towards the ambush. There were only a handful of roads leading to the spaceport, she'd been told, making the path the relief forces would use extremely predictable. And they'd be in a hurry, her trainers had added; they wouldn't take as much care as they usually would in their desperation to reach the spaceport.

She held her finger over the detonator as the first vehicles moved closer and closer to the waiting trap. They'd been told that they had to catch the first vehicle, using it to block the others from charging into the ambush and forcing them to retreat. She hesitated, then – at what seemed the best moment – pushed down on the trigger. The explosion was larger than she'd expected – the entire building shook violently, with pieces of plaster falling from the ceiling – but it worked. A military vehicle was picked up and flung against another building by the sheer force of the blast.

The sound of shooting broke out behind her as she turned and fled. None of the bullets seemed to come anywhere near her hiding place, so she guessed they were just firing at shadows. It was common practice, after all, to launch an attack after stalling the convoy – and the soldiers would expect it, which was why no attack had been prepared. The sound seemed to grow louder as she exited the house and started to run, joining other civilians as they fled the shooting. Even if the soldiers reacted fast enough to round up the civilians, they wouldn't be able to tell her from the rest of the civilians. What could possibly be suspicious about a blonde-haired teenage girl fleeing from an incident? No one would be stupid enough to hang around while the bullets were flying.

But no one came after her and the others. Eventually, the sound of firing died away. In the distance, she could hear more shooting – and explosions too. She'd been told that she wasn't the only volunteer ready to risk her life to give the police and military a bloody nose, but they hadn't told her anything else. After all, if they *did* realise that she was responsible for the blast, they would interrogate her as thoroughly as necessary to make her talk.

She kept walking, despite the risk. The rebels had given the government a bloody nose – and they would want revenge. If she didn't get out of the area before they set up roadblocks, she would have to go underground and pray the criminals didn't betray her. If they did...

Angrily, she shook her head. After her brother's death, she would risk everything – life and liberty – to make sure her homeworld was free.

CHAPTER SEVENTEEN

> In some cases, the effective power structures were marginalised by the dictates from the social scientists. Warlords, who (to be fair) could be a large part of the problem were pushed aside, even though they often possessed effective power. Naturally, they went into opposition.
> - Professor Leo Caesius, *War in a time of 'Peace:'*
> *The Empire's Forgotten Military History*

Jasmine forced herself to keep her emotions in check as the situation spiralled down into chaos. She'd seen it before, time and time again, the long chilling moments when no one knew exactly what was going on...and all seemed lost. Two shuttles were gone, two more had landed and were now under attack and she wasn't sure what she needed to do.

"Get me some images of the spaceport," she ordered, "then get me a direct link to whoever's in charge on the planet below!"

She gritted her teeth as the spaceport came under sustained attack. It was bad enough that the rebels had caught them on the hop, but with the locals under attack as well it was alarmingly easy to imagine them shooting at her people by accident. Even launching additional shuttles could be dangerous, if the locals really didn't know what was going on either. But what else could she do?

"Order a cruiser to move into position to drop KEWs," she ordered, tartly. The mortar shells were falling on the spaceport, their patterns suggesting that the gunners were switching position after firing each shell. It suggested a high level of training as well as an understanding of basic counter-battery fire. But she could drop KEWs on the launchers, if she was prepared to risk firing into an urban area. "And then launch two drones."

"I have the planet's military commander on the line," Michael reported. "Half of their system still seems to be down."

Jasmine felt a flicker of reluctant admiration as she reached for the headset. The insurgents had managed a series of successes – that much was clear, just from orbital observation – and they'd managed to put her on the defensive almost at once. She had to change that, but the only way to do it was to drop reinforcements into the planet's atmosphere, which ran the risk of being targeted by additional ground-to-air missiles. Or wait for the locals to arrive.

"This is Yamane," she said. She hesitated; diplomacy wasn't her strong suit. "I need a sit-rep, now."

"A number of military and police installations have come under attack," a strongly-accented voice said. "Our forces are responding, but the attacks on our communications and logistic networks have proven quite successful. We are having problems running reinforcements to the spaceport."

Jasmine nodded, unsurprised. She'd seen the relief force coming under attack from orbit, running straight into an ambush that should have been predicable. But then, they'd been caught by surprise too. Gritting her teeth, she checked the status display and saw that four more shuttles were ready to launch. The problem would be getting them down to the ground safely. Perhaps she should land them outside the urban sprawl...no, she saw as she skimmed the map, the closest safe place they could land was over ten kilometres away. Far too far to be of any immediate use.

"I intend to drop more troops into the spaceport," she said. An idea occurred to her and she smiled. "Perhaps if your troops surround the area, rather than trying to push into the district, we will be successful in catching the gunners when they try to retreat."

"Understood," the voice said. "Good hunting."

Jasmine felt her smile grow wider. "Launch hunter-killer drones, then send the shuttles down in their wake," she ordered. A glance at the situation board told her that Rifleman Stewart had assumed command of the troops on the ground. If that had happened in the days of the Empire, she knew, it would have caused years of inquiries and bureaucratic wrangling. In the Commonwealth, it hardly mattered. "And make sure the shuttles are prepped for ground fire."

Michael worked his terminal for a long moment. "The shuttles are detaching themselves now," he said. "Estimated ETA; five minutes."

Jasmine winced in sympathy. The shuttles would be dropping through the atmosphere like stones, violently enough to make even hardened Marines throw up in their suits. But there was no alternative. A stately descent from high orbit would merely make them targets for hidden gunners. Even if the enemy had no more HVMs to throw at the shuttles, she knew, a lucky hit with a mortar shell could be disastrous.

"Good," she said.

Looking back at the display, she thought through her options and conceded that they were remarkably limited. She would just have to improvise and keep feeding troops down to the spaceport – and hope that the spaceport wasn't assaulted heavily enough to fall, despite the presence of her troops. But if there was a Marine commanding the opposing faction…she shook her head. Surely an experienced Marine would know his forces were no match for hers in a stand-up battle.

But if he has far more men to burn than us, he might think it's worth the cost, she thought, sourly. *But will his own people let him waste their lives?*

She shook her head. There was no way to know.

Thomas ducked under cover as the mortar shells crashed down on the spaceport, doing remarkably little damage. The locals hadn't done a bad job, he had to admit; the barracks were hardened against outside attack while the runways themselves were solid and incredibly hard to damage without specialised equipment. He glanced at his HUD, then kept barking orders. It was quite possible that the mortars were intended to force him and his men to take cover while the enemy forces closed in on the spaceport from all sides.

"Get up to the fence," he ordered, as the explosions faded away. In their absence, he could hear shooting, but it was hard to tell where the shooting was coming from. It seemed as if the entire surrounding area was trapped in a civil war. "And launch two drones!"

He took another glance at his HUD, then followed his men outside. The fence surrounding the spaceport would stop petty thieves, but it wouldn't slow down a determined assault for more than a few seconds. Indeed, at least one mortar shell had come down close enough to the fence to knock part of it down. Outside, there were several metres of grass and then the start of the urban sprawl. The more he looked at it, the less he liked it. A major enemy attack could come quite close to the spaceport without being detected, as long as the enemy soldiers were careful. And then he heard the sound of incoming shells again.

"Hit the deck," he bellowed. He heard the sound of shooting growing louder too, just before the first set of shells crashed to the ground. They seemed to be firing randomly into the spaceport, rather than targeting specific buildings, something that struck him as odd. Surely they'd had enough time to range their weapons and calculate firing angles and positions properly. "Any news on the drones?"

"They're both gone," a soldier called back to him. "Five seconds of flight...and then they were taken down."

Definitely dealing with a smartass, Thomas thought. The rebels clearly understood both the value and vulnerability of man-portable drones. It wasn't as if they were difficult to hit, once the shooter had a rough idea of their location. *They must have anticipated our move.*

He glanced back, just in time to see a new shuttle fall out of the sky and come to a halt, bare metres above the ground. The noise of its engines rose to a crescendo as it lowered itself the final few metres to the ground, then popped open its hatches. A line of men ran out, half of them clearly unwell; Thomas felt a moment of sympathy, then pushed it aside ruthlessly. The reinforcements could secure the rest of the spaceport before they tried to push their zone of control outside the complex.

The sound of shooting grew even louder as the rebels started to fire into the complex from the surrounding area. They didn't seem to intend to try to actually overrun the spaceport, something that nagged at his mind; instead, they just fired whenever they saw a target.

Thomas barked orders, detailing snipers to return fire, sweeping the buildings the enemy were using as firing platforms. If there were civilians in the buildings...he shook his head, bitterly. They'd have to take their chances.

Two more shuttles landed, unloading a small battery of self-propelled guns along with additional soldiers. A third shuttle came in to land, only to be struck by a mortar shell and fall the remaining few metres out of the sky. Thomas braced himself as it struck the ground, but there was no explosion. Instead, the entire spacecraft was rapidly evacuated.

"Get the radar up and running," he ordered, as the firing grew even louder. "I want you firing back at the mortar shells!"

The gunners were well trained; they set up their guns, then opened fire, using radars to track the enemy shells back to their launchers. It was clear that the rebels were breaking down their weapons and switching position after each shot, but could they do it quickly enough to escape the inevitable response? Thomas briefly considered calling orbit and requesting orbital fire support, despite the threat to civilians caught in the battlefield, then relaxed slightly as the weight of incoming fire started to drop off. The rebels were either losing men or playing it more carefully, now the CEF was countering their shells.

He glanced back to see the remaining shuttles leaping upwards, clawing for space in a desperate attempt to outrun prospective missiles, then started barking orders to the newcomers. Thankfully, most of their chain of command had survived intact – and that they'd been trained to take orders from Marines, even if he wasn't their formal commanding officer. The person on the spot, after all, knew more about what was going on than the new arrivals. Thomas smiled briefly, then watched as the soldiers took up positions around the spaceport, shielding themselves from incoming shells as best as they could. They'd have to start advancing out from the spaceport as soon as possible.

We're going to need more protection, he thought, grimly. It hadn't been so hair-raising on Han...or Avalon, for that matter. *And probably more ammunition.*

Bracing himself, he keyed his communicator. "This is Stewart," he said, checking the live feed from the HUD. As always, orbital observation wasn't entirely useful for immediate action. "I am requesting permission to advance."

Pete had to admit, however reluctantly, that the CEF was well-trained. They'd taken heavy losses during their landing, but the survivors had secured the spaceport and were landing more troops, despite the best efforts of Pete's mortars. Indeed, they were showing a remarkable sense of restraint, compared to the Empire. If half the stories Pete had heard about Han were true, the Empire hadn't hesitated to fire KEWs into cities, just to eradicate alarmingly persistent snipers. But then, the Empire had never given a damn about civilian casualties.

"Sir," one of his spotters snapped. "The reinforcements are taking up positions outside the city!"

"Interesting," Pete mused. He didn't need to look at a map to understand what the security forces were doing. Rather than poke their heads into the territory controlled by the criminal gangs, they were sealing off the escape routes and waiting for the CEF to flush the insurgents towards them. Hammer and anvil, he noted; the tactic was older than firearms themselves. "They must have regained control of their communications networks."

He briefly considered his options, then sighed. There was only one realistic option, now the security forces were recovering and moving rapidly to block his escape.

"Launch the flare," he ordered. "And then leave the blocking force in place while the rest of us fall back."

Thomas wished, with a sudden bitterness that surprised him, that he had a whole division of Terran Marines behind him. Clearing out cities was something Marines were trained to do, even though the CEF had gained some experience of its own during the first deployment. But he knew that far too many of the soldiers who were following him had no real experience...and they were about to start learning the hard way.

He kept his head down as he led the way towards the first complex of buildings, a nightmarish mixture of transit dorms and warehouses for new immigrants and their possessions. His awareness shrank rapidly as he crossed the line and entered the complex, leaving him only truly aware of the soldiers following him. In the distance, he could still hear the sound of mortar fire and snipers taking shots in and out of the spaceport, but they didn't matter. All that mattered was his local awareness.

Bracing himself, he peered around the corner into an empty dorm. It had been stripped bare of everything moveable, leaving only the framework of bunk beds and a shower complex that had once served hundreds of people. One wall was covered with a mural, welcoming the immigrants to Thule. Thomas's lips quirked in silent amusement – it looked as though it had been painted by schoolchildren, then vandalised by young adults – before he could make his way out of the dorm. Outside, two wrecked vehicles were propped against the wall.

A shot rang out. Thomas ducked instinctively, then caught sight of the sniper, hiding in the next building. He barked orders, then led one group of soldiers towards the building while a second group covered their advance. If the sniper showed himself again, he'd be in for a nasty surprise. But no shots rang out as they reached the door and slapped an explosive charge against the metal, blowing it open. Thomas threw a smoke grenade into the building, then followed, relying on his visor to see through the smoke. If the insurgents weren't similarly prepared, they would be blinded.

The soldiers moved from room to room, advancing up the stairs and making their way through a network of offices. They saw no sign of the enemy until they reached the third floor, when another shot ran out. Thomas saw the enemy sniper and fired back, hitting the sniper in the head. He felt an odd moment of tired satisfaction as he stepped forward, examining the body from a distance. There had been insurgents in the past who had booby-trapped their own bodies, just to try to kill another soldier.

Just a kid, he thought. The insurgent had been young – around sixteen, if he was any judge – before his death. He wondered, absently, if the youngster had been an ideologue or someone who had been lured into the insurgency through a desire for fame or simple poverty, then pushed the thought aside. All that mattered, right now, was that he was dead.

They swept through the rest of the complex, then moved on to the next one. Two more snipers greeted them, one managing to wound a soldier before being killed by a grenade hurled by the soldier's comrade. The other stumbled and fell down a flight of stairs while trying to escape, breaking his neck when he hit the bottom. Thomas noted the body's position and pressed on. There would be time to sweep the battlefield later.

He paused outside the complex, checking the location of the other soldiers. They were, to all intents and purposes, advancing on a wide front, something that spread his forces very thin. He linked into the command datanet and checked on the shuttles, but he needed a reserve now. If one force ran into trouble, he didn't have much in place to provide immediate support. But he also needed to push the enemy as far back from the spaceport as possible.

"Bring in the additional shuttles as soon as possible," he ordered. He'd just have to designate one of the new units as the reserve – and hope they arrived before something went spectacularly wrong. "And request additional fire support ASAP."

We should have planned for a hostile landing, he thought, as he straightened up and began to issue the next set of orders. *Right now, we don't have enough men to secure the buildings we clear.*

He heard the sound of shuttles flying overhead and allowed himself to relax, slightly. They'd passed through the danger zone, thankfully. Now, all they had to do was keep pushing the enemy back and clearing buildings. And then they could hand the region over to the locals.

"Rifleman Stewart is requesting additional support," Michael reported.

"Send him whatever he needs," Jasmine ordered. Her conversation with the planet's defenders was distracting her from monitoring the battle, but she knew better than to override the person on the ground without good reason. "Keep me informed."

She looked back at the display, trying to understand the tactics the enemy were using. None of them quite made sense, apart from the first attack. If she'd been facing the CEF, she would have rigged half the buildings surrounding the spaceport with IEDs, just to make life difficult for the advancing soldiers. Even a handful of IEDs would have slowed her forces down long enough to allow the rebels to make their escape. Instead, they seemed to have deployed a handful of rebels merely to take a shot or two at her men before being killed. It didn't quite make sense.

The enemy CO was a Marine, one with considerable experience. He knew what he would be facing and how best to counter it. So why wasn't he doing it? Jasmine had wondered, unwilling to accept that a Marine might be involved, if he was a faker, but Colonel Stalker had assured her that he was quite real. And that meant...?

And that means there's something I'm not seeing, she thought. *A missing piece of the puzzle. But what am I missing?*

CHAPTER EIGHTEEN

> If this wasn't bad enough, the social scientists who were more aware of the political realities on Earth (not on the planet being 'assisted') proved adept at ensuring that local powers connected with their political masters were backed by the Empire's military, regardless of their local level of influence.
> - Professor Leo Caesius, *War in a time of 'Peace:'*
> *The Empire's Forgotten Military History*

In the end, they made it out just in time.

The one great advantage insurgents possessed was the ability to look just like civilians. Thousands of civilians had started to flee the area around the spaceport as soon as the shooting started; it had been simple enough to join them, even as the security forces were setting up roadblocks and cordons. It would be a while yet, Pete judged, before they were ready to start trying to detain everyone who wanted to leave the area. By the time they started, most of his people would be out and making their way back towards the Zone.

He looked back towards the spaceport as they headed northwards. Great plumes of smoke were rising up, while he could still hear the sound of shooting in the distance. It would take the newcomers some time to realise, he calculated, that most of the insurgents had broken contact completely. The only defenders of the area now were criminals, trying to keep the newcomers out of their territory. Given the nature of the defenders, Pete found it hard to care how many of them were killed by the advancing soldiers.

Another shuttle dropped down from high orbit, launching flares to distract incoming missiles...if any missiles had been launched. Pete had only a handful, after all, despite his sources of off-world weapons. He'd made the decision not to risk more than a handful of them, no matter the prize. The security forces could not be allowed to deploy helicopters and CAS aircraft without hindrance or the insurgents would operate at a heavy disadvantage. But as long as they believed the rebels had antiaircraft weapons...

He turned and joined the others, trying hard to look like a fleeing civilian. The engagement, as far as he was concerned, was over. Now, all he had to do was make it back to safety and then he could start planning the next operation.

The building looked harmless. Thomas eyed it tiredly as the soldiers surrounded it, then led the charge at the front door. It exploded inwards, allowing them to pour into the building and stare in surprise. Outside, the building looked worn down and shabby. Inside...it looked surprisingly luxurious. The floors were carpeted, the walls were decorated with paintings...each one erotic enough to make him look away, embarrassed. Some of the positions they depicted were impossible for anyone other than a trained athlete.

He heard a whimper from behind an adjourning door and kicked it open, weapon at the ready. Inside, there were seven girls, ranging in age from sixteen to twenty-five, all as naked as the day they were born. The door had been locked, he realised dully, and – judging from the marks on their wrists – the girls spent a lot of time restrained. Two of them bore the signs of a beating too. They cowered back from him and his men, gibbering slightly.

"Don't worry," he said, knowing they wouldn't believe him. "We're not going to hurt you."

Gently, he urged the girls outside as the soldiers searched the rest of the brothel. Upstairs, they found a handful of tiny rooms, each one holding a bed and a bucket of warm water. It was clear, Thomas decided, that the brothel was very low-market, probably only charging a handful of coins for its services. Compared to the legalised brothels on Avalon, it was filthy as hell and probably a breeding ground for disease. Chances were, he guessed, that none of the girls were there willingly. He'd seen the signs before, on a dozen worlds.

"Get them to the aid station," he ordered. Now the shuttles were landing in force, one of the spaceport barracks had been turned into a medical centre. Wounded soldiers, a handful of POWs and a number of civilians who'd been caught up in the fighting had already been sent there. "And see if they can be interviewed, later."

He sighed, inwardly, as he led the way out of the brothel and back onto the streets. The sound of shooting was dying away; a quick check showed that resistance had fallen to almost nothing. Instead of encountering enemy fighters, the advancing soldiers were discovering small pockets of civilians, cowering in their homes as if they expected to be shot upon discovery. The advancing soldiers reassured them as best as they could, searched briefly for weapons, then left them behind. There was no point in trying to detain them, not now.

Shaking his head, he checked his HUD again. The local security forces were responding in force now, their roadblocks firmly in place. Unlike the CEF's soldiers, they had the manpower to detain everyone who tried to leave. Still, Thomas suspected they were too late to catch anyone important. The enemy seemed to have melted away completely.

And the more we spread out our forces, he thought, *the greater the chance someone will get behind us.*

He checked the spaceport security arrangements, then resumed the advance. It wouldn't be long, he told himself, before they reached the local forces. At that point, they could return to the spaceport and get some rest while the higher-ups sorted out their next move.

"They're searching the buildings! They're searching *all* the buildings!"

Gudrun cursed her own mistake as she heard the cry. If she'd kept moving...but no, the streets weren't safe for a young woman at the best of times, not here. There were horror stories about what happened to young girls who were captured by criminals, particularly ones who had a connection to the movement. She'd decided that hiding in a house owned by a sympathiser would be a smarter move than trying to make it out of the city.

But now it had blown up in her face. She hesitated, caught between two equally unpalatable alternatives. If the building was searched by the newcomers, chances were they wouldn't have access to the security database that listed known and suspected members of the insurgency and their relatives. But if it was the security forces that searched the building, they'd have access...and they might demand to see her papers. Or, for that matter, they might insist on knowing why she wasn't on the lease. Legally, anyone who lived in a rented house had to be listed...and she, obviously, wouldn't be there.

And she might be betrayed by her host. Even if he didn't want to betray her, or wasn't tempted by the reward money, his family were at risk. Would he keep his silence if his five-year-old daughter was threatened? How could she blame him if he talked? She thought, briefly, about the pistol she'd concealed in her pocket, then dismissed the thought. It wasn't in her to kill a man and his family just because they *might* betray her. Besides, even if he kept his mouth shut, she might still be uncovered. She was too old to be his daughter, after all.

"I'll leave," she decided. Maybe she could keep her head down and escape unnoticed. "As long as you say nothing, you won't be harmed."

She considered, briefly, dumping the pistol, but shook her head. Despite her two weeks in the training camp, she was a slight girl, unable to fight off someone who really wanted to beat her down. It was better to have the weapon and not need it than need it and not have it. She nodded to her host, then headed through the door. Behind her, she thought she heard him heave a sigh of relief.

Outside, she could smell burning in the air as she made her way down the alleyway, slipping past a handful of sleeping bums. None of them so much as twitched at her passing, perhaps because they were trying to remain unnoticed...or perhaps because they had spent too much of their time drowning their sorrows in cheap alcohol. The government taxed it – the government taxed everything these days – but the bums still bought it from bootleg dealers who didn't bother to pay. There were times when Gudrun wondered if the government quietly *allowed* the alcohol to be distributed, believing it helped keep people quiet. The hell of it was that they were probably right.

"Halt!"

Gudrun almost jumped out of her skin, then spun around to see three men standing in the crossroads pointing weapons at her. They wore grey urban camouflage uniforms, she realised, but not the same design as those worn by the security forces. The off-worlders, she decided, as she kept herself very still. It was possible she might be able to bluff her way out of trouble.

"I'm just trying to get home," she stammered. It dawned on her, suddenly, that she might be in far worse danger than she'd realised. Some security force units had been reported to commit rapes, particularly when deployed to restive parts of the planet. Would the off-worlders be any better? "I…"

"Stay still," one of the men ordered. He stepped forward and frisked her with brutal efficiency. Gudrun felt her entire body tense as he found the pistol and removed it from her pocket, then aimed a kick at his knee. He dodged it effortlessly, then pushed her roughly to the ground. "Who are you, I wonder?"

Gudrun gasped in pain as her hands were pulled behind her back and secured firmly with a plastic tie. She felt him search her again, more thoroughly, then haul her to her feet and press her against a wall. His comrade said something she barely heard through the sudden roaring in her ears, the dull awareness that she was about to vanish into the system. She'd been caught with a weapon…she should have dumped it, despite the risk. They'd know she wasn't an ordinary citizen now.

She wanted to run, but there was nowhere to go.

Thomas looked up in some surprise as the prisoner was pushed into his presence. She was a young blonde girl, around twenty years old, wearing what looked like a shapeless shirt and a pair of loose trousers. The bitter resignation on her face made his heart twinge, before he reminded himself that the female of the species could be far deadlier than the male. Besides, he'd known enough female Marines to know that women were far from helpless.

"She was carrying a weapon, sir," the soldier who'd caught her said. "Personal weapons are illegal here."

"Good thinking," Thomas said. It struck him as strange – Avalon had almost no controls on who could own a weapon at all – but the soldier was right. Someone carrying a weapon in a war zone was almost certainly an insurgent. "Escort her back to the spaceport, then secure her with the other POWs. And then report to the duty officer there."

He watched them go, making a mental note to ensure that the suspected insurgent was fast-tracked for interrogation. She might well know something that could be used against her former allies...and even if she didn't, she could be probed for insight. And if she wasn't an insurgent, as unlikely as that seemed, her innocence would be proven in short order.

Sighing, he turned to follow his soldiers as they advanced towards the roadblock. Meeting another friendly force in the midst of a combat zone wasn't easy, even when both forces had trained together. Thomas had watched enough renditions of friendly fire incidents to know that it was alarmingly easy to kill someone on the same side, completely accidentally. This time, one force had never met the other before.

"Tell them we're coming," he said. "And hurry."

Jasmine allowed herself a moment of relief as she watched, from high overhead, as both forces linked up. The locals hadn't started shooting at her people, thankfully, and there hadn't been any incidents that might have produced bad feelings on both sides. And the enemy seemed to have just faded away. The only contacts for over half an hour had been criminals or people defending their homes, not insurgents.

She looked over at Michael, who looked nervous. "How many prisoners did we take?"

"Twelve, nine of whom are believed to be confirmed insurgents," Michael reported. "The other three are uncertain, but were caught in position to observe our advance."

"I see," Jasmine said.

She sighed, inwardly. They'd been meant to spend some time arguing out the Rules of Engagement for operations on Thule. The Commonwealth's might be different from the locals, after all, and there would be diplomatic incidents if her forces accidentally broke local ROE. Not to mention, she knew, the problems caused by detaining local civilians who turned out to be completely innocent. Everything had been much simpler on Avalon – or even Lakshmibai. There, they'd been free to take whatever precautions they liked without fear of setting off a diplomatic nightmare.

"Keep the prisoners under guard for now," she ordered, finally. They'd have to sort out how to handle them with the locals. "Make sure they don't see anything useful, just in case we have to let them go."

"Understood, Brigadier," Michael said.

Jasmine nodded. "Keep funnelling down our forces to the spaceport," she added. "I want the tanks deployed to provide extra firepower, if necessary."

She looked back at the display. Her forces were filtering their way back to the spaceport, while the local security forces were taking over their role on the streets. It looked as though everything had been wrapped up, but she knew it was an illusion. The insurgents had broken contact and escaped, almost without more than a handful of losses. It was impossible to escape the feeling that the war had barely begun.

"And ask for an appointment with the planetary leader and his senior officers for me," Jasmine added. "We have some issues to settle, face to face."

"The insurgents have broken contact," Adalbert reported. "But the situation is not under control."

Daniel sighed. He felt so fucking...*helpless*. His position as First Speaker had been badly undermined by the crisis, then undermined again by the insurgency. It was easy to imagine his enemies using the new disaster to unseat him completely; the only thing keeping them in check was the awareness that one of them would have to take over as First Speaker after successfully kicking him out of office. And...he hadn't even been able to do anything, but cower in the bunker when the fighting began.

"In particular," Adalbert continued, "our control over the districts surrounding the Zone has been shattered. Police stations have been destroyed – we're looking at near-total casualty rates – and most of the military and civil government stations have been wrecked. Overall, we have no effective control."

"I see," Daniel said. The insurgents were throwing down a gauntlet, he knew, challenging the security forces directly. If he left them in power, even in the Zone alone, they'd undermine his authority just by existing. And yet, if he sent his forces to engage the enemy, they'd be fighting on territory the enemy had chosen. "Is there any *good* news?"

"The attack on the spaceport was repelled," Adalbert said. "And we took prisoners."

Daniel sighed, again. Prisoners, particularly insurgent prisoners, were a contentious subject in the Senate. Half of the Speakers wanted to take the gloves off completely, using torture to break the handful of prisoners they had, the other half feared the long-term effects of using harsh methods to extract information. Their enemies accused them of either being cowards, fearing that the insurgents would torture them if they took over, or of being secret enemy sympathisers.

"We can sort that out later," he said.

"The CEF suggested the use of truth drugs," Adalbert said. "They could handle the prisoners..."

"And if something goes wrong, they take the blame," Daniel said. He hated thinking in such terms, but he had no choice. If he lost his position, his successor would either take the gloves off or surrender completely. "See to it."

"We've also managed to impose a curfew on the streets," Adalbert added. "Anyone caught outside until the state of emergency is lifted can be arrested, making it harder for the insurgents to slip out of our grasp."

Daniel made a face. It would work, militarily speaking, but it would upset the local population, most of whom were voters. If the war lasted long enough, his supporters would pay for it at the next election. And then whoever took his place...the thought kept mocking him, every time he tried to relax. He was caught in the middle, unable to avoid being pelted with charges and counter-charges from all sides.

He stood. "I'm going back to my office," he said, softly. He was not going to remain in the bunker any longer than strictly necessary. If it was safe outside, he could go to his office and think there. "Call the CEF; ask the senior officer to meet me as soon as possible. We need to discuss the future."

"I would advise having a military representative there," Adalbert said. His voice was quiet, but firm. "The Commonwealth will have its own ideas about how to conduct joint operations."

"Better I talk to her first myself," Daniel said. He knew what his friend meant, but he wanted to take the measure of the person he would have to deal with. "Can she land here safely?"

"We believe so," Adalbert said. "But if there are more HVMs out there..."

"Let them decide," Daniel said. "We will accept their decision."

Chapter Nineteen

> On Janus, the social scientists saw the shortage of food and attempted to solve the problem by shipping in food from a nearby star system. On the face of it, their proposed solution was a logical one. However, it ran into unexpected snags that eventually made it worse than useless.
> - Professor Leo Caesius, *War in a time of 'Peace:'*
> *The Empire's Forgotten Military History*

"One minute to landing," the pilot called back. "Do you want me to circle the city first?"

"No," Jasmine said, rather dryly. She enjoyed flying, most of the time, but it was hair-raising when she knew the enemy might have HVMs targeted on her shuttle, ready to fire. Besides, she really should be back at the spaceport. It had only been an hour since the area had been declared quiet, if not safe. "Just take us down as quickly as possible."

She peered out of the cockpit as the shuttle headed down towards the mansion's landing pad. It was more modest, she decided, than any of the mansions the old Council had built on Avalon, a simple blocky building within a large garden. Now, the garden was torn and broken, military vehicles spaced around the edges to provide some protection. Outside the high wall, she could see armed troops patrolling the streets, looking for any signs of trouble.

The city itself was a curious mix of styles. It lacked the elegance of the buildings she'd seen on Lakshmibai, or the simplicity of Avalon's newer buildings, but there was something about them that made her smile. A handful of churches could be seen only bare metres from the mansion; beyond them, there was a handful of large stone buildings, surrounded by more armed soldiers. Government offices, she guessed; it looked as though the centre of the city was heavily defended. Outside the offices, there seemed row upon row of endless redbrick houses. Few of them looked to be any different from the others.

She checked her weapons out of habit as the shuttle touched down, her four armed bodyguards jumping out ahead of her and sweeping the area for prospective threats. Volpe had insisted on her taking a section of Marines with her, just in case the insurgents decided to try to attack while she was on the ground. Jasmine thought he was being paranoid – and that they were likely to offend the local government – but she'd conceded the point. If she hadn't been high on the list of people the insurgents would like to assassinate, she would be by the time the CEF had finished deploying.

Outside, the air smelt faintly of burning ashes and the dead. Jasmine wondered, briefly, just how bad it had been in the city, then pushed the thought aside as a civilian flunky ran up to her. He reminded her a little of the supply officers she'd seen on Earth, right down to the slightly nervous expression on his face when he saw her and her guards. Surely, she couldn't help thinking, he'd have had plenty of time to get used to armed soldiers surrounding the palace. But some people were never comfortable with weapons in their vicinity.

"Thank you for coming," he said, with a half-bow. His voice had the local accent, but it was clear enough for her to understand. "The First Speaker is waiting for you in his office."

"Thank you," Jasmine said. "Please take me to him."

Inside, the mansion was surprisingly demure, compared to the mansions on Avalon or Admiral Singh's palace. Jasmine couldn't help noting the shortage of gilt or expensive artworks. The only real decorations were portraits of important figures in the planet's past, ranging from its founders to later First Speakers. All of them, she couldn't help noticing, broadcast steely resolve with their eyes. Jasmine had never been particularly interested in artwork, but she would have bet good money that they'd all been painted by the same artist.

"That's right," her guide confirmed, when she asked. "The previous First Speaker thought it was important for us to remember the great heroes of the past, so he had the paintings produced and hung on the walls. I believe there was quite a competition for the post of official government artist."

Jasmine listened with half an ear as he talked about the paintings, telling her a little of the history behind each one. Some of the stories were absurd enough to make her wonder if they'd been invented in hindsight, although there were stories about Avalon that certainly sounded absurd, if someone hadn't known they were real. Eighty-odd Marines landing on a war-torn planet and bringing peace within six months of hard fighting? Or the story behind *Sword's* entry into the Commonwealth Navy? Who would believe *that*?

They paused outside a pair of heavy wooden doors. "The First Speaker has granted you permission to keep your weapons," the guide said. "But your guards must stay outside."

Jasmine nodded, wordlessly. She wasn't blind to the significance of the gesture. On Earth, no one was admitted into the presence of the Grand Senate without surrendering their weapons and passing through the security scanners. But then, if she couldn't kill the First Speaker with her bare hands she'd be kicked out of the Marine Corps. The only way to be truly *safe* would be to have the conversation through the communications network.

She stepped through the door, indicating silently to her escorts that they should stay outside, and smiled as she saw the First Speaker. He was shorter than his official portrait had suggested, although that might have been because he walked in a permanent stoop. His hair was shading rapidly to gray and his suit, despite clearly being the product of careful tailoring, seemed to hang loosely on him. This, Jasmine realised, was a man worn down by circumstances beyond his control. She couldn't help being reminded of Avalon's former governor, who had retired the year after first contact with Admiral Singh.

"You may call me Daniel," he said, as he held out a hand. "We shall not stand on ceremony here."

"Jasmine," Jasmine said. His hand felt dusty to the touch. She shook it gently, then sat down where he indicated. "Thank you for inviting me."

The First Speaker laughed, humourlessly. "We try not to greet our guests with fireworks," he said, rather sardonically. "And I'm sorry for your loss."

Jasmine nodded. Overall, seventy soldiers had died in the first engagement, most of them on the destroyed shuttles. Thankfully, some of the soldiers from the shuttle that had crashed almost intact had survived long enough to be rescued. Even so, it was a major disaster – and an obvious propaganda victory for the insurgents. The fact they'd extracted most of their forces despite the best efforts of both the locals and the CEF was only the icing on the cake.

"They will be remembered," she said, quietly. "I confess, sir, that I am no diplomat..."

"I don't believe diplomacy will be of any use," the First Speaker said. He smiled at her, more openly. "You may speak freely."

"We have to take the offensive as soon as possible," Jasmine said. "The CEF is a formidable fighting force, sir, but it isn't designed to hold territory indefinitely. We also need to undermine the basis for the insurgency's existence."

"We can do one of those," the First Speaker admitted. Behind his smile, she saw a sudden hint of bitter tiredness. He would have six more years of his term to go, she knew, if he didn't get kicked out by the planet's Senate. By the end of his term, he would be an old man. "But forcing a compromise solution through the Senate...it might be impossible."

Jasmine nodded in understanding. Avalon had had plenty of room to expand, it had merely been held back by the old Council. Once the barriers had been removed, the economy and employment had expanded rapidly. But Thule didn't really have that option, unless the government invested money in trying to create busy-work. And even *that* would have its limits.

The First Speaker looked at her. "How long will the Commonwealth permit you and your men to remain here?"

"At least nine months," Jasmine said, wishing she was as confident as she sounded. If Councillor Travis had his way, the CEF would be recalled and disbanded within months, an act that would probably tear the Commonwealth apart. "After that, I don't know."

"So we have that long to produce results," the First Speaker mused. "And the insurgents might know there's a time limit."

He sighed, then looked up at her. "I believe it is time to call my advisors," he said. "We need to plan our operations with extreme care. A victory – any victory – would make it easier for us to seek a political solution."

The hanger had once been completely empty, stripped bare of everything from machine tools to personal possessions. Now, it had been taken over by the medics, who had placed blankets on the floor and used them as makeshift beds for wounded soldiers and civilians. Thomas entered through the side door and winced, bitterly, when he saw the wounded men. Half of them would have to be evacuated to the starships and returned to Avalon to recover there.

He looked over at the medic, who stepped over and led him into a private office. It was as bare as the rest of the hanger, apart from a pornographic calendar that hung on the walls that was around two years old. Thomas made a mental note to place it in the main room – it might distract the wounded – then looked back at the medic. He looked tired.

"Nine men will have to be shipped back to Avalon," the medic said, "unless we can get them proper treatment here. Their wounds are beyond field treatment, sir. There's also a handful of civilians in similar condition..."

"Place them in stasis tubes," Thomas ordered. If the locals could take them, well and good; if not, the CEF would assume responsibility. "And the others?"

"Should be back up within a week at the most," the medic said. "A couple probably should go back to the starships – I'd prefer not to treat them here if possible – but they will heal."

He paused. "There's some odd points on the civilians, though," he added. "The girls in particular. Some of them are drug addicts, others have clearly been abused as well as forced to prostitute themselves. They're frightened of men, yet any fight has been beaten out of them so completely that they're unable to offer any resistance. From what they've said, they were sold by their families and...well, if they tried to resist, they were simply beaten into submission.

"They – and most of the civilians – are also suffering the effects of starvation and poor nutrition. The drugs don't make it any easier for them."

Thomas nodded, unsurprised. War zones tended to be hellish for everyone, but it was worst of all for the helpless civilians caught in the middle.

"Treat them as best as you can," he said. "And if anyone complains, send them to me."

"Yes, sir," the medic said.

Gudrun's arms and wrists were aching, but there was nothing she could do about it. She – and around a dozen other prisoners, mostly men – had been marched into a disused hanger and told to sit by the wall, waiting for attention. Part of her wanted the waiting to come to an end, part of her knew all-too-well that when it did, she was likely to regret it. There were just too many rumours, some backed up with hard facts, about what happened to young men and women who were arrested by the security forces.

She risked a glance at the soldiers watching her, but they seemed to be paying her no special attention. One of the prisoners had made a terrible fuss, only to be gagged with a piece of duct tape and dropped in the corner; the others had kept their mouths shut. But then, cuffed as they were, there was little they could do to cause trouble. All they could do was wait and see what happened to them.

Two men marched into the hanger and walked over to her. Before she could say a word, they caught her shoulders and hauled her to her feet, then half-pushed her towards the door. Outside, more and more shuttles were landing, some of them disgorging tanks that looked larger than her father's house, before it had been repossessed by the bank. Others were unloading soldiers, more soldiers than she could possibly count. It looked as if the outsiders had brought enough soldiers to occupy the entire planet. None of them paid any attention to her as she was walked past them and into a small building that, she guessed, had once been part of the administrative centre. Now, the only occupant was a tough-looking woman wearing a black uniform and a nasty scowl.

A moment later, she was forced into a chair and her escorts headed outside, leaving her alone with the intimidating woman. Up close, her skin-tight uniform revealed an alarming amount of muscles, while her cold eyes betrayed no hint of anything, but absolute confidence she could handle anything Gudrun threw at her.

"I should tell you, just in case you have any ideas, that I have permission to maim you if you do anything stupid," she said. Her voice had a thin nasal accent that reminded Gudrun of her younger brother, who'd had his nose broken during a childhood fight. "And even if you do manage to overcome me, there is only one door and it is heavily guarded by armed men."

She plucked Gudrun to her feet with one hand, then spun her around. Gudrun yelped as she felt something cold touching her wrists, then there was a snapping sound and her hands came free. She pulled them forward and rubbed her wrists, frantically. Her captor spun her around until she was facing her, then gave her an odd little smile.

"Tell me," she said. "Are you carrying anything that could be used as a weapon?"

"I was searched twice," Gudrun said, somehow. Her voice shook as she spoke. "I couldn't hide anything."

"Good to hear it," the woman said. She stepped forward, then ran her hands down Gudrun's body, paying particular attention to her pockets. "Sit down."

Gudrun sat. A moment later, she felt something hard pressed against her neck. There was a hissing sound, a stab of pain, then her thoughts just seemed to drift away into the ether. It was hard, so hard, to focus her mind…ahead of her, she heard a booming voice. Somehow, it seemed to be the most important thing in the universe.

"Tell me your name," it said.

"Gudrun," Gudrun said. A funny feeling overcame her for a second, a feeling that suggested that perhaps she shouldn't be answering questions. But it faded rapidly and was gone. "My name is Gudrun."

"Very good," the voice cooed. Gudrun felt a rush of almost sexual pleasure, washing away her doubts. "And what were you doing when you were captured?"

The questions continued, one by one, until she had quite lost track of herself. When she finally reopened her eyes, she discovered that she'd fallen asleep. Her memories were hazy and confused...and, she discovered when she tried to move, her hands had been cuffed again while her ankles had been shackled. What had happened?

"You were injected with a basic truth drug," the woman said. Oddly, the haze still affecting Gudrun's thoughts made her want to trust the woman. "You sang like a canary."

Gudrun cringed. "I didn't..."

"You did," the woman told her. "I can show you recordings, if you like. We know everything you know, from your cell leader to your RV point for extraction. I dare say we will make good use of it."

Gudrun barely heard herself moan. She was dead. Whatever happened, she was dead. If she went to a detention camp as a young female insurgent, she would be molested by the guards – and murdered by the other prisoners, if they found out she'd betrayed them. And if the movement found out that she'd confessed everything, they'd kill her if she fell into their hands. She'd steeled herself to resist torture, to keep her mouth shut even if they flogged her to within an inch of her life, but the drug had just undermined her will completely. There had been no way to resist it.

"We have an offer for you," the woman said. "You may be able to do us a service. If so, we will provide transport off-world for you and your family at the end of the war. But it will require some willing collaboration."

She shrugged, meaningfully. "There's no shame in falling to the drugs," she added. "I've seen strong men steel themselves to resist, only to start blabbing as soon as the drug gets into their bloodstream. You could go to a camp, if you liked."

"But I'll be killed," Gudrun wailed. "They'll kill me."

"Your choice," the woman said. "Work with us, Gudrun, and you can survive. Your family can survive. Or go into a camp and take your chances."

She paused. "We won't tell anyone you talked," she added. "We can do that much for you, at least."

It was the act of kindness, more than anything else, that broke Gudrun completely. She was being manipulated, she recognised, her thoughts still – perhaps – influenced by the drug, but there was no alternative. She'd been drugged to spill everything she knew, yet now...now she was making the decision to betray her side completely.

"I'll join you," she said.

"Splendid," the woman said. She helped Gudrun to her feet. "I'll have better quarters prepared for you ASAP."

It was hard, Gudrun discovered, to walk while her feet was shackled. Oddly, concentrating on walking made it easier to forget what she'd done...and what she was going to do. But when she finally reached her new apartment, the thoughts came back full force.

What had she done?

CHAPTER TWENTY

For example, the food distribution was originally placed in the hands of Empire-backed power centres. These ranged from officials appointed directly by the Empire's representatives to outright warlords. Unsurprisingly, they tended to distribute the food in a manner calculated to benefit themselves.
- Professor Leo Caesius, *War in a time of 'Peace:'*
The Empire's Forgotten Military History

"Jasmine will be on Thule by now," Gwendolyn said.

Ed nodded as they walked into the waiting room. The hearing had lasted two weeks, with almost every officer remaining on Avalon called to testify, some multiple times. Ed couldn't decide if Councillor Travis was desperate to dig up something – anything – to justify the amount of time and effort spent on the hearing. By now, he had a private suspicion that the Councillor had burned through much of his political capital, overplaying his hand. Would he still be able to use the outcome to press for changes?

"And Wolfbane will be bare light years away," he mused. There had been more reports of intrusions across the border, reports that had been two weeks old by the time they reached Avalon. God alone knew what the situation was like now. One scenario he'd contemplated was the CEF being attacked by Wolfbane's Navy before it could disembark. "Doing what, I wonder?"

A bell rang before he could say anything else. Shaking his head, he left Gwen behind and strode into the Council Chamber and took a seat in the gallery, watching grimly as everyone who thought they were anyone on

Avalon found their places and sat down. Maybe it wouldn't be too long, he considered, before Avalon developed the ceremonies the Empire had once used to make it clear that the Grand Senate was in charge. And when that happened, when lines were drawn between rulers and ruled, something vitally important would be lost forever.

He found himself looking up at the chairs on the other side of the room. Reporters, of course – he saw Jasmine's lover among them – and family members, but there were others too. Men and women who had realised just how important this hearing was likely to be, not for what might be decided but for what might come of it. In a very real sense, the whole ideal of the Commonwealth itself was in trial.

Councillor Stevens stood and gavelled for silence. Ed leaned back in his chair as the chatter died away, watching and waiting to see what the Council might have decided. Gaby had been excluded from their discussions, but Councillor Travis – thanks to his political footwork – had not. Ed couldn't help admiring the deviousness the man had shown in organising and steering the hearing – he'd managed to both advocate it and serve as a judge – yet he wished that it had been turned to another purpose. The Commonwealth had quite a few political problems that might be solved with some fancy diplomatic footwork.

Maybe we can make him a diplomat, he thought, before dismissing the idea as absurd. They might have been trying to reinvent the whole idea of diplomacy after the fall of the Empire – the Empire had never been very diplomatic, as it had wielded the biggest stick in the history of mankind – but he was fairly sure that appointing someone adamantly opposed to the Commonwealth to the Diplomatic Corps would be a bad idea. At the very least, it would suggest that Avalon was more interested in getting rid of a nuisance than actual diplomacy.

"We are very aware of the fact that this hearing is unprecedented," Councillor Stevens said, "and that we will be setting the precedent for countless hearings to come. As such, we have been careful to go through the steps point by point, calling everyone who could reasonably be called to testify. We may have trod the same ground time and time again, but we have a reasonably comprehensive picture of everything that happened."

That was true enough, Ed knew, although it was still tainted with hindsight. But very few people could dismiss hindsight altogether, even when they were aware of the dangers of using knowledge from the future. There was always a tendency to move towards the answer the viewer knew was correct, simply through having the benefit of hindsight. It was far harder to understand that the person at the time might have thought differently.

"The Council wishes to take a moment to express its gratitude to everyone who was called to testify," Councillor Stevens continued. "It could not have been an easy experience for them, any more than it was for any of us. But their testimony helped flesh out the gaps in the record."

And wasted a great deal of time, Ed thought. There were only a handful of people involved in the actual decision. Calling junior soldiers who had first seen combat during the CEF's ill-fated deployment might have looked good, but it hadn't produced anything useful. *But then, I suppose they wanted to be as careful as possible.*

"Overall, we have reached a number of conclusions," Councillor Stevens said. "Those conclusions can now be stated for the record."

Ed felt cold ice moving through his bloodstream. A determination that he had acted poorly in making the decision to deploy the CEF, let alone accepting Wolfbane's choice of a venue for the talks, wouldn't be enough to fire him. But if his position was undermined so badly, he would have no choice but to resign. The principle of civilian control of the military was too important to allow his own feelings to interfere with his duty to uphold it. They wouldn't need to make a case for his dismissal if he resigned.

"First, the decision to use Lakshmibai was not taken by anyone on Avalon," Councillor Stevens said. "We believe that the decision was unwise, but our representatives were given few choices. Wolfbane made the decision to use Lakshmibai and we accepted it, because we were given no reasonable alternative. It is unlikely, we believe, that the people who made the original decision will ever stand trial in this chamber."

Probably, Ed thought, cynically. The Empire had occasionally tried and punished officers from independent planetary militias, but the Empire had been overwhelmingly powerful. It could have enforced compliance if the planetary militia had balked. It was unlikely, however, that the

Commonwealth could try anyone from Wolfbane...or, for that matter, that Wolfbane could insist on asserting authority over the Commonwealth. Both sides would regard it as compromising their independence.

"Second, given the security situation on Lakshmibai," Councillor Stevens continued, "the decision to deploy the CEF was not in error. Foresight shows little about Lakshmibai to like; hindsight tells us that the planet would be plunged into a full-scale war. Having the CEF accompanying the diplomats was a wise precaution, one that more than proved its value."

Ed looked up at Councillor Travis. His face was impassive, betraying none of his innermost thoughts, but he had to be outraged. The two most important charges, the ones that would have been levelled against Ed if they'd been upheld, had been rejected. Ed wondered, coldly, just what the Councillor was thinking. Did he intend to press for a retrial? Or would he merely accept there was no point in playing out a losing hand?

"Third, however, the decision to accept Wolfbane's terms of sending away the starships was a deadly mistake," Councillor Stevens said. "They may have proposed it, but we do not believe that there was any reason to accept it, particularly as they had already accepted the CEF. In future negotiations, it is our determination that if the security situation is badly unstable, we will insist on an equal number of starships being present in the star system in question.

"Fourth, the decision to take the CEF on the most direct route towards the planetary capital was the correct one," Councillor Stevens concluded. "There was no time for a more careful campaign, no time to outflank enemy defences; there was no choice, but to take the CEF straight through the enemy defences. We do not consider that anyone involved should be punished for that decision."

Ed saw Councillor Travis's face flicker, just once. He'd lost. Jasmine – or Ed himself – would not be forced to resign from the military, let alone be dishonourably discharged by the Council. There had been a reprimand, over the starships, but not enough to force him to hand in his resignation. That, too, had been something Wolfbane had demanded as part of the price for the talks. In hindsight, it suggested that Wolfbane had either underestimated the situation themselves or deliberately intended to give the locals a chance to slaughter the hated off-worlders.

"Overall..."

The first shot rang out. Ed dropped to the ground out of habit, his mind automatically calculating the number of shooters and their weapons as his hand groped for the pistol at his belt. Panic swept through the chamber as the shooter fired, time and time again, people fleeing for the doors rather than trying to tackle the shooter or get down on the ground. In hindsight – he couldn't help a flicker of dark amusement – it had probably been a mistake to largely ban weapons from the Council Chamber. Gaby had hoped to prevent her councillors from shooting at each other, but it had left them defenceless when someone else had started shooting at them.

There was a pause. Ed calculated rapidly and concluded that the shooter was using a standard pistol...and that he was probably reloading. Pistol in hand, Ed stood up and saw a young man taking aim into the crowd. He was wearing the grey overalls of an immigrant worker, something that would allow him to blend into almost anywhere in the city. Ed lifted his pistol, then called out a warning. The shooter swung round with astonishing speed, bringing his weapon to bear on Ed. Ed fired, just once. The shooter fell to the ground, blood spurting from a bullet wound in his temple.

"MEDIC," Ed bellowed, as loudly as he could. between the shooting and the crush, dozens of people were likely to be hurt. "GET MEDICS NOW, DAMN IT!"

He reached for his wristcom as he headed towards where the shooter had fallen, keeping his pistol trained on the man's body. It wouldn't be the first time someone had survived a wound that had looked fatal. But the shooter was very definitely dead, he discovered, as he prodded the body. Ed's bullet had seriously damaged his skull as well as passing through the man's brain.

"Colonel," Gwen's voice said. Security forces, soldiers and medics were starting to pour into the room. The whole scene was one of complete confusion. "I've got the QRF on the way."

"Good," Ed growled. He raised his voice, taking command. "Get everyone who isn't injured out of the building, then let the medics do their work."

———

It had all happened so *quickly*.

One moment, Emmanuel Alves had been listening to Councillor Stevens babbling on about how everything that had happened wasn't anyone's fault, the next he'd heard shots ring out in the Council Chamber. He'd had enough experience to know that the smartest thing to do was to get down on the ground, so he'd done it, just in time to see another reporter fall to the ground, a nasty wound on her throat. And then there'd been another shot and silence fell.

Carefully, summoning up a tiny fraction of the courage Jasmine routinely displayed, he rose to his feet and beheld a scene from hell. People – ordinary people – were fighting to get through the doors, while others lay on the ground, dead or stunned. Colonel Stalker and his terrifying Command Sergeant were examining another body, one with a pistol lying on the ground next to it. The shooter, Emmanuel assumed, as he staggered forward. Somehow, the sudden transition from peace to absolute mayhem had undermined his composure completely.

"Help the unwounded out of the building," Colonel Stalker snapped at him. "Now!"

The tone of command was so powerful that Emmanuel obeyed without question. Part of his mind silently took notes, plotting the story he would write later, while the rest of it concentrated on following orders. The audience seemed torn between panic and a strangely blasé reaction that bothered him, even though he knew that plenty of people on Avalon had experience in dangerous situations. But it had been five years, more or less, since the end of the Cracker War. People had had time to relax...

Outside, crowds were already gathering, watching numbly as doctors and volunteers started to carry the wounded out of the building. Thankfully, Avalon's hospitals were designed to cope with a sudden influx of patients, at least once they were actually taken to the hospitals. A line of new ambulances appeared, disgorging more doctors and nurses, allowing the patients to be loaded onboard. Several of the unwounded looked very much as though they would have liked to join the wounded in the vehicles, but there was no time.

"The President has been hit," someone said. Emmanuel gasped as he heard the rumour, running through the crowd. He'd approved of Gaby Cracker, insofar as he approved of anyone who had moved from commanding an insurgency to trying to steer politics onto a steady course that would avoid future conflict. "She's dead!"

The rumour spread faster and faster, growing in the telling. Emmanuel replayed what little he'd seen of the shooting, but couldn't determine if the President had been hit or not. How had the shooter even managed to get a weapon into the Council Chambers? He shook his head a moment later, recalling just how little security there was around the building. Gaby Cracker's insistence on avoiding the old Council's paranoia about their security had, ironically, contributed to her own injury. But she'd never taken the threats quite seriously.

Another ripple ran through the crowd as someone stepped out of the building. Emmanuel looked forward and realised, to his dismay, that it was Colonel Stalker. The Marine's uniform was stained with blood...he hadn't been bloody before, Emmanuel recalled. He'd touched someone who'd been injured...

He wanted to shout questions, but he didn't quite dare. Instead, he and the rest of the crowd watched as Colonel Stalker climbed into a vehicle and was driven off in the direction of the Main Hospital. Behind him, the security forces did their work, dragging out the body of the shooter for transport to the nearest police station. Emmanuel turned to look at the man, etching what remained of his face in his memory, then watched as the crowd moved forward threateningly. If the shooter hadn't already been dead, he might well have been lynched on the spot.

I don't know who you are, he thought coldly, *but you've won everlasting infamy for yourself.*

Ed felt oddly helpless. Command and control had been surrendered to the civil police force, although both the Marines and the Knights of Avalon had been placed on alert, ready to provide help and support if the police needed it. The intelligence service was already rushing its best men and women to the police station, where they would start the long task of identifying the shooter and trying to determine his motivations. There was nothing for Ed to do, but wait and pray that his lover survived.

He looked up as the doctor appeared and beckoned to him. Ed stood and followed the doctor through a door into an observation chamber. Peering through the window, he saw his lover lying on a bed, hooked up to a life support machine. The left side of her head was covered by a medical pack, one of the newer inventions from the Trade Federation. They'd taken standard medical nanites, Ed recalled, and improved the design considerably.

"She was lucky," the doctor said. He was a civilian, but like all of the planet's doctors he'd had considerable experience in battlefield medicine. "The bullet only grazed her skull, rather than penetrating her brain. However, her skull *was* damaged and there may be long-term mental health problems."

Ed swallowed. The feeling of helplessness grew stronger. He'd seen soldiers who'd taken head wounds...and how some of them had been unable to heal after being discharged from the military. Head wounds were dangerously unpredictable, even with the best medical technology available.

"Will..." He took a breath and tried again. "Will she recover?"

"We will try to wake her up within a few days," the doctor said. "We're keeping her under at the moment, allowing us to monitor her condition, but brain damage can be difficult to handle. She may make a complete recovery or she may never wake up at all."

Or anywhere in-between, Ed thought, mutely. He recalled one of the tours they'd taken on the Slaughterhouse, where they'd been introduced to retired Marines who had been medically discharged out of the corps. Some of them had seemed almost normal, others had had to be restrained for their own safety. Several, he'd been told, had killed themselves, unable to bear being trapped in their wounded bodies any longer. And it could be worse, he knew, for soldiers and Civil Guardsmen. *Their* superiors rarely gave a damn.

"Do the best you can," he said. Gaby looked so...*helpless* on the bed, her chest rising and falling as she breathed in and out. "And keep me informed."

"This raises a political point," the doctor said. "Who's in charge until she recovers?"

Ed gritted his teeth. "Councillor Jackson," he said. Gaby had appointed him as her second, if she left Avalon for any reason. At least it wasn't Councillor Travis. "He will be President *pro tem*."

He turned and left the room before the doctor could say another word. The political nightmare was only just beginning. If Gaby was out of office permanently, there would have to be an election to choose a new President. And Councillor Travis would be well-placed to run for office.

Shit, he thought.

CHAPTER TWENTY-ONE

> Some merely charged for the food (when it was supposed to be free), while others refused to supply food to their rivals, hoping that their rivals would drop dead from starvation. Instead, their rivals mounted constant challenges to their power.
>
> - Professor Leo Caesius, *War in a time of 'Peace:'*
> *The Empire's Forgotten Military History*

"Violet," her father called.

Violet Campbell straightened up from her desk, where she was trying to put a primitive spacesuit back together with inferior tools. Her father had told her that if she succeeded, to the point where the spacesuit could be used in a vacuum safely, he would support her when she applied to join the RockRats for a course in space engineering and habitation. But now…he sounded worried. She hadn't heard him sound so worried – and angry – since two little brats from Earth had managed to get lost in the station's storage compartments.

"Yes, father?" She said, turning to face him. He looked worried. "What's wrong?"

"There are two security officers here who want to question you," her father said. "You need to answer their questions."

Puzzled, Violet allowed him to lead her through the corridor into what had once been the briefing room, back when the ADC had operated Orbit Station. Now, it was empty, save for a single large metal table. Two people, a man and a woman, stood at the far corner of the room.

The woman's eyes went wide when she saw Violet. Clearly, Violet sneered mentally, she'd expected someone older. But spacer children learned to take care of themselves – and to work as soon as they could – even if groundside children remained...*children* until they were adults.

"Thank you for coming," the woman said. She was pretty enough, Violet decided, with short red-brown hair that looked like she hadn't bothered to comb it. Her voice suggested that she was a native of Earth, rather than Avalon. "My name is Kitty."

The man grunted, but said nothing.

"We need to ask you some questions about this man," Kitty said, passing Violet a terminal. It showed a standard Immigration ID, complete with a picture that made the subject look simultaneously mad, bad and dead. "I believe he passed through your part of the station."

Violet gave her a reproving look – there were no other parts of the station – and then examined the picture. She'd always had a good memory, but the picture was so bad it took her several moments to recall when they'd met. He'd been one of the newcomers from Bohemia, if her memory hadn't failed her, the one who'd claimed to have saved the recruiter's life. And he'd been fast-tracked to Avalon by the recruiter's company.

"He did," she confirmed. "He had an ID that was already cleared, so I sent him down to the shuttle."

The man leaned forward, suspiciously. "Already cleared?"

Violet nodded in confirmation. "He said that he'd saved the recruiter's life," she said. "It sounded like a nice story."

"Someone cleared the way for him," Kitty muttered. "What can you tell me about him?"

"He was exhausted," Violet recalled. "His clothes were ill-fitting, his eyes looked tired...I thought he would have managed to catch up on his sleep, even if he'd spent most of the voyage in a stasis tube."

Kitty's lips twitched. "It doesn't work like that," she said. "Did he pay any special attention to you?"

Violet shrugged. She was young enough to draw attention from adult groundhogs, old enough to draw attention from teenage groundhogs... some of whom had probably heard rumours and lies about sexual freedom in space. Not that she had any intention of taking up some of the offers she'd had over the years. God knew she hadn't even started her period. And if her father had heard some of them, he'd probably ban her from talking to groundhogs altogether.

"No," she said. She struggled to put her feelings into words. "He just seemed...*there*."

Kitty lifted her eyebrows. "There?"

Violet glanced back at her father, then looked at Kitty. "Some newcomers resent having to wait in line and show their ID cards," she said. "Others seem excited to see the station, even though" - she waved a hand to indicate the gunmetal grey decor - "it isn't that interesting. But this guy showed no reaction at all."

She looked down at the deck, wondering just how much trouble she was in. "What did he do?"

"Shot the President," the man explained.

Violet gaped at him. "Shot the *President*?"

"Yes," Kitty confirmed. "We're trying to retrace his steps now."

The Situation Room on Castle Rock hadn't been used much since the end of the Cracker War and the foundation of the Commonwealth, Ed knew. It simply wasn't central enough to the capital for Gaby and her Councillors to reach, while it was too obvious a location for an emergency command installation. Indeed, if an enemy *did* gain control of the high orbitals over Avalon, he fully expected Castle Rock - the home of the Marines - to be the first target they blasted with KEWs. Only an idiot would engage the Marines on the ground if there was any alternative.

He took a seat at the head of the table and waited for Gwen, Kitty Stevenson and a handful of other officers to take their places. Kitty looked as young as ever - intelligence officers had access to rejuvenation treatments denied to the vast majority of the Empire's citizens - but her eyes were tired. Ed smiled, silently grateful that the Empire had seen fit to abandon such an intelligence officer on Avalon. She'd served the Commonwealth very well.

But she looked scared, he realised, as she turned to face him.

"I was expecting to find a rogue Cracker," she said, softly. Not *all* of the Crackers had accepted Gaby's decision to come to terms with the new order and join the government. Some of them had gone underground, threatening revenge at a later date. But none of them had ever resurfaced. "But what I found was far more frightening."

Ed tapped the table. "Please get to the point," he said. He was tired himself...tired and desperate to get back to the hospital. Maybe he could do nothing there, but at least he would be with Gaby. "What did you find?"

Kitty tapped a switch. A holographic image appeared in front of them, showing a young man wearing a standard uniform. "Private Mathew Polk," Kitty said. "Born seventeen years ago on Avalon..."

Ed recognised the name. "Son of a bitch!"

"Yes, sir," Kitty said. She looked down at her terminal. "Born seventeen years ago in Camelot City, Avalon; exact date unknown because his birth was never registered. Apparently orphaned; grew up in an orphanage run by various concerned civilians. Spent a year in a work camp at after being caught stealing from a factory owned by Councillor Wilhelm. Released as part of the general amnesty that followed the fall of the old Council. Joined the Knights of Avalon when he turned sixteen; apparently, he did very well and was assigned to the CEF. Missing, believed dead, on Lakshmibai."

"Shit," Ed said.

It was a precept of the Marine Corps – one he'd introduced to the Knights – that no one was left behind, dead or alive. Battlefields had been combed for the remains of fallen soldiers, enemy records had been scanned and enemy prisoners had been interrogated, just to get a hint of what had happened to missing soldiers from the brief bloody war. But several soldiers had vanished completely on Lakshmibai, so completely that their bodies had never been found.

Ed had concluded, finally, that they'd been killed by their captors and their bodies burnt to ash or simply buried in an undisclosed location. Lakshmibai was covered in mass graves, after all, and there had been no time to open them all up before they'd vacated the cursed world. But to see one of the missing soldiers here...

"Wolfbane," he snarled.

Kitty nodded, one hand rubbing her tired eyes. "No one else could have got him off the planet," she said. "But if they *did* have allies on the surface, someone could have handed Polk over to Wolfbane and then buried their tracks."

Ed nodded, remembering the explosion that had killed Blake Coleman. Had that been a fanatic's last attempt to harm his enemies...or had Wolfbane killed off their allies on Lakshmibai, preventing them from being interrogated? Now, there was no way to know.

"His behaviour was indicative of someone who had been conditioned," Kitty said, quietly. "From the trail we've followed, he basically stayed out of sight as much as possible until the time came to act. Someone, I suspect, smoothed the way for him as much as possible."

She sighed. "His arrival clearance was processed by Theodore Smith Immigration Services," she continued. "Violet Campbell told us that he claimed his path had been smoothed by a recruiter in gratitude for saving his life. As far as we can tell, that story is nonsense – but it's impossible to be sure. The recruiter who went to Bohemia was killed in a bar fight two days after Polk arrived on the planet."

"Someone was burying their tracks," Ed commented.

"So it would seem," Kitty commented. "We traced him to McGhee Boarding House, an establishment with a reputation for discretion going all the way back to the days of the old Council. When we arrived, we found Lucy McGhee dead on the floor, apparently the victim of a break-in gone badly wrong. Her other tenants claim to know nothing about Polk's presence in the building. But then, several of the bastards had quite a bit to hide themselves."

She shrugged. "Logically, he must have had a support network on Avalon waiting for him," she added. "But, so far, all ties to them have been broken. We don't know who they are."

Ed nodded. Conditioning ensured that the victim was literally incapable of betrayal – or of betraying his former comrades, if the conditioning was applied until the victim could do longer separate right from wrong. Whatever he might have been, he wasn't any longer; Polk would, eventually, have done whatever his new masters wanted him to do. But it also interfered with a person's ability to respond to unexpected situations.

A person who had been heavily conditioned would be noticeable. No wonder Polk had stayed out of sight until the time had come for him to act...and that his masters had ensured that he'd had assistance to remain unnoticed.

"Then we have to find them," he said, although he had no idea how they could proceed. It wasn't as if Avalon was Earth, with the civilised parts of the planet subject to constant monitoring. "Before they do something worse."

He glared down at his hands, thinking hard. The picture of the dead assassin had been splashed all over the datanet; it wouldn't be long before Polk was recognised, even though most of the people who'd known him were currently on Thule. And when they did find out...there would be a demand for war. Gaby might not have been liked by everyone, but she *was* respected...and even if she'd been hated, Wolfbane had pulled off an assassination attempt that had killed nineteen innocent victims, directly or indirectly. There would be war.

But there was simply too much about it that didn't make sense. He could understand kidnapping a Commonwealth soldier for interrogation and conditioning – Polk might have only been a very junior soldier, but even a junior soldier saw more than a civilian – yet why turn him into an assassin? Unless the idea was to try to blame Gaby's death on the Commonwealth military? But that struck him as thoroughly absurd. Too many things could go wrong.

And besides, he thought darkly, *everyone knows Gaby and I are lovers.*

Wolfbane was the prime suspect. But the sheer nature of the whole plot practically *shouted* that Wolfbane was involved. It wouldn't have been too difficult to insert someone completely new to Avalon, someone who couldn't be identified the moment his DNA was checked against the Commonwealth's records...someone with no visible tie to Wolfbane. Ed could imagine a psychopath or a megalomaniac doing something so blatantly obvious – they'd practically signed their names to the crime – but everything they knew about Governor Brown suggested he was cold, calculating and not given to rash moves.

"I have to brief the Council in an hour," he said, standing up. "I want you to coordinate your efforts with the police in Camelot, but do whatever it takes to catch the operatives here. We need to be rid of them before it's too late."

Gwen frowned. "It may already be too late," she said. "The assassination attempt might be the first shot in a war."

Ed froze, chewing himself out mentally. He'd been so focused on Gaby – and the conditioned assassin – that he hadn't realised that the shit might have hit the fan elsewhere. If Wolfbane had been lucky – very lucky – they might have managed to coordinate the assassination attempt with their forces streaming over the border and attacking the Commonwealth's member worlds. It would be tricky to manage the timing, he knew, but interstellar distances ensured that there would be some room for slippage. They might just get away with it.

"Place our forces on full alert," he ordered. At least no lurking enemy fleet had appeared in the Avalon system, bent on attacking the shipyards. But it was only a matter of time. "And send an emergency signal to every planet in the Commonwealth. A state of emergency exists – and war might break out at any moment. All forces are to move to Case Theta-One."

It was risky, he knew. If they were wrong, if Wolfbane wasn't involved, he might have given his forces clearance to *start* a war. Case Theta-One authorised commanding officers to open fire if they believed their positions were threatened, without waiting for the enemy to fire first. After a few brief exchanges of fire, it would be much harder to come to terms with Wolfbane without the war spinning right out of control.

But there was no alternative. If they failed to assume the worst, they would just leave themselves vulnerable, waiting to be hit.

―――

Councillor Gordon Travis was used to violence and the threat of violence, or so he had told himself. Certainly, he hadn't taken part in the Cracker War as anything other than a supply officer, but that was a risky profession when the old Council had been quite willing to torture any Cracker they captured. But since the end of the war, he'd been at peace. Even his son had died on a wretched foreign world rather than Avalon's streets.

But the assassin had shattered Gordon's composure. One of the bullets had flashed past him and struck the wall. A centimetre or two to the left and the bullet would have punched into his head, killing him instantly. And Gaby was in hospital, fighting for her life…it was shocking, truly shocking, that anyone on Avalon would resort to violence to make their voice heard. Hadn't they realised, he asked himself, that violence only bred violence?

He watched as Colonel Stalker entered the underground bunker, looking as tired as Gordon felt. Oddly, he felt a hint of pity for the military officer. His lover was in the hospital, upsetting both his personal and professional lives. Gordon had had no time to carry out any polls, but he was sure that there would be an upswing of sympathy for the Colonel after Gaby had been injured.

"We may be at war," Colonel Stalker said, when Councillor Jackson invited him to speak. "That assassin was carefully inserted into our society for one specific action."

Gordon listened in growing disbelief as Colonel Stalker outlined what they'd discovered in the hours since the assassination attempt. A conditioned assassin? It made sense – there were countless stories about conditioned assassins getting close to their targets because they were programmed not to reveal any fear – but someone who was instantly identifiable? Someone who had vanished on Lakshmibai?

And if this was the opening move in a war, as the Colonel suspected, who knew what would happen next?

He stared down at his hands, thinking hard. He'd had his doubts about the Commonwealth for a long time, but…but it had just blown up in his face. If he pressed for Avalon to leave the Commonwealth under such conditions, his supporters would desert him in droves. Gaby had practically become a martyr already, without even dying! And…if the war had already begun, as much as he hated to admit it, the Commonwealth might be their only hope of survival.

Councillor Jackson cleared his throat. "It seems to me that we are in a state of war," he said. "Colonel, how do you believe we should react?"

"I believe that we should concentrate our forces and then prepare for offensive operations," Colonel Stalker said. "Right now, our forces along the border are spread out and vulnerable. We should re-concentrate, then force them to go on the defensive."

Gordon gritted his teeth, then held up his hand for attention. "We should send a diplomatic note," he said, "if the war has not already begun, demanding to know what the hell they're doing."

"The war began the moment Gaby was shot," Councillor Jackson snapped. Two of his compatriots howled their agreement. "It's too late to try to come to terms!"

"We should at least attempt to keep the lines of communication open," Gordon said. He'd suffer in the polls, but as long as his support didn't fall too far he wouldn't be recalled and forced to stand for re-election. "No one has fought a full-scale interstellar war in centuries, have they? We do not *know* what has already happened along the border!"

He took a breath. "They have attacked us," he said, "but do we really want a war to the knife?"

Looking at some of his fellow Councillors, he rather suspected the answer to that question was *yes*.

CHAPTER TWENTY-TWO

Eventually, this problem was noticed and distribution responsibilities were handed over to the Imperial Army. However, the forces deployed on Janus were nowhere near numerous enough to handle the task in a reasonable space of time – hence the food often went rotten before distribution – and were often attacked by local factions intent on stealing the food. A small-scale deployment rapidly became a much larger one.

- Professor Leo Caesius, *War in a time of 'Peace:'*
The Empire's Forgotten Military History

"All things considered," Pete said, "I think matters worked out surprisingly well."

He looked down at the estimates from his spies in Asgard. Most of the attacks had shocked the security forces, rather than doing any real damage, but that hadn't been the purpose of the attacks. The *real* purpose had been to give the CEF a bloody nose and *that* had been accomplished quite nicely. It had also given him a chance to watch the CEF in action, admittedly at a closer range than he might have preferred, and he had to admit that they were clearly capable soldiers. A little inexperienced, he'd noted, but still quite capable. And experience was just a matter of time.

"They pushed us back from the spaceport," one of his fellows objected. "They reacted very quickly to our attacks."

Pete shrugged. Given the shortage of time to prepare the area around the spaceport to make life miserable for the CEF, they'd done better than he'd expected. The criminals, fortunately, had kept their heads down rather than come into the open against either side, although *that* would probably change. After the planetary government had been humiliated so badly, they'd want to make damn sure the spaceport was secure in future and to hell with the criminals who thought they owned the district.

"Good for them," he said. "But we didn't give them a *real* challenge."

He looked back down at the reports. The spaceport crews had been thoroughly infiltrated long ago, with strict orders to do nothing more than report back to the movement. Judging from their reports, most of the CEF was already down on the ground, accompanied by enough Imperial-standard supplies to fight a small war. He wondered, absently, if they'd brought enough to fight the war he intended to give them, then dismissed the thought as unimportant. The government's habit of throwing money at the local defence establishment had ensured that there were plenty of supplies to go around.

But the government would be having problems of its own. Quite apart from the embarrassment, they'd discovered that the movement had infiltrated a number of police and military bases. Right now, they would be looking for spies, people who would remain quiet until the signal arrived and then start a new campaign of sabotage. The witch-hunt would utterly destroy morale, even in the most capable infantry units. No one would be able to trust anyone else for a very long time.

"They'll come here, of course," he said. "We made damn sure of that, didn't we?"

He pulled the map out from under the table and peered down at it, silently matching the buildings on the sheet of paper with the information stored in his brain. The Zone, four hundred square miles of residential buildings, shopping malls and warehouses...now the home to the displaced, the dispossessed and the rebels. It had been unsurprisingly easy to recruit all the footsoldiers the movement could possibly need from the Zone, young men desperate to prove themselves and do something useful with their lives. Pete knew that most of them were going to die, but their sacrifice would take the government down too.

Outside the Zone, the government had created a network of military and police stations, intending to try to keep the contamination in the Zone from spreading. Pete could have told them it was a waste of time, not with the economic crisis gathering steam; they'd merely created more targets for the rebels, when the time came to strike. Now, most of those police and military stations were in ruins, while the reputation of those forces had been shattered. And, while he knew it would be costly, the outsiders had committed themselves when they'd lynched stranded policemen and soldiers. The government would not forgive them for choosing the rebel side.

The longer the Zone remained outside the government's control, the weaker the government would become. They *had* to deal with the Zone... and they had to do it quickly. Whatever the CEF's commander thought, she would have to fall in line. The alternative would be surrendering the initiative to the rebels.

"Make sure the newcomers are properly screened," he ordered. Refugees had been streaming into the Zone for hours, now the war had begun in earnest. It wouldn't be long before the government started to slip spies of their own into the Zone, using the refugees as cover. "And remember to ration the food."

He smirked at the thought. The government had done nothing for the people in the Zone, the victims of a galactic crisis that was none of their making, but the movement had started to help them long before Pete himself had chosen a side. It was the movement that had started the soup kitchens, it was the movement that had restarted the schools, it was the movement that had even provided a semblance of law and order... allowing it to claim a moral authority the local government had long since surrendered. Pete hadn't hesitated to take advantage of it.

"Of course, sir," his aide said. The fact they'd managed to set up an algae-production facility under the Zone was one of their most tightly-guarded secrets. Sooner or later, someone would work out the truth, but by then it would be too late. "And the preparations?"

"Begin them in earnest," Pete ordered. "But make damn sure the children are kept away from those buildings."

He shuddered at the thought. The local government had failed in many ways, but they'd failed the children worst of all. Schools had had to close, leaving the children growing up on the streets, unable to read or write. Older children, those who had had a few years under their belt when the crisis hit, had been unable to take the exams that would qualify them for jobs...or, for that matter, to get jobs at all. Even positions like street cleaner or toilet attendant had hundreds of applicants. The movement had tried to do what it could for the children, but it didn't have the resources to give them all the attention they deserved.

Shaking his head, he looked back at the map. Bare as it was, it was easy to envisage the first line of defence. The CEF would expect it, of course – the tactic was older than the Empire – but it would have real problems dealing with it. And then the real excitement would begin.

Gudrun hadn't been quite sure what to expect after an uncomfortable night in a makeshift prison cell. She certainly hadn't expected to be woken in the morning, offered a reasonably civilised shower and a change of clothes, then an escort into a former office building that had been turned into a command centre. A dozen men and women wearing blue uniforms had set up dozens of portable computers, then started to work on them. Half of the screens showed orbital images, she realised; the others showed live feeds from a dozen cameras around the spaceport.

She recoiled inwardly as heads turned to look at her. No matter what she'd agreed to do for the CEF, her escort – who had admitted to being called Marcy – had cuffed Gudrun again after she'd showered and dressed. Marcy had pointed out, when Gudrun had complained, that she was a known danger and couldn't be allowed in a secure environment without some precautions. Gudrun had tried to object by remarking that Marcy could probably beat her to death with one hand tied behind her back, but Marcy had ignored the logic. All Gudrun could do was put up with it.

A smaller room had been converted into a private office, with two armed guards wearing helmets and body armour at the door. They insisted on running a sensor over Gudrun's body before allowing her to enter – the handcuffs set the alarms off, she noticed with some amusement – and then did the same to Marcy. Irritatingly, the overbuilt woman took it in her stride.

"You think this is secure," Marcy hissed, as they stepped through the door. "There's a secret post on Avalon where everyone is strip-searched before being allowed to enter."

Gudrun kept her thoughts to herself as she looked into the room. A small table sat in the exact centre of the room, surrounded by four uncomfortable looking chairs and a stool. The windows had not only been closed, but boarded up; the only source of light was a portable lamp someone had fixed to the ceiling. There was nothing on the table, but another portable computer attached to a series of wires that ran out of the room. She looked around, hoping to see something other than bare walls, then looked back at the room's sole occupant. The girl looked no older than Gudrun herself.

"Take a seat," she said, with a smile. "I'm Alpha."

"You must have had odd parents," Gudrun muttered, as she sat on the stool. Oddly, that small consideration made her feel weepy. "What sort of name is Alpha?"

"The kind we use when we are not allowed to disclose our real names," Marcy grated. She stood behind Gudrun, her looming presence a constant reminder – as if she needed one – that she was hardly in friendly territory. "I suggest you pay close attention."

Alpha gave her a wink, then tapped a key on the computer. The screen lit up, revealing an image from another orbiting satellite. It looked as though she was staring down at the Zone from a great height…no, somewhere outside the Zone. The green park near the houses, complete with duck pond, was a dead giveaway. No one had wasted money on beautifying the Zone, not when everyone who lived there had been expected to move out as soon as they found a job.

"This is the address you gave us," Alpha said. On the screen, Gudrun saw red letters marking the street names and house numbers. There were no such luxuries in the Zone, of course. "Will you confirm that it is the correct location?"

Gudrun leaned closer, cursing the cuffs as they dug into her hands. She'd never flown in her life, let alone been in space. It took her several moments to be sure it was the right location. Officially, the house belonged to a piano-teacher who had tried to make a living through giving lessons, allowing him to have an excuse for meeting with people like Gudrun. But inside it had been a rebel base through and through.

"Yes," she said, positively. "I'm confident it's his base."

Alpha turned to look at her. "What's the interior like?"

Gudrun shrugged. "A set of rooms, mostly barren; a toilet, a kitchen... not much there, really," she said. "I never saw the basement, though. There could be anything there."

"Yes, there could," Alpha said. A window popped up on her display and she smiled, hastily pressing her finger to the screen. "Let's see what we have here."

The image altered rapidly, zeroing in on the front door. A man had appeared, walking out of the house and onto the streets as if he didn't have a care in the world. Gudrun watched in a mixture of horror and awe as the image closed in on his face, revealing a light-skinned man with a brown head of hair and a moustache.

Marcy poked her finger into the back of Gudrun's neck. "Do you recognise him?"

Gudrun swallowed. "Yes," she confessed. "That's my contact."

Alpha gave her a reassuring look. "I'll detail the drone to follow him," she said. On the screen, a line of letters and numbers appeared beside the walking man. Gudrun had no idea what they signified. "Luckily, we can keep the entire city under observation with only a handful of drones."

"No replacement for a physical eye," Marcy grumbled. Gudrun had the feeling that it was an old argument between the two of them. "Drones just don't have the intuition of a human being."

Gudrun looked from one to the other, then back at the screen. Her contact had walked into an alleyway and started to pull off his hair. She gaped in surprise, then realised that it had been a wig all the time she'd known him...and she'd never guessed the truth. The moustache vanished a moment later, dropped into a hiding place in the alleyway. Without the hair, he looked completely different.

"I thought the moustache was a fake," Alpha said, happily. "When someone has one that big, chances are it's meant to draw attention. Given the right kind of support, no one ever bothers to question it."

She looked at Gudrun. "Did *you* ever question the moustache?"

Gudrun shook her head, embarrassed. "They were fashionable ten years ago," she said, remembering how her father had kept his handlebar moustache for years, despite her mother's endless nagging and unsubtle hints about shaving it off. "I never thought it might not be real."

"I guess you weren't taught to ask questions," Marcy said, darkly. She peered past Gudrun towards the computer. "Where's he going now?"

"Into the Zone," Gudrun said. "The border is there, roughly."

There was no formal border to the Zone, she knew. Originally, it had been intended as nothing more than a supersize transit barracks, back when anyone who wanted to catch hold of the Thule economic miracle only had to get on a starship to reach the developing world, then look around for a few days to find a job. Now, it had sprawled out of control as the government retreated, creating a morass of buildings inhabited by people with no reason to love the government. Growing up there, she thought, would be a nightmare.

Inside, there were small gangs of young men roaming the streets, carrying weapons and walking in a disciplined manner. The drone focused on a couple of them, allowing Marcy to note that they were wearing makeshift uniforms, then locked back on the original target. He walked a mile into the Zone, utterly unmolested, then entered a large warehouse through a side door.

"Lost him," Alpha said. She didn't sound too unhappy. "But at least we have a building to probe."

"So it would seem," Marcy agreed. "And you want to bet that they've taken precautions against microscopic spies?"

"No bet," Alpha said. The screen changed rapidly as the drone probed the outer edge of the warehouse. "I'm picking up hints of a commercial-grade electronic scrambler. It can probably be penetrated, given time, but I'd be surprised if it was the only precaution."

She smirked at Gudrun. "Would you like to lay a bet?"

Gudrun stared at her. She'd lost track, somehow, of the fact she'd swapped sides, to the point where she'd seen the drone's images almost as a *game*. But...but she'd betrayed her allies and would be betraying them again in future and...

Her head spun, suddenly. If it hadn't been for Marcy's hand on her shoulder, she would have fallen off the stool and landed on the cold floor. What was *wrong* with her?

"I think you need a nap," Marcy said. She helped Gudrun to her feet, then guided her towards the door. "Say goodbye to Alpha."

"Goodbye, Alpha," Gudrun said, obediently. Her head was still spinning, as if she'd drunk enough to fall into a daze. "What are we going to do now?"

"Some food and drink," Marcy said. "And then we will see."

―――

"This is not a particularly decent town," someone muttered.

Thomas tossed a glare back towards the rear of the patrol, although he couldn't really disagree. Whoever had designed the houses surrounding the spaceport had clearly been an unimaginative artist, one more interested in efficiency than actually building a community where the population had room to breathe. The houses were made from redbrick, which was marginally attractive, but they were practically identical. Very few of them even had differently-coloured doors!

It wasn't the only sign of trouble, he saw. Great piles of litter lay everywhere, as if there was no garbage collection crew within the district. Wild dogs, cats and rats darted in and out of sight, roaming through the garbage as if they expected to find food. He paused as he caught sight of a dog pulling something out of a pile of rubbish, then felt sick as he realised it had found a human body. The patrol stared in horror as the body was dragged out onto the street, then savaged by the dogs. There was nothing they could do.

"These people don't know how to take care of themselves," Private Higgs said.

"It's worse than that," Thomas said. Being a Marine, he'd seen so much more than his young subordinates. "These people are so helpless, so powerless, that they don't even care about their surroundings."

He'd seen it before, on Han and a dozen other worlds. The population were completely unable to control their lives. Either the government preyed on them or criminal gangs, flourishing in the power vacuum, took control of the area. The population sank into despair and lethargy. If any of them showed any willingness to act at all, they were generally absorbed into the criminal gangs or killed.

And such an environment was an excellent breeding ground for an insurgency.

"Stay alert," he added. It was easy for such people to turn against outsiders. They found it safer than turning against the ones truly responsible for their suffering. "We can fix this problem, given time."

Sure, a voice at the back of his head said. *Just like you solved the problems on Han?*

Chapter Twenty-Three

> Unsurprisingly, this destroyed relationships between the outsiders and the local factions. The Imperial Army's soldiers rapidly became convinced that the locals were unrepentant thugs, parasites and generally untrustworthy, while the locals became convinced that the outsiders were either covertly on the opposing side or manipulating events to ensure as many locals as possible died. They were unable to comprehend the simple incompetence of those issuing orders from thousands of light years away.
>
> - Professor Leo Caesius, *War in a time of 'Peace:'*
> *The Empire's Forgotten Military History*

"This reminds me far too much of Han," Jasmine said.

Mandy's image frowned. "You said it was bad," she commented. "Is this going to be worse?"

"I honestly don't know," Jasmine said. She shook her head. She'd hoped to help the local government win enough breathing space to cut the insurgency's ground out from under it, but she was starting to have the very definite feeling that it wouldn't be easy. "The hatred might be too deeply ingrained for anything other than a sustained bloodletting to cure."

Mandy looked shocked. "It's unlike you just to...give up," she said. "You never gave up on me."

Jasmine smiled, humourlessly. "I don't think the same solution would work," she said. "And you had less baggage than the people on this blighted world."

She sighed. Two days of consultations with the local government and military officials had left her convinced that Thule was in deep trouble. Their system had been designed for endless growth, as if they'd assumed the good times would always be there. When disaster had struck, the system had proved unable to handle it without causing major hardship and unrest. And none of the haves wanted to concede anything to the have-nots. Why was she not surprised?

Earth, she thought. Many of Earth's problems, rightly or wrongly, had been blamed on the countless billions of useless inhabitants who collected their support payments from the government while churning out the next generation of burdens on society. Once, they'd even voted for politicians who'd promised them even more benefits, before the farce that elections had become was eventually brought to an end. After all, who could trust the people to make the right decisions for themselves? Only the most insightful, caring and considerate politicians could hope to serve the population properly.

But Thule, in many ways, was a reverse of the problems facing Earth.

Mandy cleared her throat. "I believe that we're currently surplus to requirements," she said. "Unless you have a strong objection, I would like to begin my reconnaissance of Wolfbane's border systems today."

Jasmine hesitated. She did have an objection. The situation was far more complex than she'd been led to believe and she would have preferred to have as much fire support as possible under her direct command. And someone she could vent to without either compromising her position or alienating the local government. But she knew that her selfish objections couldn't be placed ahead of the urgent need to gather intelligence on Wolfbane.

"You may depart when you're ready," she said, formally. "What do you intend to do with the remainder of the squadron?"

"Battle drills," Mandy said, promptly. "We do have a fairly sizable local defence force here to test ourselves against."

Jasmine had to smile. "Trust you to find the silver lining in this dark cloud," she said.

Mandy smiled back, looking – just for a moment – like the teenager she'd been when they'd first met. "It has to be done," she said. Her face darkened for a long moment. "Take care of yourself, won't you?"

"Of course," Jasmine said. "I won't be going anywhere near the front lines."

Mandy didn't look convinced. She might not have been a soldier, but she knew enough to know that the front lines in an insurgency could be anywhere. Thule's rebels had already proved that, much to their President's alarm and irritation. Given time, they might find a way to get into the spaceport and mount an attack on Jasmine and her immediate subordinates. It would certainly be high on their agenda for the war.

"Good luck," she said, instead. "Bye."

Jasmine smiled as the younger girl's image vanished from the display, then frowned as her wristcom bleeped. The officials from the local military had arrived at the spaceport and were just passing through security now. It said a great deal about their paranoia – and their lack of faith in their own people – that they'd insisted on holding the meeting at the spaceport. They'd spun it as a courtesy to Jasmine and the CEF, but she knew better. It wasn't as if she would have refused to go to the First Speaker's Mansion.

Standing, she walked through the door and down towards the makeshift conference room. It had once been used as an office, according to the handful of spaceport workers who had remained in place since the economic crisis had begun, yet the chairs and tables the office workers had used had been stripped out long ago. Jasmine had no idea what the thieves had planned to do with them – use them for firewood, perhaps – but she'd had a handful of folding tables set up to give the impression of a functional headquarters, rather than one more interested in fancy decorations than results. The only concession to luxury she'd made was a steaming coffeemaker in the corner and a handful of plastic mugs. She'd yet to see a military installation that could function without coffee.

"Brigadier," General Erwin Adalbert said. Unlike some local planetary defence force officers, he had an air of competence that Jasmine instinctively respected, even though she had the feeling that he was in over his head. "Thank you for hosting this meeting."

He introduced his subordinates as they saluted her, one by one. A couple looked doubtful, wondering if she was really too young for the rank; the others accepted her, without any apparent objections. Jasmine wondered idly if they had read her file – at least the parts the Commonwealth had chosen to make public – or if they didn't have enough experience themselves to worry about her level of experience. The latter was a strong possibility, given the major expansion the local forces had had to undergo. Like Avalon, they had been forced to put inexperienced officers in positions of power. All of them, she couldn't help noticing, were men.

"Thank you for coming," she said, wryly. "We do have a war to plan."

They shared a look of mutual understanding. Jasmine had hardly been on the planet a day before she'd started ducking invitations to social events all over the city, hosted by the upper classes. It was absurd. Didn't the rulers of Thule know there was a war on? Or were they so blinded by their contempt for their opponents that they didn't take them seriously, even after attacks had been mounted in Asgard itself? Diplomatically, Jasmine knew, she should have gone to at least one of the events. But she had too much to do on the ground.

She tapped a switch and a map appeared on the table, projected from the projector she'd fixed to the ceiling. "The Zone," she said. "I understand you wish to mount an operation against the enemy positions in this location."

"There seems to be no alternative," Adalbert said. "But they will know it too."

Jasmine didn't doubt it. The Zone threatened to be a nightmare, an endless series of buildings that could be turned into defensible positions, then held long enough to bleed her forces before the insurgents fell back and left her to advance to the next building. She'd had her intelligence officers looking for information on the Zone, but the prisoners they'd interrogated had confirmed that the Zone no longer corresponded to the maps and building plans. Countless buildings, they'd said, had been extensively modified to suit their inhabitants. Some had been turned into several homes, others had been divided up into tiny housing compartments. It would be a completely unpredictable environment.

"We could seal the Zone off completely," she said. She used the pointer to draw lines on the map. "Knock down a line of buildings surrounding the zone, then set up barricades. Anyone who wants to come out will have to cross the barricades..."

"But that would leave the rebels in possession of the territory," Adalbert said. "They've already declared themselves an opposing government."

Jasmine sighed. She'd heard about political considerations that forced military officers to act against their own best interests, but she'd never seen it happen personally...unless one counted Lakshmibai. Here, the ideal solution was to starve the insurgents out – and it was doable. There were no farms in the Zone, no sources of food...they would have stockpiles, of course, but those stockpiles would rapidly run out.

She remembered the courses on urban combat she'd taken at the Slaughterhouse. "The combat environment is slippery and treacherous," her instructor had said. "Some insurgents will attempt to hold the food for themselves, leaving the civilians to starve. But this tends to alienate the civilians, who will forget ideology if they see their wives and children starving to death. Indeed, some insurgencies have expelled civilians to prevent them from becoming a drain on their resources."

Gritting her teeth, she looked up at Adalbert. "How many civilians are trapped in the Zone?"

Adalbert met her gaze. "Roughly nine million," he said. "But we don't know for sure."

Jasmine shook her head. She'd seen bigger cities – and each of the cityblocks on Earth had had a population in the millions – but nine million people crammed into the Zone seemed excessive. How were they feeding themselves? The logistics of feeding the CEF alone were a major headache and there were only ten thousand soldiers in the entire force. It was possible, she knew, that the figures were an exaggeration, but the Zone was certainly crowded.

"We need to try to urge the civilians out of the firing line," she said. She tapped the map. "I want to set up Displaced Person camps for them."

"Traitors," one of the officers snapped. "Why should we take care of them?"

"Because it would reduce the number of civilian casualties," Jasmine said, with a tone of patience she didn't feel. "It will also pressure the insurgents to release the women and children, at the very least, because otherwise their local support might crack."

"They might not trust us with their women and children," Adalbert observed. "But you're right. It's worth making the effort."

He looked over at his officers. "Set up the camps...here," he said, tapping the map to indicate a point seven miles from the outer edge of the Zone. "Make sure there's enough food and water on hand to keep the population alive."

"Make a register of everyone who goes into the camp," Jasmine added. "We can use it to gather intelligence. If some of them will talk to us, let them. They'll know more about what is actually happening in the Zone than us."

She sighed. The rebels were good at security, good enough to ensure that she had little specific intelligence on how the Zone actually functioned. Which building served as rebel HQ? Or was there even a formal HQ? If Jasmine had been planning an insurgency, deliberately luring an enemy force into urban combat, she would have avoided any formal HQ and commanded her men from a mobile command post. There was nothing to be gained by exposing herself to enemy fire.

"Unless we get an intelligence break," she said, "my proposed plan is to surround the Zone, seal it off and then advance along a broad front as slowly and deliberately as possible. This will make it harder for the insurgents to get around us and break up the front line. Any prisoners we take will be transported to POW camps set up near the Zone and interrogated for intelligence. Hopefully, we will be able to draw a bead on the insurgent commander."

The thought made her grit her teeth. They were looking for an experienced Marine, one who would understand and anticipate her plan for dealing with the problem. He wouldn't be stupid enough to expose himself, she knew, and he would probably have set matters up so the insurgency could fight on even without him. Unless he was mad, of course. The attacks his forces had mounted had shown a chilling lack of concern for civilian casualties.

Her own words echoed through her mind. *The hatred might be too deeply ingrained for anything other than a sustained bloodletting to cure...*

She shook her head. "In the long term," she admitted, "this is merely dealing with a symptom of the problem. You will need to come to terms with the fact there is serious discontent in your society and..."

"That's not *your* problem," the officer who'd spoken earlier snapped. "These people are *not* deserving of mercy."

"That will do, Adolf," Adalbert said. There was no mistaking the authority in his voice – or the warning. "If you feel yourself unable to work here..."

Jasmine made a mental note to find Adolf's file and read it as soon as possible. Something was bothering him enough to make him act unprofessionally, something that would have to be identified and dealt with before it caused a major problem. He didn't seem to have doubts about her youth or general level of competence, as far as she could tell; instead, he seemed to have a more personal hatred of the rebels and insurgents than she would have preferred. Hate made people do stupid things.

"I will do my job," Adolf said, stiffly.

"See that you do," Adalbert said. He turned to look at Jasmine. "The long-term solution to the crisis, I'm afraid, will depend on solving the military crisis."

Jasmine had her doubts. This wasn't Avalon. The rebels had no shortage of potential manpower – and fear and intimidation only went so far if hopelessness and despair overwhelmed them. It was far more likely, she suspected, that the Zone would be crushed...but the rebels would simply start again, somewhere else. If they moved operations to the countryside, they'd be able to settle in for a long campaign intended to starve the cities.

They'd alienate the farmers if they tried, she thought. *But would the farmers work with the government to put down the rebels?*

She sighed. Compared to Thule, solving the problems on Avalon had been simplicity itself.

"Then I propose we begin operations at once," Jasmine said, shaking herself. She'd tackle the problem she *could* tackle and hope it helped solve the other problems. "I will move advance units of the CEF to here" – she tapped a building near one of the police stations that had been destroyed during the fighting – "and start establishing lines of control. If you provide reinforcements..."

"We will," Adalbert injected.

"...We can start knocking down buildings and sealing off the Zone," Jasmine said. "We will move armoured units up in support, if you are prepared to allow them to deploy. Once the Zone is sealed off, we can start preparing the forward bases for the troops to advance."

"We can provide armoured units of our own," Adalbert said. "But yours can remain in reserve."

Jasmine hesitated, then nodded reluctantly. She would have preferred to work with her own armoured units, but she understood their reluctance to allow the Landsharks to leave the spaceport. Quite apart from anything else, moving the colossal tanks from one side of the city to the other would leave a great many wrecked buildings in their wake. And the local tanks might have been designed for counter-insurgency operations. The Landsharks had been designed for full-scale war.

"Very well," she said. "I'll start issuing the orders now."

"She's very competent," Adalbert reported. "But she put her finger on the crux of the problem. We need a political solution, sir."

"I know," Daniel said. He smiled, rather dryly. "Would you like to convince the Senate to choose one?"

He ticked points off his fingers as he spoke. "We're already reaching the limit of what make-work we can provide for people," he said. "We cannot expand our industrial base any further until off-world sales pick up, which they are predicted to do in four years. And if we did propose that we abandon the idea of determining who gets a vote...well, I'd be out of office in a heartbeat."

"The voters don't want to give up their power," Adalbert said.

"No, they don't," Daniel said. "And they may well have a point. If we concede universal enfranchisement, regardless of contributions to the community, the new government will still face the same problems I do, except they will have a much larger constituency pressing for action. They may knock down what remains of the economy in a desperate attempt to fix it."

"And then make it impossible for us to fix *anything*," Adalbert said. "There's no easy way out of this mess, is there?"

Daniel shrugged. If the projections were correct, off-world sales would increase rapidly as trade with the Commonwealth became more and more established. Given a few years of steady growth, the industrial base would start absorbing more and more people into the workforce, which would lift up the entire economy. If *that* happened, the insurgency should come to a halt as the economy started to provide jobs and opportunities for everyone again. But if the insurgents won first...

"We have to hold the line," he said. "And pray."

If the projections were wrong...he shuddered, remembering the old projections of endless economic growth. They'd been based on false figures, he recalled, figures the Empire had supplied in a desperate attempt to hide the truth. If the new projections were also wrong, the war would continue indefinitely...

...And the entire planet would be ripped apart into warring factions.

No, he thought, shaking his head. *We cannot allow that to happen.*

CHAPTER TWENTY-FOUR

Furthermore, the cost of food rapidly increased. Quite apart from the logistics of shipping food across even a relatively small interstellar gulf, the sudden demand drove prices up everywhere. Farmers insisted on being paid more for their food, shippers insisted on being paid more for their services...and local factions insisted on being paid for distributing the food or allowing it to be distributed within their territories.

- Professor Leo Caesius, *War in a time of 'Peace:'*
The Empire's Forgotten Military History

Gudrun let out a long breath as she looked at herself in the mirror. The clothes she wore were second-hand, like the clothes she'd worn ever since her father had lost his job, hanging loosely on her as if they hadn't been fitted properly. But then, no one would expect any better of someone who lived inside or just outside the Zone. Fitted clothes were a luxury no one could afford these days.

"I need a jumper," she said. The shirt wasn't as tight as she'd feared, but it still exposed the shape of her breasts. "Something to cover myself up properly."

Marcy reached into a hamper of clothing and poked around for a few moments. When her hand emerged, it was holding a tatty woollen fleece. "Will this suffice?"

"Yes, thank you," Gudrun said. She took the fleece and pulled it over her head, then inspected herself again. The trousers looked faintly odd on her, but at least they weren't tight enough to draw attention to the shape of her ass. Ironically, the Zone was fairly safe for young women, but no one could say that about the districts surrounding the rebel-held territory. "I look good enough, I think."

Marcy nodded, impatiently. "Do you remember your cover story?"

Gudrun recited it for what felt like the tenth time. "I was running after setting off the mine," she said. "In order to hide, I broke into a house and discovered an old man. The man hid me in exchange for sexual favours. I did a striptease for him, then sucked him off; he had problems performing, so he didn't ask for anything more. After two days, I snuck out and made it through the barricade under cover of darkness. No one saw me as I slipped back towards the Zone."

"Good," Marcy said. "And do you remember all the details?"

"I think so," Gudrun said. Marcy had interrogated her, time and time again, until she'd got everything straight. The level of detail the older woman had insisted on including was astonishing, right down to the colour of the old man's underwear. Gudrun had asked why she wanted to dwell on every last detail, only to be told that the insurgents might not take her back without questioning her story. "What happens if I fuck up?"

"Your former comrades will kill you," Marcy said. "And your family, if we can't get them out in time."

Gudrun swallowed. Her family – what remained of it – lived near the Zone. From what Marcy had said, they'd be taken to a camp with the other residents, then separated out and told they were leaving the planet instead. She wondered, absently, what they would make of her betrayal, before deciding it didn't matter. At least they'd be safe.

She scratched her shoulder carefully, hoping to banish the itch. When she'd woken up, Marcy had told her that the doctors had implanted a tracer and communicator under her skin, allowing the CEF to track her down wherever she went. Marcy had explained that it was intended to help them rescue her if she ran into trouble, but Gudrun hadn't missed the unspoken subtext. There would be no place to hide if she double-crossed her new masters. She couldn't see anything different about her skin, yet it *itched*.

"You will be transported to here," Marcy said, tapping a location on the map. "Once you're there, you can make your way to the Zone. I would suggest you hurried. Oh, and do try to stay out of trouble."

Gudrun scowled. The streets weren't safe; ever since the police force had turned from friends to enemies, there had been little law and order on the streets. The police could be as dangerous, perhaps more so, as the gangs of teenage thugs that roamed the districts, looking for fun. Some of them had come alarmingly close to catching her before she'd joined the insurgents. She still had nightmares over what would have happened to her if they'd succeeded. It had been one of her motivations for joining up with a force that could protect her or avenge whatever happened to her.

"I'll do my best," she said. The instructions she'd given hadn't been very precise. If she located the rebel HQ, she was supposed to use the communicator to get in touch with Marcy and tell her where it was. "If I get caught..."

"We'll still look after your family," Marcy said. "Good luck."

An hour later, Gudrun found herself walking through a deserted neighbourhood, keeping a sharp eye out for human predators. She saw nothing, apart from boarded-up windows, makeshift barricades and other signs that people were hiding in their homes, cowering in fear and horror. Rats, dogs and cats ran freely across the streets, completely ignoring her presence. She walked past the remains of a police station and shuddered when she saw the body of a policeman, hanging from a lamppost. His uniform was stained with blood.

She didn't see anyone else until she entered one of the districts close to the Zone. A handful of clergymen had set up a soup kitchen, offering free food and water to the inhabitants. One of them waved her over and she came, gratefully, even though she'd been fed before she'd left the spaceport. It would be out of character for anyone in the city to pass up the chance for a meal, no matter the price. She still felt ashamed, sometimes, of the times she'd offered her body to a man, in exchange for food. But, after a few times, the shame had slowly faded away to nothingness.

You can get used to anything, she thought morbidly, *if you do it enough*.

The priest passed her a small plate of stew and a piece of flat bread. Gudrun carefully *didn't* ask what was in the stew...but then, no one did these days. The handful of people who'd had religious taboos against certain foods were the quietest of all. It was quite possible that she was eating cat, or dog, or even rat...hell, there were rumours that some districts had even forgotten the taboo against cannibalism. She hoped – she prayed – that there was no truth to those rumours, yet they seemed terrifyingly likely. There were entire districts that seemed lost to government forces and rebels alike.

Once she had finished her meal, she passed the plate back to the priest. She felt an odd sort of envy as she met his eyes, wondering how his faith kept him going in the nightmare the planet had become. How could anyone keep believing in God when humans were trapped in an endless war zone? But somehow they kept going, despite the odds.

She turned and left, striding down the street in the hopes no one would see her as a potential victim. No one moved to confront her or try to catch her until she reached the edge of the Zone itself, where a small group of guards stood in position to block entry. Gudrun hesitated, then walked up towards them and smiled in relief when she saw the makeshift uniforms. She didn't know how the insurgents had turned young men into committed fighters, but they had a better reputation than the police and security forces. And their superiors hung fighters who stepped over the line without hesitation.

"I've come from Tarrytown," she said, when they challenged her. It was the one code her contact had given her, should she have to flee to the Zone. "I want to go to Jonesville."

The fighters exchanged glances, then one of them stepped forward. "Come with me," he said. "I'll take you to the boss."

Gudrun nodded and followed him into the Zone. She couldn't help noticing that most of the buildings seemed to have been abandoned; apart from her and her escort, there was almost no one on the streets. Some of the buildings had been extensively remodelled, turned into strongholds that looked surprisingly formidable, others seemed to have been left almost untouched. It wasn't until they had walked some distance into the Zone that they encountered a large group of other people. Somehow, Gudrun wasn't surprised to see that it was a weapons training class.

Her escort motioned for her to stay where she was as he advanced and spoke to a dark-skinned man who seemed to be supervising the training session. There was a brief exchange of words, then the dark-skinned man beckoned for her to follow him into a large warehouse that seemed to have been turned into a barracks. The ground was covered with blankets and sleeping bags, half of them occupied by men who were catching up on their sleep. Behind a thin partition, there was another row of sleeping bags. These were occupied by women.

Finally, she reached a smaller room, where two women waited for her. Both of them wore masks, suggesting she would recognise them – or that they were worried about being recognised in the future. Gudrun sighed, then submitted to the strip search, hoping that Marcy was right about the tracer being undetectable. By the time she was tossed a robe to wear, she felt as though the two women had examined every last inch of her skin. Her last boyfriend hadn't explored her so enthusiastically.

"We feared the worst when you didn't return within a day," one of the women said, apologetically. "What happened?"

Gudrun sighed as she sat down, then went through the whole cover story. Marcy had been right, she discovered, as the women poked and prodded at her words. They wanted to know everything, from the old man's name to the exact location of his house. At least she had a plausible excuse for not knowing the former, she knew, while the latter hardly mattered. The inhabitants of the area she claimed to have hidden in were being rounded up and moved to DP camps. By the time the women had finished, she was feeling perversely grateful for Marcy's torment.

"You will stay here for the moment," one of the women said, finally. She seemed to be in charge, although it was hard to tell. "There may be more debriefings in your future."

Gudrun's dismay must have shown on her face, for the woman laughed at her. "Don't worry," she added, "they won't be as bad. You just have to answer a few questions."

"And then?" Gudrun said. "What will happen *then*?"

"We will see," the woman said. "This place *is* about to be attacked, you know."

Gudrun swallowed. She didn't have to pretend to be afraid.

Thomas had seen unpleasant streets before, on Han and a dozen other worlds, but there was something about the streets of Thule that sent cold shivers of ice running down his spine. Perhaps it was the awareness that all of the other streets were in the past and he'd survived, or perhaps it was the understanding that the inhabitants had fallen suddenly and very hard, moving from riches to rags within the space of a few months. They'd had hope, he recalled, and the promise of a better life. Perhaps that, more than anything else, had fuelled the anger that led to the insurgency.

"Stay alert," he hissed, as the truck rocked. The vehicle was open-topped, rather than the heavily-armoured transports he would have preferred. Personally, he was rather surprised no one had taken a shot at them yet. "Don't lose your situational awareness."

He glanced back at his men and smiled, inwardly. For some of them, the coming war would be their first taste of combat and they relished the challenge, but – at the same time – they were seeing the evidence that they would be fighting in a zone partly occupied by civilians as well as insurgents. Many of them had grown to manhood during the Cracker War, even *fought* during the war...and some of them would almost certainly sympathise with the local population. Thomas, with the more detached perspective a Marine was encouraged to develop, was less inclined to blame outside forces. In hindsight, Thule had made a number of very poor decisions based on bad intelligence.

But at least they're from Avalon, he thought. The combat losses had made his brevet shift to combat command permanent, at least for the moment. *I don't have to worry about being embedded.*

The truck reached the remains of the police station and stopped. Thomas didn't hesitate; he hefted his rifle and scrambled over the side of the truck, dropping down to the ground. His men followed him, spreading out to pose a less vulnerable target to the enemy...but no enemy materialised. The streets surrounding the destroyed building were completely deserted, at least of human life. He winced as he saw another wave of rats running from the ruins, scared off by the sound of the truck. They'd been seeing rats everywhere for the past couple of days.

"Shit," one of his men breathed.

Thomas followed his gaze. There was a lamppost on the other side of the street, with a policeman's body dangling down from a long piece of rope. The bloodstains on his uniform seemed to have congealed around his groin, suggesting...Thomas had seen horrors before, but some of his men, judging by the sounds behind him, hadn't seen or imagined anything like it. It looked as though the lynch mob had cut off the man's balls before they hung him.

"Leave the body," Thomas ordered. He wanted to cut it down and give the man a proper burial, but there was no time. "Squad A, secure this location; Squad B, with me."

He led them towards the first intact building, eyes alert for signs that someone had left a nasty surprise in place. But there was nothing... he braced himself, then kicked open the door. Inside, a faintly unpleasant smell drifted towards him, a combination of human fear and wastes. Blocking out the distraction, he activated his goggles as he led the way into the building, peering into the darkened rooms one by one. Someone had boarded over the windows in hopes of preventing thieves from breaking into the house. Judging by the bullet holes in one particular window, the precaution hadn't made the house noticeably safer.

"The toilet's blocked up," one of his men called. "But there's no one here."

Thomas wasn't too surprised. The water supplies hadn't been cut off, no matter how badly the area had slipped out of government control. Nor had the electric power supply, something that worried him. The rebels could use the government's own power supplies against it. But surely the power would be cut off before the assault on the Zone began.

"This building will do as a FOB," he said. Their orders said to establish a number of Forward Operating Bases around the Zone, which would then be linked together to isolate the Zone from the rest of the oversized city. "But we'll search the rest of the area first."

It took several hours before the entire area had been thoroughly inspected. Most of it was deserted, as if the mobs that had destroyed the police station had hidden themselves out of fear of the government's revenge, but they did find a handful of families hiding in one or two of the abandoned houses. The soldiers searched them, as gently as possible, then started making arrangements for the families to be moved to the first DP camp. Unsurprisingly, the families had looked terrified before Thomas explained where they were going. They'd thought they were going to be taken out into the road and shot.

"Sir," one of his men said. "Are we on the right side here?"

Thomas wanted to laugh. Only years of experience kept him from snickering. The Knights of Avalon had an idealism that the Imperial Army and even the Terran Marines had long lost after fighting to uphold an Empire that had committed far too many crimes to be considered a wholly decent power. Idealism and war simply didn't go together.

He could have explained, he knew, and tried to make him understand. Instead, he merely clapped the soldier on the shoulder and grinned.

"Welcome to the true face of war," he said. He waved a hand around to indicate the destroyed building, the deserted streets and the helpless families, squatting in the middle of the road. "Ambiguity, unhelpful allies, bastards on both sides…and innocent people caught in the middle."

"Yes, sir," the soldier said. From the look he was aiming at one of the civilians, a girl barely old enough to be considered a teenager, he was having second thoughts. It wasn't a lustful look, more of a recognition that she could easily have been *his* sister. "Is there anything we can *do*?"

"End this as quickly as possible," Thomas said. "And then try to convince everyone to play nicely together."

He looked towards the Zone, an ominous collection of buildings in the distance. Some of the apartment blocks, he noted, would make excellent observation posts. It wasn't going to be easy to tackle the Zone without risking major losses on both sides.

"You did this before, didn't you?" The soldier asked. "As a Marine, I mean. How many places were more peaceful when you left?"

"Most of them," Thomas said. He hesitated, then admitted the truth. Even their success stories had had fatal flaws in the peace solutions. "But not always for very long."

CHAPTER TWENTY-FIVE

> The latter, in particular, was unexpected by the social scientists. Didn't it amount to deliberately allowing their people to starve? (Even the social scientists who understood the dangers of factions didn't comprehend that warlords might be prepared to gamble with the lives of their own people.) But when it started, relations between the outsiders and the locals collapsed further into disdain, if not outright disgust and hatred.
> - Professor Leo Caesius, *War in a time of 'Peace:'*
> *The Empire's Forgotten Military History*

Standing on top of a building was a risk, Pete knew; Marines were trained in sniping and even the Riflemen were very capable indeed. The Marine Snipers could hit targets at distances most of their targets had flatly believed to be impossible. But he needed to see for himself as the low-level war surged around the Zone. He lifted his binoculars and smiled thinly as he saw a plume of smoke rising up in the distance. Another hastily-emplaced IED had picked off a target.

Or maybe it was detonated ahead of time, he thought. Makeshift weapons could never be considered *completely* reliable, after all. Prior to his recruitment, the insurgency had lost a handful of bomb-makers when they'd blown themselves up completely by accident. Even afterwards, giving civilians a few hours of training and then expecting them to produce weapons was chancy, to say the least. *There's no easy way to know.*

He walked over to the hatch and dropped down into the apartment below, then headed down the stairs to the ground. His bodyguards appeared, as if from nowhere, when he passed through the doorway at the bottom, looking as alert as a Drill Instructor could have hoped. Pete concealed his amusement, then allowed his guards to escort him down another flight of stairs into the basement. Behind him, he heard a series of doors slamming shut as he pulled his mask out of his pocket and pulled it over his face.

"That was foolish," a middle-aged woman said, as he stepped into the room. She never bothered to wear a mask, something that suggested she simply didn't care what happened to her. Pete didn't know her story, only that she was as ruthless and determined to harm the local government as himself. Indeed, she showed a lack of concern for civilian casualties that bothered him more than he cared to admit. "You could have been killed."

Pete shrugged as he picked up a mug of coffee from the table someone had wedged into the far corner and took a swig. "Risk of our existence," he said, dismissively. There was no time to fear death in the middle of a war. "You're the one who wears no mask."

The woman shrugged. She called herself Stone. No one, as far as Pete had been able to determine, knew her real name. There were all sorts of rumours, but as some of them were contradictory and others were physically impossible Pete had just decided to wait until she decided to tell him something of her own free will.

"There are risks and then there are *insane* risks," she said. She pointed one long finger at the chair on the other side of the central table. "Take a look at this."

Pete sat, obediently.

"They're knocking down entire rows of houses and apartments," she said. "Only a few hours and they've already made quite remarkable progress."

"Standard procedure," Pete said. Privately, he was impressed. It would take weeks for a division of Imperial Army soldiers to start setting up a barricade around the Zone. "And I guess they're bringing up local soldiers too?"

"Setting up barracks here, here and here," Stone said. She pointed to large warehouses on the map as she spoke. "How long will it be until they're ready to take the offensive?"

"A few days, probably," Pete said. "Are they still mounting their propaganda offensive?"

Stone's face darkened. "As if anyone would be foolish enough to take their word for it."

Pete nodded. The offer to take women and children out of the Zone, into safety, was a cunning ploy, even if there was no intention to use them as hostages. In other circumstances, it might well have worked, either causing divisions within the insurgency or removing enough civilians from the battlefield to make the attackers more willing to use heavy firepower to clear the way. But no one in the Zone trusted the local government's promises...and besides, starvation wasn't really a possibility.

"Then we keep harassing them as much as we can," he said. He'd hidden combat units in the districts surrounding the Zone, but the tactic of sweeping up everyone into DP camps had neutralised a handful of them. "And then we wait for them to come into the Zone."

He looked down at the map and sighed. Whatever else happened, the whole battle was going to be bloody as hell. Even if the plan worked completely – and that never happened, outside poorly-designed exercises – hundreds of thousands of people were going to die. And if their benefactors had their own plans for the system...

Stone snorted. "We will give them one hell of a bloody nose," she said. "And they will not forget that we stood up and fought like free men, not cowardly shits from Earth."

"No," Pete agreed. "They won't."

"There was quite a bit of resistance from the criminal elements," Joe Buckley said, as Jasmine joined him in his FOB. "But we kicked their heads in and they decided to obey orders instead of fighting."

Jasmine followed his gaze. A line of men, mostly young, were helping to pick up the bodies and carry them to a truck the local government had provided for the purpose. Their legs were shackled and they'd been warned that, if they moved too far from the Marines, the shackles would explode, blowing their legs into bloody chunks. So far, none of them had dared to try to escape. Even if they survived the explosion, cripples wouldn't last very long on Asgard's streets.

"Good," she said. After some of the reports, she found it hard to muster any sympathy for the criminals. The insurgents might be fighting for a better world, as they saw it, but the criminals were merely making the civilians miserable. "What do you intend to do with them, once the bodies are gone?"

"There's always room for slave labour," Buckley said. He gave her a twisted grin. "Were you thinking of dumping them in the DP camps?"

"No," Jasmine said. She shrugged. "Use them as you see fit."

Another bus caught her eye as it appeared at the end of the street and stopped, waiting for its passengers. One of the Marines bellowed orders, opening up the doors to a large apartment block. A stream of people promptly appeared, many of them clutching bags of clothing in their hands as if they expected to need them. They were probably right, Jasmine considered. The local government was trying, but building up supplies for thousands upon thousands of displaced persons – refugees, in all but name – was a nightmare. At least they didn't look reluctant to go any more. Some of the early relocations had been handled by force.

"It turned out there were quite a few people who'd made themselves masters of their blocks," Buckley commented. "We had to deal with them – we added them to the labour gangs – before their former subjects would cooperate with us."

Jasmine scowled, unsurprised. There were people who talked about the virtues of a state without laws, without government…but in practice it was nothing more than the rule of the strong. No matter the situation, there was always someone who was prepared to make it worse by preying on their fellow humans, through theft, rape or even permanently making themselves the boss. Human nature, it seemed, was ill-disposed to anarchy.

But that was the Empire's justification for taking power, she thought. *How are we any different from them?*

"Keep moving as fast as you can," she said. "How are the locals coming along?"

"A mixed bag," Buckley said. "Most of their infantry units aren't too bad, though there's a high degree of hatred for the rebels, but their security units are fucking awful. They shouldn't be allowed anywhere near prisoners, let alone helpless civilians."

"Understood," Jasmine said, although she knew she wouldn't be able to influence the local government enough to convince them to spare a competent unit to guard POWs. The level of hatred was worrying, though. People did stupid things because they hated their enemies and allowed that hatred to override their common sense. "Would they have been booted out of training on Avalon?"

"Oh, probably," Buckley confirmed. "But then, most of them simply don't have enough training or have pretty crappy officers who don't know what the fuck they're talking about either. Maybe they've stripped the recruiting pool pretty bare."

Jasmine wouldn't have been surprised. Like Avalon, Thule had had to expand its infantry units in a hurry and simply hadn't had enough competent and experienced officers to command all the new units. Given time, the problem might go away...or it might swell up into a looming disaster that would rip the army apart. It had happened to particular regiments in the Imperial Army, regiments so incompetent that even other regiments had feared being forced to fight beside them. What sort of disasters would happen on Thule?

"Yeah," she said. "And there isn't much we can do, is there?"

"Not unless you want to cause a diplomatic rupture," Buckley said. "I had an officer from one of the local units come right out and tell me that he reported to their High Command, not me or my commander. Can we legally arrest one of their officers?"

"I don't think so," Jasmine said. "It might be a diplomatic disaster to try."

She scowled. The Empire's views on command authority had been very simple – the Empire was in command at all times, with local officers subordinate to the outsiders – but the Commonwealth had a more nuanced view. They'd been too idealistic, Jasmine realised, and never considered that there might be problems integrating Commonwealth forces with local forces. An oversight, she realised, that stemmed from the Marines' approach to war.

"I think someone's put you in position to be fucked up the ass," Buckley said, spitting. "Probably with Tabasco-covered cucumbers. Did they do it deliberately?"

"I've got to have a girl-to-girl chat with Lila," Jasmine said. Buckley's dark face reddened, but he held his ground. "What *do* you two do when you're in bed together?"

She smiled at Buckley's expression, then changed the subject before he told her something she didn't want to hear. "I don't think the Colonel or anyone else set me up deliberately," she said, firmly. "But it's clear that there's a lot going on we didn't know about before we departed Avalon."

"No surprises there," Buckley commented. "When have we ever been fully and completely and absolutely briefed before we were dumped into the shit?"

Jasmine heard the sound of another explosion in the distance and glanced down at her terminal, then glanced back up at her friend. "Never," she said. "And just try to bear that in mind at all times."

The building was a seven-story apartment block, almost completely stripped of everything that would have made it habitable. Thomas hadn't been surprised, when the soldiers had searched it, to discover only a handful of people living there, cowering on the topmost floor. The soldiers had helped them out, reassured them as much as possible, then handed them over to the local security forces handling the Displaced Persons. Once the building was empty, the demolitions experts went forward to take a look.

"This building would probably have collapsed on its own within a year or two," the expert called, when she returned to where Thomas was waiting. "You know just how poorly they set up the support structures? I swear they were rotting away into dust before my very eyes."

She gave him a slightly-manic grin. "But the charges are in place," she added. "You want to push the button?"

Thomas shook his head, inwardly rolling his eyes. Marine Auxiliaries were a little strange – and often resentful, no matter how hard they tried to hide it – but Elzandra was the strangest he'd encountered. From her file, it sounded very much like she'd fallen in love with demolishing things with high explosives at a very early age and attempted to join the Marines because they would provide her with the opportunity to do it legitimately on a regular basis. Given her slight build, he honestly wasn't sure how she'd managed to make it through Boot Camp. Someone must have seen promise in her that had ensured she made it to a specialised training centre rather than the more general path through the Slaughterhouse.

"No, thank you," he said. "Have fun."

Elzandra gave him a smile that made her look as stunning as the video stars the Empire had used to try to distract the population, then reached into her pocket and produced a flat terminal-like device with a large red button on the top. Thomas watched as she slotted a datachip into the device, then looked up and stared at the apartment block as she pushed the button. There was a dull series of booms, so close together that they merged into one sound, then the entire building simply collapsed into a pile of rubble with a loud roar. Thomas shook his head as Elzandra started to giggle. She was having the time of her life.

"We could have done this with orbital weapons," he pointed out, just to rile her. "It would have been quicker."

"There would also be more collateral damage," Elzandra said, sweetly. "And it would be much less fun."

Thomas shrugged.

Over the next two hours, they knocked down twenty more buildings and started establishing a network of small FOBs surrounding the Zone. With a combination of automated sensors and human eyes, Thomas was fairly sure, nothing would be able make its way out of the Zone without being detected and engaged. If a heavy assault happened to materialise, a QRF unit was based just behind the line to provide immediate reinforcements, while an artillery battery would provide fire support. A handful of shots rang out of the Zone – enemy snipers trying to harass the soldiers – but they tended to fade away as Buckley's Marines returned fire.

He watched the local soldiers with a wary eye, but most of them seemed reassuringly competent, if unpolished. His terminal noted that the unit assigned to his section of the front had seen plenty of action and held together remarkably well, although he'd seen too many assessments like that which had been taken on faith until they'd been proven to be unfounded. Besides, invading a fortified city would be very different from guarding sections of the city, keeping roads open or whatever else they'd been doing. He'd just have to keep an eye on them when the signal came to advance and hope they didn't break and run the moment they ran into serious resistance.

"They're saying two days before we can advance," he said, when one of his men asked him. It seemed remarkably fast, too fast. But from what he'd heard, the local government was desperate to hit back at the insurgents. After what had happened in Asgard itself, Thomas found it hard to blame them.

But he couldn't escape the feeling that they were doing precisely what the enemy wanted them to do.

After an uneasy sleep, Gudrun had been wakened and told – after a short breakfast – that she'd been assigned to the hospital. She'd hoped for something a little more interesting, something that might have allowed her to have a look around, but apparently that wasn't an option. Her attempt to point out that she knew nothing about medicine hadn't done her any favours. The doctor had promptly given her a whole series of unpleasant tasks to do, starting with cleaning bedpans.

She was midway through her fifth bedpan – and every time she forgot to breathe through her mouth she ended up feeling sick – when she heard one of the patients talking to a visitor. Carefully, she slipped closer and listened to their voices, despite the risk. She was there to gather intelligence, after all.

"They're saying the attack will begin in two days," one voice said. "Our source in the mansion confirmed it."

"I'd better be out of here by then," the other voice said. Gudrun almost smiled as she heard the typical reluctance to stay in bed any longer than strictly necessary. The doctor had threatened to tie some of her patients to their beds. "Have they made any threats or demands?"

"Just an offer to take our women and children for safety," the first voice said. He sounded rather scornful. "As if we'd make such a mistake."

"The outsiders might mean it," the second voice countered. "But the local government has never kept its word. They'd use our people as hostages – or simply re-educate them to become good little slaves."

Gudrun hesitated, then sneaked away back to the table as she heard footsteps down the hall. She had a piece of information now, something Marcy needed to know. And yet part of her wondered if she should share it at all...

And then her shoulder itched, answering her unspoken question. She had no choice. She'd given up her choice the moment she'd accepted Marcy's offer. And all she could do was pass on what she heard and pray it was enough. But would it *ever* be enough?

She waited until she'd finished cleaning most of the bedpans – some of them really just needed to be dumped – and then headed towards the nearest toilet. It was private enough, she hoped, for her to try to send a message. She could only place her faith in Marcy's claim that the communicator was undetectable. If she was caught...

...Death was the least she could expect.

CHAPTER TWENTY-SIX

> But, perhaps worst of all, when the outside food no longer arrived (the intervention force had run out of funds), the result was a far harsher famine. The arrival of free food had destroyed what remained of the planet's farming industry, even the relatively healthy sections that could have been put back to work in short order with the proper outside support. By the time the intervention force pulled out, half the planet's population was dead or dying and civil war was ripping what remained of order apart.
> - Professor Leo Caesius, *War in a time of 'Peace:'*
> *The Empire's Forgotten Military History*

"I always liked the sunrise," Daniel said, softly.

Beside him, Brigadier Jasmine Yamane nodded, impatiently. She was an odd person, Daniel had decided; intensely focused, determined to win and, at the same time, aware of the underlying causes of the conflict that had to be removed to bring the conflict to an end. But, like so many others who weren't involved in politics, she had no idea of the practical difficulties of actually proposing and implementing solutions. The best ideas she'd had would result in Daniel's immediate impeachment if he proposed them in front of the Senate.

Daniel shrugged. The sunrise had always given him hope that, no matter what happened, the sun would come up in the morning, banishing darkness back to the pits of hell. Even as a grown adult, he had clung to the whimsical childhood superstition, despite knowing that the sunlight sometimes illuminated the damage done during the night. But now...he turned and looked at her, wondering briefly how she'd joined the Marines. Her file hadn't been very clear on personal details, all of which were considered classified.

"The forces are in position," Jasmine said. Her voice was oddly flat, almost completely atonal. It made her seem more robotic than feminine. Every time he looked at her, he couldn't help thinking of a viper poised to strike. In some ways, she was far more intimidating than the muscular guards who followed her everywhere. "We can move on your command."

Daniel let out a breath. The Senate had been demanding strong action against the Zone for years, even before the arrival of the CEF and savage bloodshed in Asgard's streets. Now, they were about to get their wish...but only at an appalling cost in lives and equipment. He'd seen the estimates put together by the High Command, stating that thousands of soldiers and civilians were about to lose their lives. Part of him wanted to refuse the military permission to advance, part of him knew there was no choice. The war had to be brought to an end as quickly as possible. As the very least, the insurgency would need years to rebuild itself after the Zone was crushed. He could use that time to nurse the economy back to health.

"Tell me," he said, very quietly. "Is this going to work?"

"We will handle the Zone," Jasmine said, confidently. "The short-term problem will be removed. In the long-term..."

"I know," Daniel said. He sighed, feeling the weight of power and authority pressing down on him. His cowardly opponents, no matter how much they hated him, wouldn't try to remove him as long as he didn't try to change too many policies, purely out of fear of having to tackle the problems themselves. "You can order the attack as soon as you return to your HQ. Just...keep me informed of progress."

"Understood," Jasmine said, crisply.

Jasmine would have preferred to command operations from the spaceport, or the FOB nearest the Zone, but the locals had insisted on placing the command post in a building right next to the mansion. It wasn't a decision Jasmine cared for – local politicians had already come to visit more than once, demanding full explanations of what was going on – yet she'd had no choice. The locals had overall command, after all, even if they'd ceded tactical command to Jasmine for the duration of her deployment.

The bunker was too elegant for her taste, despite her best efforts. There was little sense of immediacy in the room; it was comfortable, elaborately furnished and generally decorated in a manner that was staggeringly unmilitary. She'd seriously considered ordering her subordinates to scrape the gilt off the walls, as well as replacing the comfortable chairs with tacky ones borrowed from the spaceport. The only concession to practicality she'd been able to enforce was the removal of the installed tables and their replacement with tables designed for the CEF's command staff. They were now covered with computer terminals, communications equipment and a handful of weapons.

She didn't bother to sit. Instead, she looked down at the display on the main screen, showing the live feed from the five drones as they orbited the Zone. Each one could pick out and track hundreds of individual fighters; combined, they could pick the Zone apart, at least the parts of it visible from high overhead. Jasmine knew that the full capabilities of the system hadn't really been touched by the Empire, but the CEF had turned the use of drones into an art form, one that bore no risk to the pilots. Beyond them, a network of orbital satellites kept a sharp eye on the area around the Zone. It was easy to understand, she realised, why so many of the Empire's commanders fell prey to the temptation to micromanage. They seemed to have a god's-eye view of the entire battlefield.

"Send the order," she said, curtly. "The advance is to begin at once."

Thomas felt sweat trickling down his back as he heard the order, then glanced back to inspect his troops. They looked grimly determined to do their best, but the wisecracking and sardonic remarks had completely evaporated. Thomas grinned at them all, remembering just how many times he'd risked his life and come out intact, then turned and led the way towards the Zone. They'd already moved the rubble from the destroyed buildings aside, working it into the barricades. The only downside of creating a kill-zone for the enemy was that the enemy could use it in reverse.

"Snipers ready and waiting," a voice hissed in his ear. "Mortars online, ready and waiting; drones on the prowl."

He heard a dull roar behind him as the first local AFV – he wouldn't dignify it with the term *tank* – started to advance forward, machine guns searching for targets. There was no hope of surprising the enemy now, but in all honestly no one had actually expected to surprise the insurgents and catch them on the hop. They probably had their own sensors monitoring the cleared area as well as visual contact.

But nothing moved to intercept them as they reached the first set of buildings. Thomas tensed, then keyed the sensors built into his suit. There were traces of high explosives, faint hints that the entire building had been turned into an IED. Muttering curses under his breath, he ordered the building to be marked for later attention, then led his men towards the next one. It was, if anything, coated in traces of high explosive. A nasty suspicion nagged at his mind – the sensors were easy to fool, if one knew how to do it – but he knew he couldn't take the risk of assuming the traces weren't real. The enemy might have hoped he'd do just that and walk right into a blast.

He led the way towards the first barricade, weapon in hand. He'd expected savage street-fighting, or even the enemy mounting suicidal charges towards the advancing infantry, but there was nothing. Just an eerie quiet that seemed almost deafening. The roar of the AFVs seemed almost muted as they reached the barricade and started knocking it down. Behind it, there was nothing but empty streets. A faint series of titters ran through the command net as tension released, abruptly; he barked orders for them to shut up and stay alert. The enemy might have chosen to avoid an immediate engagement, but that didn't mean they'd conceded the battle. They were lurking, deeper within the Zone, and preparing to strike.

"Bomb disposal teams are on their way," the coordinator said. Thomas checked; nearly fifty buildings had been marked as being primed for demolition. If the bombs could be remotely detonated, the advancing forces might be in for a nasty surprise. "Hold the line until they arrive."

"Understood," Thomas said. "Hold the line against *what*?"

Another AFV appeared, prowling past them and driving down the exact centre of the road. It encountered nothing, but slowed rapidly as the driver saw the amount of rubbish on the road, just waiting for him to drive over it. Thomas knew, all too well, just how easy it was to conceal an IED under a pile of rubbish, let alone rubble or dead bodies. The rebels had slowed them down without even bothering to engage the advancing soldiers. Defusing the various buildings and turning them into strongpoints would be utterly time-consuming.

And, by the time they show themselves, we will be exhausted, he thought, grimly. *This* is *not going to be easy.*

There had been no point in using radios, let alone microburst communicators within the Zone. Pete knew, even if his fellows didn't, just how easy it was to track such emissions and arrange for a missile to be dropped on the transmitter. Indeed, he'd set up a few decoys to activate when the time was right, knowing that they would distract the government forces at the worst possible time. The telephone system he'd had set up was primitive compared to a modern radio, but it had the advantage of being almost completely undetectable. It also allowed him to keep the location of his HQs reasonably secret.

He smiled as the operator put down her phone and made a quick mark on the map. It was nowhere near as capable as an electronic display – there were certainly no force-tracking systems to tell him where his men were – but it had a certain charm. Besides, like the telephone, it was completely undetectable. He just had to keep reminding himself that the situation on the ground would be fluid and the map would be out of date within minutes, at most.

"They're prodding their way through Line A," the operator said. "So far, they haven't entered any of the houses."

Pete wasn't surprised. No one in their right mind would enter a house that might be rigged to explode at any moment. Removing the explosives would take time and effort, something that would slow the advancing forces down considerably. But he needed to act quickly himself, just to make sure he kept the loyalty of his own forces. Simply falling back and *letting* the enemy take command of the outer edge of the Zone wouldn't sit well with them.

"Check the passive sensors," he ordered. "Do we have a lock on the drones?"

He smiled as he looked down at the screen. There were two types of drones deployed by the Marine Corps; handheld drones that could be picked off by a reasonably competent sniper and large aircraft that could hover for hours over the battlefield, their unblinking eyes tracking his forces with exquisite precision. They were untouchable with the weapons owned by most insurgencies; even HVMs had problems reaching them before they deployed countermeasures and evaded contact. But his off-world allies, whoever they were, had given him something to even the odds.

"We do," the operator confirmed. He would have sold his soul for a trained team, but he'd forced the people he had to drill mercilessly until they could deploy the weapon in their sleep. "They're not trying to hide."

"They couldn't hide," Pete said, smoothly. "Pass the word to the gunners. They are to engage ASAP."

Alpha didn't really consider herself a soldier. She'd been recruited from the Avalon Technological Institute as a drone operator and computer programmer, streamlined into the military's support arms rather than being put through Boot Camp. It was something that relieved her; she might have been forced to undergo firearms training and basic exercises with the rest of her unit, but she knew she would never make a soldier. But it hardly mattered, she believed. She might not fight, yet merely by working the drones she helped to multiply the fighting power of the CEF.

Few people really understood just how much data flowed into the drones at any one time. It was hard, even for the advanced computer programs they'd developed, to separate out the important data from the torrent and forward it to the people who needed it. Alpha had seen the drones confidently identify brooms as guns and vice versa, while sometimes they could lose track of a person simply because he donned a pathetic false moustache. It was the reason for the human element in the system, she knew, and why she couldn't leave the drones to handle requests for data alone. She needed to monitor the system personally.

A display flashed red, then went black. Alpha gaped – she'd heard of a drone's communicator failing, but there were multiple backups in place – and then ran a diagnostic program. Moments later, the remaining four drones failed too. Alpha stared in disbelief, then hit the alarm button as she hastily scrolled through the final few seconds of transmissions from each of the drones. All five of them had reported a sudden rise in temperature before they'd lost contact.

Marcy burst into the room, her face worried. "What's happening?"

"We've lost the drones," Alpha said, dully. She dug through the final few seconds of data, but found nothing. "They shot down the drones."

Marcy walked up behind Alpha and peered over her shoulder. "How?"

"I think a laser or a directed-energy weapon," Alpha said. "The drones aren't built of hullmetal. A few seconds would be more than enough to blow them out of the sky."

"I see," Marcy said. "You'd better report it to the CO."

Jasmine swore under her breath as the report came in, followed by a report that several satellites had also been targeted by the laser. Who would have thought that an insurgency had somehow managed to get its hands on a planetary defence laser? And who would have thought of using it against drones?

"Take the weapon out," she ordered. The only advantage to the whole affair was that they'd been able to locate the weapon. Once destroyed, it wouldn't be able to do any more harm. "And then warn the troops to prepare to repel attack."

Her mind raced as her subordinates scrambled to do her bidding. The insurgents had blinded the command posts, which would have been disastrous if she'd been commanding an Imperial Army unit, let alone the Civil Guard. By taking out the drones, they'd crippled her ability to contact and direct her forces. But it wouldn't last, she knew; once they recovered from their surprise, the locals could direct their satellites to provide coverage. It wouldn't be as good as the drones, but it would be enough to direct the offensive. And the enemy would know that too.

No, she thought. *They mean to counterattack now.*

The ground shook, violently. Pieces of plaster dropped from the ceiling and fell on the map, only to be swept off the table by the operator. Pete looked up at the ceiling, then forced himself to relax slightly. The building was as secure as they could make it, but if the invaders dropped a KEW on their heads there would be no hope of survival.

"They took out the big gun," the operator said. Thankfully, the telephone network had multiple levels of redundancy built into the system. Wires could be cut – wires probably *would* be cut, once the invaders caught on – but the network would remain usable. "And an entire block of flats."

"Unsurprising," Pete commented.

The thought made him smile. He hadn't expected to be allowed to keep the gun, once the enemy knew it was there. It was just a relief to have taken out the drones before committing his forces to the first counterattack. There was no way to know how many drones the CEF had brought to the party – the local government hadn't realised their value, thankfully – but he doubted they had many replacements. Apart from the Empire, there had been few governments producing drones of their own. Would Avalon have produced more of their own?

"Call the forward posts," he ordered. "The counterattack is to begin in five minutes."

He watched the young women leap to obey, issuing his orders, and muttered a prayer under his breath. He'd given his people as much training as possible, attempting to impart the lessons learnt over years of fighting insurgents rather than joining them, but he knew that hundreds of young men were about to die. There was no alternative, he knew, yet it didn't sit well with him. And there were civilians caught up in the maelstrom...

Your wife is dead, his thoughts reminded him. *Don't you want revenge?*
Yes, his own thoughts answered him. *But at what price?*

───────

"We've got a definite report," Michael said. He sounded shocked. "Mortar fire is coming out of the Zone in all directions."

"Understood," Jasmine said. She pushed her emotions into the back of her mind and sealed them there. "Order the counter-battery units to engage, then alert the troops to prepare to withstand attack."

She looked down at the map, feeling helpless. Command had just slipped out of her hands, to all intents and purposes. The communications network had been restored quickly, but the all-seeing eyes were gone. Her forces wouldn't be operating as a unified machine so effectively until the drones were replaced. And who was to say there wasn't another anti-starship weapon hidden in the Zone?

Not us, she thought, sourly. *We didn't anticipate it at all.*

CHAPTER TWENTY-SEVEN

> In hindsight, local understanding, combined with freedom of action on the part of the intervention force, might have actually helped the locals. Protecting local farmers, a pragmatic response to local authorities and building up unified power structures would have proved far more successful. However, it was not to be.
> - Professor Leo Caesius, *War in a time of 'Peace:'*
> *The Empire's Forgotten Military History*

"Incoming fire!"

Thomas swore as warnings blinked up in front of his eyes. The enemy had taken advantage of the sudden confusion, all right; they were firing mortar shells towards the advancing infantry and tanks, as well as towards the FOBs outside the Zone. And probably mounting an infantry attack of their own, he guessed, as the sound of shooting grew louder. They'd caught the platoon in just the right place to do some real damage.

"Check the house," he snapped, as the first wave of shells crashed down. One of them came down alarmingly close to an AFV, scattering pieces of tarmac everywhere; the remainder hit houses or struck the ground with terrifying force. One of his soldiers was struck by flying debris and sent falling to the ground, blood spurting from his chest. "Look for traps."

Another wave of shells could be heard as they double-timed it towards the house, then checked the door. It *had* been struck by a shell, but nothing had detonated; the ground shook as another house, further down the road, exploded into a fireball. The odd-coloured flames suggested, not entirely to his surprise, that the enemy had used non-standard chemicals to make the explosive mix. Chemical warfare was far from uncommon, after all. But most of his men had treatments to make the chemicals less effective.

One of his men kicked open the door, allowing them to slip into the building and take shelter inside. Thomas's blood ran cold as he saw the detonator on the ground, then realised that the explosions had accidentally disabled the IED. Hastily, he dismantled the rest of the device and ordered his men to search the house as the sound of shelling got louder, hammering the road hard enough to shatter the tarmac into pieces of debris. It would make it harder for wheeled vehicles to advance into the city, Thomas noted absently as his men returned. The remainder of the building was thankfully safe.

He looked back outside and swore. One of the AFVs was nowhere to be seen, but the other two were burning wrecks. There was no sign of their crews, all of whom should have been able to bail out in time if the vehicle came under attack. Had the enemy managed to get lucky or had they loaded their mortar shells with armour-piercing warheads? If so, they'd given up the advantage of HE to try to take out a few dozen vehicles. But it would certainly dent morale to see burning vehicles.

"We should get the body, sir," one of his men said. The sound of mortar shells was dying away, probably because the counter-battery officers were taking them out. If *Thomas* had trained the mortar gunners, he would have prepared them to fire one shot and then switch position before the return fire came howling in to extract revenge. "Clive's out there..."

"There's nothing you can do for any of them now," Thomas said, gently. The enemy wouldn't content themselves with a small amount of shelling, not when they'd never have a better chance to inflict major damage on the advancing forces. "We have to turn this place into a strongpoint."

It wasn't a very well-built building, he discovered, even though it had survived the mortar shell with impressive fortitude. From what he'd heard, no one had been intended to stay in the Zone for longer than a few months, which explained the complete absence of shops, parks and everything else a growing community might need. The buildings might as well have been mass-produced and dumped in the Zone *en masse*, making it harder for him to identify their building to his superiors. In the end, they just had to hope that they would be relieved before the enemy finally overran the building.

He peered out of the shattered window and smiled, darkly, when he saw the first enemy troops come into view. They looked surprisingly impressive for insurgents, he decided; their formation was almost military, although there was a sloppiness about it that didn't surprise him in the least. The insurgents probably hadn't had access to a proper training ground and some excellent Drill Instructors. Still, they might be advancing, but they weren't committing suicide by charging towards the guns.

"Take aim," he muttered, just loudly enough to be heard. "Conserve your ammunition. I don't want a single wasted shot."

The insurgents paused as they saw the burning vehicles, then kept moving towards the house. Thomas wondered, absently, if they knew the house was occupied, before deciding they probably didn't. None of them seemed to pay the houses any special attention, apart from keeping their distance from the ones that might be primed to explode. IEDs were not discriminatory weapons, after all. The IEDs Thomas had seen on Han had taken out enemy fighters as well as their enemies.

"Fire," Thomas snapped.

Seven shots rang out in quick succession. Five insurgents fell to the ground, dead; one more dropped, clutching his shoulder. The seventh insurgent gaped for a long second, then threw himself to the ground and started crawling backwards with speed. Thomas felt a flicker of sympathy, which didn't stop him from firing another shot. The insurgent jerked and lay still.

"That won't be the end of it," Thomas warned, as he heard the sound of mortars firing in the distance. Shells passed over their heads and headed towards the edge of the Zone. "They'll know we're here now."

The next group of insurgents were more professional, he noted, as they appeared at the end of the road. Two of them advanced towards the house, moving from cover to cover, while their remainder fired short bursts of fire to force Thomas and his men to keep their heads down. It wasn't a bad tactic, Thomas decided, as he unhooked one of the grenades from his belt and set the timer. But it had the weakness of forcing him to use other tricks to get rid of the two intruders. He threw the grenade and had the satisfaction, a few seconds later, of hearing it explode. There was a yell from outside, followed by screaming.

Poor bastard, Thomas thought, as he took a peek. One of the insurgents had taken the brunt of the blast; he'd literally been blown into pieces of flesh, scattered all over the road. The other had been hit badly by flying debris; Thomas winced as he saw blood pouring from a wound in the man's lower chest. Even the best medical clinic on Avalon wouldn't be able to save him.

The remaining insurgents opened fire, violently. Thomas kept his head down as bullets cascaded over the house, blasting through the windows and slamming into the far walls. The sound was deafening as the bullets started to punch through the redbrick; desperately, he crawled out of the room before one of the bullets could score a hit through sheer bad luck.

He pressed his communicator and called for support. Moments later, he heard the sound of a mortar shell, followed by an explosion that made the entire building shake. It had taken enough abuse, he realised, to finally start collapsing into debris. Quickly, he ordered his men to evacuate the building, despite the risk. They didn't dare lose anyone in a pile of falling debris.

Outside, there was a smoking crater where the insurgents had stood. Thomas looked towards it, satisfied himself that they were no longer under attack, then half-ran, half-crawled towards the wounded insurgent. The man had gone into shock, Thomas discovered as he reached the insurgent; he didn't have long to live. If the shock didn't get him, the bleeding out definitely would. Thomas hesitated, then reached into his medical kit and produced a sedative tab, which he pushed against the man's head. It would at least ensure his final few moments were peaceful. Half-annoyed at himself for such sentimentally, Thomas stood up and headed back towards his men. They'd pulled the bodies from the vehicles and placed them at the side of the road.

"They'll be picked up," Thomas assured them, as he heard more shells racing over his head. The enemy, it seemed, either had plenty of mortars or *very* capable launch crews. "But we have to report back to higher authority."

He heard an engine sound and turned to see a pair of AFVs nosing their way towards their position. Hastily, he signalled that they were friendly. It would be all too easy, in the confusion of a battle, for friends to be mistaken for foes. But the AFVs stopped just past the burning ruins of their comrades and opened their hatches, disgorging reinforcements.

"We have orders to pause here to regroup, then press onwards," the leader said. "You held this position?"

"Yes," Thomas said, flatly.

"Others were killed in the houses," the leader explained. "They sought cover..."

Thomas gritted his teeth. The enemy CO – treacherous former Marine or not – was cunning. He'd known that the natural response to mortar bombardment was to seek cover...and the houses had all been mined. When the soldiers had tried to hide, they'd run right into the blasts that had killed them.

"I see," he said. "What are our orders?"

"Take forty winks, then get back into the fight," the leader said.

Thomas nodded. At least the enemy wouldn't be getting much sleep.

"Two hundred and forty men – thirty-seven of them ours – killed or wounded," Volpe said. "Seventeen AFVs, nine trucks..."

Jasmine held up a hand. "Spare me the rest of the figures," she ordered. She'd been played, right down the line. She hadn't realised the implications of a former Marine directing the enemy preparations...and she damn well should have done. Instead, she'd been assuming – without ever quite realising it – that she was facing a standard insurgency. "Have the satellites been moved into place?"

"They have," Volpe confirmed. "But they're not as capable as the drones."

"I know," Jasmine said, tartly. She'd been a Marine before Volpe had started to shave, let alone joined the military. "But we have to make do with them."

She wished, with a sudden intensity, that Mandy was there. They could talk openly. Instead, she was on her own.

"I will suggest that we start demolishing the buildings as we come across them," Jasmine said. Some of the local magnates had wanted to redeem the Zone, rather than smash it flat, although Jasmine had pointed out that the rebels were hardly likely to leave the Zone intact by the time they were defeated. "The IEDs can be detonated ahead of time, allowing us to advance forward quickly."

She sighed, then turned to look down at the live feed from the satellites. Her forces had held the line, but they'd been pushed back in places and morale had been dented quite badly. Thankfully, the enemy's one major attempt at a large-scale counterattack had been detected and engaged with long-range weapons before they got into firing position. It had put them off launching another such attack.

"And then we can keep pushing them until they stand and fight," she added. "Let the bastards try to stop us then."

Gudrun had never worked so hard in her life before her first stint in the hospital when the fighting began. Hundreds of wounded, mostly men but some women, were dragged into the complex and dumped on the floor. The handful of trained medical personnel were utterly overwhelmed within minutes, leaving Gudrun and the other nurses – if they dared use that title to dignify themselves – to do what they could for the wounded. She had cleaned and bandaged wounds, wrapped up broken bones and watched helplessly as some of the wounded had died. And she didn't really know what she was doing!

She wanted to cry as a young man, no older than her brother, was brought into the room, bleeding from a nasty wound to the stomach. He made a noise of protest as Gudrun pulled open his shirt, then started to choke up blood. Gudrun had long since lost the squeamishness she'd felt when she'd first seen a wounded body, but she felt sick when she saw the full extent of the damage. She'd hoped she could bind the wound long enough to give him a fighting chance, yet she couldn't convince herself that it was possible. The man – practically a boy – let out a gurgling sound and sagged. Moments later, he was dead.

A hand fell on her shoulder and shook her, roughly. "There's no time to cry," the doctor snapped. She was a shrew-faced woman who seemed to have developed an aversion to everyone on sight. Gudrun disliked her and knew that most of the other nurses felt the same way. "Get the body out of here, then move on to the next patient."

Gudrun pulled herself to her feet, signalled the orderlies and moved over to the next person. The doctor looked from wounded man to wounded man, then pointed to one of the less-wounded men and directed her orderlies to take him into the operating room. Gudrun gave her a puzzled look, which earned her a sarcastic scowl and an order to get back to work. The doctor didn't seem to be concentrating on the most badly wounded at all.

She was binding up a man's stump – where his leg had been before the fighting started – when it hit her. The doctor was choosing to spend her time with the least critical patients because those were the ones with the greatest chance of survival. Their limited medical supplies couldn't be wasted on patients who were certain to die. Sickened, she finished binding the man's leg and then turned and fled from the ward. There was nothing she could do for them, for any of them. She didn't even know if she was doing more harm than good.

Outside, she saw a couple of young men sitting just outside the door and smoking something aromatic. Both of them looked shattered; one of them held the rolled-up piece of smoking paper towards her, as if he expected her to take a sniff for herself. Gudrun shook her head, firmly. One lesson she'd learned from her father was never to trust drugs, if only because there was no way to know where they'd come from or what had been done to them. The drug business had been booming ever since the economic crisis had begun, but the pushers had had a nasty habit of mixing the pure drug with other substances, trying to make it last longer.

Instead, she sat down next to them, put her head in her hands and started to cry.

"There, there," one of the smokers said. He pointed towards the nearby buildings. "It will all be over soon."

Gudrun followed his pointing finger. The buildings looked intact, but there was smoke rising up from all over the Zone. In the distance, she could hear the sound of shooting and explosions, blurring together into a hellish background noise. Kilometre by kilometre, the CEF and its local allies – the force that had blackmailed her into working for them – was making its way through the Zone. When the wave of destruction washed over them, everything the residents had created would be swept away.

"I hope so," she said, wiping her eyes. "I really hope so."

The smoker patted her knee, awkwardly. "It will be," he said. "We're all about to die. May as well get our living in while we can."

He grinned at her. "You want to come raving with us tonight?"

Gudrun started at him, then found herself starting to giggle. She'd raved quite a bit as a younger girl, even if her district hadn't been as fond of them as the Zone. But then, her district had largely been composed of people who had believed in the system. It hadn't been until the system crashed that disillusionment had set in. Despair had followed soon afterwards.

She was tempted, she had to admit. Go to a rave, dance like a crazy woman, take something to dull the pain, find a boy, push him against the wall and have mad passionate loveless sex…but she'd grown up over the last few days. She couldn't simply throw herself away any longer. Not now.

"No," she said, standing up. Drug users could switch moods with terrifying speed. If he thought she'd rejected him, his drug-addled mind might be offended. "I have too much work to do."

"And there I was thinking you were covered in blood as a fashion statement," the smoker said. He smiled at her. Despite his scruffy appearance, she couldn't help thinking he was surprisingly handsome. "Come if you want. We don't mind."

Gudrun smiled, then turned and walked back into the building. The lines of wounded had grown worse, she realised, as she started to work on the first in line. He, at least, didn't seem to be seriously wounded. In fact, he kept demanding to be released and sent back to the front lines.

"You can go as soon as I've bandaged your wounds," Gudrun told him, tartly. "And not a moment before. You really should stay in bed."

The man eyed her, menacingly. "You really think anyone here will have time to recuperate?"

Gudrun shook her head, but said nothing. He was right. Besides, there were hardly any beds in the hospital. The doctor had given up trying to assign people to anything more than a pallet on the floor.

"Silly girl," the man said. "*Of course* no one will have any time to recuperate."

CHAPTER
TWENTY-EIGHT

On Stan's World, the conflict was more understandable...until the social scientists became involved. Indeed, their involvement was against the will of both parties in the conflict; the corporation saw them as the tools of their political enemies on Earth, while the miners saw them as the tools of the corporation. It didn't help that their proposed solutions were outrageously favourable to one side or the other, although there was no hope of a real compromise.

- Professor Leo Caesius, *War in a time of 'Peace:'*
The Empire's Forgotten Military History

Ed had always hated hospitals.

It was the duty of a Marine officer, he'd been told more than once, to visit his wounded while they were recuperating. And he'd done it too, apart from the time before their hasty departure from Earth. He still wondered, sometimes, what had happened to the wounded they'd had to leave behind. If Earth had really been destroyed...

He pushed the morbid thought aside as he watched Gaby and the doctors. One of them was holding a monitor to her skull, the other two were carefully monitoring her condition. It had taken a considerable amount of arguing to convince them to let Ed watch as they woke her up and they'd given him strict orders to stay out of the way, whatever happened. Even so...he watched, feeling cold ice congeal around his heart, as Gaby gasped, struggling for breath.

If he'd been asked, he couldn't have pinpointed the moment he'd fallen in love with her. Their first meeting had been after the Battle of Camelot and she'd been a prisoner, caught between hope and fear. Hope that Ed meant it when he offered her the political terms to end the war, fear that it was all a trap to destroy the remaining Crackers. Even then, she'd been beautiful and determined...and caught between warring factions. Bringing them to heel had been a truly impressive achievement, one that had cemented her reputation in Ed's eyes. And then he'd fallen for her.

He'd done his best to ignore the rumours, some of them mischievous, some of them downright worrying. Some people had wondered if Ed and Gaby intended to start a dynasty, despite writing laws that should have made it impossible; others had wondered if they intended to leave Avalon after Gaby completed her term in office, saying goodbye to politics once and for all. Ed would have liked to do that, he admitted privately to himself, but he couldn't simply dismiss his responsibilities to the Marines. Jasmine was in no position to take over as supreme commander, not yet. Besides, anyone they met from the Empire would know her as nothing more than a Rifleman.

The thought bothered him more than he cared to admit. He'd come to Avalon with eighty-seven Marines, fifteen of which were dead and twenty-seven had been inserted into various positions where their skills were required. It wouldn't be long, he admitted privately, before the remaining Marines simply faded away into the Knights of Avalon. There would be no replacements, no continuation of traditions that had held strong for over three thousand years...just an ignoble end. They'd fade away into nothingness.

Gaby let out another gasp and opened her eyes. Ed stood, just so he could see what was happening as the doctors examined her. Her entire body shook alarmingly, then convulsed once. Ed stared in horror as she sagged, then looked up at him. For a long moment, her face seemed utterly blank. And then she smiled at him.

"Ed?"

"Gaby," he said.

"Lie still," one of the doctors said. "You are not out of danger yet, Madam President."

Gaby met Ed's eyes as she lay back. He could read the impatience in her face as the doctors passed various devices over her, examining her brainwaves and commenting quietly amongst themselves, using technical terms Ed couldn't even begin to understand. It was impossible to escape the feeling they were trying to conceal her true condition from him – and that he should call for the interrogators and get answers out of them, by any means necessary.

"What happened?" Gaby demanded. "And why am I here?"

The doctor turned to look at her. "How much do you remember?"

Gaby hesitated, her brow furrowing in thought. "I was in the Council Chamber," she said. "They'd just brought the hearing to an end. And then..."

Her face darkened. "I don't remember," she said. "What happened?"

The doctor looked at Ed, then back at Gaby. "There was an...incident," he said. "Someone tried to assassinate you and the rest of the Council. Several died, you were wounded – we had to keep you out until we could repair the damage."

Gaby sat up, so quickly she almost slammed her head into the doctor's nose. "I have to go to the Council and..."

"You have to stay here," the doctor snapped. He looked over at Ed. "I can give you a few moments of privacy while we tabulate our results, but you need to stay in bed."

Ed watched the doctor make a hasty exit, then sat down beside the bed. "It isn't good news," he said, softly. Gaby would never have forgiven him for keeping it to himself. "We're on the verge of war."

He ran through the entire story, starting with the shooting in the Council Chambers and the discovery of the shooter's identity. "It looks very strongly as though Wolfbane deliberately attempted to assassinate our society's leaders," he concluded. "War is a very strong possibility."

Gaby looked at him. She'd always been good at reading his expressions, right from the start.

When she spoke, her voice was weaker than he'd feared. "Do *you* believe it?"

"I don't know," Ed admitted. "On one hand, it's hard to think of any other candidates for the assassination attempt. Wolfbane might well have prepared the uprising in hopes of capturing one or more of our people for interrogation."

"They could have kidnapped someone from Avalon without risking so much," Gaby countered. "The whole uprising on Lakshmibai couldn't have been intended merely to snatch a single soldier."

Ed shook his head. "There was probably more than one objective," he said. "Grab a soldier, test how far we were prepared to go to make a treaty with them, get a look at the CEF in action, cause a political nightmare here on Avalon...overall, there were plenty of ways they benefitted from the whole uprising."

He shrugged, expressively. "I convinced the Council not to send an immediate declaration of war," he added, "but what they *did* send wasn't much better. They're demanding a full accounting of Wolfbane's territory, an end to probing missions across the border, open trade and negotiations in a planet we choose...overall, the message was about as diplomatic as a punch in the face."

"And rather less effective," Gaby observed. "How do you think Wolfbane will respond?"

"It depends," Ed said. "The message didn't leave much room for evasion. Either they admit to deliberately undermining our government – including your assassination – and accept the terms we demand or they start a war. Councillor Jackson wanted to start a war right away."

"Jackson always was a hothead," Gaby said. She looked down at her hospital gown for a long moment, then back up at Ed. "I have to get out of here."

Ed understood. He hated spending time in hospitals as a patient almost as much as he hated visiting the sick or wounded. But he also knew that Gaby needed proper medical treatment after she'd been wounded. A brain injury was nothing to laugh at, not when it could cause all kinds of long-term problems.

"See what the doctors say," he said. "They'll make the final decision."

Gaby glowered at him. "I thought you were on my side," she said. Her lips quirked, revealing she didn't entirely mean it. "I have a war to prevent."

"Or fight as effectively as possible," Ed said.

He hated being blind, he hated the sheer mass of unanswered questions surrounding Wolfbane...and the cold knowledge that a war was almost certainly about to start chilled him to the bone. No one had fought a major interstellar war in over a thousand years. Ed had plenty of experience fighting on the ground, or tackling pirate bases in deep space, but a major war? What would such a war, fought with modern technology, be like? The simulations kept producing different answers, depending on what assumptions were used as the baseline, but all of them agreed that it would be disastrous.

"Another good reason to get me out of here," Gaby said. "The doctors can't hold me prisoner forever."

The doctor reappeared before Ed could say a word. "Madam President," he said. "We have collated the data."

There was a long pause. "We have successfully repaired the damage to your skull," the doctor continued. Gaby reached up to touch the side of her head, where her hair had been cut away to allow the doctors to work. "As far as we can tell, there is no lasting damage to your brain. However, the brain is still full of surprises for the unwary doctor. You may well suffer effects from the blow."

Gaby leaned forward, her eyes sharp and cold. "Like what, Doctor?"

"Headaches, mood swings, bouts of forgetfulness and suchlike," the doctor said. He held up a hand before Gaby could say a word. "I know it isn't a very precise answer, but head injuries are notoriously unpredictable. You might suffer no further problems at all or you might be plagued with headaches and other problems. My very strong advice would be to spend the next few days here while we monitor your condition."

Gaby shook her head, firmly. "I've got work to do, Doctor," she said. "I can't simply stay here."

"So I understand," the doctor said, with a sigh. "I would suggest, then, that you kept a medic with you at all times. If you start to suffer problems, come back here at once."

He hesitated. "You might also want to consider taking a leave of absence," he added. "I believe you can stand down for a few weeks on medical grounds..."

"I think that would be a very bad idea," Gaby said, tightly. She swung her legs over the side of the bed, then stood. Her long red hair cascaded down her back. "Do you have some proper clothes for me or do I have to walk out in this skimpy hospital gown?"

"In the bedside cabinet," Ed said. He opened it to reveal one of the long dresses that had recently come back into fashion. They were handmade by farmwives, from what he'd heard, but fashion had never made much sense to him. Underneath, there were a pair of panties and a bra. "You'll have to look your best when you walk into the Council Chamber."

"Councillor Rubens would probably faint if I walked in wearing the gown," Gaby muttered, as she pulled the gown over her head and dropped it on the bed, then reached for her panties. She didn't seem to have any trouble with coordination, Ed noted with some relief. A concussion alone could screw up someone's ability to use their hands properly. "But it would certainly win me a few thousand votes."

Ed rolled his eyes. "What happened to the woman who insisted that councillors should wear unflattering uniforms?"

Gaby snorted, rudely, as she pulled the dress on. She'd been courted by hundreds of young Crackers, according to her, many of whom claimed to be motivated by nothing more than the desire to ensure that Peter Cracker's legacy was passed down to yet another generation. Ed recalled just how one of her assistants had clung to her, only to go back to his farm when Gaby had taken up with Ed. The young man had had an intense crush on Gaby, something that had left him torn in two. It was easier, Ed decided, to leave romance and sex out of the equation. Insurgencies, however, didn't have the luxury of intensive training for their people.

"She got shot in the head," Gaby said. She finished buckling up the belt, then peered at herself in the mirror. A quick few motions brought her hair under control. "And right now she needs to avoid any questioning of her ability to do her job."

She turned and strode out of the room. Ed followed her hastily, understanding exactly what she meant. Without her, the Council was divided. Councillor Jackson wanted immediate war, Councillor Travis seemed torn between war and peace, Councillor Stevens wanted to know just what had happened before making up her mind...and Councillor Rubens seemed to have nothing to say. God alone knew how the old man had won election in the first place, Ed had decided, a long time ago. He had less energy than an Imperial Army supply officer and far fewer incentives to do anything.

"There's an aircar waiting just outside," he said. "I'll take you to your office."

Gaby paused long enough to look back and smile. "Aren't you worried that someone will think you're abusing your authority?"

"I don't mind, right now," Ed said, honestly. "And besides, an aircar will get you there quicker than a street car."

Someone must have blabbed to the media, Ed decided, as they stepped out of the door. A small army of reporters stood there, holding up sensor pads and shouting out questions. Gaby seemed to freeze for a long moment, long enough that Ed started to worry, before catching herself and stepping forward with icy determination. The reporters parted before her like the Red Sea before Moses, remembering – suddenly – just how many privacy laws there were in Avalon's constitution. Reporters might be tolerated – a free press was the key to freedom, according to Professor Caesius – but they weren't treated as little tin gods. If Gaby chose to file suit against one or all of them...

She stopped as she reached the aircar and turned to face the reporters. "As you can see," she said smoothly, "rumours of my injuries are greatly exaggerated. I am alive, well and looking forward to resuming my duties."

Ed wondered, absently, how she knew there had been exaggerated reports of her injuries, then remembered that Gaby hadn't just been a fighter. She'd directed the propaganda war against the Old Council with as much icy determination as she'd brought to bear on the battlefield. And it had worked, too. No one believed a word of the official dispatches, which had helped, but she'd largely ensured that the Crackers told the truth. And, because of it, they were believed.

"Thank you for your time," Gaby concluded, with a winning smile. Ed couldn't help wondering how long it would take the reporters to realise that she'd really told them next to nothing. "And goodbye."

Ed helped her into the aircar, then moved around and slipped into the pilot's chair. Aircars were still staggeringly rare on Avalon, not when the excess productive capability to produce them simply didn't exist. The vehicle shook as he activated the engines, then rose up smoothly into the air and headed out over the city. From overhead, there was a charm about Camelot, Ed had always felt, that was lacking in older cities. It helped, he decided, that no one had authority to issue guidelines for buildings beyond ensuring that their buildings were actually *safe*.

"There may well be war," Gaby said. She reached out and touched his hand, lightly. They rarely allowed themselves any romantic touches outside their apartments, not when it would give rise to more rumours. "Ed... can we win?"

"I wish I knew," Ed admitted. He wanted to take her in his arms and kiss her, but he resisted the impulse. "There are just too many ways the war can develop."

"May *already* have developed," Gaby said. She'd grown used to the time lag between star systems quicker than anyone else he knew outside the Imperial Navy. "They could already be attacking our star systems."

Ed nodded. One scenario – the nightmare scenario – was a sudden attack on Avalon, Corinthian and the handful of other star systems with industrial nodes. Wolfbane wouldn't even have to occupy the systems, merely destroy their industrial centres. The Commonwealth Navy would be unable to resupply itself and would eventually run out of everything from missiles to spare parts. How long would their supplies last if there were no more coming in from the industrial centres?

But no such attack had materialised, while the assassination attempt had put his forces on their guard. It made little sense, tactically speaking, unless Wolfbane had decided on a more steady advance across the border. Maybe that *was* what they had in mind, he considered; Wolfbane would know that sending fleets deep into Commonwealth space was asking for trouble, if something went wrong. Better a slow and steady advance than a sudden blow that might easily miscarry and leave entire squadrons stranded in interstellar space.

"We will win this war," Gaby said, with icy determination. She looked down at the city, then past it towards one of the makeshift planetary defence centres. "Whatever it takes, Ed, we will win this war. I am not going to let the ghosts of the past overwhelm the future."

Ed smiled to himself as he guided the aircar down towards the Council Chambers. *There* was the Gaby he had fallen in love with, the indomitable will mixed with an understanding and a pragmatism that had allowed her to make an alliance with her hated enemies. Whatever was coming, he hoped, she would be a match for it. She certainly had far more moral fibre than the Grand Senate had ever shown.

Because she's right, he thought, grimly. *The dream of the Commonwealth, of a new interstellar order, cannot be allowed to die.*

CHAPTER TWENTY-NINE

The miners steadfastly refused to go back to work until they were provided with ironclad guarantees of better treatment and a share in the proceeds, which would be reinvested in Stan's World. This was supported by some of the scientists, but opposed by others. Caught in the middle, the corporation refused even the smallest compromise. There could be no political solution as the politics had expanded well beyond the conflict zone.

- Professor Leo Caesius, *War in a time of 'Peace:'*
The Empire's Forgotten Military History

The only inhabitants of the Titlark System were a handful of asteroid-dwellers, members of a half-mad religious order that had secreted themselves away from the Empire after their messiah had warned them of the looming disaster. Or so they claimed, when Admiral Singh's troops had rounded them up, loaded them onto a cargo ship and sent them back into Wolfbane-held territory. Rani found it hard to care about their beliefs, not when she needed their star system for her own purposes. Besides, a few years of re-education and their children would become good little peons on Wolfbane.

She sat in her office on *Orion* and read the update from Avalon. The courier had almost burned out her drive rushing it to Titlark, but it had definitely been worth the risk. Rani's assassin had made it through the defences, such as they were, and launched an attack right in the heart of the Commonwealth itself. It had misfired slightly – the President of the Commonwealth was apparently wounded, rather than dead – but it had succeeded in its principle objective. There could be no peace between the Commonwealth and Wolfbane.

Using Private Polk as her assassin had been a gamble, one that could have easily gone spectacularly wrong. Someone might have recognised him, despite some facial alterations, or his conditioning might have broken at the worst possible time. Or he might have been identified as a conditioned person, which would have led to him being taken into custody and his identity uncovered when the Commonwealth checked his DNA against their records. Or...someone might have checked his DNA anyway when he tried to enter the planet's orbital station, which would have been disastrous. But everything had worked out better than she'd had a right to expect.

And, best of all, Governor Brown knew nothing about the assassination attempt.

Rani herself had held the plan in reserve for several months, hoping she could talk the Governor into authorising a strike against Avalon and Corinthian as the opening blows in the war. A successful strike against either or both of them would have crippled the Commonwealth, all the more so when the attack came out of nowhere. But when Governor Brown had refused to permit her to take the risk, she'd put her second plan into motion instead. The Commonwealth, after discovering that one of their own had been turned into an assassin, would be in no mood to talk peace. They'd make outrageous demands on Wolfbane, demands that would be automatically rejected. The message from her spies had made that clear.

Governor Brown was an odd mix of traits, even Rani had to admit. He was bold enough to take power for himself, playing various factions off against one another until they all supported his supremacy, but there was a strong streak of caution running through him that made him reluctant to stick his neck out too far. Rani could understand the fear of losing power – if Brown lost power, he would lose his life soon afterwards – but she also understood the dangers in refusing to gamble when one was holding most of the cards. Brown thought, she suspected, that if the war went badly, he could come to terms with the Commonwealth and declare the war over. Rani knew better. The mere existence of the Commonwealth

– and the Trade Federation – was a dagger pointed at the very heart of Wolfbane. There could be no peace.

The Empire had never really tolerated any interstellar power that wasn't firmly subordinate to its own agenda. It was far from uncommon for the Grand Senate to interfere, openly and often, in their affairs, manipulating events until their independence was nothing more than a sham. Indeed, many of the brushfire wars the Empire had had to stamp on towards the end of its existence had been caused by meddling from Earth in the first place. But they hadn't really had any choice. The existence of a rival system, one that worked better than anything the Empire had produced, would raise uncomfortable questions in the minds of the Empire's citizens. Why couldn't *they* have such political and economic freedoms?

Governor Brown might have understood just how important it was to maintain corporate control of the sector – and the Empire. Without it, why...the great corporations might be undermined and eventually driven out of business by a horde of local competitors. They would be forced to fight to survive. It was no surprise to Rani, who understood just how wide the gap between the Empire's government and its population had grown in the final years of its life, that it seemed easier to manipulate the laws rather than remaining competitive. But that would change, now the Empire was gone. Unless, of course, Governor Brown managed to keep tight control over his fragment of the Empire.

There *would* be war, Rani knew. The Commonwealth had been eager to discuss terms, so eager that they'd let themselves be manipulated into a trap, but their mere existence was a threat to the newly-established order. Planets would be tempted by the promise of control over their own internal affairs, spacers would be tempted by the offer of political independence and freedom from burdensome regulations...hell, there were even faint rumours that the Commonwealth's scientists had made a number of new breakthroughs. If *they* were true...

Rani hated to think about the implications. Scientific research and development in the Empire had slowed down to a crawl, reducing itself to tiny improvements that were barely worth the effort. Scientists had even asked, openly, if humanity had reached the limits of the possible. Dreams such as FTL communications, matter transference and direct energy-to-matter duplication – to say nothing of freeform nanotechnology – seemed nothing more than science-fantasy. But now...the Commonwealth was claiming to have started to improve its technology radically. The prospects for the future were alarming.

Once, as a young trainee, she'd simulated a battle between a modern squadron and an entire fleet of battleships from the Unification Wars. The battleships had been wiped out, effortlessly. Their missiles were clunky compared to modern designs, their armour was pathetic and their sensors almost blind. What would happen if the Commonwealth made an unimaginable breakthrough and perfected something that would make Wolfbane's entire fleet obsolete? The war could be over in less than a month. Maybe she was being paranoid, but she'd learned the hard way not to underestimate the Commonwealth. They'd kicked her out of Corinthian, after all.

Shaking her head, she took one final look at the message, then keyed her console and called an immediate staff meeting. Half of her staff officers were spies, of that she was sure, appointed either by Governor Brown or her rivals on Wolfbane. If she held a meeting without making sure they were *all* called, they would go crying to their masters and mistresses about the *secret* meeting she'd held. She rolled her eyes at the thought, then stood and walked through the hatch into the conference room. Her officers were already gathering there.

"Be seated," she ordered, as they stood to greet her. There was no shortage of discipline, she had to admit, and most of the incompetent officers had been purged by Governor Brown and his allies. But half of them were still spies. "There are two days until we begin our staggered departures. How do we stand?"

"All starships are in excellent condition," her ops officer said, at once. "The training battalions and conscripted units have turned out a lot of good technicians to maintain the systems. The latter have actually managed to fit in quite well, with a little prodding. Overall, there are no major problems that would delay our departure."

Rani smiled. There was almost nothing, even a battleship unable to enter Phase Space, that she would have deemed sufficient to delay their departure. It was hard enough planning a series of simultaneous strikes against a multi-star opponent without delaying matters any longer than strictly necessary. By now, most of the Commonwealth would know that their President had been the victim of an assassination attempt. Rumour would probably make her dead even if she wasn't literally dead. They'd be going on the alert, expecting war. But Governor Brown wouldn't know it...

Risky, she thought. *But worthwhile.*

She had no illusions about her position as his subordinate. Brown hadn't been interested in her personally or sexually. He needed her – and he would use her – but he wouldn't underestimate the depths of her ambition. If the war ended quickly, or both sides agreed to a truce, he would have no further use for her. Rani knew her fall would lead rapidly to her execution. It was what she would have done.

But if the war continued, Governor Brown would need her more than ever.

The ops officer continued speaking, unaware that his mistress wasn't quite paying attention. "Overall, training and exercise schedules have worked out fairly well," he continued. "Most of the crewmen have proved themselves adaptable, even when dealing with unscripted exercises and unexpected surprises. Those that haven't have been relieved of duty and shipped back to Wolfbane, with a strong suggestion they be reassigned to somewhere a little less challenging. In particular, speedboat crews have proven themselves in exercises, but we do not yet know how they will work out in practice."

Rani smiled. Speedboats – tiny spacecraft intended to assist long-range missile targeting – had been a concept the Imperial Navy had experimented with, but never managed to get to work. Perhaps the Commonwealth and Trade Federation wouldn't be the only innovators in future, she knew, because Wolfbane had actually made the concept work reasonably well. It would have to be tested in combat before she approved completely, but it would give the enemy an unpleasant surprise. The major downside was that it was regarded as almost certain suicide.

"And the crews?" She asked. "How are they coping?"

"They seem to be considered heroes everywhere," the ops officer said. "Several of them were placed on report for...unscheduled sexual congress."

"How *terrible*," Rani said. Her lips curved into a smile. "Sexual congress we didn't authorise."

The ops officer looked embarrassed. Rani understood; there were certain matters that were meant to remain below decks, not brought to the attention of the fleet's commander. But then, she had *been* an ops officer herself. She knew, all too well, that the men she commanded weren't paragons. God knew just how many mistakes she'd made by allowing her men free reign on Corinthian. People who might have supported her, or at least tolerated her rule, had been driven into opposition. It was a mistake she wouldn't allow herself to make again.

"Inform them that there are pleasure units for such matters," Rani said. "And remind them that it isn't a good idea to distract other personnel from their duties."

The ops officer didn't look any better, but he pressed on anyway. "Overall, stockpiles of weapons, spare parts and fuel are in place," he said. "The fleet train is ready to accompany us, with enough stockpiles to allow us to fight several battles without finding replenishment within the Commonwealth. In addition, a flight of courier boats are also ready to spread the word of our conquests and upload propaganda into the Commonwealth's datanet, as well as carrying word back to Wolfbane."

Rani nodded, then turned to her ground forces commander. "General?"

General Haverford was a tall, powerfully-built man who had – in the style of Imperial Special Forces – shaved his head, then had it treated so his hair wouldn't start to grow out again. It gave him a slightly sinister appearance, which he cultivated to get the best from his officers and men. Rani had read his file carefully, but she honestly couldn't say she knew the man all that well. Chances were he had secret orders to move against her in the event of Governor Brown deciding she had outlived her usefulness. Rani had considered trying to manipulate him, but she hadn't been able to get enough of a measure of his personality to devise a plan of attack that might work.

"Our troops are loaded and ready, Admiral," he said. They'd had to modify a number of colonist-carrier starships to transport the troops, but it would suffice. "They will be able to occupy Thule and our other principle targets as soon as the high orbitals are secured. We have devised plans to deal with both the local government and the insurgent leadership within hours of landing."

Rani nodded. Both the local government and the insurgents would be surplus to requirements, once Thule was occupied. The insurgents, she hoped, would simply assume that they could just link up with the newcomers, which would allow them to be snatched and transported to a penal island before they could realise the error of their ways. They might have believed they would be allowed to keep their world as an independent system, but Thule was simply too valuable a prize to allow it to slip out of her hands.

"The only problem is the presence of the Commonwealth forces," General Haverford continued, coldly. "I intend to allow them the chance to surrender, once we control the high orbitals. They will be treated as prisoners of war, in accordance with the Articles of War, rather than insurgents, terrorists or traitors. Governor Brown has agreed to support me in this matter."

Governor Brown lacks the killer instinct, Rani thought, coldly.

It wasn't exactly a surprise, though. Mistreating prisoners would rebound on them, disastrously. No one would surrender if they felt they could expect to be killed out of hand by their captors. Instead of taking their place in the Wolfbane Consortium, the Commonwealth's military and armed civilians would fight to the death. No, General Haverford was correct. They had to take prisoners, if the prisoners actually chose to surrender.

But would they believe us, she asked herself, *once they know what happened to Polk?*

"We do need to consider the value of intelligence," she said, carefully. "If enemy officers are taken captive..."

"They are unlikely to know enough to make interrogating them worthwhile," General Haverford said. "In any case, the Governor has made up his mind."

Rani kept her face expressionless, refusing to show any trace of the anger that was slowly bubbling its way through her mind. It was...irritating to have such an important issue forced on her at the last possible moment, even if she hadn't found the timing suspicious. There was no time to send a request to Wolfbane for the Governor to rethink his decision before they had to mount the offensive. No, she would have to accept it for the moment. And, in truth, she didn't really disagree with it.

Bide your time, she told herself. *Your day will come.*

"Very well," she said, out loud. "I will leave such matters in your capable hands."

"We will occupy one hundred vitally important locations on Thule within hours of landing," the General said. "Our space forces" – he didn't say *Marines*, Rani noted – "will occupy sites around the system, including industrial nodes and cloudscoops. Once the occupation is completed, the locals will have no choice but to cooperate with us. Should they refuse, they will be shipped out-system to re-education camps."

Rani nodded. Governor Brown's system of re-education camps had been surprisingly effective at turning enemies into allies. Being separated from their families and half-starved until they submitted, the cynic in her noted, probably had something to do with it. But Thule wasn't one of the minor Wolfbane worlds. There were other considerations.

"They will be more effective on Thule than anywhere else," she pointed out. "You will need to try to push them into cooperation, rather than simply removing them if they refuse to work at first."

"We will take care of it," the General said.

Rani smiled, coldly. "I have prepared the departure schedule for you all," she said, addressing the table as a whole. "We will start dispatching starships and squadrons within two days. I want to take this opportunity, however, to impress on you all that some of the targeted systems are *not* as vitally important as your starships. If you should happen to run into opposition you cannot hope to defeat without risking your ships, you are to pull out and abandon the system."

Several officers looked mutinous. She pushed on anyway. "I expect you to use your best judgement of what constitutes a major threat," she continued. "But I will not be best pleased if some of the targeted systems cost us one or two ships. Thule is important; the others…are just propaganda. They will not be particularly useful to us for years to come."

She sighed, inwardly. Too many of her officers had served in the Imperial Navy, where retreat was considered disgraceful even if one was badly outgunned. But there was no point in wasting a starship merely to lay claim to a farming world. Several of their targets had been chosen merely to make it look as though the Commonwealth was going to lose and lose quickly. Civilians, largely unaware of the realities of interstellar war, would see the tidal wave of red icons overrunning the green and panic.

"This war will last for far longer than a few days," she added. "We cannot afford heavy losses, not when the prize isn't worth the cost. Do you understand me?"

There were nods, some enthusiastic, some reluctant. She made careful note of who did what.

"Good," Rani said. She rose to her feet. "Dismissed."

CHAPTER THIRTY

> But, on Morningstar, the social scientists took a bad situation and made it a great deal worse. It is notable that none of the scientists proposing solutions had ever visited Morningstar, let alone spoken to any of the military officers involved in the actual operation. The only locals they spoke to were refugees and representatives from the various factions who had come to Earth to find backers amongst the Grand Senate.
>
> - Professor Leo Caesius, *War in a time of 'Peace:'*
> *The Empire's Forgotten Military History*

The first star system *Sword* had entered, as covertly as possible, had yielded nothing apart from the discovery of a previously unknown asteroid-mining complex that seemed to be supplying the planet with more ore that it could possibly need. Mandy had spent longer than she should have done watching the planet and trying to determine what it was doing, before finally deciding that they were attempting to bootstrap themselves into space. If they had received any help, it was more likely to have come from the RockRats rather than Wolfbane; the technology they were using, while serviceable, was primitive.

They hadn't found anything more interesting in the second system they'd examined, either, apart from traces of a brief battle and a large orbital weapons platform in position to bombard the planet if necessary. Mandy's intelligence officers suggested that the locals were resisting Wolfbane's occupation forces, but there was little else they could determine apart from attempting to capture someone who might have answers and there was no way they could do that without risking exposure. Reluctantly, Mandy ordered the ship to sneak out past the Phase Limit and return to Phase Space.

She'd had a hunch after that, one that had nagged at her mind until she'd finally given into the impulse to act on it. The Imperial Navy had always used inhabited star systems as forward bases, simply because even a stage-one colony was capable of feeding itself and a whole fleet of unexpected guests. But would Wolfbane feel the same way? There was enough cross-border trade, no matter how illicit, for a forward deployment to run the risk of being noticed by a trading ship...and for the ship to have a chance to escape, before it was too late. No, logically, if Wolfbane was planning to cause trouble they would have based themselves on a star that was less likely to receive visitors.

Titlark seemed perfect. According to the somewhat outdated files from the Imperial Navy, Titlark had been visited once, briefly surveyed and then simply abandoned. There was nothing there, apart from a handful of asteroids and a couple of comets the red star had captured thousands of years ago. It might attract pirates or survivalists, but not the Imperial Navy...and not the Commonwealth Navy either. But, if one ignored the absence of anything usable, it was within a handful of light years of Thule.

"The Phase Limit is unusually close to the star," the helmsman commented, as they dropped out of Phase Space a light year from Titlark. "It actually seems to be constantly fluctuating, which is odd."

Mandy frowned. A star's gravity well should remain stable at all times, but they tended to be slightly distorted by the presence of large planets. The Phase Limit was, therefore, a slightly flattened sphere surrounding a star. But she'd never seen one that seemed to be constantly fluctuating. A glance at the files told her that the survey team had noted it in passing and then...as far as the files suggested, no one had shown any interest, even if it was a very odd system. But the Empire had long lost interest in pure science.

She leaned forward. "Does it pose any danger?"

"I don't think so," the helmsman said. "The only real danger would be using the Phase Drive inside the system and...well, if we tried I think the drive would simply fail. But it is odd."

Mandy nodded. "Take us towards the system, but drop out a safe distance from the limit," she ordered. "And keep one eye on it at all times."

She waited, impatiently, until *Sword* returned to normal space once again. There was still nothing special about Titlark, nothing that suggested the presence of a sizable enemy fleet. But her instincts kept nagging at her as the crew deployed the passive sensor arrays, ready to pick up even the slightest hint of intelligent life within the system. Something was deeply wrong.

There was a chime from the console. "We're picking up snatches of low-level radio communications," one of the officer reported. "It looks like ship-to-ship communication protocols, but garbled."

Mandy nodded. They were some distance from the source, but it looked as though there *were* a number of starships within the system. Or had been, she warned herself. They were still light hours from the signal source. Something could easily have changed between the time the signal was sent and it being picked up by her ship. But there was a constant stream of radio transmissions now, suggesting at least a dozen ships lurking deeper within the system.

"They're close to the asteroid field," the sensor officer noted. "They must have turned them into a base."

"Or simply set up a fleet train," Mandy commented. It was how the Commonwealth Navy had trained to operate, rather than remaining dependent on a network of naval bases like the Empire. The loss of a single naval base could cripple the Empire's ability to respond to a sudden emergency. "Are we likely to discover more at this distance?"

"No," the sensor officer said, after a brief consultation with her fellows in their compartment. "I think we need to slip closer."

"Yeah," Mandy commented. She sat back in her chair. "Me too."

Slowly, *Sword* slipped further into the system, passive sensors alert for any trace of an enemy presence. The signals seemed to grow stronger as they moved closer, several of them becoming clear enough for the crew to identify them as station-keeping signals. Mandy felt sweat trickling down her back and forced herself to remain calm, to appear to be in control at all times. She couldn't afford to allow her crew to see her weak.

How, she asked herself, *does Jasmine make it look so easy?*

"I think we can launch a drone here," the sensor officer said. "It would slip past the enemy ships on a ballistic course, letting us have a good look at them without risking the ship itself."

Mandy nodded. The enemy didn't seem to be taking many precautions, but if they were feeling paranoid they would have scattered passive sensor beacons all around their anchorage, watching for the merest trace of an incoming ship. If they detected a hint of *Sword's* presence, they wouldn't lock onto her with active sensors, but track the ship passively until she flew right into a trap. She didn't dare assume that the enemy *hadn't* been paranoid, not when they were clearly preparing for *something*.

"Launch the drone," she ordered. "And keep a laser link fixed on its communicator."

Piece by piece, the system started to reveal its secrets as the drone moved closer and closer to the enemy fleet. A number of asteroids, all clearly hollowed out and converted into living space; fifty-seven starships, including five battleships and two battlecruisers...and a number of colonist-carrier ships. Their presence puzzled her until she realised they were actually troopships. The troops could be held in stasis until they reached their target, whereupon they would be brought out of the stasis pods, loaded onto shuttles and sent down to fight.

"There are nine heavy colonist-carriers there," the sensor officer said. "Assuming they have their full complement of stasis pods, we could be looking at nine hundred thousand soldiers armed and ready to fight."

Mandy shivered. The hell of it was that the colonist-carriers she was studying weren't even the largest the Empire had produced. But they were large enough to carry thousands of settlers, willing or unwilling, away from Earth. And now they were converted into troopships, allowing Wolfbane to flood a designated target with armed soldiers.

"They'd be easy targets without an escort," she muttered. "But they have enough of an escort to take out almost *any* target short of Corinthian or Avalon itself."

She shuddered at the thought as the display constantly updated. None of the signs that suggested ill-maintained starships were visible, as far as the drone could tell. Instead, the fleet appeared to be in perfect working order, armed and ready for action. Mandy knew, with a cold certainty that overwhelmed any other thoughts and feelings, that the fleet was preparing itself for an assault on the Commonwealth. Nothing else made sense.

Nothing to defend here, she thought, coldly. *And nothing to gain, save by being a few light years closer to the border – and Thule.*

"How long," she said, turning to the analyst, "before they launch their offensive?"

"Unknown," the analyst said. "We simply don't have enough data."

Mandy knew she wasn't being fair, but pressed ahead anyway. "Give me your best guess?"

The analyst looked up at the display, reluctance written over his face. "There's no hint they're waiting for anything other than the order to attack," he said, finally. "They could probably leave now..."

"And be on top of Thule within a few hours," Mandy said. If they pushed their drives to the limit, Thule was only nine hours from Titlark. It would be costly, if one or more drive components happened to fail, but they could do it. "Do you know what they're waiting for?"

"No," the analyst said.

Mandy considered it, briefly. Thule was in a state of war, with an insurgency draining the lifeblood of the planet, an insurgency that had support from off-world. Logically, Wolfbane was the only real suspect, the only power that would have the ability and motivation to ship in enough supplies to make the conflict far worse. But if they were planning an offensive at the same time...could it be that they intended to overwhelm and destroy the CEF? Or did they want to burn the insurgency and the local forces out before they took over? It did make a certain kind of sense.

She shivered, remembering a very old problem from her captivity. Someone had supported the pirate chieftain, a man who had called himself the Admiral. For all of the time she had spent on *Sword*, Mandy had never been able to gain any idea of who had been supporting him – or why. The Admiral had had delusions of grandeur, plans to build an empire of his own, and he'd come alarmingly close to succeeding. But, even after his defeat, his supporters remained a mystery. Had it been *Wolfbane* who had provided the practical support?

Admiral Singh had seemed a more likely candidate, she knew, but Admiral Singh's records had been carefully scrutinised after Corinthian had been pushed into rebellion and she'd been forced to flee. There had been nothing in her files relating to pirates, apart from reports of pirate ships destroyed or captured by her forces. Mandy didn't recall anything, even a minor hint, that suggested that Admiral Singh had backed *the* Admiral. But Wolfbane hadn't been linked to her...hell, no one had even been aware of Wolfbane's existence until eighteen months ago. Or, at least, no one had known that it had become the centre of a new interstellar power.

"Get me a full rundown on their ships," she ordered. There *was* a formidable force there, she saw, formidable enough to overrun her squadron, given time. The force shields would give them a slight advantage, but not enough to guarantee a victory. "And then prepare to withdraw from the system."

She smiled at her crew's puzzlement. *Sword* had sneaked close enough to see what the enemy were doing, but not close enough to draw all the data they could from the enemy fleet. But they'd already learned the most important piece of data, one they *had* to take back to Thule. There was an enemy fleet within striking distance, preparing to move against the Commonwealth. There could be no other explanation. The war the Commonwealth had dreaded since Wolfbane had been discovered was about to begin.

The data flowing back from the drone kept mounting in the holographic display. Mandy had to admit, reluctantly, that it looked like Wolfbane knew how to take care of their ships. The battleships alone took plenty of maintenance – as the Commonwealth had discovered after capturing a handful from Admiral Singh – but Wolfbane seemed to have enough technicians on hand to do the work. Mandy really didn't like the implications; given the resources of a more developed sector and a complete lack of interference from the Empire, just how far could a Governor go? Far enough to train up new technicians who actually knew what they were doing? Or was he conscripting spacers and anyone else who might have the skills he needed?

We should hope it's the latter, she thought, sourly. *They might be tempted to rebel.*

"I think we've reached the limit of what passive sensors can tell us," the analyst said, finally. "The drone cannot alter course without running the risk of being detected."

"Let it go, then set the self-destruct to destroy it on contact," Mandy said. The beancounters would probably have a fit when they realised she'd sacrificed an expensive drone, but Admiral Delacroix was a serving officer herself. She would understand Mandy's decision and override any complaints from the bureaucrats. "Helm, take us about and back to the Phase Limit, best possible speed while avoiding detection."

She kept a wary eye on the enemy fleet as it receded into the distance, seemingly unaware that it had been located. If they had realised that *Sword* was there, she knew, they would have attempted to trap her... wouldn't they? Or would they simply bring their plans forward and arrive at Thule hard on Mandy's heels? That was what *she* would do, she knew, if she was commanding the other side. Surprise would have been lost, so the only real option was to attack before the defenders were ready to withstand attack. Thule wasn't undefended, not by a long shot. Her defences would take one hell of a bite out of an attacking formation.

But there was no sign they'd been detected as they crossed the Phase Limit. "Take us FTL," she ordered, shortly. "Set course for Thule, best possible speed."

She yawned, despite herself, as the flickering lights of Phase Space appeared on the display. They were safe now – it was extremely difficult to track or intercept a starship in Phase Space – and on their way back to Thule. Once they were there, she would have to devote all of her attention to preparing the planet to withstand a siege...or withdraw, if the entire enemy fleet came to Thule. There was no way she could sacrifice the entire squadron merely to delay the enemy for a few hours.

"XO, you have the bridge," she said, standing. Another yawn threatened to escape, but she held it down, somehow. "I'll be in my office."

"Aye, Captain," the XO said. "I'll alert you as soon as we reach Thule."

Mandy nodded, stepped through the bridge hatch and into her office. As soon as the hatch had hissed closed, she lay down on the sofa and closed her eyes. Tension drained out of her mind slowly, to be replaced with fear, fear of what would happen if they were unable to reach Thule in time. But somehow, eventually, she managed to calm her thoughts and fall asleep.

"There was a contact," Rani stated.

The sensor operator looked uncomfortable. She was young; like most sensor operators with genuine talent, she had been rushed through the training course and pushed into active service, rather than being given the seasoning of other officers. And she wasn't even remotely comfortable in Rani's presence. But it didn't matter.

"Just a rough contact on the passive sensors," the operator confirmed. "But it could easily have been a starship."

Rani considered it as the operator showed her the readings. The contact had been very brief, brief enough to make her think it was just a sensor glitch...but there was something about it that bothered her. Reaching out, she minimised the star system on the display and sucked in her breath as she realised the contact was real. It had been on a least-time course to the Phase Limit...and on a course that would allow it to fly directly to Thule.

"Thank you," she said, finally. She was too experienced an officer to expect *all* of her plans to work perfectly, but it was irritating to have to change operational plans at such short notice. But there was no alternative. The Commonwealth knew the shit was about to hit the fan. "You may go."

She watched the operator leave her office, then keyed a switch. "General signal to all ships," she ordered. "Our plans have to be moved up. I want all ships ready to depart to their assigned targets within an hour."

"Yes, Admiral," Carolyn said. At least *she* didn't sound surprised. "I'll alert the fleet at once."

Rani smiled. There would be opposition, of course. Changing the plans so close to their scheduled departure date would cause one hell of a lot of confusion...and some of the spies would wonder just what she was doing. But there was no choice. If the Commonwealth had time to prepare, the fighting would be far more costly than either she or Governor Brown wanted. Their plans for a quick victory were about to be tested in fire.

"And then summon a courier boat," Rani added. "Someone has to inform Governor Brown that the war is about to begin."

She paused, then continued. "And assign a second one to me personally," she said. "I want to send a message to our operatives on Thule."

CHAPTER THIRTY-ONE

> This ensured that the best of the social scientists, the ones who did the most 'research,' still had a very skewed view of the crisis. Their perceptions were often at variance with reality. For example, the principle aggressor in the conflict, despite being responsible for genocide, attempted genocide and a number of other war crimes, was constantly referred to as responding to outside aggression. Small incidents (post-war investigations suggested they were staged to serve as causes for war) were used to 'justify' the war in the eyes of the Grand Senate.
> - Professor Leo Caesius, *War in a time of 'Peace:'*
> *The Empire's Forgotten Military History*

Thomas ducked as a bullet cracked through the air above his head, then unhooked a grenade from his belt and tossed it towards where he estimated the shooter to be lurking. There was an explosion; he jumped up and ran down the corridor, weapon in hand, looking for the enemy combatant. But there was nothing left of him, apart from bloody stains on the wall.

He sighed as he caught his breath. Four days of hard fighting had allowed them to penetrate the next set of fortifications within the Zone, which the insurgents were fighting desperately to hold at all costs. Each building had been turned into a fortress, with multiple firing positions and reinforced walls, linked into a series of interlocking defence posts. Clearing them out cost time and lives, while the enemy fell back, then counterattacked with increasing force. They'd even dug a warren of tunnels under the Zone, allowing them to slip their people past the front line and pop up in the rear. One attack had nearly wiped out an entire local formation that wasn't watching its back carefully enough.

"Got a hatch there, sir," one of his men said. Thomas didn't know him personally; he was a CROW, a Combat Replacement Of War, sent into the unit to replace a man he'd lost days ago. Normally, Thomas knew, it would be hard for a newcomer to be accepted until he'd proven himself. Now, the fires of war made it easier for the newcomer to join a unit. "Want me to do something about it?"

Thomas shrugged as he eyed the tunnel, lying temptingly open. Going down was almost certainly a mistake, though. The tunnel would be difficult to explore while the enemy, who would know it very well, would be lurking in ambush. Or maybe they would simply have rigged the tunnel to fall in when the CEF troops advanced into the darkness.

"Drop a couple of grenades down there," he ordered, instead. "I want you to collapse it, if possible."

There was a dull roar as the grenades exploded, followed by a series of crashing sounds that suggested the tunnel had caved in on itself. Thomas dropped a motion sensor down into the darkness anyway, just in case, then keyed his HUD for updates. The advance had slowed almost to a halt as the soldiers had encountered the new defence zone, but higher command seemed to believe the rebels couldn't hold out for long. Thomas had his doubts; so far, the rebels had fought savagely and very well.

He motioned to his unit to follow him as they swept the rest of the makeshift fortress. For once, the remaining enemy seemed to have fallen back, either out of fear of being cut off from their fellows or because they were planning a counterattack as soon as the invaders relaxed. Thomas had to admire their determination, no matter how irritating it was to him personally. The remainder of the house was empty, so he called for reinforcements so it could be converted into a makeshift FOB. Not a perfect arrangement, he knew, but it would provide some shelter to advancing troops before they returned to the fight.

"Incoming!"

He cursed as another wave of mortar shells echoed through the air and came down on the other side of the front line, explosions shaking the entire area. Moments later, he heard a series of more distant explosions as the counter-battery fire went to work, trying to kill the mortar teams before they rushed their weapon to a new firing location. Either the enemy teams were *very* good, Thomas had decided long ago, or the insurgents had thousands of the weapons. No matter how many shells the invaders fired, the enemy still launched mortar shells towards the advancing troops. And they were extracting a price from the CEF...

A dull rumble caught his attention and he turned to stare through a gap in the wall, just in time to see one of the massive apartment blocks in the distance collapse into a pile of rubble. For a long moment, silence seemed to fall over the battlefield, as if both sides were stunned by the sudden collapse, then shooting resumed, greater than ever before. Gritting his teeth, shaking off the tiredness that seemed to pervade his bones, Thomas motioned for his troops to follow him. Surely, sooner or later, the rebels would run out of men to throw at the CEF.

But it didn't seem likely, he admitted, in the privacy of his own mind. The discipline the rebels were showing, even under extreme pressure would do credit to *any* military unit, even the Marines. And they were brave too, he knew; brave...and dreadfully misguided.

Poor bastards, he thought.

A quick check of his HUD revealed that a local infantry unit was moving into position as backstop, ready to support his unit if necessary. Sighing, hoping it was one of the good units, he turned and led his men onwards, back into the fight.

"They took down the Rosetta," Stone said.

"It took them a while," Pete said. So far, the advancing force had hesitated to fire on the largest buildings, even though their snipers had been quite effective at clearing *his* snipers from the building. "I think it might have been an accident."

Stone eyed him, dubiously. She hadn't hesitated to tell the troops that the advancing forces had looting, raping and burning on their minds, in that order. With so many families, including wives and daughters, within the Zone, it had proved hellishly effective at preventing the fighters from surrendering. But it was also giving rise to a worrying amount of savagery. Despite his strict orders, a Commonwealth soldier who'd been captured had been beaten to death rather than handed over to him and his enforcers. But how could he blame his men after what they'd been told?

"An accident," Stone repeated. "And how do you know that?"

Pete shrugged. "You know how accurate their guns are," he said. The CEF had been alarmingly precise, precise enough to wipe out over two dozen mortar teams in the last few days of fighting. "If they'd wanted to bring down all the buildings, they would have done so by now."

He looked down at the map, mentally collating the latest series of reports from his observers and placing them on the chart. There was no way to deny the simple fact that the Zone's defences were starting to crumble, no matter how desperately his men fought to keep the invaders back. Logistics, once again, had proven the bane of a military operation. The high-intensity fighting was sapping his stockpiles of ammunition faster than they could hope to replace them. If the invaders ever realised that he'd run out of HVMs to fire at their aircraft...

"I think it's time to consider withdrawing the lighter units," he said. "They can go through the tunnels and then fade away into the countryside."

Stone's head snapped up. "You propose to abandon the Zone?"

"I propose to withdraw some of our forces," Pete countered. The operation had succeeded, in one sense; the Zone was absorbing more and more of the forces available to the government. Judging from how one regiment had come apart at the first hint of gunfire, they were even throwing completely untrained units into the maelstrom. But he knew there was no point in fighting till the bitter end. "They will go into position for the next phase of the war."

Stone sneered. "You plan to join them?"

"No," Pete lied. He had no shortage of bravery, but he knew, without false modesty, that he couldn't meet his death in the Zone. The movement needed him to help guide the war. "I will stay here until the bitter end."

"See that you do," Stone said, darkly.

Pete eyed her back as she turned and stamped out of the room. She was a fanatic, unsurprisingly; she'd executed cowards – or men she'd seen as cowards – with an enthusiasm that disturbed him. He had already decided that Stone wasn't going to survive the war, hopefully breathing her last as a martyr – although he was quite prepared to shoot her in the back if necessary. Any hope of rebuilding the planet along more peaceful lines would be lost if Stone took power. She would start by purging the government and civil service – and whatever remained of the military – then move on to eradicating all members of the movement who didn't live up to her standards. By the time she'd finished, her reign of terror would leave scars that wouldn't heal for years to come.

Shaking his head, he lifted an eyebrow as a pretty blonde girl – one of the messengers – knocked on the open door. "Message for you, sir," she said, her entire body trembling. "Will there be a reply?"

Pete took the message, wondering if she was shaking because she was scared of him or if she was more worried about the constant shooting that kept everyone awake. The children were having real problems...indeed, he had seriously considered calling a ceasefire long enough to get them into a DP camp. But Stone and the others would never have agreed, either out of fear of what would befall their women and children or simple reluctance to let go of even a shred of their power.

He scanned the letter quickly, then nodded. "Tell them to take no action," he said, sticking the piece of paper in his pocket. One piece of the defences had crumbled – and a number of fighters had surrendered. The gunners wanted to drop a mortar shell on the defenceless POWs before they were taken out of range. "Pass on those words – and nothing else."

The blonde girl nodded, still trembling. She was pretty enough, Pete noted, the type of girl who should be attending college or university rather than being trapped in a warzone. Guilt tore at him as he realised she was the type of person the Terran Marines existed to defend, even if they weren't always grateful for the military's mere existence. Hell, the girl was old enough to be his daughter, if his daughter had lived. She shouldn't have been in a warzone. But the war on Thule had been brewing long before he'd joined the movement...

He smiled at her. "What is your name?"

"Gudrun," the girl said.

Pete sighed as she looked down at the ground, perhaps expecting him to make an indecent suggestion. Some of the smaller resistance groups had had too many footsoldiers who'd done just that, trading on their position to talk girls into bed. But Gudrun was really too young to be interesting. She should be innocent.

But she probably isn't, Pete thought. It was astonishing just how quickly reluctance to open one's legs vanished when one was confronted by starvation. Or worse; one of the reasons he'd joined the movement was to prevent exploitation far worse than simple prostitution. In the end, he knew he hadn't entirely succeeded. It was quite possible that Gudrun had already traded her body for food and protection before joining the movement. Or…

And she wasn't really his daughter.

"Take the message back, quickly now," he said. He didn't miss the brief expression of relief crossing her face, an expression that horrified him more than he cared to say. "And then take a break. You need it."

Gudrun turned and practically ran out of the chamber. Pete shook his head. In a sense, the movement had become parasites, no matter the rightness of their cause. They had complete power over the Zone, power to do whatever they wanted with its inhabitants, with the only thing holding them in check being an awareness of their own weaknesses. After all, if everyone who wasn't part of the movement rose up against them, the movement would be doomed.

Poor girl, he thought. His daughter…would his daughter have been like Gudrun, if she had lived? Or would his daughter have wanted to stay out of the fighting? Or would she have been intimately involved with the fighting? Or…what?

He shook his head, again. There was nothing he could do for Gudrun, not now. All he could do was pray that she survived the fighting without harm.

Gudrun had believed, the moment she set eyes on the movement's leader, that he would know just how badly she'd been compromised. She'd lowered her eyes, unable to stop her entire body shaking with fear...and he'd sent her away with kindly words. It was odd, but there was no time to wonder about what he'd been thinking. All she could do was use the communicator to tell Marcy where the leader was hiding...and hope like hell it was enough to win her freedom. She didn't want to be a spy any longer.

She sent the message, then hurried over to where the gunners were waiting under a protective awning. They didn't seem pleased with her words, but they accepted them without demur. As soon as they banished her, Gudrun left and sneaked back towards the hospital. Maybe, if she was lucky, she would be able to keep her head down until the fighting came to an end.

Her shoulder itched. No, she knew, that wouldn't be a possibility.

"They flew two helicopters over the Zone," Michael said. "Neither of them were engaged with anything other than rifle fire."

"Interesting," Jasmine mused. Could it be that the Zone's defenders had run out of HVMs? The last one they'd fired, at a drone she'd sent in a day ago, had missed its target and exploded harmlessly in midair. "How low were they flying?"

"Low enough to be hit within seconds," Michael confirmed. "They couldn't have hoped to escape."

Jasmine nodded. HVMs – High-Velocity Missiles – had been developed to give ground forces a chance to keep enemy aircraft away from them, which they did very well. A helicopter flying near an HVM launcher was almost certainly doomed, with jet aircraft and drones faring only slightly better. Even a Marine Raptor would have difficulty surviving a direct hit from an HVM...not that it mattered. The handful of Raptors they'd brought to Avalon were all out of service now, after being worked to death.

"It's worth considering," she agreed. Bringing up CAS aircraft would certainly speed up the fall of the Zone, but it would be giving the enemy easy targets if they were playing possum. After everything that had happened, she wasn't going to underestimate the rebels again. "Do we have any confirmation from intelligence?"

Michael shook his head. "Nothing," he said. "Just...indirect evidence."

Jasmine looked up as the door opened, revealing Marcy. "We just received word of a High Value Target," she said, shortly. She dropped a datachip on the desk, which Jasmine took and slotted into the projector. "Our former comrade himself."

"Good," Jasmine said. She looked down at the satellite images, thinking hard. The rebel HQ – if it *was* the rebel HQ – was a small building, completely inseparable from the others surrounding it. It was tempting, awfully tempting, to drop a shell on the building and blow it into dust. But if she did, they would never know what – if anything – they'd hit. "You want him alive?"

It was a silly question, she knew. *She* wanted the former Marine alive. *She* wanted to ask him what the fuck he was thinking, joining up with a rebel group of uncertain motives, working for an outside power that was almost certainly hostile. *She* wanted answers.

"Get me Lieutenant Buckley," she ordered. She glanced down at her wristcom, then looked through the windows at the darkening sky. The raid would have to be launched very quickly or not at all. "I need to speak to him."

If she'd stayed in command of the platoon, she would have agreed at once. But she knew it wasn't her choice to make, not really. It was Joe Buckley, the man with a talent for getting into trouble and then getting out of it, who would have to make the final call. She couldn't make it for him, or force him to act against his better judgement. Everything would depend on him.

"Brigadier," Buckley said, as his face appeared on the screen. "What can I do for you?"

"I'm shooting you the details now," Jasmine said. "We have an HVT that needs captured – or taken out."

There was a long pause as Buckley reviewed the intelligence summary, then the raw data. "Chancy," he said, finally. "What can we call upon?"

"Anything you need," Jasmine said. Buckley would be the CO on the ground, after all. "If we have it, you can use it."

"I'll start planning now," Buckley said. "Kick-off in an hour suit you?"

Jasmine nodded. It was unlikely they could launch the operation any quicker, no matter what happened. They'd done better on Han, towards the end of the war, but then they'd had QRFs scattered all over the planet.

"Have a good one, Joe," she said.

"Thank you," Buckley said. He touched his forehead in a mock salute. "*Semper Fi!*"

And, Jasmine thought, in the privacy of her own head, *wasn't that more than a little ironic?*

Chapter Thirty-Two

> But, from Earth, such incidents looked relatively small. The death of a few hundred locals was minor – incidents had to kill hundreds of thousands to register on the Grand Senate's collective radar – and easily dismissed on Earth. They simply could not comprehend that a few hundred deaths might easily encompass an entire tribe or extended family grouping, thus the deaths might be classed as genocide.
>
> - Professor Leo Caesius, *War in a time of 'Peace:'*
> *The Empire's Forgotten Military History*

Joe Buckley knew his strengths and his weaknesses very well. After all, a succession of commanding officers had drummed them into his head from the moment he'd entered Boot Camp to the day he'd been given command of 1st Platoon. He was capable and flexible, very good at reacting to unexpected situations...but also very good at getting into trouble. If he hadn't been good at getting *out* of trouble, he knew, he would probably be dead by now.

"You have a strange kind of luck," the Commandant had said, years ago. "I seriously considered failing you, even though I couldn't point to a rational reason *why* I should fail you."

He pushed the memory aside as he glided towards the Zone, followed by the other nine Marines who made up 1st Platoon. Sneaking their way into the Zone on the ground would be incredibly challenging, even for Marines; Joe knew, all too well, that they would almost certainly be detected and have to fight their way out of the urban zone. Coming in by air, however, would at least get them to their target before they were noticed. The gliders were silent, very hard to detect even with active sensors...and almost invisible in the gathering darkness.

The Zone itself looked thoroughly weird from high overhead. There were flashes of light and explosions from the front lines, but the interior of the complex was almost completely dark. Joe's helmet sensors reported a number of heat signatures on the ground, men and women moving from place to place under cover of darkness. A number of larger signatures were probably cooking fires, he guessed, or heating elements. It grew cold at night on Thule and, now they'd been cut off from the planet's electric network, the inhabitants would be resorting to fires to warm themselves. But they still definitely had power.

Someone must have stockpiled batteries...or even a fusion core, he thought. He wouldn't have expected an insurgency to hide a portable fusion core somewhere within their territory, but the insurgents on Thule had already pulled off a whole series of surprises. They'd clearly been planning the uprising and consequent civil war for quite some time. But their commander knew, all-too-well, just how his counterparts would think.

Gritting his teeth, he twisted the hang-glider slightly, altering course, his gaze tracking their destination. It looked almost completely defenceless from high overhead, which was almost certainly an illusion. Unless they had been grossly mistaken, the rebel HQ would have plenty of hidden defences, even though having the defences out in the open would have told the enemy gunners precisely where to aim. His altitude dropped rapidly as he fell towards the building, feeling a rush of the old tension and excitement from when he'd carried out his first parachute jump. He'd once been told that a number of Boot Camp recruits managed to make it as far as their first jump and stopped, dead. If they couldn't jump out of a plane, they didn't have a hope of performing a combat drop on a heavily defended planet.

"Get ready to deploy the gas grenades," he ordered. Using microbursts this close to the rebel HQ was a risk – he dared not assume that the rebels didn't have equipment capable of picking them up, no matter what the techs claimed – but there was no choice. A few seconds of warning wouldn't make that much of a difference. "Drop them as soon as we land."

The roof came up towards him at terrifying speed. Joe twisted the hang-glider once again, slowing his fall, then dropped the last few metres onto the roof. A pair of guards, half-hidden under the awning, came into view, gaping in horror at the men who had just landed on top of the building. Joe picked them both off before they could react, then led the way towards a hatch in the rooftop. Underneath, the rebels were waiting for them.

"Grenades away," one of his Marines said. There were a series of pops as the grenades fell down around the building. Unusually, the gas was clearly visible, even in the darkness. But its purpose wasn't to stun or kill, merely to keep the enemy penned up inside the house. Assuming, of course, that their intelligence wasn't completely wrong. "Sir?"

Joe smiled. "In we go," he said. He activated his communicator. "We're entering the house; I say again, we're entering the house."

―――

Pete had long ago mastered the trick of sleeping, despite the sounds of gunfire and explosions from outside the house. His Drill Instructors had pointed out that sleep was so important that the Marines would have to sleep wherever and whenever they could, even if there were shells and bullets whistling all around them. They'd meant it too, Pete recalled; one of the more sadistic training drills at the Slaughterhouse had played the recruits the sound of combat while they were trying to sleep. Later, on training deployments, they'd slept in places as varied as muddy fields and captured enemy houses. He still had nightmares about the foxhole that had caved in on him during the first live-fire combat drill he'd endured.

But he was also a very light sleeper, much to the amusement of his wife. If something moved too close to him, he jerked awake. He'd always woken her in the middle of the night, normally after she snuggled up to him and shocked him out of his rest. Now...he jerked awake, convinced that *something* was badly wrong. His training had included lessons in listening to his intuition, even though it wasn't something that could be quantified. The human mind often picked up danger signs without quite realising what it was picking up.

He sat upright and reached for the pistol he'd hidden under the bed. It wasn't uncommon for an insurgency to come apart into civil war; Pete knew that quite a few of the other leaders didn't appreciate his plans or trust him without reservation. Stone, among others, might have decided to launch a coup. They all had men who were loyal to them personally, rather than the movement as a whole. But if it had been Stone, she would probably have blown up the whole house rather than risk trying to take him alive.

Stumbling to his feet, pistol in hand, he ran over to the far wall and pressed his hand against the plaster. There was only one door into his bedroom, something that had bothered him when he'd first seen it. Long experience had taught him that having only one way in or out of a room could turn the room into a trap, so he'd looked for an alternate way out as soon as the building had been designated one of his headquarters. The plaster was thin, thin enough for him to smash with his bare hands, if necessary. It ran the risk of making noise, but there was no longer any choice. Outside, he could hear the sound of running feet and gunfire. It was quite clear that *someone* had decided to take him out.

Bracing himself, he struck the plaster and smiled as it broke under the blow.

The interior of the building didn't match the plans they'd been given, Joe noted, as they spread out through the building, but he wasn't particularly surprised. They'd designed the buildings for rapid reconfiguration if necessary and, when it had become clear that they would be trapped in the Zone for the foreseeable future, the original inhabitants had started to redesign it to suit themselves. The Marines would just have to search the building floor by floor.

"Got several small units running towards the building," his communicator hissed. The drone, high overhead, was watching the building and providing top cover. "Gunners standing by."

"Tell them to engage," Joe ordered, as he entered another room. A pair of young men scrambled away from him, only to be shot down before they could escape. "And tell them to be damn careful where they aim their weapons."

The building shook violently, seconds later. Joe swallowed a curse as they plunged into the next room, discovering a handful of datachips, a paper map and little else. He marked the room down for later attention, if they had time before they had to run for their lives, then moved into another room. Outside, the gunners had dropped antipersonnel rounds into the area surrounding the building, catching the rebels on the hop. Or so he hoped. Between the shellfire and the gas, the rebels should have real problems responding to the sudden intrusion.

"Top floor cleared," one of his men snapped.

"Down to the next floor," Joe ordered. "Hurry!"

Some of the enemy soldiers had clearly managed to get organised, Joe realised, as they reached the top of the stairs. They'd set up an ambush, firing madly up towards the Marines. Joe barked orders; the Marines used high explosive to shatter the floor and drop down on top of their enemies. The insurgents barely had time to react before the Marines sliced through them, taking them all out. Joe led the Marines onwards into the next set of rooms. Inside, he discovered several young women staring at the intruders in horror. Judging from their appearance, they were probably rebel coordinators rather than whores or any other kind of sex slave.

"Stay here," he ordered. It was stupid – the female of the species could be just as dangerous as the male – but he wasn't going to shoot down girls in cold blood. "Stay here and don't move."

They confiscated a handful of weapons from the girls, then ran on into the next set of rooms and discovered a small barracks. The beds were empty, suggesting that the room had been occupied by the men they'd killed. Joe muttered a curse under his breath and led the way down to the next floor. They were running out of rooms to search.

And then he heard the noise.

———

Pete forced his way through the plaster and stopped, listening carefully. The sound of gunfire – precise gunfire – from outside suggested that the attack wasn't a coup, but a SF raid on a HVT. Part of his mind was mildly impressed, noting that the attackers had dropped into the centre of the Zone to carry out their attack, the rest of him was horrified. They'd managed to effectively surround his building and isolate him. He heard the sound of running footsteps and turned, beating a hasty retreat towards the emergency exit. If there were shells falling around the building, the only way out would be the underground tunnels.

And then someone came after him.

Gritting his teeth, he turned and found cover. If they wanted him, they wouldn't take him without a fight.

Joe Buckley knew, beyond a shadow of a doubt, that the man diving for cover was their target. No Marine could conceal his identity from another, not when they'd had the Slaughterhouse in common. Pete Rzeminski might have retired before Joe himself had graduated and donned his Rifleman's Tab, but the training remained identical.

"Halt," he bellowed, reaching for a stun grenade. It would have to be his first resort, even though he wasn't entirely sure it would work. Rzeminski had been out of service for a long time, but his immunisations and enhancements would still be in play. "Halt or I shoot."

He threw the grenade without bothering to wait for a reply, then cursed under his breath as two shots came back at him. Clearly, Rzeminski was still immune to the knock-out gas. Joe muttered a quick update into the radio, then threw himself forward at breakneck speed. His target had been inching backwards, but came up to fight as soon as he realised there was no point in trying to evade Joe any longer. Joe ducked a punch, then slammed the stunner into Rzeminski's chest and pulled the trigger several times. Rzeminski staggered, somehow remaining on his feet for a handful of long seconds, then collapsed. Joe let out a breath, then rolled the body over and checked its face against the records, then the DNA. It wouldn't be the first time an insurgent leader had left an underling to take the fall.

But the face was correct, as was the genetic code. Joe hesitated, then yanked Rzeminski's hands behind his back and bound them with a plastic tie. He wrapped another tie around the man's ankles, just to make sure he was immobilised, then picked the insurgent leader up and slung him over his shoulder.

"Enemy captured; I say again, enemy captured," he said. "Requesting immediate extraction."

"Understood," the coordinator said. "Choppers inbound now; I say again, choppers inbound now."

Joe could hear the sound of shooting outside as he met up with the remainder of the Marines and headed back to the roof, taking a few moments to sweep the floors for anything that might be useful for intelligence purposes. Somewhat to his disappointment, there was very little, apart from clear evidence that a paper disposal system had been used to destroy documents over the past few days. Rzeminski, it was clear, had known the dangers and practiced strict communications security. There probably wouldn't be anything sensitive on the datachips they'd recovered, Joe decided. It wouldn't be the first time the Marines had captured datachips, only to discover they were loaded with entertainment programs – or porn.

Outside, the Zone seemed to be seething with anger. The live feed from the drone revealed several more groups of insurgents making their way towards the house, while others were trying to bring mortars to bear on their former HQ. Joe had to admire their determination, even though it was clear they'd given up all hope of recovering their former leader. Maybe their other leaders wanted to get rid of him too, he wondered, as shells started crashing down on top of the mortar positions. This time, there would be nothing held back.

"Keep your fool heads down," he barked, as bullets started to crack over the rooftop. Thankfully, the enemy didn't seem to have snipers in place to fire down at them, but it was only a matter of time. 1st Platoon had been on counter-sniper duty for the last few days and he had to admit the rebel snipers were alarmingly good. They'd probably been hunters in the countryside, like some of the Crackers. "I don't want to lose anyone now!"

"Warning," the drone operator said. "They're setting the building on fire."

Joe swore. If the enemy were reluctant or unable to engage them directly, setting fire to the building was a simple way to kill the intruders. Or maybe the operator was wrong and one of the shells fired to deter intervention from outside had accidentally started the fire. Not, in the end, that it mattered in the slightest. All that mattered was getting out of the Zone before the flames caught them or they had to make a run for it through streets crammed with angry insurgents.

"Helicopters inbound," the coordinator said. "I say again, helicopters inbound."

Joe looked up as four helicopters swooped down over the city, firing down into the streets as they approached. One of them came to a halt over the building, then dropped down rapidly until it was hovering just above the roof. The others started to orbit the building, firing burst after burst towards anyone who tried to fire on the helicopters. Joe ran forward, tossed Rzeminski into the helicopter, then motioned for his men to board. As soon as they were onboard, he climbed in and slammed the hatch shut behind him. The helicopter pilot didn't hesitate; the helicopter rose sharply, dropping flares behind it.

Joe felt his stomach clench as he sat down on the metal deck. There wouldn't be a better moment – a worse, from his point of view – for the enemy to reveal a final HVM. They would never have a better shot at a whole platoon of Marines...and their former leader, who they could expect to be bled dry of everything he knew about the insurgency. But as the helicopter clawed for sky, the only opposition was a handful of bullets, which dinged off the armour harmlessly.

He pulled himself to his feet and peered out the porthole as they raced away from the Zone. Flames were rising up behind them, spreading to a number of other buildings. It was clear, part of his mind noted, that the designers hadn't even bothered to give lip-service to the Empire's rules and regulations on fire prevention. Not, in the end, that it mattered in the slightest. Either the rebels managed to put out the fire or it would spread, destroying the Zone.

Success, he thought, as he looked over at Rzeminski. The former Marine was slowly waking up, his enhancements countering the stunner bursts. He might have been able to shrug off one or two bursts, Joe knew; he'd hit him several times just to make sure it worked. By the time Rzeminski woke up properly, Joe told himself, he would be in a secure cell. He grasped the stunner in his hand, just in case. If Rzeminski woke up too quickly, he might be able to cause real trouble before they made it back to the spaceport.

And then, Joe thought, looking directly at Rzeminski, *we will find out just what made you turn against your oaths.*

Chapter
Thirty-Three

> Nor did they see the details. The mass slaughter of military-aged males (which often ranged from ten years old onwards), the rape and then murder of women (unless the women were lucky enough to be taken as slaves instead), the forced kidnap and adoption of younger children...all of these details were simply not visible from Earth. Indeed, given what passed for entertainment in the final centuries of the Empire, it is possible that these details were considered titillating rather than shocking.
> - Professor Leo Caesius, *War in a time of 'Peace:'*
> *The Empire's Forgotten Military History*

It had been six years, more or less, since Jasmine had endured the dreaded Conduct After Capture course at the Slaughterhouse. The Empire's military – at least the part of it that actually fought wars – had no illusions about how captured prisoners would be treated by their captors. It was unlikely, they'd believed, that prisoners wouldn't be tortured and forced to disgorge information, no matter what precautions were taken. After all, the Empire was rarely merciful towards captured insurgents.

She shuddered at the memory as she stared through the one-way glass at Pete Rzeminski, sitting in a metal chair with his hands and feet firmly cuffed and a solid metal band around his waist. The Conduct After Capture course was far from pleasant; she'd been beaten, deprived of food, drink and sleep...and threatened with all kinds of horrific sexual abuse. It was a mark of some pride to her that she hadn't broken, any more than any of the other Marines, and successfully misled her captors. But Pete

Rzeminski would have done the same himself, she knew. It was unlikely they could get him to talk.

"We ran a full physical examination," the medic said. His voice was very quiet. "He's physically healthy, in better than average condition for someone of his age. No major implants or additional non-standard enhancements, as far as we can tell. There wasn't any sign of starvation rations either."

Jasmine wasn't surprised. Somehow, the insurgents had clearly managed to stockpile enough food supplies to feed *everyone* in the Zone. Or had they set up an algae farm? There were none on Thule, she knew, but they were hardly difficult to establish. Hell, the local government could have established a few years ago and used them to feed the poor and starving. It would have cut some of the ground out from under the insurgency.

She made a mental note to mention it to the First Speaker, then looked at the medic. "Does he have any implants that might enable him to resist interrogation?"

"He does," the medic confirmed. "They weren't removed when he left the corps."

"I see," Jasmine said. "Can the implant be removed?"

The medic shook his head. Jasmine sighed. Unless there was something non-standard about the implants, they would activate if they believed Rzeminski was being interrogated, killing him before anyone could react. Everything from drugs to outright torture ran the risk of activating the implants. They were normally deactivated when someone no longer needed to take precautions, but Rzeminski had clearly kept his. What secrets had he had, she wondered, that had made him take the risk?

"Then there's no way to interrogate him," she said, out loud. "Unless..."

She hesitated, then stepped through the door. Rzeminski lifted his head to look at her, his eyes flickering over her uniform. Jasmine wished, suddenly, that she'd thought to wear the *Marine* BDUs, but he would have no difficulty in recognising her service. The Slaughterhouse left its mark on everyone who passed through its doors.

Surprisingly – and in defiance of the Conduct After Capture course – Rzeminski spoke first.

"Why are you here?"

Jasmine knelt down beside him, resting her arms on her knees. "Why are *you* here?"

Rzeminski snorted. "Why should I not fight for what I believe in?"

"What do you believe in?" Jasmine asked. "What made you fight?"

"I retired," Rzeminski said. "I came out here to live with my family. I had a wife and children. There was a government sweep just after the crisis began, hunting for the first set of insurgents. My family were killed in the crossfire."

"You have my sympathy," Jasmine said. She wasn't quite sure what to feel. Part of her *did* feel sorry for the retired Marine, part of her hated him for betraying the Corps. But had he *really* betrayed the Corps if he'd been retired at the time? "And so you went to war?"

Rzeminski looked up at her. "Why are *you* here?"

Jasmine considered her answer carefully before speaking. "The Commonwealth sent me here," she said, finally. "Because the local government asked for help."

"The very same local government that has pissed on everyone who lost their source of income?" Rzeminski asked. "And the one that allows the remaining corporations to dominate the economy?"

He had a point, Jasmine knew. It wouldn't be the first time Marines had been sent into battle to uphold an unpopular or even downright evil government. In some ways, she'd escaped the worst of it – her first action had been on Han – but she'd heard the stories. Somehow, Marines would go in, kick ass and withdraw...and the problems would resume within weeks of their departure. And she knew, from her discussions with the First Speaker, that it was unlikely Thule's government would make any major concessions. They wanted to end the war on their terms.

"I was under the impression," Rzeminski said, after a long moment, "that the Commonwealth had forsworn interference in local affairs. What – exactly – do you call this?"

"We were invited by the legitimate government of the planet," Jasmine reminded him. She knew it was a weak argument, if only because only ten percent of the planet's population were enfranchised. "And we had other reasons to want to keep Thule within our sphere of influence."

"And what would you do," Rzeminski asked, "if Thule decided to go elsewhere?"

Jasmine suspected that the Commonwealth would – reluctantly – accept Thule's decision, if it was made freely. The Commonwealth couldn't hold a member world against its will, not without risking the complete collapse of the entire system. Too many worlds had only joined on the promise their internal autonomy would be respected. And the Commonwealth had certainly intended to *keep* that promise...

That's the problem, isn't it? Her own thoughts asked. *The promises we made ran into reality. And reality is that we need all the industrial base we can get.*

"I wish I knew," Jasmine said, out loud.

"And the vast majority of the planet's population has been disenfranchised," Rzeminski pressed. "How are they meant to vote in a new government when they can no longer vote?"

"The age-old problem," Jasmine muttered. She'd undergone theory classes at the Slaughterhouse as well as intensive physical training. People who were denied legitimate ways to change government policy had the choice between accepting the status quo or outright rebellion. "But surely if the economy improved..."

"If it did," Rzeminski asked, "would that make up for the loss of my family?"

"No, it wouldn't," Jasmine said. The file had been barren about just *why* Rzeminski had joined the movement. "But does the loss of your family justify the mass slaughter you unleashed in the streets of Asgard?"

She pressed on, without bothering to wait for his answer. "Why did you make contact with outsiders?"

"We needed weapons," Rzeminski said, with a shrug. "And where else could we get them?"

Jasmine nodded. "And what, I wonder, was the price? Do you even know who you're dealing with?"

Rzeminski shrugged. "Does it matter?"

"I'd say it does, yes," Jasmine snapped. Deliberate stupidity had never sat well with her. "What do they get in exchange for helping you?"

"And I say again," Rzeminski said. "Does it matter?"

Jasmine looked at him for a long moment, then straightened up. "I think they'll have a price for their help," she said. "I think they'll demand it from you, sooner or later. And I think you may discover that their motives are far from friendly. You may find yourself in a far worse position by accepting their help."

Rzeminski shrugged, again. "Does it matter?"

Jasmine controlled her irritation with an effort. "I have not yet told the local government that we have you," she said. Her voice grew harder as she spoke. "Once we do, I imagine they will demand that you be handed over to them. If they don't trigger your implants through interrogating you, they'll execute you publically as one of the rebel leaders. A sad end for someone who once wore a Rifleman's Tab!"

"You don't have any good options," Rzeminski said, softly. Oddly, he was looking down at the concrete floor, rather than up at her. "Nor do you have any good arguments to use against me. We wanted to be free, we wanted to be decent citizens, not...not peons, not the victims of a galactic collapse utterly outside our control. We wanted..."

"You wanted revenge," Jasmine snapped.

"If it had been just me, I would have gone on an assassination spree," Rzeminski said. "But it isn't just me, is it?"

Jasmine turned and marched out of the cell. Outside, she took a long moment to calm herself, analysing her own thoughts and feelings. The hell of it was that she *did* understand his motivations, she understood them all too well. What would she do, she asked herself, if her husband and family were killed by accident? Or if she watched as the planet she loved became a nightmare? Marines weren't trained to sit on their asses and do nothing. She'd been taught to take the initiative at all times.

So was he, she thought, morbidly.

She understood him, more than she cared to admit. But she also knew that, no matter his pretensions to decency, the war had turned savage long before the CEF had arrived. The war was an endless litany of horror, from assassination attempts that killed families as well as the intended targets to mass counter-terror sweeps that penalised the innocent as well as the guilty. Entire villages had been rounded up on suspicion of being involved with insurgents, families of government workers and the lucky enfranchised had been exterminated; men, women and children were all dying, slaughtered in a war that was rapidly becoming more and more pointless. By the time the Zone was completely destroyed, the local forces would be so badly gored that they'd be almost useless. And the CEF wouldn't be much better.

We could withdraw, she thought, grimly.

She *did* have authority to withdraw, if she deemed the situation beyond repair. But the situation wasn't beyond repair, not if the local government stepped up its act and actually tried to bring the fighting to an end. It wouldn't be difficult to set up algae farms, she reminded herself, and feed the starving. And it wouldn't be *that* hard to help people to retrain and take advantage of the opportunities the Commonwealth was bringing to Thule. Hell, given a few more years, most of the economy might well recover.

But the local government was being stubborn.

She understood, too, their feelings on the subject. Their whole system had been designed on the basis that those who paid the bills made the decisions. Taxpayers were allowed to vote, others – people who weren't earning money – got no say in how the money was spent. It was a simple system, a response to the crisis that had overwhelmed and eventually destroyed Earth, but it wasn't designed to cope with a crisis that tossed millions of people out of work and enfranchisement. They were unmanned at the same time as they lost the work that gave their life meaning.

And even if the local government wanted to make changes, the voters would rebel against it. Why should *they* make concessions, they would demand; *they* were the ones who made the system work, the ones who actually paid the bills. They wouldn't want to surrender what they had, even though their survival was largely a matter of luck, rather than judgement. No, trying to make concessions would rip the local government apart.

She considered, very briefly, allying herself with the rebels. They could overthrow the local government...and then what? There would be pogroms and purges as the hatred of five years of bitter war spent itself, while the Commonwealth collapsed into chaos and Wolfbane surged across the border to destroy it while it was weakened. Maybe she could arrange matters so she was the only one who was blamed...but it wouldn't matter. The Commonwealth would still be doomed.

The thought made her snort. She doubted that one in a million Commonwealth citizens had even *heard* of Thule. God knew she hadn't until she'd started reading up on new member worlds, worlds that might – one day – become a battleground. But Thule might become the catalyst for a war that would rip the Commonwealth apart. Or perhaps there would be no war, merely...an end to the united government.

Councillor Travis will be pleased, she thought, darkly. *Whatever decision I make here is almost certain to be the wrong one.*

"Brigadier?"

Jasmine looked up to see Michael standing there, looking worried. She had to fight down an insane urge to start giggling inanely, then gathered herself and stood upright. He'd seen her distracted and started to worry...

"Yes?" She said. "What's happened now?"

"A courier boat has just entered the system," Michael said. "She sent a message requesting a secure laser link with you as soon as possible."

"Understood," Jasmine said. Courier boats were the fastest ships in known space, but their range was short and they were almost defenceless. "How long until she enters laser range?"

"Three hours," Michael said. "She's coming in hot."

"Very hot," Jasmine agreed. She glanced at her wristcom. It was 0123, but it felt like she'd kept herself awake for days. "I'll take it in my office."

She turned to face the two guards. "The prisoner is to remain here," she said, flatly. "You are to take every precaution in the book when dealing with him. He is to remain cuffed firmly at all times. His feeding will be done through IV tubes rather than though his mouth. Whatever he says or does, he is not to be released at all without my permission. If you take risks with him, he is likely to take advantage of your mistake and kill you."

The guards looked nervous, which was understandable. Jasmine knew they'd be embarrassed about it later, but better embarrassed than dead. A Marine was also trained to take the slightest opportunity to escape, just as Jasmine herself had done on Corinthian. Rzeminski could not be permitted to escape her custody, particularly when she hadn't decided what to do with him. Perhaps they could use him to put together a peace agreement of some kind.

And pigs will fly, she thought, crossly.

She walked back to her office, then spent the next three hours reviewing the latest reports from the Zone. Apart from some minor trembles, the defenders still seemed to be holding themselves together, despite losing their leader. Of course, they also had nowhere to go, as far as anyone knew. They could only fight or surrender. And surrender didn't seem to be an option.

Jasmine sighed. She'd had to assign companies of infantry from the CEF to serve as POW guards, despite the fact she needed them on the front lines. Some local units treated prisoners reasonably well, others...others were not much better than the rebels she'd worked with on Lakshmibai. They'd wanted to slaughter all the prisoners and had to be prevented from doing so at gunpoint. It wasn't much of an improvement from what the Lakshmibai rebels had wanted to do.

"Message packet downloading now," her terminal said. Jasmine rubbed her tired eyes as the compressed packet flowed into the buffer, then started to decrypt itself. "Confirm ID."

Jasmine pressed her palm against the terminal, allowing it to scan her ID.

"Identity confirmed," the terminal said. "Message packet open. Nine messages inside, opening now."

The first message was a personal note from Colonel Stalker. "Jasmine," he said, "this message may reach you too late, despite the orders I've given the two courier boats. We may well be at war with Wolfbane by the time you read this and you may already have been attacked. There was an attack mounted on the Council Chambers..."

Jasmine listened to the remainder of the message in stark disbelief. She'd never been particularly fond of Gaby Cracker, although she'd understood and appreciated her achievement in converting the Marine tactical victory into a long-term success. Hell, Thule needed someone like her to bring the war to an end. But now she was wounded, perhaps dying...

And the shooter had been Private Polk!

Jasmine had always hated to lose people under her command, but it was worse – far worse – when she had no idea what had really happened to them. Private Polk had vanished on Lakshmibai and then...there had never been any trace of him. Jasmine had concluded, finally, that he'd been murdered by his captors and his body burned to ash. But instead he'd been conditioned and turned into an assassin? It wasn't just an assassination attempt, it was a deliberate slap in the face to the Commonwealth. The coming war – and the Colonel seemed to hold out no hope that it could be averted – would be merciless.

She keyed her wristcom. "Inform the local government that I need to meet with the First Speaker, at once," she ordered. "And then prepare a helicopter for me."

Closing the channel, she forwarded the message packet to the remaining starships and her senior officers. They had to know what was happening – and that war might be about to break out. The closest Wolfbane-occupied star was bare hours away in Phase Space. How long would it be, she wondered, before an enemy fleet arrived? Or had their timing misfired, somehow?

She didn't dare, she knew, take that for granted. All hell was about to break loose.

CHAPTER THIRTY-FOUR

> Instead, the social scientists saw a version of the locals that bore little relationship to the truth. Instead of bloody murderers, they saw noble savages; instead of rapists, they saw quaint local customs; instead of child soldiers (forbidden by the Imperial Charter), they saw children fighting to defend their faith. These delusions proved impossible to surmount, not least because the social scientists never even tried to come face-to-face with reality.
> - Professor Leo Caesius, *War in a time of 'Peace:'*
> *The Empire's Forgotten Military History*

Daniel heard the knocking and jerked awake, half-convinced that the rebels had finally burst into the mansion and intended to kill him. It took him several moments to sort out the nightmare from reality and establish that he was safe and warm in his own bed, rather than anywhere else. The last tendrils of the nightmare faded away as he sat upright and keyed the switch that opened the door. Outside, one of his secretaries was waiting for him.

"First Speaker, there has been an urgent message from the spaceport," she said. "The CEF's commander is on her way to speak with you."

"At...whatever time this is?" Daniel asked. He glanced at his watch and swore. It was still earlier than he'd thought. "What for?"

"She didn't say," the secretary said. "But it is apparently urgent."

Daniel pulled himself to his feet and reached for a dressing gown. "Have some very strong coffee prepared for us," he ordered, as he pulled the dressing gown over his pyjamas. He never quite dared sleep naked in the mansion, not when there was almost no privacy at all. "And some stimulants, if the doctors will authorise them."

The secretary looked doubtful. Daniel sighed, inwardly. He was, at least in theory, the most powerful man on the planet...and he couldn't get stimulants without permission from his doctors. Didn't they *know* he couldn't afford to make decisions while he was half-asleep? But they never listened to him, even when he told them he barely slept at nights. There was just too much to think about...

He pushed the self-pity aside as he stumbled into the small office and sat down on the comfortable chair. There was a large pile of reports he had to read, reports he took a certain private pleasure in ignoring as long as possible. Didn't anyone know how to think for themselves these days? Of course they did, he answered himself crossly; they just feared the consequences of making a mistake. It would cost them their jobs, their status and quite possibly their lives.

A door opened, revealing a maid wearing a traditional little black dress. Daniel was too tired to notice the generous amount of cleavage she was showing, or her long shapely legs; his attention was firmly fixed on the jug of coffee. She poured him a mug, bowing deeply enough to expose far more of herself than he cared to see, and placed it in front of him. Daniel sipped it gratefully and waited, feeling the caffeine moving through his system. It was about the only drug the doctors would allow him to use without ticking him off for it.

Another door opened, revealing Brigadier Jasmine Yamane. She looked disgustingly alert, even though she'd probably been awake for hours. Daniel rose to his feet, waved her to a chair facing his desk and poured her a mug of coffee. She took it gratefully, her every motion that of a predator rather than one of the society ladies who would have fainted at the thought of being served by the First Speaker.

"There have been developments," Jasmine said, without preamble. She dropped a datachip on the desk. "The short version of the story is that there has been an assassination attempt on Avalon – and that we may already be at war with Wolfbane."

Daniel considered it, tiredly. He knew next to nothing about interstellar power projection, but he *did* know that Thule was right next to the border. Surely, the planet represented enough of a prize – and a threat – to be considered a primary target. And yet no enemy starships had materialised in his skies.

"I see," he said, finally. "What do you want us to do?"

"Two things," Jasmine said. She crossed her legs as she leaned forward to meet his eyes. "I want you to put the planet's orbital defences on alert – and I want you to call a halt to the campaign in the Zone."

"I see," Daniel repeated. "Is that all?"

A ghost of a smile crossed Jasmine's sharp features. "For the moment," she said. "I know it won't be easy."

Daniel snorted, rudely. *That* was an understatement. There had been so much pressure in the Senate to do something about the Zone that it was unlikely they would understand, let alone accept it, if he ordered the troops to hold in place. And yet, the cost of reducing the Zone had been staggering, in both men, material and buildings. If the fighting continued at the same intensity, there would be nothing left but bloodstained rubble.

But some of the Speakers are already planning its replacement, he thought, slowly. *They don't care if the entire Zone is flattened.*

"No," he said. "It won't be easy."

Jasmine sighed. "We could be attacked here at any moment," she said. "If Wolfbane attacks, the last thing we need is so many units involved in a ground combat campaign that will make them very obvious targets. We need to start thinking about dispersing our military units..."

"Which will run the risk of allowing the insurgents to claim a victory," Daniel pointed out, after a long moment. "They're already winning the propaganda war."

"We could lose the war against Wolfbane if we allow too many of our units to be destroyed on the ground," Jasmine pushed. "And you may *need* the rebels, if the shit hits the fan."

Daniel shook his head. "There's no way we could work with them," he said. "The Senate would never allow it."

He held up a hand. "I'll allow you to hold in place, for the moment," he added. "But you need to understand the political realities. We cannot allow the insurgents time to recover, not now, not after all we've lost. And they know it too."

Jasmine sighed. "At least put the orbital defences on alert," she urged. "You'll need them if Wolfbane comes here."

"I will," Daniel said. "And thank you."

"Review the data," Jasmine said, pointing to the datachip. "I think we only have days, at best, before the war begins."

"The *next* war," Daniel corrected.

Mandy let out a sigh of heartfelt relief as *Sword* returned to normal space on the edge of the Thule System. She'd feared the worst; *Sword* was an older ship, no matter how many improvements the Commonwealth Navy had worked into her systems. It was vaguely possible that the fleet she'd detected had outrun her, if they had left at once. But there were no emergency beacons on the edge of the system, squawking their alarm.

"Send the signal I prepared," she ordered. "And then take us back to the squadron, best possible speed."

"Aye, Captain," the communications officer said.

Mandy settled back in her command chair, silently reviewing the situation time and time again. None of her conclusions had changed, no matter how much she poked and prodded at her thoughts. Wolfbane was preparing to strike, she knew, and the blow could fall at any moment. Everything was about to go pear-shaped.

She'd compressed everything they'd picked into a single signal, which she'd had beamed towards both the squadron and Thule. Jasmine would know what was coming, she knew, although she was damned if she knew what Jasmine could do. Maybe she'd have a better idea, Mandy hoped, but all *Mandy* had been able to devise was loading the CEF on its transports and abandoning Thule. There was no way she could hold the world if the entire fleet she'd detected came calling. Endlessly, while she waited, she waged the Commonwealth-Wolfbane War in her head. But there were just too many possible opening moves for the enemy side.

"Captain," the communications officer said sharply, "we're picking up an emergency signal from the squadron."

Mandy glanced down at her console...and swore as she saw the summary. An assassination attempt on Avalon, war threatened...and, she knew, an entire enemy fleet within striking distance. The war was almost certainly about to begin within the next few days.

"Order the squadron to form up on *Sword*, once we rendezvous with them," she ordered. She had to compose a new message, one for the courier boat. "And alert me the moment something – anything – happens."

There was a bleep from the console. "Captain, a courier boat just entered the system," the sensor officer said. "It was on the same course as ourselves. And it just sent a message into the system."

Mandy gritted her teeth. Somehow, she was sure that message was intended for the insurgents on Thule. But, right now, there was nothing she could do about it.

"This is the situation," Jasmine said, an hour after Mandy's message had arrived and she'd read her sealed orders. They hadn't included anything she hadn't expected, given the situation. "An enemy fleet is within striking distance, an enemy message was beamed into the system and everything has suddenly become suspiciously quiet."

She looked around the small office, meeting the eyes of her subordinates. "I don't need to tell you, I think, what this might mean for us," she continued. "Thule is heavily defended, but she won't be able to stand off the enemy fleet alone. Furthermore, we cannot risk heavy losses in starships ourselves. This leaves us with a major problem."

They all understood the implications. The only thing preventing either the local government or the CEF from heavy use of KEWs to obliterate rebel formations was concerns about collateral damage. Once the orbital defences fell – and Wolfbane took control of the planet's high orbitals – any resistance on the surface could simply be destroyed from orbit. If the CEF failed to disperse by then, it would be wiped out too.

That's why they lured us into the Zone, Jasmine thought, in sudden cold realisation. *They wanted us to mass the local units so they could be destroyed. When the CEF arrived, they merely updated the plan to include our forces too. And destroying the CEF in the opening moves of the war would be a grievous blow to Commonwealth morale.*

"I was granted authority to withdraw, if necessary," she said. She dropped the datachip with the orders on the table, inviting her officers to examine them. "I want you to start working out plans for withdrawing as much of the CEF as possible through the spaceport and up to the transports. The equipment can be replaced, men cannot be. Once they are on the transports, they are to withdraw towards Avalon."

"The local government will have a fit," Joe Buckley observed, mildly. "They will claim they're being abandoned."

And they'd be right, Jasmine thought.

She slapped the table, loudly enough to catch their attention. "Every previous war we have been involved in was localised," she said. "We fought to put down an insurgency, subvert a military dictatorship or relieve our comrades who were under siege. There hasn't been a real interstellar war for over a thousand years...and *that* interstellar war was on a very small scale. The Empire simply built up a colossal fleet and overwhelmed its target.

"*This* is going to be different. Wolfbane may be bigger than us, but it is hardly the size of the Empire. The coming battle for Thule may determine the planet's fate, yet it will not determine the victor of the war. I will not waste resources fighting for Thule when they can be preserved to continue the fight elsewhere. If the Colonel feels that I have made a mistake, I have no doubt I will hear about it. Until then, my orders stand."

She took a long breath. "I do not want to inform the locals of our decision, if possible," she admitted. "We have been planning to rotate units back through the spaceport in any case. This...will merely be another such movement."

"If they don't attack," Buckley offered, "you will be rather embarrassed."

Jasmine smiled. "I know," she said. "But does anyone here believe they *won't* attack?"

There was no answer.

Silence fell over the Zone as the sun rose in the sky.

Gudrun slipped out of the hospital at daybreak and wandered through the streets, feeling almost as though she were in a dream. *Something* had happened at the HQ, according to the rumours, although no two rumours agreed on what had actually taken place. There had been gas and fire and helicopters and...Gudrun had a terrible feeling that the CEF had mounted a mission which had succeeded alarmingly well.

And it was quiet. The endless shooting from the front lines had come to an end. Insurgents thronged through the streets, looking around in bemusement. There had been no surrender, no end to the war, just...a sudden pause in the storm. No one quite seemed to know what to think about it. Gudrun looked at some of the children, their faces pale and terrified, and shivered. Maybe the war would come to an end and the children would be safe, no matter where they went. Or maybe the sudden silence was just a pause in the storm.

Pete Rzeminski disliked being a prisoner. He knew how to wait, he knew how to be patient...but there was nothing at the end of the line, apart from death. The planetary government wouldn't hesitate to execute him for his crimes, even though they'd committed the crime that had brought him into the war. Would the fighting have been so bad without him and his allies? Perhaps so...or perhaps it would have been worse. Hundreds of tiny movements rather than one big one, all trying to outdo their rivals as well as fight the government.

He tested his cuffs again, but there was no hope of escape. His captors had undergone the same courses as himself, he knew; they understood how best to keep him prisoner. He was mildly surprised they hadn't knocked him out or stuffed him into a stasis tube, which would have rendered escape completely impossible. But they had probably decided it didn't matter, he told himself. There was no hope of escape.

The door opened, revealing the young female Marine from earlier. Pete wondered, absently, if his words had made an impact on her, but suspected it didn't matter. If he'd been on active service, he probably wouldn't have switched sides no matter the cause. Even if she wasn't loyal to the local government, she would be loyal to the ideal of the Corps and her comrades, the men and women she fought besides. And then she squatted down next to him.

"This planet is about to be attacked," she said, quietly. "By Wolfbane."

Pete lifted his eyebrows. "Wolfbane?"

"You must know that they are the ones who supplied you with weapons," the Marine snapped. "Or didn't you bother to ask for any ID?"

"I didn't choose to ask," Pete said, softly. "We were *desperate*."

"I suppose you were," the Marine said. "Listen carefully."

She briefly explained about the assassination attempt on Avalon, the identity of the would-be assassin and the discovery of an enemy fleet within striking distance of Thule. "You have to know they probably want more from you than just your neutrality," she concluded. "Like it or not, your world is one hell of a prize."

"I see," Pete said, when she'd finished. "And what would you like me to do?"

"I have an offer for you," the Marine said. "When their fleet arrives – if their fleet arrives – I am prepared to release you. In exchange, I want you to ensure that your people don't join with Wolfbane when they land."

"That might be tricky," Pete observed. "You do realise they might suspect I was conditioned, while I was in your custody?"

"It's a possibility," the Marine agreed. "But we're running out of options."

"You must be," Pete said. Inwardly, he was impressed. Marines were always *brave* – that was a given, after Boot Camp and the Slaughterhouse – but it took guts to make a decision that could easily bring her career to an end. Hell, the local government might demand her head on a platter after she let him go. "I also don't command *all* of the insurgent cells."

"Do what you can," the Marine said. She stood. "If the shit hits the fan, you will be released. I would suggest, quite strongly, that you took your people out of sight. If they walk up to the newcomers..."

"They might be exterminated," Pete said. Years ago, he'd served on a world that one of the giant interstellar corporations had wanted to bring under its wing. One particular group of rebels had been supported until they'd won the war, then they'd been quickly captured and shipped to penal worlds by their backers. "I don't know how many will follow my lead."

He paused. "But I can give you a suggestion," he added. "When you disperse your forces, disperse them into Riverside."

She frowned. "Why...?"

"The people who live there are the people they'll want to take alive," Pete said. "And you might be able to use them as human shields."

Her face twisted, disgust warring with the grim understanding that it might be the only thing between her people and a quick death. He understood; human shields were weapons of the weak and dishonourable, not Marines and other honourable men. But there might be no alternative. Orbital bombardment would shatter her units if the enemy took control of the high orbitals.

"We shall see," she said, finally.

Her wristcom buzzed. She glanced at it, automatically.

"I think we're out of time," she said, after a moment. Pete sat up, despite the cuffs. "A large enemy fleet has just entered the system."

CHAPTER THIRTY-FIVE

Their solutions, as such, relied on far too many assumptions, starting with the simple assumption that it was possible to appease the aggressors. The social scientists created plans for reservations for each ethnic group, which were then forwarded to Imperial Army commanders with instructions to implement them immediately. Unsurprisingly, the reservations could not have been created save by the mass relocation of tens of thousands of people – which would be bitterly resisted. The plan floundered upon reality.
- Professor Leo Caesius, *War in a time of 'Peace:'*
The Empire's Forgotten Military History

It felt *good* to command a fleet once again.

Rani allowed herself a tight smile as the fleet shook itself out and advanced towards Thule, making no attempt to hide its presence. She had wanted to command a fleet in action since she'd joined the Imperial Navy, but few of her fellow officers had ever had that chance. The Imperial Navy had been so overwhelmingly powerful, at least on the surface, that few had ever dared to challenge it directly. She wasn't just commanding a fleet, she was starting the first true interstellar war for over a thousand years. It was the very pinnacle of her professional career.

"Launch drones," she ordered. "Get me a direct laser link with the hidden sensor pods."

She watched as the display rapidly filled up with information. Thule *was* a valuable prize, by almost any definition. It wouldn't need years before the system became a productive part of the Wolfbane Consortium;

it would only require a small number of occupation troops and some deals with the local corporations. Rani had no doubt the corporations would play ball, not when the alternative was mass deportations and the installation of a new ruling class. No corporate CEO had ever shown a trace of integrity. They'd sell out their workers in a heartbeat if it gained them one more iota of power.

And they will work for me, she thought. She'd learned a great deal from her stint as a military dictator – and, she wasn't afraid to admit, from Governor Brown himself. People without integrity could be manipulated into doing the dirty work, without forcing Rani too get to closely involved. They'd try to profit for themselves, of course, but it didn't really matter. All that mattered was that they did as they were told to do. *And I will use this system as a base for my expansion.*

She cast a greedy eye over the hundreds of asteroid mining stations and industrial nodes. A few weeks of occupation and they would all be working at maximum capacity, fuelling the assault on the Commonwealth. Rani had a great deal of confidence in her fleet train, but having a base of operations a few light years closer to their ultimate target would be very useful. And it would even benefit Thule itself to become a war production node. The insurgency she'd supported would no longer have a cause for war.

Her lips curved into a cruel smile. There was one great advantage of supplying the insurgency; it ensured that the local government's forces were drained before her forces ever started to land. And it pushed the local government to confiscate weapons, disarming a population that might become a major threat, given time. And it weakened the insurgency as well...weakening the CEF was just the icing on the cake.

"Admiral," the sensor officer said. "The long-range sensors report a Commonwealth squadron in high orbit near the planet."

Rani nodded, pleased. She'd half-wondered if the Commonwealth would have pulled out completely – it didn't take a genius to work out that Thule was high on the list of principal targets – but having a chance to catch and destroy a small squadron of enemy starships was definitely something to exploit. It took months to construct even the smallest starship, ensuring that any losses she inflicted now might not be replaced before the war came to an end. And the Commonwealth would have the choice between fighting – and being destroyed – or abandoning the planet.

And if they take that option, she thought coldly, *their allies will not trust them to defend their worlds.*

"Keep us heading towards the planet," she ordered. "Let them come to us if they want a fight."

It would be hours, she knew, before the two fleets entered weapons range. The Commonwealth ships could avoid engagement easily, if they chose to do so. It wouldn't be difficult at all. But if she kept heading towards the planet, they'd have to choose between abandoning Thule and making a stand. And if they picked the latter, she would have a definite opportunity to destroy their entire squadron.

More data kept flowing into the display as they moved closer and closer to Thule. The planet was surrounded by orbital stations, some armed to the teeth. No one had attacked such a heavily defended world for hundreds of years, unless one counted the sneak attack on Corinthian. She couldn't help feeling a hint of tension running through her body as she contemplated testing the tactics the Imperial Navy had devised over hundreds of years, but never used in action. It was quite possible, she knew, that she could die in the coming engagement.

She'd thought herself used to the thought of a violent death. The Imperial Navy was hardly a safe occupation, even in its glory days. Even if there had been no enemy to fight, there were still accidents, dangerous rescue missions...and the very real threat of being knifed in the back by a senior officer. Hadn't *she* been exiled to Trafalgar for refusing to open her legs for her commanding officer? But that commanding officer was dead now – she'd issued the kill order personally – and her ambitions had taken her far. Maybe she had suffered a reversal along the way – more than one, really – but she kept climbing her way back up the ladder towards her goal.

Her lips quirked. *Empress Rani*. It had a ring to it.

Certainly more than the Childe Roland, she thought, wryly. She sometimes wondered what had happened to the teenager who should have taken the throne. Was he dead on Earth or had he escaped, taken by his security officers to a hidden redoubt? She suspected she would probably never know...not, in the end, that it mattered. If she ever met him again, she would have him executed before he could appeal to any of the loyalists on Wolfbane. For once, she and Governor Brown would be in perfect agreement. Roland would have to die.

She watched the display as dozens of freighters, some clearly interstellar designs, broke loose from Thule and started to flee. Most of them headed up or down, away from the system plane, hoping to reach the Phase Limit before they could be run down by the advancing enemy fleet. Rani had no intention of giving chase, in any case. It would divert her forces from their primary task; securing the planet and its priceless population of trained technicians. She had ambitions for those trained men and women, ambitions she knew Governor Brown shared. They'd be very helpful when it came to building Wolfbane's industry to a point it rivalled the once-great network surrounding Earth.

And what, she asked herself, *happened to Earth's industry?*

The mistakes of the past, she vowed, would not be repeated. Maybe her subordinates – Governor Brown's subordinates – would build their own power bases, but there would be limits. They would not be allowed to bully their own subordinates, let alone force them into bed, not when it would create resentments that would tear Wolfbane apart. There would be struggles for power – Rani was a strong believer in survival of the fittest – but there would be rules. And the struggles would not be allowed to turn violent. People tended to be less rational when there was a strong possibility that they would end up dead.

She settled back in her command chair and watched the fleeing freighters. They'd be back soon enough, she knew, once the war was over. There would be nowhere else for them to go, not after the Commonwealth and the Trade Federation were destroyed. They'd come back to civilised space and Rani would welcome them back. They wouldn't even face the crippling taxes and fines the Empire – at the behest of its corporations – had piled on independent shippers. There was no point, Rani had learned the hard way, in killing the goose that laid the golden eggs.

"Launch a second flight of drones," she ordered. "I want you to keep a close eye on that squadron."

Mandy sat in her command chair and watched doom advancing slowly towards Thule. It wasn't the entire fleet she'd seen at Titlark, but it was large enough to crush her fleet in open battle. The absence of a handful of ships, including two battleships, was actually quite worrying in its own right. Where had *they* gone?

Plenty of other targets along the border, she thought, as the enemy fleet grew closer and closer. *They could be overrunning them all by now.*

She watched the display as the drones revealed the full extent of the enemy fleet. Three battleships, each one clearly in excellent working order. Twelve heavy cruisers, nineteen destroyers and four colonist-carriers that probably served as troopships. The calculation of just how many troops the newcomers could land on Thule was not remotely reassuring, not when the enemy would have enough firepower to take and hold the high orbitals. They'd be outnumbered, but they'd have vastly superior firepower.

The enemy were playing it smart, she noted. Instead of trying to chase Mandy all over the star system, they'd selected a target they knew she had to defend – or abandon the system completely. If she stood in defence of Thule, she ran the risk of losing her entire squadron; if she pulled out, she disgraced the Commonwealth and risked denting its reputation as a defender of its member stars. And yet, if she fought a close-range battle, she would almost certainly lose her entire squadron.

Assume they don't have force shields, she told herself. *Could we win the coming battle?*

She scowled as she ran through the options in her head. Maybe they could, if they were lucky, but the enemy capital ships could produce gravity shields, if not proper force shields. Her fleet wouldn't be *equal*, no matter what she did; the sheer level of ponderous firepower bearing down on her was enough to overwhelm her, force shields or no. The irony – her modern cruisers could probably have danced rings around the older ships – was chilling. All she could do was delay the enemy for a few hours, if that.

And if they're willing to soak up losses and keep coming, she thought, *they will be orbiting Thule within four hours.*

She switched the display to monitor the loading. It was difficult, moving troops at such short notice, but the CEF was slowly pulling out of

Thule. But it would take far more than four hours to evacuate the entire formation, assuming the locals didn't object. No matter what she did, Mandy realised, the incoming attack fleet was going to catch at least two-thirds of the CEF on the ground.

If she stood and fought near the planet, she could combine her firepower with the planet's defences. It was a tempting thought, she knew, but it would also doom her fleet. They'd be unable to run as the invaders bore down on them. And she knew she didn't dare risk heavy losses.

Silently, she made the decision she knew had been inevitable right from the start.

"We'll go with Omega-Three," she said. A couple of her officers looked shocked, but the others understood. They didn't dare risk a close engagement with the enemy fleet. "Alert the crews. We will leave orbit in thirty minutes."

She stood and walked towards her office. Jasmine needed to be informed…Mandy felt her heart clench in pain as she realised Jasmine wouldn't leave until all of her people were safely loaded onto the transports. And there was no time to load them all before the enemy reached orbit. No matter what she did, Jasmine – the person who had straightened her out and prepared her for life on Avalon – was doomed. There was no way out.

Perhaps they'll accept surrenders, she thought, as the hatch hissed closed behind her. *But will Jasmine consider surrender?*

The alarms had started to howl while Daniel had been in the middle of an emergency meeting with his Cabinet. It hadn't been a very productive meeting – not all of them had been prepared to believe that there was an incoming threat that justified pulling back from the Zone – but he disliked it when his meetings were interrupted. His objections had faded away, however, when he'd been escorted back down to the secret bunker, just in time to see red icons appear on the deep space tracking display.

"We have a large fleet of unknown origin heading towards us," the operator said. "I don't think they're friendly."

"That's a least-time course from Titlark," another operator added. "They're from Wolfbane."

Daniel sat down and stared at the display, feeling his mouth suddenly become dry. An enemy fleet, a *real* enemy fleet, was in his system, advancing towards his planet. Suddenly, bitterly, he regretted the loss of the Empire. They'd all thought the days of interstellar war were in the past.

A thought nagged at his mind. *But would we have been allowed to remain autonomous indefinitely?*

It was possible, he knew, that the answer to the question was *no*. The Empire's Grand Senate hadn't cared for autonomous worlds, let alone independent star systems. Thule might have been wealthy, by the standards of the nearby sectors, but she was quite poor by the standards of the Core Worlds. Daniel's predecessors had known there was a risk that, one day, a corporation might push the Empire into making a grab for Thule. But even that would have been preferable to outright war.

"I see," he said, swallowing hard. "Do we have an ETA?"

"Four hours, assuming they maintain their current speed," the operator said.

"Alert the orbital defences," Daniel ordered. "The enemy fleet is not to enter orbit."

He turned to see General Erwin Adalbert striding into the compartment. "General?"

"It doesn't look good," Adalbert said. "We can only assume the worst."

Daniel nodded, contemplating his options. Could they force the enemy fleet to stay away from the planet? It didn't seem likely – and even if they did, the enemy ships could simply obliterate the asteroid mining stations, the cloudscoops...and everything else Thule needed to keep going. Hell, they could just sit outside engagement range and hurl rocks towards the planet's defences, draining their supplies as they struggled to intercept each and every rock before it hit something vital. Or would they threaten the planet itself?

It was easy, shockingly easy, to depopulate an entire planet. Daniel hadn't known the half of it until his first briefings, after being elected into office. Long-range strikes with asteroids pushed up to a fair percentage of light speed, engineered viruses, radioactive warheads...there were no shortage of tricks a ruthless enemy could pull. But there had been no planet-killing strike for thousands of years. Even the Nihilists on Earth had never tried to slaughter an entire planet's population.

But if they did that, he thought, *surely the Commonwealth would retaliate in kind?*

He sighed. "Have they contacted us at all?"

"No," Adalbert said. "They haven't even tried to demand our surrender."

Daniel sat back in his chair and watched, feeling a growing sense of helplessness, as the enemy fleet slowly closed in on the planet. The Commonwealth's squadron was pulling away from the planet, heading out on a course that would allow it to enter engagement range of the enemy fleet, but somehow Daniel knew it wouldn't be enough. He envied the operators in the bunker, wishing that he had something to do, something that would distract him from the doom advancing towards his world. What would *happen* to Thule if Wolfbane occupied the planet?

"Picking up a signal," one of the operator said.

"Put it on the screen," Adalbert ordered.

A dark-skinned woman materialised on the display, sitting on the bridge of a starship. "This is Admiral Singh, speaking on behalf of the Wolfbane Consortium," she said. "A state of war exists between the Commonwealth and Wolfbane. You are ordered to surrender your star system to my fleet or face attack. You have five minutes to signal your surrender."

Daniel frowned. The name was familiar. "Admiral Singh?"

"She used to rule Corinthian," Adalbert said. "Assuming it's the same woman, of course."

Daniel swallowed. "We can't surrender," he said, finally. "Order the defences to repel attack."

Adalbert nodded, wordlessly. "Yes, sir," he said. "I'll send the orders at once."

Five minutes passed slowly. The enemy fleet didn't bother to send a second message demanding surrender. Instead, it launched another flight of drones and picked up speed, shortening the time to engagement, Daniel watched, helplessly, as the two fleets converged on one another. Somehow, he was sure it wouldn't be enough.

Another set of alarms sounded. "Intruder alert," someone snapped. "I say again..."

The entire bunker shook, violently. Someone had attacked the mansion, Daniel realised in horror, as half of the displays went blank. They'd been cut off from the planetary datanet! The bunker shook again, and again...and then cracks appeared in the ceiling. Daniel looked up, shocked, as pieces of debris began to fall to the ground. They'd told him the bunker was utterly secure. Had the enemy sneaked a starship into orbit and dropped KEWs or armour-busting warheads? Or...

"Get out of here," Adalbert snapped, yanking him to his feet. "Move..."

There was a thunderous roar as the roof caved in. Daniel had a moment to think about his wife and child...and then nothing, nothing at all.

CHAPTER THIRTY-SIX

> Undeterred, the social scientists tried again. This time, they focused on the issue of shipping guns to the various warring factions and convinced the Grand Senate to order an embargo on weapons shipments. The Grand Senate was bitterly hoplophobic, fearing (quite reasonably) that weapons would end up being pointed at their servants, so this was not a hard sell. Unsurprisingly, this decision also failed to take note of certain local realities.
>
> - Professor Leo Caesius, *War in a time of 'Peace:'*
> *The Empire's Forgotten Military History*

Jasmine heard the explosion in the distance and swore out loud. "What was that?"

Michael looked down at his terminal. "Explosion – a major explosion – in the city centre," he said. There was a long pause. "Brigadier, the First Speaker's mansion is gone!"

"Shit," Jasmine said. The enemy had clearly had plans to decapitate the government as soon as it refused to surrender. If the blast had been powerful enough, it might have destroyed the bunker under the mansion...or had they managed to sneak someone through vetting and trigger the bunker's self-destruct? It didn't seem likely. "Do we have anything, anything at all, from the First Speaker or the local military?"

"No," Michael said, after a long moment. "And a chaos virus is infecting their systems."

And we taught her how to do it, Jasmine thought, bitterly. She'd used similar tactics to break Admiral Singh's grip on Corinthian. Now, Admiral

Singh had returned – and she'd learned from Jasmine's tactics, using them against her. The Admiral might have superior firepower, but she was playing it carefully, unbalancing her opponents as much as possible before entering engagement range. All hell was about to break loose.

Michael muttered a curse under his breath, then looked embarrassed. "We have reports of shootings, bomb attacks and mortar fire at a dozen local government bases," he added. "And no one seems to know who is in charge."

Jasmine gritted her teeth. Thule didn't stand a chance, not now. Even if they located someone in the chain of command who was still alive, they wouldn't be able to re-establish control until long after Admiral Singh was in orbit. By then, it would be far too late. She glanced up as she heard a handful of explosions in the distance, then looked back at the display. There wasn't much time to act…if, of course, there was anything they could do.

"Keep funnelling men up to the transports," she ordered, shortly. "Contact the units near the Zone and order them to make their way back to the spaceport, through Riverside. All heavy equipment is to be abandoned in place."

Michael blinked. "Brigadier?"

"There's no time to transport it home," Jasmine snapped. Losing it would be irritating – it would be costly to replace everything they'd brought to Thule – but she needed the trained manpower more than she needed the equipment. Assuming the Colonel left her in command of the CEF after this. She hated to admit it, yet there was no choice. She'd screwed up rather badly more than once. "Send the orders."

She stood and strode out of the room, towards the makeshift prison cell. Joe Buckley and two of his Marines stood guard outside the cell, exchanging grim looks. They were all experienced enough to understand just how bad the situation had become.

"Go see to the loading," Jasmine ordered, shortly. None of her men had practiced loading under pressure. It was possible, alarmingly so, that discipline would break down as the enemy fleet grew closer. "Leave me here."

Buckley gave her a surprised look. "Jasmine…"

"Not now," Jasmine snapped. "I need you to handle the loading."

She waited until they were gone, then opened the door and stepped inside. Pete Rzeminski was seated on the chair, looking up at her curiously. Jasmine hesitated, then knelt down beside him and met his eyes. He looked...more curious than afraid.

"Going to leave me with a pistol and a single bullet?" He asked, finally. "Or are you going to execute me yourself?"

"There's a large fleet bearing down on the planet and the First Speaker is dead," Jasmine said, shortly. "Or at least we *assume* he's dead. There's nothing left of his mansion, but a big heap of smouldering rubble."

"You should know the dangers of assuming anything," Rzeminski said, dryly. "What do you want from me?"

"We're withdrawing from the planet – or trying to," Jasmine said. "I'm going to let you go, in exchange for you going underground. When Wolfbane starts abusing the planet's population, I want you to lead resistance to their occupation."

Rzeminski smiled. "Don't you think you're taking one hell of a chance?"

Jasmine smiled back, coldly. "The alternative is shooting you in the head now," she said. "I think my career has just hit a roadblock anyway."

"A large enemy fleet would be one hell of a roadblock," Rzeminski smiled. "But what will your superiors say?"

"Under the circumstances," Jasmine sighed, "I may never find out."

She stood and stared down at him. "I have no more time," she warned. "Decide now; death or resistance."

"Resistance," Rzeminski said.

Jasmine started to undo the cuffs securing his hands. It was one hell of a chance, just as he'd said, but there was no alternative apart from executing him herself. Besides, she suspected that it wouldn't be long before the planet's population grew tired of Wolfbane's presence and started plotting a second insurgency. Rzeminski would be able to train up new insurgents and give them a fighting chance.

"That feels much better," Rzeminski said, as he rubbed his wrists. "Do you think whoever designed this chair was a bondage freak?"

Jasmine scowled as she released his legs, keeping a wary eye on him as she moved. "I remember breaking out of a prison cell when I had half a chance," she countered. "We didn't want to lose you, did we?"

She straightened up, allowing him to pull himself free of the straps and stand. "And yet," he said, "you're letting me go now."

"Yes," Jasmine said. "I think you'll cause as much trouble for Wolfbane as you caused for us, perhaps more. But I'd advise you to be careful with their weapons. You never know what they might have included in the software."

She led him out of the building, then escorted him towards the gates. "Have a good one," she said, as they stopped and waited for the guards to open the barricades. "And try not to get caught before the planet is occupied."

"Thanks," Rzeminski said, dryly. He smiled at her. "Can I tell you something?"

Jasmine nodded.

"You were promoted too far, too fast," Rzeminski said. "I'd bet you're at your best in small-unit actions – most Marines are. But large-scale operations are a little different. You let me lead you by the nose more than once."

Jasmine gritted her teeth in frustration, but said nothing. He was right.

"Goodbye," Rzeminski said.

Jasmine watched him walk away from the spaceport, then turned and strode back towards her office. Despite her glib words, she knew she might well have destroyed her career by letting him go. But she did have wide authority and besides, there were few other alternatives. Admiral Singh, she knew, wouldn't have shown him mercy when she occupied the planet, if he'd still been a prisoner.

Absently, she wondered just how Admiral Singh had linked up with Wolfbane and become a commander in their navy. Perhaps she'd escaped Corinthian with enough ships to make her a major player, despite her non-existent supply base. Or perhaps she was the best Governor Brown had been able to find. She *had* managed to take and hold a small empire of her own until Jasmine had taken it from her, through subversion and a careful plan to hit her at her weakest point. And it had worked.

And if she catches you now, she thought coldly, *she will kill you.*

Michael looked up as she entered the office. "I've got several units on the way back from the Zone," he said, "but others are taking fire from enemy positions. They're having to cut their way through."

"Understood," Jasmine said. "Keep me informed."

She shook her head. There was nothing she could do, save wait and pray she managed to get enough men out before Admiral Singh entered orbit. After that...she'd have to make a choice between going underground on a planet that largely hated the CEF or surrendering to Admiral Singh. And *that* wouldn't be a pleasant experience at all.

Let's hope Mandy manages to deter her, she thought. *Even a day's delay would be enough to get everyone out of the trap.*

―――――

"Sniper!"

"I see the bastard," Thomas snapped, as he ducked behind an armoured car. The insurgents either hadn't realised the CEF was retreating or were intent on hounding them as much as possible. They'd been hit by snipers, IEDs and even a rush of fighters that had been swiftly wiped out. "I'll get him."

He took aim as the sniper revealed himself again and fired, once. The body fell from the rooftop and landed somewhere in the alleyway. He gritted his teeth as he swept the weapon over the rest of the houses, looking for targets, but found nothing. The local civilians, he hoped, were either keeping their heads down or had had the common sense to evacuate the entire area.

We should have moved them into the DP camps, he thought. But the last thing he'd heard from the camps had claimed that there were riots in three of them, along with one of the POW camps. The guards had had to seal the fences and then start their own trek towards the spaceport. *Or maybe we should just have flattened the Zone from orbit.*

He jumped back into the AFV as the driver gunned the engine, sending it rushing forward at high speed. The handheld drone he'd launched showed no sign of anything large enough to bar their way, as far as he could tell, but it hadn't spotted the sniper either. But at least they could rush through any other sniper attacks, rather than having to slow down to deal with them.

His communicator buzzed. "IED strike; AFV 34," it said. "Vehicle disabled; I say again, vehicle disabled."

Thomas swallowed the vilest curse he knew. The front line – what had once been an organised front line – was dissolving into absolute chaos. Some local units had maintained their discipline, others had fragmented into individuals or simply started firing into the Zone, as if they wanted to crush the insurgents before Wolfbane's forces arrived. The shattered communications net didn't help; Thomas had tried to contact one unit, only to be told he didn't have the right communications codes and if he tried to contact them again he would be fired upon. Judging from the other comments on the radio, several units *had* ended up firing on other friendly units.

Friendly fire isn't, he reminded himself.

He keyed his communicator, then glanced at a map. "Abandon the vehicle," he ordered. Normally, he would have preferred to recover the AFV – the vehicles were designed to be cannibalised, if they couldn't be repaired – but there was no time. "Get out of the area ASAP."

He rubbed his forehead as he heard the acknowledgements from the vehicle's crew. If there had been time to do some proper planning...but there hadn't been any time, not really. Instead of an orderly withdrawal, they were heading out along roads that might well be mined, operating in scattered units rather than as a group. Hell, if they kept spreading out, they'd be completely isolated soon enough. And then they'd be overrun piece by piece.

The AFV lurched to a halt as a group of insurgents appeared ahead of them, firing rifles towards the armoured vehicle. Its gunners returned fire with machine guns, no longer bothering to conserve ammunition; the insurgents, caught by the bullets, were literally ripped apart into chunks of bloody flesh. Behind them, one of their fellows launched an RPG, which – thankfully – went wide of its intended target.

"Contact the spaceport," Thomas ordered, grimly. They would be delayed...and the delays would keep mounting up until it was too late. "Give them our revised ETA."

———

Mustapha Wellington hadn't found it hard to blend into Thule's society. Unlike the world of his birth, Thule prided itself on being cosmopolitan; as long as someone was prepared to work they were more than welcome. There were so many different faces – natural faces as well as the results of bioengineering – that it was quite hard to be actually *noticed*. He'd kept his head down, worked as a waiter in a criminal-run dive and kept himself in readiness for the moment the call arrived.

When it did, he walked out on his employer and returned to his apartment, where he recovered the HVM from the hidden compartment under the floorboards. Keeping it so close had been a risk, particularly since the local forces had begun random sweeps for weapons, but there hadn't been anywhere else he'd cared to hide it. A HVM in usable condition would be worth enough credits to his employers to encourage them to take it from him, perhaps putting a knife in his back if he dared to complain. But no one apart from him knew that it was there.

He took the weapon and walked up the stairs to the rooftop. The manager had padlocked it closed before leaving the building years ago, but a swift kick got rid of it in a hurry. Smiling at what some people considered secure, he stepped out onto the rooftop and looked towards the spaceport. The sound of gunfire in the distance – and the explosions from a handful of mortar shells – was almost drowned out by the sound of shuttles landing and taking off from the spaceport. Mustapha allowed his smile to widen as he watched another shuttle lift off, then took aim before activating the seeker head. As soon as it had locked on, he pulled the trigger, launched the missile and started to run.

Behind him, a shuttle staggered, then exploded in midair.

———

"Shuttle Twelve is gone," Michael said. "They just blew her out of the sky."

"Understood," Jasmine said. Cold ice lodged itself in her heart. "Order the other shuttles to deploy decoys constantly, then contact the QRF and tell them to sweep the area."

She looked down at the map, knowing it was a waste of time. The area was just too large to sweep without more men than she had, which meant that there was no way she could guarantee that there weren't more HVMs lurking nearby. And if they were...each shuttle she lost not only killed a number of soldiers – she promised herself she'd mourn later – but crippled her ability to move more troops up to orbit.

"Keep moving the troops as fast as you can," she ordered. "And then contact the counter-battery units. I want a maximum fire pattern on the source of any further missiles or shells."

Michael looked shocked – a maximum fire pattern would almost certainly guarantee civilian causalities – but nodded and sent the message.

We're going to need to rethink all of our procedures, she thought, grimly. *We rarely had to land shuttles in a hot zone while we fought for the Empire.*

She looked over at Michael and sighed. He'd been born on Avalon; he didn't have the assumptions she'd developed over her years of fighting for the Empire. And he'd done very well in his previous battles, even though he'd started young.

"Assign yourself to the next shuttle," she said. Avalon would need him, perhaps, more than it needed her. "And get your ass out of here."

Michael stared at her. "I should stay..."

"That's an order," Jasmine said. "You're going to be needed in the future."

Gudrun kept her head down as she ran towards the edge of the Zone. The sheer level of devastation stunned her; buildings that had once housed dozens of family members had been shattered, bodies lay everywhere to mark where the movement and the invaders had fought for control of bare metres of ground. All the old landmarks had been utterly destroyed. The only way to tell she'd moved out of the Zone was when she started encountering intact buildings once again, even though they were all badly damaged.

She paused long enough to catch her breath, then resumed running. Marcy's message had been far from encouraging, but it was all she had. If she made it to a specific location in time, she would be evacuated along with her family. But if she failed to reach it, she would be left behind. She'd heard, as she'd walked out of the hospital, that a powerful fleet had entered the star system. The Commonwealth was running and...someone new had arrived.

"Hey," a voice shouted. "Stop!"

Gudrun glanced back and cursed, out loud. A group of soldiers wearing local uniforms were waving to her, bottles of alcohol in their hands. Gudrun blanched as she saw their expressions, realising that they had rape on their minds. She turned and fled as fast as she could, drawing on reserves of strength she didn't know she had. The soldiers gave chase, catcalling as they followed her, promises of what they would do once they caught her. Somehow, Gudrun kept running, leaving them behind until she tripped over something on the road.

She hit the ground hard enough to stun her. Desperately, she tried to scramble to her feet, but it was too late. One of the soldiers landed on top of her, holding her down, as his comrade grabbed her arms and wrenched them forward. Moments later, they had her on her back and started to pull at her clothes. Gudrun kicked out, but missed them completely.

Two shots rang out. The soldiers fell on top of her. Gudrun managed, somehow, to push them aside and sit upright. A man – a very familiar man – was standing there, holding a pistol.

"Well," Rzeminski said. "What are you doing here?"

Gudrun swallowed and tried to think of an answer. But what could she say? The movement wasn't much kinder to deserters than it was to traitors. And she was, technically speaking, both.

"Not that it matters," the movement's leader said. He helped her to her feet, then smiled. "I think it's time we went into hiding, don't you?"

CHAPTER THIRTY-SEVEN

> Put simply, the aggressors were already armed to the teeth. They'd had years, prior to the start of their grand crusade, to secure all the weapons they needed. (They'd also shipped in various production machines, allowing them to keep pace with demand for both weapons and ammunition.) The net result of the embargo was to disarm the victims of aggression, while allowing the actual aggressors free reign. Also unsurprisingly, the aggressors managed to make vast gains in a relatively short space of time.
> - Professor Leo Caesius, *War in a time of 'Peace:' The Empire's Forgotten Military History*

"The enemy fleet is leaving orbit, Admiral."

Rani nodded, unsurprised. It *was* their smartest move, although she had yet to determine if the Commonwealth ships intended to try to delay her or simply cut and run. Either one would be defensible, although she had no idea what sort of commanding officer would deny himself a long-range engagement. It was their best chance of inflicting some kind of damage, without risking total disaster in a short-range battle.

"Monitor their course," she ordered. "And launch an additional flight of drones."

She watched as more data started to flow into her display. The Commonwealth's new class of cruisers seemed to have an alarmingly high acceleration rate, higher than anything their size within the Empire. It was actually quite impressive, she decided, as the drones started to report back. They must have discovered some way to modify the drive chambers, perhaps even to produce newer and improved drive systems. It boded ill for the future.

Rani was a military officer. She had little time for theorists who promised revolutionary scientific developments, provided their pet projects were funded without intensive supervision. When she'd been the ruler of Corinthian, she'd insisted that development be concentrated on improving current technology. Had the Commonwealth done the same, she wondered, or had they come up with something completely new? There was no way to know.

"Special orders," she said, softly. "If possible, I want one of those modern cruisers disabled for capture."

"Understood," the tactical officer said.

Rani had to smile at the enthusiasm in his voice. Disabling a starship wasn't easy – and the Commonwealth would presumably have installed a self-destruct system in their cruisers, one capable of vaporising the entire ship if it seemed likely she would fall into hostile hands. But there was no alternative. If they captured such a cruiser largely intact, they could start to unlock its secrets without having to begin from scratch.

She settled back to watch as the Commonwealth ships arced around, then started to advance towards her fleet. It was to be a long-range engagement then, rather than an attempt to block her way towards the planet. Somehow, she wasn't too surprised. Normally, the planet's defences would have made her a tough customer. Now, with the chaos virus running through its systems, every defence station would be operating on its own.

You'd think they'd take precautions against their own tactics, she sneered, mentally. *Who says you can't steal ideas from your enemies?*

Thule wasn't a Commonwealth world at the time, her own thoughts answered her. *They may not have realised the implications of Corinthian's fall.*

The tactical officer looked up from his display. "Admiral, they're sweeping us with tactical sensors," he said. "But they're still out of engagement range."

Known engagement range, Rani knew. Had the Commonwealth designed a long-range missile as well as fast cruisers? It was possible… but unless they'd developed a completely revolutionary form of drive technology, they'd only make it easier for her point defence crews to track and destroy the missiles before they reached her fleet. Or were they merely trying to make sure all of her ships had been detected? They were presumably wondering what had happened to the other two battleships. Or, for that matter, the rest of the fleet they'd seen at Titlark.

"Sweep them in return," she ordered. There was no point in trying to hide anything, not now. "And bring up our point defence."

She smiled, coldly. The first major space battle for nearly a thousand years...and she was one of the commanders. Did her opponent think the same way, she wondered, or was she more focused on her mission? Or was she inexperienced enough to panic, when the shit hit the fan? Or...

Smiling, she watched as the two fleets converged.

"Weapons range in two minutes," the tactical officer said.

Mandy felt an odd little pit in her stomach as she watched Admiral Singh's fleet. The message had confirmed the enemy commander's identity beyond all doubt, worrying her more than she cared to admit. Like Jasmine, she'd researched Admiral Singh thoroughly after the first encounter and little of what they'd found had been good. Admiral Singh had been a skilled officer who'd once beaten a scripted exercise she'd been supposed to lose. It had taken Mandy some time to understand that Singh was competitive, competitive enough to risk damaging her career by not following the script.

And she won't be dependent on the same basic tactics, Jasmine had said, dryly. *She will innovate when necessary.*

Mandy sighed, inwardly. There seemed little room for innovation now, as far as she could tell...but could Admiral Singh see opportunities Mandy had missed? The equation was very simple; the fleet would enter orbit in less than an hour, unless Mandy managed to delay her for a few hours. But if she placed herself between the planet and the oncoming fleet, she'd be squashed flat and destroyed. The only way to win was to hope that Admiral Singh found them sufficiently irritating, enough to force her to change course and engage the fleet.

If she does that, Mandy thought, *I can lead her on a wild snipe chase indefinitely.*

As far as her analysts could tell, Admiral Singh's fleet was in excellent condition, but there didn't seem to have been any non-standard modifications. Mandy wasn't surprised – Avalon's embrace of modifications had come from its decidedly non-standard crews and the alliance with the Trade Federation – yet it still struck her as odd. *Her* ships were fast enough to decide the time and place of an engagement, as long as Admiral Singh didn't isolate a target the Commonwealth Navy *had* to defend. But the advantage wouldn't last indefinitely.

"Deploy missile racks," she ordered, as the range closed sharply. "Prepare to engage the enemy."

Admiral Singh showed no signs of being worried as Mandy's fleet closed in...but then, she didn't have to do anything. All she had to do was wait while Mandy waltzed into weapons range. And *that* wouldn't take very long at all.

"Missiles locked and ready," the tactical officer said.

There was a bleep from the display. The fleets were now within missile range of one another.

"Fire," Mandy ordered.

Seconds later, *Sword* fired the first broadside of the Commonwealth-Wolfbane War.

———

"Missile separation," the tactical officer snapped. "Missile separation!"

"Point defence is to engage the enemy," Rani said. "Analysis?"

"Missiles do not appear to have a higher acceleration rate than models designed prior to the Empire's fall," the analyst reported. "There appear to be minor improvements to the ECM warheads."

Rani smiled. The Empire's standard warheads had been designed over five hundred years ago and hadn't been replaced since then. Rani had been told, back at the Academy, that the warheads were perfect, but she suspected the stagnation had something to do with the corporation that had designed the missiles using its influence to ensure that no one else managed to get into the missile-production business. But maybe they'd been right after all.

Or maybe they haven't sent improved missiles to this system, her thoughts mocked her. *What if you're wrong?*

She studied the missile throw weight for a long moment, then nodded. It looked as though the Commonwealth Navy was using external racks, despite the risks. But then, if what she'd heard about the Commonwealth was true, there would be fewer risks for an interstellar power that taught its technicians how to actually *think*. They'd be able to make non-standard repairs if necessary. Wolfbane wasn't in that league yet, but it was getting there.

"Return fire," she ordered. The enemy did have yet another advantage – they could get out of missile range fairly easily – but there was no real alternative once again. "And stagger our firing sequence."

The enemy missiles closed in on her ships, switching their ECM patterns to make it harder for her point defence to track them. But, one by one, they started to die as the point defence picked them off, hacking them out of space. Only a handful of missiles made it through the point defence to detonate, sending ravening beams of nuclear fire against her gravity shields.

"*Gamma* has been hit," the tactical officer reported. "Her crew reports minor damage to her lower sections."

Rani smiled. If the Commonwealth Navy wanted to do more damage, after shooting off their external racks, they'd have to come closer. Much closer. And she would be waiting.

Mandy silently watched as her point defence hacked through the waves of incoming missiles, noting how Singh seemed to have decided to stagger her launches. It didn't quite make sense, something that nagged at her mind. Was Singh testing her, mocking her or did she have something very nasty up her sleeves?

"Two direct hits on *Portsmouth*," the tactical officer reported. "The shields took the brunt of the blasts."

"Good," Mandy said. But she couldn't help wondering what Singh's tactical officers would make of it. The force shields weren't as obvious as gravity shields, yet it would be obvious that *something* had interdicted the bomb-pumped lasers. "And her generators?"

"Stable, for now," the tactical officer said. "But several more hits would probably burn them out completely."

Mandy nodded, thinking hard. Should she close the range...or simply fire at Singh's ships at extreme range, knowing it was unlikely that she would score any hits?

"Take us around them," she ordered, finally. "Get us into a position where we can target the troop transports."

Rani kept her face very still as she studied the odd sensor reports. She knew, better than anyone else, just how easy it was to spoof sensors at long range. Hell, the Commonwealth had spoofed *her* sensors before, making her think an entire fleet was bearing down on her. But now...what had they done?

"It looks as though they might have improved the gravity shields," the analyst said, reluctantly. "The blasts should have burned into that ship's hull."

"Maybe," Rani said. If someone had solved the age-old problem of bending a gravity shield around a starship, without crippling the starship's ability to manoeuvre and fight, the war was very likely to be short and end badly. Nothing, not even a bomb-pumped laser, could burn through a gravity shield. "But it can't be something like that, can it?"

She knew, beyond a shadow of a doubt, what *she* would have done if her starships had been wrapped in invincible gravity shields. It would have been easy to close the range and tear the enemy ships apart, while they lashed out helplessly. But the Commonwealth ships weren't doing anything of the sort, which meant they were far from invincible. Of that, she was very sure.

"Enemy fleet altering course," the tactical officer reported. "Moving out of weapons range."

No, Rani thought, as the enemy course became clear. *They're going for the transports.*

"Move our ships to cover the transports," she ordered. "But keep us on course towards Thule."

The enemy wanted to delay her. She was damned if she was letting their fleet slow her more than strictly necessary. And, unless they wanted to close the range, she didn't have to slow her fleet at all.

And there would be time, later, to figure out what they'd done to protect their ships.

Mandy gritted her teeth as the enemy ships altered their position, careful to keep a number of ships between her and their troop transports. It wasn't a bad tactic at all, she knew, and it would serve its purpose very well. And it would prevent her from slowing the enemy fleet enough to make a difference.

She glanced at the live feed from Thule and swore, inwardly. Jasmine's last update had told her that several shuttles had come under attack, crippling their ability to get troops to orbit and board the transports. Two-thirds of the CEF were in serious danger of being destroyed or captured in the opening moves of the war, yet there was nothing she could do. If she closed to a range that would allow her to score hits, she knew, the enemy would be able to score hits on *her*. And their advantage in launchers would prove decisive.

This isn't over, she thought. But she knew the battle couldn't go much further.

"Twenty minutes to orbit," the helmsman said.

Mandy took a long breath. "Order the transports to break orbit at the ten minute mark," she said. Given their relative speed compared to the enemy warships, even that was pushing it. If Admiral Singh gave chase after that, Mandy would be practically *forced* into a short-range engagement just to give the troop transports a chance to escape. "And remind them, should they feel inclined to object, that it is an *order*."

Bitter hatred welled up in her breast as she contemplated her actions. She was abandoning her best friend, the woman she had grown to look up to as an older sister, the woman who had made her what she was today. Jasmine would understand, she knew, but somehow that was no consolation. It only made it worse.

"And then break contact completely," she added. "Take us back to the planet, best possible speed."

———

"Enemy fleet is withdrawing," the tactical officer said.

Rani smiled. The enemy fleet definitely had improved drive units, she decided, as the range opened rapidly. There was no way she could catch them if they decided to run. Heading back to the planet was an interesting choice…did they intend to scatter mines in her path or were they merely planning to escort their troopships away from Thule? Either one would be more than a little annoying.

She considered, briefly, trying to run down the troopships. Thule wouldn't be going anywhere, after all. But the situation on the ground, according to her agents, was chaotic, with several different factions battling for supremacy. If they didn't manage to land quickly, everything they needed from Thule would be destroyed in the civil war. It was worth allowing the troopships to leave, she decided, if it meant she captured Thule.

"Contact General Haverford," she ordered. "Have him prepare the troops for immediate landing…and warn him they might well be jumping into a hot zone."

———

"Move it," Buckley snapped. "Now!"

Michael wanted to hesitate as the shuttle docked with the troopship, but the Marine – his face dark with fury – was too intimidating. He hurried through the airlock and into the starship, where a handful of crewmen were hastily directing the refugees to their sleeping compartments. The interior of the ship seemed to have turned into a madhouse.

The entire ship shuddered as the drive came to life, then he felt a faint sensation that told him the ship was underway. Several people started cursing out loud, or shouting angry rebukes at the bulkheads, protesting that they were abandoning everyone on the planet. But it made no difference. By the time Joe Buckley crashed through the compartment, bellowing for silence in a tone that dared anyone to challenge him, the truth had sunk in.

Michael sat down, leaning against a bulkhead, and pulled his terminal out of his pocket. It still had an automatic link to the Commonwealth datanet, allowing him to see everything that wasn't marked classified. The enemy fleet was advancing towards the planet, threatening to overrun the transports as well as the planet's high orbitals. And when they took control of the orbitals...

He shuddered, thinking of the Brigadier. She was stuck down there, along with two-thirds of the men under her command. They would soon be prisoners – or dead. The last reports Michael had heard, as he'd waited to board the shuttles, had said that the streets were dissolving into chaos. By the time someone restored order, anyone wearing a CEF uniform would probably be lynched by the mob.

Switching the terminal off, he closed his eyes. There was nothing he could do now, but wait and hope they made it out of the system. The war wouldn't be won or lost here, he knew; they'd have to hope and pray the Commonwealth managed to recover from the surprise and fight back. One day, he promised himself, they would attack Wolfbane itself. Until then, they could do nothing, but fight.

"Enemy troopships are leaving orbit," the tactical officer said. "Should we give chase?"

"No," Rani said. The planet was the most important prize, by far. "Prepare to clear the planetary defences."

She settled back in her command chair and watched, grimly, as they slipped into engagement range. The defences were tough, even without their communications networks, but her fleet had the firepower to remove them without serious risk to her ships. Behind the fleet, the troops were already preparing to land.

"Fire as soon as we enter range," she ordered. "Sweep the skies clear of all hostile material, then launch boarding parties to the industrial nodes. I want them all under our control within the hour. Take prisoners if possible; remember, we need these people. Anyone who harms them without permission will end up breathing hard vacuum."

She smiled. They *did* need these people...and if they wound up seeing Rani as their saviour, so much the better. Loyalty was always welcome. And besides, her former allies on the planet below were expendable.

Moments later, the fleet opened fire.

CHAPTER
THIRTY-EIGHT

The third and final course attempted by the social scientists, after reports of increasingly bloody slaughter made their way to Earth, was to insist on a major intervention by the Imperial Army. On the face of it, the combination of superior technology and orbital fire support should have made it a fairly easy operation for the Imperial Army. However, there were several problems.

First, every faction now regarded the outsiders as enemies. The aggressors wished to continue their crusade until the destruction of their rivals. Their rivals, on the other hand, saw the imperials as the ones who had arranged for them to be disarmed. The net result was a series of increasingly bloody encounters between locals (of all stripes) and the off-world forces.
- Professor Leo Caesius, *War in a time of 'Peace:'*
The Empire's Forgotten Military History

"They're engaging the orbital defences now."

Jasmine nodded as she stepped outside, looking up towards the darkening sky. Flashes of light could be seen high overhead, followed by trails of fire as pieces of debris fell into the planet's atmosphere and started to burn up. Admiral Singh's forces were launching kinetic projectiles towards the unmanned platforms, while firing missiles at the manned orbital defence stations. With their datanets contaminated and every defence station forced back on its own resources, the end could not be long delayed.

"Start dispersing the remaining troops," she ordered. The spaceport would be a primary target the moment the attacking fleet got into range to hit the planet with precision weapons. "And then prime the computer cores for self-destruct."

She thought, briefly, about the insurgent leader. Had releasing him been a wise decision – or a mistake? She would find out in time, she assumed. Or she would die when Admiral Singh ranged in on the planet. Mandy's ships were already well out of her range, escorting the transports away from Thule. At least something would be saved from the growing disaster.

"Understood," her new assistant said.

Jasmine sighed, inwardly. On any other Commonwealth world, her troops could disperse into the countryside and continue the war, but Thule would be extremely hostile territory for them. A smart enemy commander wouldn't hesitate to use the locals against the CEF, offering all sorts of incentives to win hearts and minds. Hell, given how tightly Wolfbane had worked with the local insurgency, they already had enough ties to ensure their troops received local knowledge…at least until the sheen wore off. But it wouldn't be quick enough to save the CEF. They were in the very definition of an untenable situation.

And Admiral Singh will want revenge, she thought. Did Admiral Singh know who Jasmine was…and what she'd done on Corinthian? She'd been a prisoner for a few scant hours, more than long enough for a DNA sample to be taken. Marine records were generally classified, unavailable to officers outside the Corps, but it might not matter. Jasmine's DNA could easily have fallen into the Admiral's hands. She might be willing to treat the others as legitimate POWs, yet she might make a special exception for Jasmine. Losing a pocket star empire to a handful of Marines had to be irritating.

She sucked in her breath, watching the live feed from orbit. One by one, the orbital defences were being blown out of the sky.

It wouldn't be long now.

———

"Shuttles dispatched," the operations officer said. "There's no sign of weapons on the industrial nodes."

Rani nodded. She would have been surprised if there were, even in a system that had thrown so many of its tax credits at the local defence establishment. Thule's industrial network was its pride and joy; the planet's defence planners wouldn't want to turn the industrial stations into targets, not when they could use the stations to bargain for better treatment. They'd get it too, she knew, as long as it suited her to treat the locals well. And, if they behaved, they would *always* be treated well.

She watched, dispassionately, as a hail of missiles tore a large orbital defence platform apart, sending pieces of debris flying in all directions. Orbital space would be a minor hazard for a while, part of her mind noted, although it wouldn't last long. The chunks of debris that didn't fall into the planet's atmosphere would be vaporised by the starships or simply knocked out of orbit. It wasn't as if there were enough of them to do serious damage to the planet's ecosystem, not like there had been in orbit around Earth. If half the stories were true, every asteroid in Earth orbit had fallen on the planet below. Earth wouldn't just have been depopulated, it would have been pulverised beyond reason.

Good, Rani thought. She'd worked her way up the ranks, without taking advantage of her good looks and charm. If only ten percent of the population of Earth had shown themselves ready to work to save their world, the Empire would never have fallen. *Let us survive without the worthless parasites.*

"Send the surrender demand," she ordered, looking over at the communications officer. "And repeat it until we have secured complete control of the high orbitals."

"Aye, Admiral," the communications officer said.

Rani smiled. The ground-based stations appeared to have been badly hit by the insurgents or her commando squads. They were already at a major disadvantage, being at the bottom of a planetary gravity well, but they could still have posed a problem. But not if they were already hammered long before her fleet entered orbit. Hopefully, enough remained to allow her troops to secure them, without forcing her to bombard them from orbit. Not, in the end, that it would make any difference. Thule was doomed. The only question was just how badly battered the world would be when their time ran out.

"The commandos have secured the orbital stations," the operations officer reported. "They're reporting back now, Admiral; the locals have surrendered rather than fight."

"Remind them to treat the locals gently," Rani said. She cared little for the great mass of unemployed on the planet below, but trained technicians were always useful. "I'll have the head of anyone who mistreats one of them without extremely good cause."

"Aye, Admiral," the operations officer said.

Rani smiled. "Is there any response to our surrender demands?"

"Negative," the communications officer said. "I'm trying to track their communications, but it's proving impossible. I don't think there's anyone left in command on the planet below."

The plan worked too well, Rani thought, then laughed at herself inwardly. Not being able to demand a formal surrender from the planet paled compared to losing one's planet to an outside occupation force. The problems she was facing were the problems of *victory*. She could guess the horror and despair gripping the remaining planetary defenders, defenders who knew they could do nothing to stop her taking Thule. All they could do was bleed her a little.

"Contact General Haverford," she ordered. "Inform him that he has permission to land his advance forces."

Thomas looked around Riverside and shuddered, inwardly. It looked far more civilised than the Zone, even though most of the houses were still quite small. They had gardens, parks and even a library, as well as a healthy degree of separation from their neighbours. It was easy to understand that the people who lived in Riverside were the ones who had jobs and employment, the ones who had survived despite the economic crash...and the ones who had silently supported the local government's refusal to find a compromise.

There were hardly any civilians in sight. Thomas hoped that meant they were keeping their heads down, although he wouldn't have put money on their chances if – when – the mobs started rampaging through

Riverside. The radio channels were a non-stop litany of horror, an endless series of reports of fighting right across the giant city. No one was in command, it seemed, on either side. The insurgents they'd fought were pushing out of the Zone, while police and military units fought hopeless battles for survival.

"Enemy fleet launching shuttles," a voice said, through his radio. "I say again, enemy fleet launching shuttles."

Thomas sighed, considering his options. Nearly two hundred men had made it to Riverside and dispersed through the district, abandoning their vehicles in the middle of one of the giant parks. They'd be targeted from orbit, Thomas knew, as soon as the enemy fleet took the high orbitals. He would be very disappointed with the enemy commanders if they wasted time trying to capture the simplistic vehicles instead of destroying them.

But what were they going to do?

He'd been in bad spots before. Serving in the Marines during the last days of the Empire had involved moving from bad spot to bad spot, pissing on fires long enough to put them out and declare victory before moving to the next one. But this was different. Offhand, had there *ever* been an Imperial unit in such a dire position in the last thousand years? The Empire normally controlled space so carefully that outright defeat was rarely a possibility.

His men could fight, when – if – the shuttles landed in Asgard. Hell, they had a handful of HVMs they could use, giving Wolfbane a taste of their own medicine. But then...they'd be obliterated, along with the civilians in the district. It crossed his mind that that wouldn't be a bad outcome, a thought he angrily dismissed. Maybe it would help the Commonwealth if trained and skilled manpower were to die, rather than fall into Wolfbane's hands, but it wasn't something he could countenance. If they started thinking like that, they might as well start depopulating whole planets. And no one would win such a war, apart from the RockRats. They'd probably be relieved.

He passed the word to his men, then waited. It was all they could do.

Jasmine looked down at the portable terminal, then up at the operator. "They're not coming near the spaceport?"

"Doesn't look like it," the operator said. He looked nervous, but pressed on anyway. "As far as I can tell, half of their shuttles are heading for the centre of the city and the other half are heading for Riverside. They're dropping decoys and flares everywhere, though."

"I see," Jasmine said. It made a certain kind of sense; secure the remains of the planet's government and the most valuable sections of the population, then deal with everything else. At least they weren't dropping Marines out of orbit onto the city, she noted; Wolfbane didn't seem to have any trained Marines, at least no one comparable to the Terran Marines. Or maybe they were just holding them in reserve. "Warn the locals, if possible."

She shook her head, inwardly. The local defence network had fallen apart, completely. It was unlikely that any resistance could be organised, at least in time to matter. Besides, the invaders would have orbital fire support to clear any large obstacles out of their way. She was mildly surprised they hadn't destroyed the spaceport already, along with her command post. Did they think the command post had already been destroyed?

"That's another flight of shuttles," the operator added. "I think these are heading for the edge of the city."

Jasmine nodded, wordlessly. In the distance, she could hear shuttles dropping through the planet's atmosphere, heading towards their targets. There was a flash of light in the distance, followed by a fireball that billowed up into the darkening sky and slowly faded away to nothingness. She didn't need the operator to tell her that the KEW had struck the remains of one of the major military garrisons in the city. Two more died in quick succession, obliterating what remained of the military infrastructure. The local troops – all that was left of them – were doomed.

In an entertainment flick, she knew, the Marines would come riding to the rescue at the last possible moment. Or, if the producers preferred the Imperial Navy, a large battlefleet would appear out of nowhere and save the planet from certain destruction. But there would be no miracle, Jasmine knew; they rarely happened in the real universe. And, even though Mandy was a competent officer, she had strict orders to withdraw rather than engage superior forces and risk losing her fleet. There was no hope of rescue.

And the end could not be long delayed.

―――――

General Mark Haverford distrusted Admiral Singh more than he cared to admit. Governor Brown might have been a corporate hack, rather than a military officer, but Mark knew that he'd done an excellent job of holding the Wolfbane Sector together after the Fall of Earth, when chaos had threatened to tear them all apart. He might not have been someone Mark would have expected to respect, yet he'd saved the sector from chaos. Admiral Singh, on the other hand, had come begging for succour and somehow parlayed a handful of starships into a position of considerable power. Mark suspected she was ambitious enough to do whatever it took to gain supreme power.

But he pushed his concerns aside as the shuttle dropped through the planet's atmosphere and fell towards the centre of the city. The advance elements were already on the ground and reporting minimal resistance, which wasn't entirely surprising. Between the shock of commando assaults in their own city and the massive deployment to the Zone, the enemy troops were definitely caught out of place. There would be no time to recover before his forces held all of their targets and deployed to suppress resistance.

The shuttle lurched, then hit the ground with a loud crash. Mark pulled himself from his chair as soon as the craft stopped shaking, then followed his troops towards the hatch and out onto the local ground. The smell struck him as soon as he took his first breath – every planet had its own smell – but he ignored it as he looked around. Hundreds of years of work had been reduced to piles of rubble.

He smiled, darkly. The first major planetary invasion of the post-Empire era and it was going according to plan. His troops had already fanned out, securing the remains of the central government, while a number of prisoners were held firmly in the middle of one of the grand parks. There was a dull roar behind him as the shuttle took off, clawing frantically for the sky before an isolated enemy unit could try to fire an HVM at it. Mark allowed his smile to grow wider as he strode over to the newly-established command post. The enemy were so badly hammered that they couldn't even mount a counterattack in the heart of their own city.

"We've secured all of the approaches, sir," Major Hodge reported. "Limited contact with roving bands of soldiers and a handful of armed civilians, but not much else. They didn't even manage to shell our landing zones."

"Let's hope it stays that way," Mark said. A single mortar shell at the worst possible time could do a great deal of damage. The downside of having shattered the enemy command network so thoroughly was that the bands of soldiers wouldn't get any orders to surrender, if the local government had sent any. It was much more likely that any survivors would try to blend into the local population to continue an underground war. "Start transmitting the message for the civilians on all bands. We want them all to hear it."

"Yes, sir," Hodge said.

Mark nodded. The message was simple enough, just informing them that Wolfbane had taken over the city and urging them to remain indoors, where they would be safe. It was hard to know just how well they'd take it – civilians were mindless sheep at the best of times, in his opinion – but Thule *had* been in the grips of a civil war. Surely the civilians would have learned when to keep their heads down by now.

"And then raise the Commonwealth forces," Mark added. There had been a reason the spaceport hadn't been targeted, quite apart from the value of having the facility intact for his own forces. "Tell them...that we wish to discuss their surrender."

Jasmine found herself wrestling with a dilemma that she had never considered, not outside her worst nightmares. On her own, she could and would continue the fight as long as possible, no matter what happened. She had escaped from captivity once before, after all, even though it should have been impossible. But she was responsible for over two thousand soldiers, all of whom would die if she continued the fight. And there were the civilians who were likely to be caught in the middle.

She looked down at the terminal as the message started to repeat itself. It was very simple, she noted sourly, but effective. The Wolfbane commander had pointed out that their position was hopeless, ensuring their rapid destruction if they tried to fight. But if they surrendered, he'd continued, they would be treated as prisoners of war under the pre-Unification Wars conventions. Jasmine had had to look them up; they'd be imprisoned, unless they were traded back to the Commonwealth, but they wouldn't be harmed, interrogated or forced to betray their comrades.

But could Wolfbane be trusted? Her impression of Admiral Singh had been that she was pragmatic, but also completely ruthless. Even if she didn't know who Jasmine was, she might well interrogate Jasmine and her subordinate commanders for intelligence on the Commonwealth. It would kill Jasmine if she tried, Jasmine knew; her implants simply wouldn't let her be interrogated thoroughly. Would Admiral Singh see the benefits of keeping her word, despite the golden intelligence opportunity that would fall into her lap?

She stared down at her hands for a long moment, mentally searching for options. But there were none.

"Contact their commander," she ordered. Her mind felt numb, as if she had passed beyond sensation. "Tell them...tell them that we would like to surrender."

She took a breath. "And then destroy the computer cores," she added. "I don't want even a scrap of useful data to fall into their hands."

CHAPTER
THIRTY-NINE

Second, the social scientists who had established themselves as 'advisors' were still exercising huge influence over the conflict zone. In particular, they put restrictions on how the military could conduct its operations. For example, given the nature of most aggressor armies, a program of targeted assassination aimed at their leaders would have rapidly rendered them headless. Such a program, however, was declared verboten – forbidden.

Third, there was a colossal refugee crisis on the surface of the planet. Imperial Army units found themselves tied down defending the refugee camps, which (at least in the case of the less well-disciplined units) rapidly resulted in mass abuse of the refugees. Worse, the limited manpower available to the operation's commanders forced them to limit their commitments, which meant that refugee camps often became targets for the aggressors.

- Professor Leo Caesius, *War in a time of 'Peace:'*
The Empire's Forgotten Military History

"They surrendered," Rani said. "Excellent news, General."

"Yes, Admiral," General Haverford agreed. His face smiled at her in the display. "With your permission, I will prepare them for immediate transport to the POW facilities."

Rani hesitated. "You don't want to interrogate them?"

"Admiral," Haverford said, "I gave my word as a military officer that they would be treated according to the conventions. And I expect you to honour my word."

Rani kept her face under tight control as she thought rapidly. She wanted – needed – intelligence on whatever contingency plans the Commonwealth had for war with Wolfbane, but the General had neatly pre-empted her from pulling information out of the prisoners. It would be simple enough to appeal to Governor Brown, but he might well take the view that harming prisoners would damage their cause more than gaining information would benefit it. And besides, he had to be wondering about her role in starting the war...

"Very well," she said, tightly. "I expect you to take the utmost care with them, General, while my forces secure the outer system. And if they cause trouble, you are not to hold back."

"Understood," the General said.

His face vanished from the display. Rani glared down at it for a long moment, then looked up at her crew. There was still much work to be done before the system could be declared secure. Besides, the enemy fleet had yet to abandon the system completely.

"Two destroyers are to remain in orbit to provide fire support for the troops on the ground," she ordered. "The remainder of the fleet is to prepare for immediate deployment."

Her crew, sensing her vile mood, hastened to obey.

Rani settled back in her command chair and forced herself to relax. Losing custody of the prisoners was annoying, but it paled in comparison to the sheer scope of her success. The war had begun, Wolfbane had claimed the most important prize along the border...and she'd ensured that there would be no hope of a negotiated peace. Governor Brown would need her more than ever, now that the Commonwealth was hopping mad over the assassination attempt on their leader. Rani had hoped it would kill her – a person who could broker a durable truce between warring factions was clearly not someone to underestimate – but it had worked out well enough. For a plan executed across light years, with so much that could go wrong, it had been damn near perfect.

She smirked. No matter the problems on the planet's surface, there was no escaping the simple truth. The war was halfway to being won. All they had to do was keep up the pressure and the Commonwealth would crumple and collapse into chaos. And then Rani would be well-placed to unseat Brown and take power for herself.

———

Mandy had known it was coming, but it still shocked her.

"She surrendered?"

"Yes, Captain," the communications officer said. "The CEF has surrendered."

Mandy gritted her teeth. At best, Jasmine would go into a POW camp, either on Thule itself or somewhere deeper in Wolfbane's space. There would be little hope of escape, even for a Marine. But at worst, Admiral Singh would know just who was responsible for unseating her from Corinthian and extract a little revenge. Jasmine might be tortured to death...

She pushed the thought aside as she considered her options. There was no point in lurking around the outskirts of the system, not now. Admiral Singh would just keep tight hold of the planet and wait patiently for Mandy's force to run out of supplies. But if she was leaving the system, maybe she could deliver a parting blow before she left.

"Send the transports out of the system," she ordered. "And then alter course towards the gas giant."

She smiled, humourlessly. These days, replacing a cloudscoop wasn't quite the time-consuming task it had been in the days of the Empire, but losing the cloudscoops would still delay Admiral Singh's attempts to turn Thule into a supply base for Wolfbane. It would still take months to rebuild the scoops, even the newer ones. Mandy was reluctant to engage them at all – spacers hated the thought of running out of fuel – but she saw no alternative.

"And broadcast a message across the system," she added. "Anyone who wants to seek refuge from Wolfbane with us is more than welcome."

It was impossible to know just how many people would take her up on the offer, or if she *could* get them all away from the out-system bases and industrial nodes. But any trained manpower was welcome...and it would deny Admiral Singh the chance to make use of them. Besides, if she threatened the cloudscoops...

She shook her head. An officer as experienced as Admiral Singh would know there was no point in trying to save the cloudscoops, not now. There was no hope of distracting her from Thule long enough to slip around her and pick up Jasmine and the CEF. All they could do was take out the scoops and pray it was enough to score a minor victory.

"This is bullshit!"

"As you were," Thomas snapped. He was just as shocked himself, but he had to maintain discipline. "You have your orders, *soldier*."

The soldier looked mutinous. Thomas didn't really blame him. None of them had prepared for the prospect of surrender, not really. Going into Wolfbane's hands would be risky – the promise of good treatment might easily be broken – but the alternative was disobeying orders and trying to go underground. Anywhere else, Thomas would have considered it a viable tactic; after all, as long as it wasn't completely hopeless, Marines were meant to carry on the fight. But here, on Thule, he knew it had become hopeless.

He looked from face to face. "If any of you believe that you can survive on this planet, you may leave now," he added. "But if you understand the real situation, you will stay here with me and wait for them."

The sound of more shuttles echoed through the air as Wolfbane's reinforcements arrived. An eerie quiet had fallen over the city, despite the noise of the shuttles, as if the entire planet was holding its breath. Thomas suspected that most of the civilians were praying that Wolfbane would bring an end to the war, if only by providing a common enemy. Or simply by putting the leadership of both sides down. Thule might not have been hopeless, but the actions of both parties to the conflict had made it beyond redemption.

It was a sad end, he told himself, to an inglorious deployment. But they'd been played, right down the line. And maybe, in the end, they would learn from the experience. Maybe the next conflict would be left to burn itself out.

In the distance, he heard the sound of approaching troops. It wouldn't be long now.

Jasmine still felt numb as she watched the two armoured cars and a handful of trucks making their way towards the spaceport's gates. Wolfbane's soldiers didn't look *that* different from her own, she noted, although there were definite hints that they hadn't fought a major engagement before landing on Thule. It wasn't something she could put into words, just a sense that they were...less aware of their surroundings than they should have been. But in the end, it didn't matter.

"Open the gates," she ordered, quietly.

The armoured cars passed through the gate and came to a halt, while the trucks stopped outside and began to disgorge troops. They fanned out, holding their weapons with an easy professionalism that would have been impressive under other circumstances, but was downright worrying now. Not, she thought with a flicker of humour, that it was likely to matter. She probably wouldn't see Avalon again.

She'd been conditioned, in Boot Camp and then the Slaughterhouse, never to give up. She was psychologically incapable of it. No matter what they did to her, she would retain her grim determination to keep going, but she couldn't think of a way out. And yet there would be one, of that she was sure. Sooner or later, there would be an opportunity to escape.

A man, wearing a combat uniform without any rank badges, strode over to face her. Jasmine was mildly surprised to discover that she didn't recognise him, although she wasn't sure quite why she should have expected differently. They'd gone through the files of officers who might have joined Governor Brown, but there had been literally *billions* of officers and men in the Empire's military. At least it wasn't a known sadist, Jasmine considered, as the man came to a halt in front of her. There were officers she would never have surrendered to, no matter the situation. But would she have preferred an *unknown* sadist?

"Brigadier Yamane," the newcomer said. "I am General Haverford."

Jasmine nodded, not trusting herself to speak.

"On behalf of Wolfbane, I accept your surrender," the General continued. Behind him, his men kept spreading through the spaceport. "You have my word that you and your subordinates will be treated well."

"Thank you," Jasmine said, tightly.

She'd failed, she knew. If she'd realised the trap in time, she might have encouraged Colonel Stalker not to deploy the CEF. Or if she'd taken a firmer hand with the local government, she might have been able to talk them into making concessions that would have prevented the civil war from spiralling out of control. Or if she'd prevented the assault on the Zone. Or if...

It wouldn't have mattered, she thought, dully. *The war would have begun with or without our presence on Wolfbane.*

She offered no resistance as the newcomers bound her hands behind her with a plastic tie, then searched her quickly and efficiently. One by one, her men were given the same treatment and then herded into a corner of the spaceport to wait, squatting on the ground. No one objected, at least not out loud. Jasmine was proud of their discipline; they held together, even when they were forced to surrender. But she knew it might be the end of the line for all of them.

It was nearly an hour before they were escorted onto a shuttle and launched into space. Jasmine wasn't too surprised. Thule was hardly a safe place for POWs, particularly POWs who might be lynched by the planet's population. They'd probably be shipped to an isolated world and left there. Or, perhaps, dropped onto a penal world. Or would that be too rough a prison for POWs?

It doesn't matter, she told herself. *We are not going to give up. We're going to make it home.*

"The cloudscoops have been destroyed," the tactical officer said.

Mandy nodded. The cloudscoops were fragile and almost completely undefended. A handful of kinetic projectiles had obliterated them, once their crews had boarded shuttles to escape the incoming missiles. She'd invited them to join her fleet, but a third of the crews had refused her offer.

"Take us back towards the Phase Limit," she ordered. They'd been picking up other shuttles, crammed with technicians who refused to work for Wolfbane, but there was no longer any time to delay. "And then set course for Avalon."

She wondered, absently, if she would still be in command of the squadron after they got home. Her father had once pointed out that the Empire had a nasty tendency to blame the messenger for the message, which was at least partly why it had collapsed. Colonel Stalker wasn't like that, Mandy thought, but he wasn't the one making the decisions. God alone knew what the Council would say about the disaster. There was no way the Battle of Wolfbane could be spun as anything other than a defeat.

Wars generally don't start well for the defender, she told herself, firmly. *But we can counterattack – and we will. All we need is time to get back on our feet.*

"They took out the cloudscoops," Rani said.

"Yes, Admiral," the communications officer said. He looked hesitant to say anything else, but kept on anyway. "And they picked up at least three dozen shuttles from the various asteroid facilities."

Rani scowled at the display. The further they were from the Commonwealth ships, the longer it took to track their activities. It was simple enough to imagine her ships being forced to give chase, then outflanked as the Commonwealth ships raced around her fleet and then slip into bombardment range of the planet. They wouldn't have time to recover their people – half of them were already being shipped to the transports that would take them to the POW camps – but they could still inflict colossal damage. And there would be nothing she could do.

"Dispatch two cruisers to track their passage, but hold the rest of the fleet," she ordered, bitterly. They might have captured the planet itself, yet losing the cloudscoops and technicians would hurt. "And then start deploying the automated weapons platforms."

She couldn't keep the fleet at Thule indefinitely, she knew. Wolfbane did have an advantage in hull numbers, but the Commonwealth's technology might well even the balance. They'd have to leave soon, within days, just to strike deeper into the Commonwealth before Governor Brown tried to order them to consolidate their gains. And yet...she didn't dare leave the planet completely uncovered. After the assassination attempt, it was unlikely that a Commonwealth officer would hesitate to bombard their positions on the planet's surface.

But it didn't matter, she told herself. Thule was *hers*. She'd won.

And, she added in the privacy of her own mind, it was only the beginning.

The safehouse was right on the edge of Asgard, the perfect position – once upon a time – for meetings between the urban and rural divisions of the movement. Now, Pete decided, it might well have turned into a trap. Wolfbane's forces had landed on the outskirts of the city and sealed the roads, preventing the population from fleeing out into the countryside. He was trapped too, at least until darkness fell completely.

He glowered at the radio. There had been nothing, but Wolfbane broadcasts since their troops had started to land, each one warning the civilian population to stay in their homes, no matter the situation. It wouldn't be long, Pete suspected, before Wolfbane started registering the civilian population, exercising a degree of control that even the previous government had been unable to mount. And then...somehow, he had a feeling that his former captor had been right. Instead of calling the movement out to take the reins of power, Wolfbane seemed to be securing the city for themselves.

"It's almost dark," Gudrun said, from where she was seated on the couch. She'd barely spoken a word since he'd saved her life, just stared at him. Pete couldn't help wondering if she thought he'd saved her purely to take advantage of her himself. Her voice was very soft when she spoke. "Are we going to make a run for it?"

"Yes," Pete said, shortly.

It was easy to see her apprehension. She was a city girl, born and bred; she'd probably never seen the countryside, even when she'd been in school. It was just another reason to dislike the local government, Pete considered; they'd never given the children room to grow. But then, the population was really too large for the ideal balance between urban and rural environments. If it had been up to him, the children would all be brought up in the countryside, where they would learn to take care of themselves. But it was probably logistically impossible.

"Don't worry," he said, finding it in himself to reassure her. There was no point in letting her worry if he could make her feel better. "The countryside isn't full of dangerous animals who want to eat you."

But the most dangerous animal walks on two legs, he thought. Law and order had broken down completely, save where Wolfbane held sway. Parts of the city, even the fairly civilised parts, had collapsed into anarchy. Shops would be looted, women would be raped, men would be killed...all hell was breaking loose. Even where Wolfbane had a strong presence, he suspected, their troops would have real problems keeping order. Soldiers weren't police, after all. The units that had been trained to play peacekeeper had never been very good at serving as the tip of the spear.

He sighed. His wife and children were dead and his planet was occupied. And he had played a role in making that possible, no matter how much he wanted to deny it. In hindsight, it was clear that Wolfbane had done a lot more than just supply weapons. If the reports were true, they'd inserted commando teams who had shattered the chain of command, just as their fleet was entering the system. And they'd taken his planet.

Not for much longer, he told himself. *Whatever it takes, we will evict these people from our world. We will be free.*

CHAPTER FORTY

Unsurprisingly, the entire operation rapidly dissolved into chaos. With the Imperial News Media looking over their shoulder, the operation's commanders were forced to pretend to be in control, which resulted in colossal embarrassment when it was proven, time and time again, that they were nothing of the sort. In the end, the outcome was inevitable. The Empire abandoned Morningstar, unfortunately evacuating the social scientists along with their military personnel.

It was these failures that played a role in the slow collapse of the Empire. Pointless military operations, long-distance command and control, the baleful influence of the unenlightened upon the uncomprehending...all problems that our Commonwealth must attempt to avoid. But can we avoid such problems as we expand further towards what were, once, the Core Worlds?
- Professor Leo Caesius, *War in a time of 'Peace:'*
The Empire's Forgotten Military History

Ed Stalker gazed down at the report, half-wishing he could smash the terminal against the wall and forget what it had said. Disaster. Thule occupied, five other systems believed to be occupied...and the CEF either prisoner or destroyed. Compared to some of the losses suffered during the Unification Wars, it was tiny, but it was the greatest disaster in the Commonwealth's short history. And it was far from over.

In hindsight, it was clear the enemy's timing hadn't worked out perfectly. At a guess, they'd intended to kill Gaby at the same time as launching their offensive, relying on her death to throw the Commonwealth's political leadership into chaos. But it had worked out well enough, he saw; their invasion of Commonwealth space had begun, forcing the Commonwealth to go on the defensive. It would be very hard to recover their balance, let alone take the offensive themselves. But there was no alternative.

And the losses were grievous. Avalon was proud of the CEF, despite Councillor Travis...hell, he'd concentrated his attacks on the leadership, rather than the CEF itself. But now the CEF was gone, along with its commanding officer. Four more Marines were dead or captured too, losses he could ill-afford. And Thule – and its priceless industrial nodes – had fallen behind enemy lines. The cloudscoops might have been destroyed, but Ed had few illusions. It would be months, at most, before they were replaced and Thule started churning out war material for Wolfbane. Absolute disaster was looming over the entire Commonwealth.

He stood, thinking hard. Gaby and the Council would have to be informed; hell, they would already have heard rumours. He'd put a block on the information as soon as he'd realised the sheer magnitude of the disaster, but something would have leaked out. It always did, he knew, no matter the security. The return of Mandy's squadron and the absence of much of the CEF had made sure of *that*. A formal announcement would have to be made soon, no matter what else happened. Or the rumours would grow completely out of control.

"Get me a flight to the mainland," he ordered, as he stepped out of his office. "And inform all senior officers that I wish to meet with them at Churchill Base, after I meet the Council."

It was going to be brutal, he knew. The attack on Gaby showed just how ruthless Wolfbane was prepared to be...and the attack had caused widespread anger across Avalon and the Commonwealth. Gaby was popular; she'd been the person who'd forged a lasting peace *and* started building the Commonwealth. No one, even her enemies, had taken the attack on her lightly. Her name would be used in cries for revenge that would echo over the entire world.

And there was no longer the guarantee of overwhelming force.

The Trade Federation will support us, he thought, as he followed Gwen over to the helicopter. Using a military aircraft as a personal taxi wasn't his preferred choice at all, but there was little alternative for a hasty trip. *And we have support from the RockRats.*

And there were the improvements in technology. The irony was chilling; even if the most pessimistic projections were accurate, Avalon would have a staggering advantage within five years. If the more optimistic projections were closer to the truth, the old Imperial Navy wouldn't have been able to stand up to a squadron of Commonwealth ships. But there was hardly any time to get the new innovations into play. They'd have to make do with what they had. They still had some advantages...

But would they be enough? All their information on Wolfbane was little more than educated guesswork, at best. How many ships did Governor Brown have at his disposal? What work had he done to improve his tech base? How many trained technicians did he have working for him? How many...there were just too many questions and too few answers.

And Admiral Singh had returned, out for revenge.

And there was a spy ring on Avalon, still undiscovered. Who knew what it was sending to its off-world masters?

No, Ed told himself. *It will be hell.*

Rumours had raced through the city at the speed of light, each one wilder than the last. The Commonwealth had suffered a great defeat; no, the Commonwealth had been victorious, but at a terrifying cost. Wolfbane had been attacked by the Empire; no, Wolfbane *was* the Empire and the Commonwealth was facing overwhelming force. By the time he joined the crowds outside the Council Chambers, Emmanuel Alves had heard so many rumours that he couldn't have said which one was most likely to be the truth.

The crowds looked angry, he noted, as he found a place to watch. They'd already seen their President attacked – anger against Wolfbane had been terrifying to watch, after Gaby Cracker had been shot – but now it was worse. If the rumours were true...

He heard silence fall as Gaby Cracker stepped out of the Council Chamber. They'd been meeting in urgent – and confidential – session, according to the rumours, a meeting that had been called just after the squadron returned to Avalon. Emmanuel leaned forward, hoping to see Jasmine, but there was no sign of her. Had she returned to Avalon or...or what? Was she dead?

"We have been attacked," Gaby said. Her voice was quieter than Emmanuel remembered; he shivered as he realised the woman who had once been able to master a crowd could no longer speak with full force. "Two weeks ago, Wolfbane's forces rolled across the border and attacked seven Commonwealth star systems. Six of them – including Thule – have fallen to the enemy. There have been very heavy losses."

The crowd seemed to shiver, rage and fear warring for supremacy. Emmanuel felt cold ice running down his back. Jasmine had been deployed to Thule, along with the CEF. Was she one of those losses? Somehow, he couldn't imagine her abandoning Thule and her people if there was a hope of saving them. Or, for that matter, abandoning her men to captivity.

"Wolfbane wishes us to surrender our independence to their Consortium," Gaby continued. "They want to turn us into their slaves, to enforce a servitude on us that will be far worse than anything we experienced under the Empire. Everything we have built over the last five years will be forced to work for Wolfbane. It will not be tolerated."

There was a long pause. "Today, the Commonwealth Council formally declared war on Wolfbane," Gaby said. "We will not surrender, we will not submit ourselves to them; instead, we will fight like free men and women, fight until we are safe once again.

"It will not be easy. There will be many battles to come and there will be serious losses. But we have powerful allies, an important cause and justice on our side. We will defeat the advancing enemy fleet, we will send them back across the border and we will take the war to Wolfbane itself.

"There will be those who will want a limited victory, a truce rather than unconditional surrender. To those people, I say that these are the days in which empire are formed. Will it be us, with our freedom and self-determination, or Wolfbane's corporate tyranny that determines the shape of the future? If we lose this war, freedom itself will vanish from the galaxy. We will fight and we will win."

She stopped speaking and waited. The crowd went wild, cheering her words and shouting their outrage and hatred of Wolfbane into the skies. Emmanuel allowed himself a tight smile, even though he knew the coming war would be very bad. But there was no alternative to fighting, he recognised. Governor Brown was unlikely to be content with just a handful of worlds. No, he'd come for them all.

Afterwards, he approached Colonel Stalker before the Marine could make his escape. The Colonel looked unsurprised to see him, merely... irked. Emmanuel asked the question as quickly as possible, as soon as they were out of earshot of the crowd.

"Colonel," he said, "what happened to Jasmine?"

"She's been taken prisoner," the Colonel said, quietly. "We don't know what will happen to her."

Emmanuel stared at him. "But..."

"I believe she will cope with the situation," the Colonel assured him. "And she may well find a chance to escape. But until then..."

"I understand," Emmanuel said. "I'll wait for her."

Two kilometres away, a pair of grim eyes watched the newscast as the reporters competed with one another to come up with the vilest names and suggestions for Wolfbane. The watcher couldn't help finding it more than a little amusing, even if it was completely uncontrolled. It would have to be changed in the future, she knew. The mindless sheep who made up the vast majority of the galaxy's population needed to have their opinions steered in the right direction, not allowed to pick and choose what information and attitudes they wanted to listen to for themselves. Not, in the end, that it would matter.

The spy allowed herself to relax. No one had come near her, not as far as she had been able to determine; she was, in their eyes, a complete non-entity. But now...she could finally begin to retake what had been hers by right, no matter the cost. She hadn't spent years on Earth, trying to build up a power base, just to abandon her dreams completely when the

Empire collapsed. No, she still wanted power. And she was damned if she was abandoning her quest now.

She sat up and poured herself a glass of sherry. Let the mindless sheep call for war, she told herself, even though there had been defeats rather than victories. They'd be disillusioned soon enough when Wolfbane arrived, forcing the entire planet to surrender. And she would be waiting to step back into the limelight and take power for herself. This time, she wouldn't be dependent on a well-meaning, but inept husband. This time, she would rule in her own right.

Maybe she would be a satrap, she conceded. But she would still have power.

And, in the end, power made it all worthwhile.

Governor Brown sat alone in his office on Wolfbane, thinking hard.

The first reports had come in, hard on the heels of an official note from Avalon that had been so undiplomatic that he'd been surprised it hadn't burst into flame. Someone had attempted to assassinate the President of the Commonwealth…and *he* was being blamed. But why would *he* have attempted to kill someone he wanted to negotiate with? If Gaby Cracker had seen sense, she could have taken on a high position within his administration. He would have welcomed someone with so much ability to get hated enemies to work together.

Instead, she'd been shot – and wounded – and he had a war on his hands.

It was more than he'd wanted, he knew. There had been nothing personal in the war – or at least there hadn't been. Now, Gaby Cracker and her subjects wanted revenge; they were unlikely to see sense and make concessions, rather than force him to crush the Commonwealth completely. And yet he hadn't ordered the assassination attempt. Maybe it had been one of her political rivals, he wondered, or maybe it had been a lone wolf. It wouldn't be the first time someone, acting completely on their own, had attempted to kill a major political figure.

Or had it been someone else?

He wasn't blind to the ambitions of his underlings. Some of them wanted power for themselves, others wanted to restore the Empire. Either motive would give them a reason to try to lash out at him, to take power... or to provoke a war. So far, Wolfbane had been victorious at very little cost. But it wouldn't be long before the Commonwealth and the Trade Federation began striking back. The war was far from over.

Bitterly, he shook his head. There was no point crying over spilt milk. Instead, he would have to bend every effort to win the war before it was too late. If nothing else, the advances the Commonwealth had shown were truly worrying. What would happen if they were given time to put their new developments into mass production? No, the war had to be won... which would make him all the more dependent on his military advisors.

Standing up, he walked over to the window and peered out over Wolfbane's skyline. So far, the locals knew nothing about the war, but that would change soon enough. How would they react, he asked himself, once they knew the truth? Would they be pleased that their empire was winning battles or would they fear the outbreak of interstellar war? Perhaps they would be both, he thought sourly. Winning battles was always popular. But long wars were never so welcome.

We'll just have to win, he told himself. *The alternative is unthinkable.*

But he couldn't help the feeling that he'd started something he could no longer control.

The transport might not have been designed for prisoners, Jasmine decided, but it did the job admirably. It was nothing more than a starship hold, lined with solid metal, with an isolated life support system and a small amount of ration bars. There was no way in or out, save for a hatch that would need a cutting laser or a molecular debonder to break. The prisoners had nothing, but their bare hands.

Jasmine had organised them as best as she could, once the hatch had been closed. Morale had been low, but she'd talked to her subordinates and encouraged them, all the while contemplating ways to escape. In some ways, she felt better about no longer being responsible for the CEF, being responsible for actually running a large-scale war. Now, she could forget the bigger picture and concentrate on escape.

Her interview with General Haverford – her second interview, technically – had been brief, formal and edgy. He'd promised to ensure that the Commonwealth received a list of prisoners, then admitted that the POWs were being sent to an isolated stage-one colony world. Jasmine wasn't too surprised. Putting POWs on Wolfbane itself, no matter the security, might well have been asking for trouble. But an isolated world... they couldn't cause much trouble there. Or so Wolfbane might have good reason to believe.

She looked around the compartment, illuminated by a single light source embedded in the metal, and smiled to herself. She knew next to nothing about Meridian, but she knew one thing. It wouldn't be enough to hold her and her personnel. They would escape, then .. they would make their way home.

The thought made her smile, despite the sad tinge that came with it. Avalon was home now, no matter where she'd been born. And the Commonwealth was worth defending.

She closed her eyes and made a silent vow. *I shall return.*

To Be Continued...

AFTERWORD

There is an unspoken and unchallenged assumption in society – particularly those parts of society content to have their history and current affairs spoon-fed to them – that only crazy or stupid people start wars. Such versions of history demonise people who start wars – not always, I will admit, without good cause. But such versions of history choose to skip over the reasons someone might conclude that war is actually a good idea. The concept of the warmonger actually being a rational actor is too disturbing to contemplate.

In some cases, this is not surprising. Adolf Hitler has been demonised, with very good reason, so badly that anyone who suggests that Hitler was *right* to go to war is automatically branded a Nazi-sympathiser. This may be understandable, but it is not conductive to good and careful consideration of the background to any given war. We prefer to think of Hitler as crazy. But this forces us to overlook the simple fact that Imperial Germany also went to war in 1914 and modern-day Germany is slowly moving to dominate the EU.

Is there, therefore, something wrong with the state of Germany? Or are there deeper factors at work?

Let us consider the German position. Prior to German Unification (after the Franco-Prussian War) Germany was effectively a battleground, fought over by France, Austria and Russia. None of the German states could muster the military power to keep themselves out of the fighting, or to prevent their destruction by their stronger neighbours. Once the Germans united, they possessed greater power than any of their neighbours – but did they possess greater power than *all* of their neighbours?

Seen from Berlin, Germany was encircled by hostile powers. While Austria was largely neutralised (and fought on the same side in the Great

War), France and Russia were irreconcilable enemies. German planners concluded that they might beat France, only to be stabbed in the back by Russia (or vice versa). In fact, both France and Russia were growing stronger as Germany moved into 1914 – and France and Britain had concluded an alliance that bound them together against Germany. From the German point of view, there would be war – and it was better for Germany that the war came sooner, rather than later.

To us, looking back over eighty years of history, this seems absurd. History records that Germany lost the Great War, after four years of bloody slaughter, and Imperial Germany vanished from Europe. But Germany itself did not die and the Allies failed to splinter it into its component fragments. It was unsurprising that Germany would grow powerful once again and seek to avenge itself on Europe. Hitler was, in this view, nothing more than a tool of history. His decisions were taken within a framework that existed outside of his regime.

The same could be said, to some extent, for Imperial Japan prior to Pearl Harbour. Japan had good reason to feel constrained – and good reason to view the American build-up with alarm. US sanctions on Japan were forcing the Japanese into a corner. They could either seek a decision through war or submit tamely to American demands. In hindsight, the latter seems the better option; in foresight, it was far less clear-cut. If the Japanese conceded to the US, they asked themselves, what guaranteed that the US would not make further demands? One simple rule of life is that giving in to blackmail invites more blackmail. Why should the Japanese have conceded anything?

I imagine that a few readers will write angry comments about Imperial Japan being a thoroughly unpleasant state, one deserving of sanctions. The Japanese Army looted, raped and burned its way across China. When unleashed to the south, they carried out a series of atrocities that outdid the Nazis themselves. I am not disputing any of that, but the morality or lack thereof of any specific point in history is immaterial. The point is that Japan was constrained and tried to break out. This should have been predictable to planners in Washington, London and Moscow.

However, the Japanese were quite unable to actually win their war. They could not hope to out-produce the United States, they could not occupy American territory and they could not destroy the American factories that became the arsenal of democracy. Nor, for that matter, could they occupy Britain or Russia. The constraints that forced Japan to choose between war and submission were, in the end, fatal to Imperial Japan. In short, the course of World War Two was largely determined by geopolitics.

———

Defining geopolitics is a complicated business. It is the interaction between dozens of factors that determine a country's relative strength compared to other countries. Some of these factors are immutable, while others can change depending on technology, investment and even government and attitudes.

Let us consider, for example, the treacherous maps that show Canada as being largely equal in land surface to the United States. A more careful look would reveal that the vast majority of Canada's population lives to the south. Furthermore, Canada's military is in no way comparable to the United States, being outclassed in almost every category. Put bluntly, the United States is vastly more powerful than Canada and this is unlikely to change in the near future.

A second deceptive map would show Russia. Russia is one of the largest countries on Earth, but much of its interior is undeveloped, slowing the country's economic growth. In some ways, the sheer size of Russia works to its advantage (in absorbing invading armies) but in others it makes it hard for the Russians to mobilise their potential resources. Russia requires massive investment in infrastructure before it can begin to live up to its potential. However, this required a level of investment that neither the Tsars nor the USSR was able to provide.

Russia is actually indicative of geopolitical factors that can change with stunning speed. In 1914, the Russian Army was regarded poorly after the disasters of the Russo-Japanese War; the Germans calculated (wrongly) that the Russians couldn't mobilise in time to save France from defeat. Russia's defeat and the rise of the communist regime meant that Russia was largely excluded from post-war settlements. In 1939, the Russian failure to crush Finland turned them into a laughing stock, convincing

Hitler that the Russians were a paper tiger and encouraging him to attack the USSR. But, by the end of 1945, the Red Army was feared throughout Europe.

And yet, when the USSR collapsed, the Russian Army collapsed with it. During the Yeltsin years, once again, NATO acted without regard for Russian feelings, let alone their geopolitical priorities. This led directly to Putin's determination to re-establish Russian predominance in Eastern Europe, a program that has proved highly successful.

Each country has a set of geopolitical priorities that it must maintain to keep itself safe and unconstrained. It was these geopolitical priorities that convinced Imperial Germany (and later Hitler) that war would come – and better it be fought sooner than later. After all, if both France and Russia grew stronger, Germany would be trapped between them. When a country fails to take care of its geopolitical priorities, the country is imperilled.

These patterns exist regardless of the government. Russian history shows the same pattern repeated by Tsars, Communists and Putin's brand of quasi-fascism. All three of them have moved to keep control of the countries surrounding Russia, knowing that failure to do so causes problems for Russia – and eventual disaster. This seems thoroughly unpleasant of the Russians; their post-WW2 domination of Eastern Europe was neither desired nor gentle. But the Russians, following their geopolitical priories, had no choice. The states that made up the Warsaw Pact were, in effect, colonies that shielded Russian territory from invaders.

It shouldn't surprise anyone, sadly, that the advance of NATO eastwards was viewed with alarm by Russia – and that they would take every opportunity they could find to undermine NATO's position, reputation and general trustworthiness. NATO meant no harm – but, from the Russian point of view, its advance eastwards was constraining...and threatening.

The study of national and international geopolitics, thus, is vitally important. If you understand a country's geopolitics, you can predict, to some extent, just which way that country will jump. The government may be led by a seeming madman, the population might be roused by cries of 'death to America,' but they are often more rational than they seem.

Let us consider North Korea. The pattern of each successive nuclear crisis is largely identical. North Korea rattles the sabre, everyone takes them seriously for a while...and then the whole crisis quietens down. There has been no repeat of the Korean War, at least partly because the North Korean Government understands that such a war might lead to their complete destruction.

Or let us look at Iraq and Iran. Saddam's government repressed both the Shia and Kurds savagely. This was noted in the West, with appropriate sounds of horror, but the deeper implications were ignored. The Kurds were determined to keep hold of their freedoms after Saddam was removed, while the Shia gravitated towards Iran, giving the Iranians a shot at taking control of Iraq.

Or...following the end of the Iraq-Iran War, Saddam demanded that the Arab states give Iraq free loans and other support. Kuwait refused. This might have been legally permitted, but Iraq was far more powerful than Kuwait and the refusal was foolhardy. What guarantee did Kuwait have that would ensure the US would intervene? Indeed, if the Iraqis had mounted the invasion of Kuwait a year or two earlier, they would probably have gotten away with it.

There are other examples, of course. During the Cold War, geopolitical priorities demanded that the NATO countries hang together, despite disputes that could easily have turned into catfights without a common threat. Now, without the looming Russian Bear, America and Europe have much less binding them together. Can NATO be a significant power again?

―――――

The failure to consider geopolitics is perhaps the greatest weakness of the current crop of governments in the West. Their behaviour, in many ways, shows a complete *lack* of awareness of geopolitics. When it comes to intervening in the Middle East, playing games with Russia and adjusting positions in the Far East, Western governments frequently seem blind to the underlying costs and consequences of their actions.

There are no shortage of places in the world that could serve as a flashpoint for a general war, no matter how seemingly suicidal. Will Taiwan declare independence, with US backing, forcing China to either accept its permanent separation or start a war? Will Eastern Europe's treatment of Russian minorities convince Russia to intervene with force? Will Indian involvement in Afghanistan trigger a war with Pakistan? Will Syria turn into a black hole sucking in forces from all over the world? Failing to think two or three steps ahead, as NATO did when it absorbed Eastern Europe, could be lethal.

When it comes to geopolitics, the United States is the most blessed country in the world. The US has a friendly neighbour to the north and a far weaker neighbour to the south, while giant oceans protect the country's coasts. There is no way that any hostile power could mount a seaborne invasion of the United States. The USN is so staggeringly powerful that it could stand off the entire combined naval power of the rest of the world. In short, the United States does not really *need* to think about geopolitics. Unlike Russia, which needs to tend to its geopolitical knitting constantly, the US can forget about it.

This tends to cause problems for the US outside North America. When the US has no real awareness of the geopolitical realities of the Middle East, or Europe, or the Far East, the US can and does blunder around like an elephant in a china shop. Worse, perhaps, the US can lose interest very quickly. While states like Pakistan and Iran cannot avoid confronting problems spreading over the border from Afghanistan, the US can always simply withdraw, leaving the locals behind. And then the US has a tendency to complain about local treachery, when the truth is that the locals are trying to stabilize their own positions in anticipation of the inevitable American withdrawal.

Those who do not learn from history are condemned to repeat it.

Those who do not study geopolitics are condemned to have their fingers mashed in gears they cannot see.

So why don't our politicians study history and geopolitics?

Christopher G. Nuttall
Manchester, United Kingdom, 2014

The Empire's Corps will continue in…

THE THIN BLUE LINE

Historian's Note
The Thin Blue Line starts one standard month after *When The Bough Breaks*.

PROLOGUE

"It doesn't look very comfortable from up here, does it?"

Captain Kevin Vaughn – who was only a Captain by courtesy – turned and smiled at his sole crewmember. Cynthia was a bright young thing, a girl from a diehard Marine family who had insisted on becoming a spacer rather than a groundpounder like her father, brothers or cousins. He had to admire her resistance to peer pressure, even though he privately doubted that she would have survived the Slaughterhouse. It chewed up and broke an alarmingly high percentage of young recruits who made it through six months of Boot Camp.

"The Slaughterhouse isn't meant to be comfortable," he said, feeling his legs itch. It was psychometric, the shrinks had said; he'd lost his legs on an operation that had gone badly wrong and had to have them regrown in a tube. "It's meant to push its victims to the limits."

He sighed as he gazed down at the planet below. The Slaughterhouse was a confused patchwork of environments, each one possessing its own nasty surprises for unwary recruits, the result of a failed terraforming program. By now, keeping its environment as uncomfortable as possible required a full-time crew, who did everything from replace topsoil to introducing nasty critters from right across the Empire. The Slaughterhouse might break far too many of the recruits, but those who survived were the best damned soldiers in all of history.

"Everything is in working order," Cynthia assured him. "How long do we have to remain here again?"

Kevin shrugged. The Commandant's orders had been clear. *Polly* was to remain behind in orbit after the evacuation, watching and waiting, until something happened. Something had already happened, Kevin had thought rebelliously when he'd been given his orders, but he'd done as he was told. The empty planet below was living history, even if it was a part of history most of the Empire would prefer to forget. Watching it from high orbit was not a particularly unpleasant task.

"As long as we are ordered to do so," he said, patiently. Cynthia was young. She'd learn patience soon enough. "Besides, it does give us a chance to run all those checks we never managed to do before the state of emergency was declared."

He sighed, inwardly. The reports had been all too clear. Earth had been destroyed, her society ripped apart by social conflict, then smashed flat as pieces of debris fell from orbit and struck the surface with terrifying force. Kevin had no particular attachment to Earth – he'd been born on a planet hundreds of light years away – but it was still horrifying. Mother Earth might have been a poisoned, polluted mess, home to literally billions of civilians who did nothing but suck at the government's teat, yet she was still the homeworld of humanity, the planet that had birthed a hundred thousand colony worlds. To know she was gone was terrifying.

Something has been removed from our lives, he thought. He'd heard any number of rumours before the Commandant had ordered the Slaughterhouse closed down, with all of the staff and recruits moved to a secure – and secret – location. *And nothing will ever be the same.*

"I could bring you a cup of coffee, if you're busy wool-gathering," Cynthia said. "Or would you like to find something else for me to do?"

"Coffee would be nice," Kevin said. "And..."

He broke off as an alarm sounded. "Contact," he snapped. "Man your station!"

Cynthia obeyed, scrambling into her chair and bringing the sensor console online. *Polly* was really nothing more than a handful of passive sensors and stealth systems, mounted on a squashed drive unit that had been pared down to the bare minimum. Kevin had no illusions about what would happen if they were detected, even by something as small as a gunboat or a corvette. He and his ship would be blown out of space before they knew they were under attack.

"I have five contacts, all coming out of cloak," Cynthia snapped. "They must have realised there's no one here to greet them."

Kevin nodded, unsurprised. The Slaughterhouse was barely defended, compared to Earth or Terra Nova. No one in their right mind would consider attacking the Slaughterhouse when the reputation of the Marine Corps reached right across the galaxy. But Earth was gone and nothing would ever be quite the same. Who knew what was about to happen now?

"That wouldn't have been hard," Kevin said. They weren't in the best position for optimal observation, but they were close enough to separate individual targets. It helped that the newcomers weren't even trying to hide. "Give me a complete breakdown, if you can."

"Three destroyers," Cynthia said. "All *Falcone*-class, I think, but one of them has been heavily modified. The other two are light cruisers, probably *Peacock*-class. They appear to be standard specification, sir."

"From a self-defence force, then," Kevin said. That proved nothing. A number of star systems possessed semi-independent self-defence forces. The Grand Senate had regularly considered bills to disarm them, only to run into the threat of outright rebellion. "There aren't any *Peacocks* left in the Imperial Navy."

"Ship-spotter," Cynthia accused. On the display, the small flotilla moved into orbit, scanning aggressively. "What are they doing here?"

"Good question," Kevin said. "I have a feeling we're not going to like the answer."

The unknowns, whoever they were, were thorough. It was nearly forty minutes of constant scanning before they decided, apparently, that the planet was abandoned. Kevin wouldn't have taken that for granted, not with the Slaughterhouse; he'd seen entire army divisions carefully camouflaged against orbital observation. There were no shortage of places where the Marines could have hidden their personnel, if they'd remained on the planet. Planets were big, after all. Spacers had a nasty habit of forgetting just how difficult it could be to move from one place to another.

Particularly if there's an enemy force trying to stop you, Kevin thought, with grim amusement. *It can take days to move from one system to another, but it can take weeks to move a hundred kilometres if the enemy is willing to do whatever it takes to slow you down.*

Cynthia tapped his shoulder. "What are they doing?"

"I don't know," Kevin said, shortly. "I..."

An alarm sounded. "Missile separation," Cynthia said, swinging her chair back to her console. "Multiple missile separations...sir, they're firing on the planet!"

Kevin swore. The Slaughterhouse was living history. Hundreds of thousands, perhaps millions, of Marines had emerged from the Slaughterhouse to fight for the Empire. The structures on the surface contained histories and relics the rest of the Empire, even the military, had chosen to forget. And it was part of a tradition he'd embraced with all his heart, long ago. To be forced to watch it die...

"Airburst detonations," Cynthia said. "Sir...I don't understand."

"Radioactive poison," Kevin said. Planet-killing weapons were forbidden, full stop. Bombarding a planet was one thing, but actively rendering it uninhabitable...the entire galaxy would rise up in horror. "I..."

He gritted his teeth in bitter frustration as lethal radiation spread through the planet's atmosphere. Within days, there would be nothing left alive on the surface, unless it was *very* well protected. Even combat suits would be hard-pressed to shield their users against such levels of radiation. It would be years before radiation levels dropped to the point that anything could be recovered from the surface, then it would need intensive decontamination before it could be touched safely. He sought, frantically, for options, but found nothing.

There was nothing he could do but watch, helplessly, as the Slaughterhouse died.

CHAPTER ONE

> The law, as the old saying goes, is the true embodiment of society. One can tell a great deal about a society by what it chooses to forbid and what it chooses to permit – and, perhaps more importantly, how it handles crimes.
> - Professor Leo Caesius, *The Decline of Law and Order and the Rise of Anarchy*

Earth was gone.

Marshall (Detective Inspector) Glen Cheal shook his head bitterly as the unmarked van made its way through Terra Nova's darkened streets. The sun was setting in the sky, the remaining shoppers hurrying home for fear of being caught outside after curfew. Everywhere he looked he could see the signs of decay and despair; closed shops, abandoned vehicles and armed guards everywhere. It wouldn't be long, he thought as they drove past a soup kitchen, before Terra Nova followed Earth into the fire.

He caught sight of his own reflection in the wing mirror and shivered. His brown hair was turning grey, his skin leathered and lined after too many stressful years as an Imperial Marshal. It was impossible to escape the feeling that he was old, old and tired. After Hazel had died, after his unborn daughter had died with her, part of him had just wanted to give up on life. Or maybe it was just a reflection of the lost Earth. What was humanity without its homeworld?

"Sandy's been volunteering at her local kitchen," Marshall (Detective) Isabel Freeman said, softly. "She says it's getting harder to find anything, even processed algae."

Glen nodded, unsurprised. The soup kitchens were the only places still feeding vast numbers of people who had been rendered suddenly destitute by the economic crash, when they'd discovered that all the money they'd invested in the imperial banking system had suddenly evaporated. But with funds drying up everywhere, it was getting harder to ship food from the farms and growth facilities into the cities. It would *definitely* not be long before the first food riots started, even without the Nihilists pouring fuel on the flames.

"Tell her to stay indoors in future," Glen said. He rather envied Isabel her skill at managing her work along with a personal life, but right now it just gave her hostages to fortune. His daughter would have been fifteen two days ago, if she had lived. "The shit is heading towards the fan."

He rubbed his eyes as they passed a school, now shuttered and dark. In his early years as a Marshal, he'd been called to deal with one riot or another on school grounds when the permissiveness of Imperial society finally led to its logical conclusion. Now, the children were either on the streets or cowering at home, mesmerised by the thought of the onrushing tidal wave of destruction. Earth was gone. There were no longer any certainties in the universe.

Isabel nodded. She was tough, Glen had to admit, certainly tougher than she looked. He'd been astonished when she'd been presented to him as a new graduate, one of the last before the Marshal Academy had been closed for the duration of the emergency. At the time, he'd looked her up and down and concluded she'd slept with one or more of the examiners. Now, he knew better. Isabel was tough enough to survive anything. And warm enough to join a group marriage and become a part of something greater than herself.

Something else greater than herself, Glen thought, tiredly. It was late; he would have preferred to go back to his apartment and sleep until his next shift was about to begin. But the tip-off had been urgent, urgent enough for him to forget the idea of going home and arrange for a raid without waiting for clearance. The Nihilists, God damn their black little souls, had a nasty habit of moving around at short notice before popping up to cause chaos.

The handful of people on the streets faded away completely as they drove into the tangled network of warehouses surrounding the nearest spaceport. Most of the warehouses were completely empty, he knew from the reports. Anyone with access to a starship had boarded it and set out for somewhere safer, somewhere isolated from the coming storm. He didn't blame them, any more than he blamed the endless lines of civilians waiting to book starship tickets, or even taking short hops to asteroid settlements. Terra Nova, Earth's oldest colony world, was less densely populated than Earth – than Earth had been, he reminded himself sharply – but it couldn't support itself indefinitely. Law and order were teetering on the brink of falling into absolute chaos.

"I hope your informant was right, Glen," Isabel said quietly, as they reached the RV point and parked the van. "The boss isn't going to be very happy if this is a fuck-up."

"There's no point in taking chances," Glen said. The tip-off had been too good to ignore – and besides, part of him would be grateful if he *was* suspended or fired. He could have left the star system with a clear conscience. "And besides, if we'd waited for approval from our superiors, someone might have tipped off the bastards."

He gritted his teeth as he checked his pistol, then carefully stashed it beneath his trenchcoat and opened the door. It was an open secret that criminal gangs had made connections to senior officers within the Civil Guard, paying them for everything from advance warnings of any raids to military-grade supplies. And the criminals often had their own links with the Nihilists. The terrorists wouldn't give a damn about crime, regarding it as yet another manifestation of the hopelessness of existence, but they'd be happy to trade with the crime lords. If someone had advance notice of an attack, they could use it to hide something while the law enforcement forces were distracted.

Outside, the air smelt faintly of oil and burning hydrocarbons. Glen glanced around, spotted the other vehicle some distance from the target warehouse, then made a hand signal inviting Isabel to join him outside the van. Surprisingly, the Civil Guardsmen had actually managed to be discrete when they moved their SWAT team into position. Normally, there was nothing so conspicuous as a Civil Guard force trying to hide.

Glen smiled to himself, then led the way to the other vehicle. Inside, it was a mobile command and control centre.

"Marshal Cheal," a tough-looking man said. "I'm Major Daniel Dempsey, local CO."

"Pleased to meet you," Glen said. "Status report?"

He allowed himself a moment of hope. Dempsey looked surprisingly competent for a Civil Guard officer and, more reassuringly, he was wearing nothing more than a basic uniform. The only trace of vanity was a hint that the uniform was tight enough to show off his muscles. Compared to the lines of fruit salad many officers wore, Glen was quite prepared to excuse it.

"Stealth drones reveal the existence of a low-power scrambler field within the warehouse," Dempsey said, tapping the console. "Passive scans have turned up nothing, Marshal, but the mere presence of a scrambler field is justifiable cause for a raid."

Glen nodded, shortly. A scrambler field would make it impossible to slip nanotech bugs inside the warehouse – and, unsurprisingly, civilian ownership was thoroughly illegal. The citizens of the Empire had nothing to fear as long as the Empire was allowed to spy on them at will, Glen had been told. But he'd also been a Marshal long enough to know just how easy it was to take something innocent, something that certainly shouldn't be a criminal offense, and use it as evidence to get someone condemned.

And merely using the field suggests they have something to hide, he thought. *But are they really terrorists...or just smugglers trying to get their goods off-planet?*

"I will be sending in two teams," Dempsey said. "And I *will* assume tactical command."

"I want prisoners," Glen said. "Tell your men to stun without hesitation, Major. The Nihilists are rarely taken alive."

"And one of them might trigger a bomb," Dempsey agreed. He picked up a helmet, then placed it on his head. "I would prefer it if you two remained here while we carried out the operation..."

Glen made a face. The Civil Guardsmen had made a good showing so far, but the real test would begin when the raid started. He wanted to be on the spot, yet he knew he hadn't trained beside the Civil Guardsmen. It was quite possible he'd be shot by accident if he inserted himself into the scene before the bullets stopped flying. The Civil Guardsmen were low on enthusiasm and even lower on training.

"Very well," he said. He took one of the chairs and began studying the views from microscopic cameras inserted around the warehouse. If everything had gone according to plan, the Nihilists had no idea a SWAT team had surrounded them and taken up positions to launch a raid. "Good luck."

Isabel elbowed him as soon as Dempsey had made his way out of the command vehicle. "You don't want to take command for yourself?"

"He's the guy on the spot," Glen said. In theory, Imperial Marshals had supreme authority to take the lead on any investigation, if they felt like it. But, in practice, it was normally better to let the locals handle it unless there was strong evidence the locals were likely to screw up, deliberately or otherwise. "And his men know him."

He settled back in his chair and forced himself to watch as the display updated, rapidly. The team had done a good job of surveying their environment, he noted, as well as obtaining the warehouse's plans from the rental authority. There was only one way into the warehouse, a large pair of double doors on the north side of the building. But, as the Nihilists would almost certainly have the entrance rigged to blow if the wrong people came through, Major Dempsey intended to assault from the rear and blow his way through the walls. Glen rather doubted there was any better options, given the short time they had to mount the raid. God alone knew when the Nihilists would try to move to another location.

And we could try to grab them when they moved, he thought. *But that would be too risky.*

"They're moving," Isabel said. "Team One is assaulting the wall; Team Two is moving to seal the doors."

Glen took a breath as explosive charges blew holes in the walls. Moments later, armoured troopers ran forward, spraying stun bursts ahead of them. It ran the risk of stunning their own people, Glen knew, but it was the quickest way to clear the building. The prisoners would be moved to the cells, where they could be searched and then woken safely. They would have no opportunity to present a threat to their enemies.

He swore as he heard the sound of gunfire echoing out from the warehouse. Caught by surprise or not, the Nihilists had clearly been prepared – and ready to fight back. He wondered, absently, if someone had tipped them off despite the speed the raid had been organised, then decided it wasn't likely. The Nihilists were mad, but they weren't stupid. If they'd expected the raid, they would have rigged the warehouse to blow or cleared out before the shit hit the fan. They had to know that not everyone was as fanatically committed to destroying everything, purely for the sake of destruction, as their leadership.

"Two men down," Isabel said. "One more injured, but still fighting."

Glen ground his teeth, helplessly. He *hated* the waiting, hated having to watch helplessly as other men fought and died. If he'd had a choice, he would have taken a weapon himself and gone into the building, rather than watch the Guardsmen die. But all he could do was wait...

The sound of shooting grew louder. Pushing his thoughts aside, Glen reached for his terminal and began to type out an emergency update. The shooting would attract attention, even now. No one in their right mind wanted to run the risk of one group of Civil Guardsmen turning up to engage another group of Civil Guardsmen. Besides, he had to explain himself to his superiors when they demanded answers. He'd lost quite a bit the moment they opened fire.

"Take the com, tell them to send reinforcements, forensic teams and ambulances," Glen ordered, as the shooting finally came to an end. One way or another, he was definitely committed now. He would have to pray that the raid had been a success or that his boss was feeling merciful. "I'll be out there on the spot."

He jumped out of the command vehicle and strode towards the warehouse, stripping off his trenchcoat to reveal a glowing yellow jacket. No one liked them, particularly the Marshals who had seen military service before making the jump to law enforcement, because they attracted attention, but the risk of being shot by one of his own snipers was far too high without some clear means of identification. He paused long enough to allow the snipers to eyeball him, then walked towards the hole in the wall. Dempsey met him as he reached the gap into the warehouse.

"It's a mess, sir," Dempsey said. "Four of my men are dead, two more badly injured."

Glen made a face as the Civil Guardsmen carried their dead comrades out of the building and laid them, as respectfully as possible, on the roadside. The two wounded were escorted out next, their wounds already being tended by their fellows. In the distance, Glen could hear the sound of sirens as the emergency services converged on the warehouse. He sighed, then followed Dempsey into the building. Inside, it was definitely a mess.

There were hundreds of shipping pallets everywhere, some already broken open and spilling their contents on the ground. One of them was crammed with rifles, a knock-off of a design that was older than the Empire itself, another held SAM missile launchers, although there didn't seem to be any missiles. *That* was odd, Glen noted, as he walked deeper into the building. Normally, the missile launchers were single-use fire and forget weapons. But their mere presence boded ill for the future.

"There are over a hundred crates in the warehouse," Dempsey said, as several dead bodies were carried past them and out into the open air. "If they're all crammed with weapons…"

"We might have had a serious problem," Glen finished. Terra Nova was, in theory, a gun-free zone. In practice, the planet was awash with illegal weapons, mostly bought or stolen from the Civil Guard. But the stockpile before him was enough for a major war and it had all been in the hands of the Nihilists. What had they intended to do with it? "Where did they get them from?"

"This is a transhipment warehouse," Dempsey said, dryly. "Someone must have shipped the weapons in from out-system, then smuggled them past the security guards."

Glen shook his head in disbelief. Every year, more and more security precautions were added to sweep everything and everyone heading down to the surface. Every year, more and more visitors were irritated or outraged by body-scans and even close-contact searches. Every year, the number of tourists visiting Terra Nova declined still further, damaging the planet's economy…and yet, the Nihilists were able to smuggle hundreds, perhaps thousands, of dangerous weapons though security without setting off any alarms.

But we caught them, he told himself. There was no way his boss could refuse to say the raid wasn't justified, not now. *We caught the bastards before they could start distributing the weapons.*

He turned to look at Dempsey. "How many did we take alive?"

"None, so far," Dempsey said. He didn't seem flustered by Glen's accusing look. It was far from uncommon for terrorists who had killed policemen or Civil Guardsmen not to make it to the station after being taken into custody. "They all had suicide implants, sir. They died moments after they were stunned."

"Make sure the place is secured, then have the forensic team go through every last inch of the building," Glen ordered. "I want every one of them identified, I want to know just who let them through security and why..."

"If we have the manpower," Dempsey cut him off. "Will your boss authorise such an effort?"

Glen swore. With the threat of food riots, nearly every law-enforcement official on the planet had been diverted to patrolling the cities. Even the backroom experts who made the service work had been forced to remember their basic training as they donned armour and set out to try to make the streets a little safer. It was a recipe for disaster, everyone knew, but there was no alternative. They just didn't have the manpower to flood the streets with officers, let alone Civil Guardsmen.

His terminal bleeped, loudly. It was Isabel's ringtone. "Excuse me," he said, removing the terminal from his belt. "Glen here."

"Glen, I just got called by the boss," Isabel said. "She's sending a team of experts over here, but she wants you to report back to the station at once. I think you're in the shit."

"Come back this evening...tomorrow morning and dig me out," Glen said. He wasn't surprised. The raid had been a great success, but he would still have to answer a great many hard questions. "And bring coffee."

"Will do," Isabel said. "What would you like me to write on your gravestone before I dig you up and put you back to work?"

Glen laughed, tiredly. "Something witty," he said. "Take over here; let me know if we took anyone captive. We need answers from them."

He stepped back out of the warehouse and walked over towards the line of vehicles screeching to a halt. One of them would take him back to the station, probably far too quickly for his peace of mind. He needed coffee and a rest, not a lecture from the boss.

But an Imperial Marshal's work was never done.

Chapter Two

> The definition of crime is, of course, part of society. Throughout history, there have been no shortage of acts that we would unhesitatingly deem as criminal, yet were not considered crimes at the time.
> — Professor Leo Caesius, *The Decline of Law and Order and the Rise of Anarchy*

Belinda closed her eyes. When she opened them, she saw the city.

It was an ugly sight. Dozens of gray cookie-cutter houses, each one completely unremarkable, completely indistinguishable from the others. There was nothing to separate each of them from their partners, no trace at all of individuality. Whoever had designed this suburb, she decided as she started to walk, had no intention of allowing human sentimentality to affect their design work. There were no shops, no schools...nothing, but endless rows of houses...

...And there were no traces of any living beings, none at all.

Alarm bells rang in her mind as she started to run. The mission was simple enough, which meant, in her experience, that there was a nasty sting in the tail. All she had to do was get from one end of the city to the other, without allowing anything to impede her path. She'd run countless such missions before, when she'd been nothing more than a Marine Rifleman, but then she'd been surrounded by the rest of the company. Now, she was alone.

Her enhanced senses, such as they were, probed the darkness as she ran faster, keeping to the shadows as best as she could. If someone was setting an ambush ahead of her, she was reasonably sure she could hear them lying in wait before they realised she was there, unless they knew what she was. Or they were just being paranoid. Even the most enhanced humanoids known to exist couldn't hear something if it wasn't making a sound, even breathing. Belinda had set enough ambushes in her time to know how the ambushers were thinking. They'd try to lure her into a killing zone and do whatever it took to stop her.

She darted down an alleyway, then out into the next street, ducking into the shadows long enough to scan for anything out of place. The soulless buildings seemed to mock her, casting dark shadows that were almost completely shrouded, even to her enhanced senses. She hesitated, then ran onwards, trying to keep the sound of her footsteps to the bare minimum. And yet, she knew she was making noise, too much noise. If someone was lying in wait…

I should have asked for more time, she thought, as she entered another alleyway and jumped over a set of garbage cans. *Enough time to run around the city, rather than through the buildings…*

A sound caught her attention and she froze, listening carefully. It sounded like someone was crying, very softly, and trying not to be heard. Belinda turned, using her enhanced senses to triangulate the source of the sound, then crept forward. It was coming from a nearby alleyway…

It's a trap, part of her mind yammered. The rest of her told that part of her mind to shut up. She couldn't leave someone in pain, all alone in the dark, not if she wanted to live up to the Marine ideal. And besides, she knew – all too well – what it was like to be alone. She peered into the alleyway and frowned as she saw the girl lying on the ground, her arms and legs akimbo. Belinda's eyes narrowed as she moved closer. She'd seen too many horrors wrought by mankind on its fellows, but this was odd. There had been no sign that anyone lived within the city…

A sudden motion flickered behind her. Belinda ducked instinctively as something flashed overhead, through where her head had been seconds ago, then swung around to see a gangbanger standing there. She didn't hesitate. Before he could take another swing at her, she lashed out herself and slammed a punch into his chest. She felt his bones breaking under the impact, but he staggered forward, his arms flailing rapidly. Belinda darted back, then watched dispassionately as he fell to the ground. And then she sensed the others shimmering into view.

Personal cloaks? She thought, surprised. *Where did a bunch of gangsters get their hands on personnel cloaking devices?*

There was no time to consider the mystery, not when she was surrounded by at least five gangsters. None of them seemed to be carrying projectile weapons, which surprised her, but they all moved as if they had some degree of martial arts training. Belinda considered trying to negotiate, then dismissed the thought impatiently. Falling into their hands would be a fate worse than death, even if they merely took her captive and traded her to their backers for additional weapons and supplies. And besides, she had no intention of surrendering – ever.

The first gangbanger lunged forward. Belinda triggered her enhancements, then leapt up and over his head. He didn't seem surprised as she landed behind him and started to run, rather than stopping to fight. Instead, he barked a command and three of his men started to follow her, back out onto the street. Belinda ran faster, calling on her enhancements, then swore mentally as she realised they were keeping up with her. It should have been impossible...

And then one of them threw himself forward and slammed into her back.

Belinda fell, twisting around to land on her back and bring her legs up to kick out at her captor. Her boot caught him in the head, which snapped backwards with a satisfying cracking sound. There was no time to be pleased with her success. Belinda jumped back to her feet as the other gangsters advanced towards her, their hands suddenly sprouting a mixture of knives, clubs and steel bars. Belinda smiled, feeling truly alive for the first time in far too long, then allowed them to close before she started to fight with enhanced strength and determination. Two of the gangsters fell before her fists, then the leader slammed *something* into her back. There was a sudden shock that send her falling to her knees, as if she'd been struck with an weakened stun beam.

A neural whip, the analytical part of her mind pointed out. *You've had your nerves jangled...*

She gritted her teeth and started to force herself to her feet, but it was too late. One of the gangbangers caught her arms and yanked her back to the ground, while two more caught her legs and wrenched them apart. Belinda struggled, feeling panic bubbling at the corner of her mind, as the leader produced a sharp knife and went to work on her trousers. He wasn't fool enough to have his men let her loose, she realised numbly. It was clear he had a good idea of just who and what she was. And then she felt cold air on her exposed skin...

"Lie still," the gangbanger ordered, as he started to undo his trousers. "This will be..."

"End program," another voice said.

Belinda cursed under her breath as the droids holding her went limp, then looked up. Major General Jeremy Damiani, Commandant of the Terran Marine Corps, was standing to one side, looking disapproving. His bulldog-like face was twisted into a scowl that left her feeling as though she'd disappointed him, which she probably had. At the peak of her prowess, before the Fall of Earth, she could have cut her way through any number of gangbangers without a second thought. But a great deal had changed since then.

"Well," the Commandant said. "I've never seen anyone almost *raped* by the simulators before."

"No, sir," Belinda said. She stumbled to her feet, ignoring the remains of her trousers as they fell off her legs. Dignity wasn't something permitted to Pathfinder Marines. She'd carried out missions buck naked, once upon a time. Maybe she would again, one day. If she managed to recover from the Fall of Earth. "I wanted to test myself."

"You set the simulator to extreme levels," the Commandant said. "I believe the medical corpsmen will want a few words with you."

Belinda shrugged, refusing to show any of the bitter despondency that threatened to overwhelm her as she turned and started towards the hatch. Her emotions had once been tightly controlled, but no longer. She'd lost count of just how many times she'd found herself in tears since Earth had died, since Prince Roland had been sent to the Safehouse. It was almost a relief that he was no longer with her, even though she missed him more than she cared to admit. At least he wouldn't have to see how far she'd fallen from the dispassionate Marine he'd met on Earth.

The Commandant cleared his throat. Loudly.

"You were badly injured on Earth," he said, following her through the hatch. "I don't expect you to regain your health so quickly."

"I was always an overachiever," Belinda said. She started to strip off her uniform jacket, boots and panties, heedless of his presence. The *Chesty Puller's* simulator had left her sweaty and uncomfortable. It had really been too real for comfort. "And I will not surrender to despair."

"Good," the Commandant said. His tone was artfully flat, so carefully controlled she knew it had to be an act. "But you are also pushing yourself too hard."

"I don't think so," Belinda said. "The medics have always erred on the side of caution."

She finished undressing, then stood naked in front of the mirror. Physically, she looked normal; a blonde-haired young woman with a heart-shaped face and a body that was healthy and fit without seeming unnaturally muscular. Her long blonde hair alone would have made it hard for anyone to believe she was a Marine, not when almost every Marine in the Corps shaved their hair to keep it from getting in their way. But Pathfinders had always been allowed a certain level of latitude, particularly when they were operating undercover. They couldn't afford to *look* like Marines...

But her blue eyes were haunted and her skin was unnaturally pale...

"The medics are trying to keep you alive," the Commandant said. "We don't want to lose you because you pushed yourself too hard."

"I have to *know*," Belinda said. Giving up wasn't in her nature. Her family had seen to that a long time before she'd ever heard of the Terran Marine Corps. But, at the same time, she'd never been so weepy and upset over nothing before. It was hard to escape the sense that something was badly wrong with her mind. "Earth is gone. Is there any point in further struggle?"

"The human race lives on," the Commandant said. There was something in his voice that caught her attention. "Although not for much longer, perhaps."

Belinda looked up, surprised. "Sir?"

"Someone attacked the Slaughterhouse," the Commandant informed her. "The entire planet is dead."

Belinda recoiled in horror – and disbelief. The Slaughterhouse was more than just another badly-terraformed planet, she knew. It was the heart and soul of the Terran Marine Corps, the place where Marines were created, sent out to fight on behalf of the Empire and laid to rest when they died. If, the cynical side of her mind reminded her, there was enough of their bodies left to be buried. The Corps would do everything in its power to recover bodies, even trading with the enemy if necessary, but it sometimes wasn't possible to bring the dead home and lay them to rest properly.

It couldn't be gone. Centuries of tradition, of iron discipline and loyalty to the ideal of Empire, couldn't be gone. But she knew the Commandant wouldn't lie to her.

"Shit," she said, finally.

"Yes," the Commandant agreed.

Belinda looked down at her unmarked hands. She'd seen them bleeding and broken on the Slaughterhouse, when she'd forced herself to go on and on until she'd found herself unable to even *think* about quitting. Others had taken far worse injuries and kept going, daring the universe to try to stop them. And even those who had failed the final hurdle had found a home with the Corps. The Corps couldn't function without the auxiliaries in the background, the men and women who were still devoted to the Corps, even if they couldn't wear the Rifleman's Tab. It was hard to escape the impression that the Slaughterhouse was irreplaceable.

She looked up at the Commandant, feeling cold anger blossoming to life within her breast and turning to rage.

"Who did it?"

"We don't know," the Commandant said. "There's no shortage of suspects."

Belinda nodded, ruefully. The Grand Senate had feared the Marines, knowing the Corps couldn't be controlled as easily as the Imperial Army and Navy. They'd done their level best to weaken the Corps long before the Fall of Earth and, she had to admit, they'd done a very good job. And then there were the countless secessionists, terrorists and other rebel factions that had good reason to want to cripple or destroy the Marine Corps. The Nihilists, in particular, would seek to take advantage of the chaos caused by the Fall of Earth.

She took a breath. "Survivors?"

"The planet was evacuated as soon as I sent word of the Fall of Earth," the Commandant said, shortly. "Everyone on the planet was moved to escape ships and transported to the Safehouse, which is in another system entirely. The only people left in the system were a handful of observation staff, watching from a safe distance. They could do nothing as the planet was rendered uninhabitable."

Belinda swore. "Uninhabitable?"

"They used planet-scaled enhanced radiation weapons," the Commandant said. "It will be hundreds of years, perhaps longer, before the planet can be considered habitable once again."

"If ever," Belinda said. The Slaughterhouse had started its existence as a terraforming mistake, after all. Whatever polity replaced the Empire, if any such polity came into existence, would have to invest vast resources in restoring the planet. "What about the records? And the Crypt?"

"We have copies of the former," the Commandant said. "The latter...is lost to us, for now."

Belinda gritted her teeth in bitter rage. She'd spent time at the Crypt, when she'd been a recruit, learning about the Marines who had given their lives in service to the Empire. She'd wondered, at the time, if there was anything she could learn from men and women who had died in the course of their duties, and it had taken her some time to realise that *was* the lesson, that there were people who had made the ultimate sacrifice for the Corps. They hadn't fought for the Empire, in the end, but for their buddies, for the Marines on either side of them when they'd gone to war. And now their legacy was lost forever.

"Fuck," she said, finally. She wanted to hit something. But there was nothing to hit. "Just...fuck!"

"Quite," the Commandant agreed.

He looked her up and down, his gaze contemplative rather than unpleasant. "I may have a mission for you," he said. "It isn't one I am comfortable assigning to you. Quite frankly" – his voice hardened – "you are in no state to do anything, beyond slowly recuperating to the point you can be assigned to a line company or redirected to the auxiliaries. Under the circumstances, we would even accept your resignation."

Belinda eyed him, fighting down a surge of hope within her heart. "I can do it, sir," she said, quickly. "Whatever you want me to do..."

The Commandant met her eyes. "Last time I assigned you to a mission, I told you that I had doubts," he said. "Do you remember?"

"Yes, sir," Belinda said. "I remember."

She winced in memory. She'd been the lone survivor of an operation that had gone badly wrong from the start, thanks to Admiral Valentine and his cronies. The medics had told her she was suffering from Survivor's Guilt and had urged her to take a long rest. Instead, she'd been given a mission that should have been a milk run. And it had almost killed her.

And it did kill eighty billion people on Earth, a voice reminded her. *You watched helplessly as the planet died.*

"This time, I have more doubts," the Commandant said. "If I had another Pathfinder available, I would send him instead and keep you here, where you can recover safely. But I don't and so I have to rely on you. If you feel you cannot complete the mission, after I brief you, I expect you to tell me so."

"Yes, sir," Belinda said, already knowing she wouldn't. She didn't know how to quit – or how to rest. "What do you want me to do?"

"Get dressed, then report to Briefing Room A," the Commandant said. "I'll brief you there."

He paused. "And you might want to consider writing a new will afterwards," he added. "I do worry about you."

Belinda kept her face expressionless with an effort. The Commandant wouldn't normally have expressed concern about any of his Marines. For him to do so, openly, suggested that he felt he had good reason to worry, over and beyond the normal call of duty. Her medical records were sealed, but she'd had a look at them once her neural link had been repaired, allowing her to hack into the computer networks. She'd come far too close to death on Earth, they'd stated, and she would never be a fully-functional

Pathfinder again. There was no way to replace some of her burned-out implants without risking brain damage.

Or more brain damage, she thought. She hadn't told anyone she sometimes heard the voices of her dead teammates. Perhaps the Commandant *did* have good reason to worry. *But I won't give up now.*

Sighing, she reached for her uniform as he walked out of the hatch, leaving her alone. She'd get dressed, then hear the briefing. But she already knew she wouldn't refuse the mission, even if it was certain death. She just didn't know any other way to live.

Printed in Poland
by Amazon Fulfillment
Poland Sp. z o.o., Wrocław